SHADOWRUN:
VEILED EXTRACTION

R. L. KING

SHADOWRUN: VEILED EXTRACTION
By R. L. King
Cover art by Victor Manuel Leza Moreno
Design by Matt Heerdt and David Kerber
Editing by John Helfers

Published by Catalyst Game Labs,
an imprint of InMediaRes Productions, LLC
7108 S. Pheasant Ridge Drive • Spokane, WA 99224

ONE

Vyx never felt more alive than when she was in motion.

All around her, the familiar sounds echoed: the thundering roar of the train rumbling through the subterranean tunnel, the whines and growls of bikes as they zipped along beside it, the echoing whoops and yells of the others ahead and behind her. The lights from their bikes threw crazy patterns against the ancient, scarred concrete of the curving walls.

They flung themselves through the darkness with the supreme confidence of familiarity: they knew every twist and turn of these tunnels, every pile of rubble, every support column. Vyx grinned as Virago neatly shot the gap between two strewn piles of chunked concrete without reducing her speed in the slightest. Her girlfriend's tricked-out Suzuki Mirage wasn't as well suited to this kind of thing as Vyx's modified Yamaha Rapier, but her skill was nearly unmatched among their little chapter of the Ancients.

Nearly.

"C'mon!" Vyx teased over the comm as in a split-second she identified a narrow strip of 'crete, shifted her weight to bring the Rapier's front wheel up, and launched with effortless grace over the pile. "You're ridin' like your granny!"

"My granny's in the slammer, ya fraggin' showoff!" Virago's brash voice was full of cheerful bravado. *"Watch what yer doing so I don't have to peel yer ass off the fraggin' train!"*

"Pay attention, you two!" came another voice from behind them. *"Comin' up on the station."*

Vyx gunned her Rapier and surged ahead, keeping pace with the train. At only three cars, it barely qualified as a train at all. She didn't know what was inside it—none of them did. They weren't being paid to know things like that. Their job was to escort it safely to its destination, and discourage anyone who might show up to prevent it from getting there.

Ahead, the tunnel opened up, a wider platform appearing off to their right. Someone had long ago erected a makeshift ramp leading up to the platform, and Vyx mounted it quickly to make room for the others.

"Your spirit see anything ahead, Grey?" Virago asked.

"Not yet. Clear so far."

Vyx didn't let herself relax at his words—she rarely relaxed anyway, and especially not now, with this being the first real job she'd been allowed to come along on with the Ancients crew. She didn't have to look at Grey, riding pillion on the back of Falcon's bike in case he had to sling the mojo, to sense his disapproving eyes on her. He didn't say anything, though—he was too much of a pro to put the job at risk—but she was sure she'd have to endure his jibes after they were done and back at Kustom Rode Bykes. Falcon's, too.

And they wouldn't be the only ones. Sure, the Ancients had backed down on their "elves only" policy after the wall went up and they'd lost too many of their people, but that didn't mean Vyx's lack of pointed ears didn't get her noticed, and not in a good way. It didn't even matter that her mother was an elf. That made it somehow worse—she'd inherited inferior genes from her unknown father. A day didn't go by when she didn't hear somebody muttering about "breeders" and "norms" and worse from the shadows. They didn't try to hide it from her, either.

Screw 'em all, was Vyx's philosophy. She pulled her weight, and it wasn't like anybody had to coddle her. Hell, she was faster than most of them, and better and more reckless on a bike after three months than some of them who'd practically been born on the fraggin' things. They'd get used to her. Some of them already had—hence Lucky Liam's grudging agreement to let her go on the job. You couldn't waste talent, even when it didn't come in the right package—not in the Zone, where it was a vanishing commodity the longer the quarantine stayed up—and the Ancients' leader damn well knew it. That, and Virago was his cousin. Never look a little nepotism in the mouth, if it gave you the chance to prove you had what it takes.

Bad luck they'd had to take Grey along too, given his opinion of Vyx, but real magical punch was thin on the ground these days. They'd had intel that something might go down this time, and the beefy Dog shaman was the best mojo they had left after those Bane Sidhe bastards had taken out Bryce in an ambush at near Riverdale Park two weeks ago.

"Nervous, babe?" Virago's mocking voice came through again. She was still down alongside the track, where she zipped past only

centimeters away from the train's side. Her green synthleather jacket and bright green hair stuck up above the edge of the platform, a shocking contrast to the dull steel and faded graffiti.

"Hell, no!"

"If Mommy could see ya now, huh?"

"Shut up!" Grey's voice cut into their banter. He and Falcon were on the platform now too. *"I've got–"*

A loud *BOOM* ripped through the tunnel up ahead. The train shuddered and slowed. Suddenly the air was full of dust and sounds: creaks, crashes, the whine of more bikes, and amplified laughter. A staccato burst of SMG fire roared, stitching a line of holes along the train's side and pockmarking its armored windows.

"Bane Sidhe!" Falcon yelled.

"Fuck!" Virago peeled off away from the train, spun her bike on its back wheel, and zipped back up the ramp on the other side of the station. She was already drawing a Predator from beneath her jacket.

The train slowed further, its wheels screaming on the old metal rails, but didn't stop. More figures on bikes emerged from the darkness beyond the platform, their familiar green, orange, and white jackets marking them as members of the Ancients' rival gang.The Bane Sidhe were a human-only outfit affiliated with the Knights of the Red Branch, which meant they had a particular hatred for elves.

Vyx gunned her bike again, zigzagging across the platform's blasted-out floor and behind a support column as gunfire followed her progress. "I see five!" she said over the comm.

"Stay with the train," Falcon snapped. *"Might be a diversion."*

The train had slowed, the rigger inside and its own automated defenses reacting to the obstruction on the track, but whatever the Bane Sidhe ambushers had done to create the blockage hadn't been enough to stop it.

Ahead of Vyx, fire bloomed around one of the Bane Sidhe riders. Screaming, he erupted into flame, his momentum carrying him forward and over the edge of the platform. Vyx didn't turn to see what became of him, but the loud crash was enough. She spun her bike around and headed back for the far ramp, gripping tightly with her knees as she pulled her extendible baton from a sheath on her back and flicked it out to telescope into twice its length. Her muscles sang as power and adrenaline coursed through her.

Behind her, gunfire roared again, and the whines of bikes grew closer. Falcon was right—this was only a diversion.

"*C'mon!*" Virago yelled over the comm. "*Let the backup take these guys! Stay with the train!*"

A Bane Shidhe rider headed straight for Vyx, his passenger spraying fire from an SMG. Vyx planted one foot, zigged the light bike to her right, and ducked down over the bars. She hit the gas and the Rapier leaped forward, closing the distance between her and her opponent fast. As she zoomed past, the quick flash of the rider's startled expression rewarded her when she swung the baton at his neck. It hit with a satisfying *thud,* neatly clotheslining him off the bike.

His passenger yelled something Vyx couldn't hear and tried to bring the SMG around before the his ride went down, but Vyx was already gone, making a wide, sweeping turn that took her behind another support column and back in the direction of the train.

"*Get your asses back up here!*" the train rigger's voice came over the comm. "*More up ahead!*" This was followed by the sound of more gunfire—the train wasn't without its own defenses, but it was no match for the Bane Sidhe's ambush without the Ancients to reinforce its efforts.

Vyx risked a quick glance around. The rider she'd clotheslined writhed on the ground, clutching his neck—not dead, but probably out of the fight. His bike lay next to him. She couldn't see the passenger anywhere. Virago had come back up the ramp and was circling around to get behind the train.

Muzzle flashes split the darkness from the guns mounted on the top of the train, which was still moving slowly. It was a few seconds from the station's exit now—if it reached it, the tunnel would narrow again and the bikers wouldn't have as much room to maneuver. If there were more Bane Sidhe waiting ahead, they might already have another ambush ready, or a more effective way of stopping the train.

"Come on!" Vyx called to Virago. She grabbed a handful of throttle and the light bike surged under her, leaping forward. She loved the feel of its rumbling power under her command—it almost felt like an extension of her own body with the effortless way she threw it around. She wondered sometimes if this was how riggers felt when they were jacked into their vehicles. Sure, she couldn't see all its readouts and feel its tires like her own limbs as they could, but she didn't need to. It was fast and fearless and maneuverable, and so was she.

"*Careful, Vyx!*"

Vyx just laughed. Virago didn't get it. Sure, the elf was lithe and athletic, and she even had some 'ware to help give her an edge, but she didn't know what it was like to have the mojo coursing through her veins. She didn't know how it felt to be absolutely sure of every movement her body made: where her limbs would go, how high she could jump, the precise way to balance herself so she'd land exactly where she meant to, how to avoid obstacles and projectiles like the rest of the world was moving in slow motion. She thought maybe Jet and Keno, stuffed full of wires and all kinds of artificial enhancements, might understand better—but she didn't figure she'd ever get around to asking them, since whenever they turned up they looked at her like she was something on the bottom of their boots.

A Bane Sidhe on a battered Yamaha Nodachi, its red color barely visible under a thick coating of scrapes and dents, darted out of a side tunnel, trying to cut her off. Instead of braking, she whooped and gunned the engine, aiming straight at him. He had a gun in one hand, a heavy pistol from the look of it, but he was having a hard time dealing with his own bike, the gun, and an opponent who wasn't doing what she was supposed to. His shots went wide as Vyx roared up to him.

She shifted her weight forward, hit the front brake, executing a perfect stoppie and whipping the Rapier's rear wheel around. She adjusted her balance without conscious thought as the wheel smacked across the side of the Bane Sidhe rider's bike, hitting him hard in the leg and knocking him sideways. The human ganger yelled, trying to grip the other handlebar without dropping the gun, and then Vyx was roaring off, crouched low over her own bars, cutting an erratic path away as the ganger crashed.

Behind her, she heard the echoing chatter of more SMG fire, along with Virago's and Falcon's bikes. *"Got him!"* Virago's voice called.

Vyx grinned. She and Virago made a damn good team. She flung the bike forward again.

She didn't see the figures lurking in another niche off the side of the tunnel until she was nearly upon them. As she flashed by, they leaped forward and threw not one, but three small, spherical objects at her.

Two thoughts simultaneously went through Vyx's mind as the tiny grenades flew at her and everything shifted into slow motion.

The first was *Frag! How'd I miss him?*

The second was *Yeah! Now I'll show 'em what I can do!*

Three grenades. They spread out as they flew, and she calculated that by the time they reached her, they'd be about half-meter apart. Without conscious thought she made the simultaneous adjustments: goosed the throttle to increase the bike's speed, shifted her weight to throw the back wheel sideways, ducked low over the handlebars, and swept out with her staff. If the grenades were set for impact she might be in trouble, but only from one, not three. One she could handle.

Her fierce grin widened as her evasive maneuvers went off exactly as planned—just as they almost always did. The first grenade sailed past the rear of the speeding bike, the second one flew over her back, and the third one—which was not, as it turned out, set for impact—rocketed back toward the thrower, who scrambled madly to one side in an effort to avoid being made into chunky salsa by a grenade blast in a brick tunnel niche.

But then another voice rose in terror: *"What the–?"*

The grenades went off—*boom boom boom.*

It was only then that Vyx remembered that Virago, Falcon, and Grey had been following close on her tail, and her blood chilled.

Virago shot past unharmed, but before Falcon could react, two grenades slammed into the side of his bike and detonated. Falcon was thrown forward over the handlebars, where he tumbled head-over-heels and rolled to an awkward stop against curved tunnel wall.

Grey, on the back, wasn't so lucky. As Vyx watched in horror, he too flew off the bike, but his forward momentum sent him careening not into the tunnel, but directly in front of the accelerating train following behind them. His agonized scream echoed through the tunnel, rising above the train's rumble and the bikes' whines, and then was abruptly cut off as the train, unable to stop, smashed into him and rolled inexorably over.

"Grey!" Virago screamed.

Vyx didn't stop to consider her next action, but likely even if she had, she wouldn't have changed it. They still had the remaining Bane Shidhe to deal with, up ahead. "Cover me!" she yelled, and gripped the throttle. The bike flew forward.

The Bane Sidhe ambushers had piled chunks of concrete a meter high next to the track, no doubt to slow down the bikes while letting the train through. Vyx gritted her teeth in a grin that had nothing to do with pleasure. The sight of Grey's body going under the train's grinding wheels flashing across her mind's eye, she channeled her rage and grief into action. Even after what happened, if she and the others didn't stop the Bane Sidhes, they'd kill the rest of the group too. Did they think they could stop her? Did they think some crappy pile of rocks would prevent her from getting to them?

These tunnels were old—some of the oldest in Boston—close and claustrophobic, with curved sides and a low, arched ceiling.

There wasn't much room for bikes to roll alongside the trains, and Vyx was sure the Bane Sidhes were counting on the fact that the Ancients would have to come in behind the train, or try to beat it to the barrier and make themselves easy targets in the glow of the train's powerful headlights.

Vyx never liked the expected options.

Crouched low over the bike's tank, her steely glare fixed forward, she effortlessly calculated the angles without conscious thought. She barely heard the chatter of gunfire from behind her as Virago and Falcon laid down covering fire. She didn't glance behind her.

As she approached the barrier, she abruptly nudged her bike to the right, angling it toward the edge of the tunnel. Any second she expected Bane Sidhe rounds to tear into her, but she didn't stop.

She gunned the bike up the curved side of the tunnel, over the side of the barrier and past the crouched Bane Sidhes behind it. As she went by, she lashed out with her booted foot and caught one of them in the jaw as he tried to aim at her. His SMG's muzzle bucked upward, spraying the ceiling with rounds and sending puffs of dust and chunks of concrete cascading down. The other, with feathers and fetishes pinned to his green, orange, and white jacket, spun around and began gesturing. To Vyx, he looked like he was moving in slow motion. But then, a lot of the world moved in slow motion as far as she was concerned.

She flew forward, ahead of the train now. Once she was clear, she executed a stoppie that lifted the bike up onto its front wheel, then shifted her weight to bring the back end around so she was facing the ambushers. As the bike dropped back down onto both wheels, she pulled a flash-bang grenade from her pocket and whipped it toward the barrier. "Flash!" she called over the comm.

From the other side, Virago had apparently done the same thing, and nearly at the same time. The twin *booms* and bright flashes went off almost simultaneously, dropping the two remaining Bane Sidhes to their knees as the train rumbled past the barrier.

Falcon, still shaky and bleeding from his unexpected ejection, had mounted the back of Virago's Rapier. His face was twisted, dark with rage. As they rolled up next to the concrete pile, he aimed his pistol downward and double-tapped the Bane Sidhe with the feathers, right in the face. Blood sprayed, covering the barrier, the side of the train, and the ganger's buddy, who was now trying to scramble backward, still stunned and half-blind from the grenade's flash.

Virago put a hand on Falcon's arm as he prepared to plug the other one as well. *"We gotta stay with the train,"* Vyx heard her say over the comm.

"Fraggin' assholes're gonna pay," he muttered. He took aim and dispassionately put another pair of rounds into the back of the other ganger's head.

Virago was listening to something else on her comm. "Backup's just up ahead," she said. "They have visual on the train. We're good."

"We ain't good." Falcon glared at Vyx, who'd climbed off her bike and was staring at the back of the train as it faded into the darkness. "Fraggin' breeder slitch was showin' off again. That's what got Grey killed."

Vyx stared at him. Had she really just heard what she thought she heard? "You're blaming *me?* What was I supposed to do, let those grenades hit me?" Her body shook with excess adrenaline as what had just happened caught up with her, but even so, she knew he was right. It *had* been her fault. She'd gotten Grey killed because, as usual, she'd gone for a flashy move when a simple one would have worked. Right now, though, she was so wound up that Falcon's words sounded more like an attack than an accusation.

"Yeah," Falcon said, taking a step forward, reaching inside his jacket. "You got armor. And your norm ass ain't worth a fraction of Grey's, anyway."

Virago stepped between them, her face twisted with anger and grief. "Knock it off, both of you," she ordered, brandishing her SMG. "We're done here. You heard 'em. Get back on your bikes and let's go."

Vyx glared back at Falcon, but nodded. "Yeah," she said, deflating as the adrenaline began to fade. She thought the whole elf-chauvinism thing the Ancients had going was a lot of bullshit, especially now, but that didn't do anything about the fact that she'd been reckless.

Virago gripped her arm. "It's okay. This is the way it goes sometimes," she said gently, while still keeping an eye on Falcon. She brushed a lock of sweaty hair off Vyx's forehead. "You gonna run with us, you gotta see that. This ain't like that fancy college stuff. This is real life." She spat dust. "And sometimes it sucks."

"Yeah." All the energy that had coursed through Vyx a minute ago, making her body sing, had drained out of her as Grey's abruptly silenced shriek of agony replayed itself in her mind. The guy hadn't liked her, hadn't given a damn about whether she lived or died. Probably would have been happy to see *her* fall in front of that train. But he damn well had done his job. He'd backed her up, just like he'd backed up the others.

And now he was dead, and it was her fault. Her limbs felt like lead, her head like someone had grabbed it and squeezed. She pictured the irregular spray of blood on the front of the train, and how that and a few mangled remains were all that was left of the best mage they had. Just like that—a bloody smear in a filthy train tunnel under a hellhole of a city where they were all trapped like animals.

Virago pulled her close. "Come on," she said. "Let's get outta here."

"We can't just leave—"

"Yeah. We can." Virago's voice was normally brash, loud, boisterous, but now it was soft and understanding. "They'll send somebody over. We can't do nothin' for him now, 'cept hoist a few in his memory."

Falcon's eyes narrowed. "Yeah. Maybe that's all we can do. We'll see." Before either of them could reply, he turned and stomped over to one of the Bane Shidhes' fallen bikes. He stared down at it for a moment, spat on the scarred emblem on its side, and then mounted it and roared off into the darkness of the tunnel.

TWO

Two Weeks Earlier

Winterhawk liked McKinley's Bar, just outside downtown DeeCee. It wasn't because the drinks or the ambiance were any better than any of the other upscale watering holes in the area. No, he liked it because both the clientele and staff knew him well enough to leave him the hell alone when he was working. The bartender had a sixth sense about when he wanted another drink, sending it over before he thought to put in an order, and rarely got it wrong. Maybe it was due to the impressive tips Winterhawk left, but in any case, that kind of attention—or lack thereof—was worth paying a premium for.

He set his datapad down and took a long drink from his half-full glass. He should quit soon, maybe even try to get a decent night's sleep for a change. The planning for the upcoming expedition into the Boston Quarantine Zone still had a lot to hammer out, but he could afford to let it go for the night.

He'd just stowed the datapad and was about to rise when his comm buzzed. He pulled up the number idly. *Probably Wu with some last-minute question.* The woman was as driven as he was—maybe even more so. But no, the LTG number was blocked.

Odd. "Yes?"

No image, either. Even odder.

"Alex?"

He went still and carefully set his drink down. "Who is this?" He kept his voice deliberately calm and inflectionless, though warning bells were going off in his mind. That was a name he hadn't gone by for many years—and one not many people knew anymore. He didn't recognize the voice.

"I'm sorry," the woman said. *"Winterhawk, I guess it is now. You're a hard man to get hold of, no matter what you're calling yourself."*

She sounded maddeningly familiar—someone who belonged to his past as much as the name did—but he couldn't put his finger on the specifics. "Who is this, and what do you want?"

"It's Olivia Crane," she said. *"Do you remember me? I know it's been a long time."*

His hand tightened on his commlink. A face swirled in his memory, all windblown hair and smooth skin and sparkling, merry blue eyes. A figure, tall and lithe, clad in jeans and a bohemian sweater, a backpack swung jauntily over one shoulder. Some of the details had faded—he didn't remember every woman he'd ever known with perfect clarity, especially when it was that long ago—but the highlights resided uncomfortably in some part of his mind that he tried his best to file away without further examination.

"This is...unexpected," he said at last.

"That's very diplomatic," she said. There was an odd edge to her voice, a kind of stressed amusement. *"How have you been?"*

He remembered his drink and took a healthy swallow. "Is there something I can do for you, Olivia?"

There was a pause. *"I'd like to see you, actually,"* she said at last. *"I understand you're in DeeCee. There's something I'd like to discuss with you, if you can spare the time."*

And now she knew where he was. That ramped up his awareness another step or two. "Olivia, I don't know what this is about, but I'm quite busy. Can't you just tell me—"

"No," she said. *"I really can't. It's not the sort of thing I want to talk about over the comm."* Another pause. *"Please, Alex. It's very important. I know—things didn't end well with us, but this isn't easy for me, either. If you could just spare me an hour..."* When he still didn't reply, she added, *"I'm at the Four Seasons downtown. We could meet at the bar there. Can you come?"*

There was no mistaking the stress in her voice now, though the amusement had vanished in favor of a hint of pleading. Whatever she wanted, it was indeed important to her. "Tonight?" He glanced at the chrono on his commlink: nearly eleven.

"If you could, I'd appreciate it. I promise I won't take much of your time."

He considered. She was right: things had not ended well with them. But that was a long time ago. They'd both been young and foolish. He was a different person now—she almost certainly was as well.

"Fine, then," he said at last. "I'll meet you there in an hour."

"Thank you, Alex. It...will be good to see you again."

She broke the connection before he could answer, which was probably good, since he couldn't in all honesty say he was looking forward to seeing her.

He finished his drink and ordered another, then pulled up an AR window and, after narrowing the search down a couple times, found the information he was looking for. He didn't know what, exactly, he'd been expecting—from what he'd known about her from their previous association, perhaps that she'd become an artist, or was working for some social cause. She'd always cared about that sort of thing, despite her comfortable upper-class background.

He'd certainly never expected to see her face looking out at him from a slick corporate PR site. It was all general information—anything more specific was certainly hidden behind protections he'd need a lot more expertise to break than his simple commlink—but it was enough for now.

If anyone had asked him where he thought Olivia Crane might have ended up in the intervening years since he'd seen her, this would have been low on his list of options—lower even than a few he wouldn't have mentioned in polite company. She worked for Ares now? Not only worked for them, but apparently was some kind of executive vice president. He skimmed the sanitized corporate bio, noting that she'd joined the corp shortly after she left university, and had remained with them, rising steadily through the ranks, for the last eighteen years. The bio included nothing about her personal life. Had she married? Had children?

He supposed he didn't care. He was curious about what she wanted to talk about, but he didn't have time to spare much thought for it. The preparations for the trip into the Boston Quarantine Zone, locked down tight after the dragon Eliohann, in an attempt to escape from a secret MIT&T facility, had crash-landed into Fenway Park and started the spread of Cognitive Fragmentation Disorder, were taking up all his time, and he still had a lot to finish before the expedition began. The lockdown itself was frightening enough, but the team would have to be doubly careful to avoid getting letting the highly contagious CFD overwrite their brains with nanites and turn them into mindless zombies. Leave it to technological mad science to come up with a situation that made Bug City look like a walk in the park by comparison.

He shut down the window with Olivia's information and pulled the QZ files back up, his gaze flicking over the list of supplies they'd need to gather. The group wouldn't be able to take much with them—getting over the wall was going to be hard enough without having to keep track of a lot of gear—so everything that went with them had to justify its presence, preferably in more than one way.

As he examined the items and began paring them down, his mind drifted to thoughts about the QZ itself. He couldn't decide whether he was pleased or disappointed that he'd decided not to accompany the expedition. Ten years ago, he'd have jumped at the chance. The formation of a brand-new ley line—one apparently aspected toward dragon magic—had intrigued him since reports had begun trickling out from behind the wall shortly after it went up. His first impulse had been to form an independent team composed of researchers and a few handpicked shadowrunners, but when the DIMR had approached him with its own interests in the project, he'd signed on without regret.

Only as a consultant, though. Officially he was in charge of the team, due in equal parts to his academic credentials and his years of practical field experience in what they called "unusual operations." He chuckled when he thought of that—in the arena of magical field research, where the old saying about doing six impossible things before breakfast was part of the job description, getting something labeled "unusual" meant it had to be pretty fragging extraordinary.

Unofficially, though, his job was merely advisory. He was there to offer suggestions on whom to include on the team, what they should take with them, and the tests they should be doing when they got there, as well as tips on doing research in hostile environments. The others listened to him, and by all accounts seemed to value his contributions highly, but all of those who would actually be performing the research had developed a kind of camaraderie that he wasn't a part of. It was subtle, but not surprising: all of them were at least ten years younger than him, eager and excited to get out in the field and perform the kind of research that could make a career for years to come.

He finished his drink, closed his files, and got up. Had he made a mistake by choosing not to accompany the group? It wasn't too late to include himself if he wished, but doing so would require the kind of bureaucratic wrangling he found tiresome, not to mention the very real possibility of upsetting the team's balance just as they were making their final preparations.

No, much as he regretted it, it was probably best for him to sit this one out. They were a good group, and they'd gather good data. If they made it out again (a big *if*, to be sure, if the walls didn't come down soon), he'd have plenty of chances to analyze their findings. Without any particular conceit, he knew those ten years he had on the rest of them would likely result in inferences and discoveries that would elude most of the others. He didn't need to go inside, subject himself to the chaos and danger and uncertainty that he used to thrive on.

That was what he was trying to convince himself of, anyway.

THREE

Olivia was waiting for Winterhawk when he arrived, which surprised him. Back in the day, she used to be late for everything.

The bar was one of those old-money places that had been around for at least a hundred years, all polished wood and tasteful old paintings and vintage bottles arranged neatly in front of a mirror depicting a pastoral scene. It was the kind of place where power brokers made deals over liquor that was probably older than the bar itself. Even the AR iconography fit the overall scheme: muted, elegant, unobtrusively understated.

Winterhawk's first impression as the host led him to the table in the private dining room was that Olivia looked older. Of course it wasn't a physical thing: not much, not even after all this time. Near-eternal youth was, after all, the most desirable component of the genetic lottery all elves won. Especially if they took care of themselves as well as she obviously had.

He studied her as he approached: she had the same luxuriant red-gold hair, though she wore it in a short, corp-chic bob now instead of long and wild as he remembered it. Same trim figure, clad in a tailored Zoe suit of deep red now rather than the ripped jeans and that ridiculous studded synthleather jacket she used to favor. Same deep blue eyes, regarding him with half-lidded intensity from beneath perfectly sculpted brows.

"Well," he said, making a little bow that might or might not have been mocking. "It *has* been a long time."

She nodded, once, without changing expression. "Thank you so much for coming," she said. "Please, sit down."

The holopic he'd seen when he'd pulled up the file on her had shown her smiling, in one of those standard-issue, carefully manipulated headshots every corporate bigwig had to sit for when their career reached a certain stage. She wasn't smiling now. Her expression had an odd stillness that made her smooth, flawless face look like a mask. He paused to assense her, immediately noting the tension in her aura. She might look calm and unruffled on the surface, but underneath something was troubling her. Something big, from the look of things. She never could hide anything from him.

He sat down across from her. A waiter appeared from nowhere and filled his wineglass, then glided back off. "I took the liberty," she said, indicating the glass with a quick twitch of her elegant chin. "I remembered you used to like Bordeaux."

He took a sip. It was a much finer vintage than what they'd shared during their brief time together back in New York. "You're looking well."

"So are you." Her aura twitched again, and he got the impression that an unspoken *better than I expected you to* hung in the air. He might have found it flattering, except the connotation was more surprise than approval. Given the circumstances of their last meeting, that wasn't entirely unexpected.

"What can I do for you, Olivia? I can't imagine this is a social engagement after all this time."

"No," she said. "No, it isn't." She toyed with her fine linen napkin, twisting it between long, red-nailed fingers, and then her gaze came up to meet his. "I understand you've been doing some work for the DIMR."

"Here and there," he said. "Why?"

"I've also heard rumors that you're assembling an expedition to enter the Boston Quarantine Zone to do some sort of research."

"Where did you hear that?" he asked, keeping his tone carefully neutral.

She smiled, just a brittle lift of one side of her thin lips, but didn't reply.

"Suppose it's true," he said. "Why should you care?"

"If it's true," she said, "I want to hire you."

Winterhawk narrowed his eyes and let his breath out slowly. So that was it. He supposed he shouldn't have been surprised—when the quarantine had dropped over Boston, a lot of things got stuck on the wrong side of the barriers. In many cases, they were the sorts of things some very rich people would pay a lot of money to get back on the *right* side of the barriers.

"Ah," he said. "Now it becomes clear. Ares put you up to this, then, did they? They dug up the fact that we knew each other twenty years ago, and sent you, hoping you could exploit the connection."

Her hand tightened on her napkin. "Even if they did find the connection," she said, "I hardly think they'd consider it something I could exploit. Do you?"

"I wasn't the one who left," he said, sipping his wine to hide an edge in his voice. "That was all on you."

Her smile this time had a clipped quality. "It doesn't look like you've done anything to prove me wrong in all those years, does it?"

"While you, on the other hand, seem to have settled in nicely to your gilded little corporate cage."

"I grew up, Alex," she said. "Or should I call you 'Winterhawk' now?"

"Suppose you just tell me what you want," he said. "For curiosity's sake, if nothing else. Even if I were planning such an expedition, you can't expect me to start taking on side jobs."

"You haven't heard what I'm offering yet," she pointed out.

"It doesn't matter."

Something in her aura changed; a bit of her impervious corp-exec armor shifted. "Please," she said. "Just hear me out. I don't have any other options."

He tilted his head. *That* was something he'd never heard any corporate Mr. Johnson admit —and make no mistake, if she was trying to hire him to do some job in the QZ, that was exactly what she was, regardless of their previous history. Even if it were true, it didn't matter: the first page of Johnson 101 started out with "Never let them see you sweat."

Olivia Crane was most certainly sweating, even though she'd never manifest such a vulgar physical reaction on her perfect elven face.

If he hadn't been curious before, he was now. "All right," he said, picking up his wineglass and leaning back in his chair. "Let's hear it. But please make it fast. I've got quite a lot I still need to do tonight, and this meeting has cut into the time I'd planned to do it in."

She only nodded, which increased his curiosity. The old Olivia would never have let that go without some sort of snappy comeback. Instead, all she did was remove her commlink from her stylish, genuine leather bag, twiddle a couple settings, and set it on the center of the table next to the tiny, mushroom-shaped white noise generator.

It displayed a holopic of a young human woman, obviously cropped from a larger image. It was hard to tell her exact age, but Winterhawk guessed perhaps eighteen to twenty. Tall and athletic, she had the slim build more often found in elves than in humans. Her short, dark hair swept back from delicately rounded ears sporting numerous earrings, and she fixed the camera with a challenging stare and a wide grin. Something about her looked familiar, but he couldn't identify what it was. He studied the image for a moment, then returned his attention to Olivia without speaking.

"She's inside," Olivia said, nodding toward the commlink. "In the QZ. And I want her out."

Winterhawk continued examining the image. "Who is she?"

"I'll give you the details once you've agreed to take the job," she said. "I'm authorized to pay you fifty thousand nuyen for her safe return."

Something in her voice caught his attention. "What aren't you telling me?"

She remained still in her chair, her corp-trained mask of impassivity firmly in place. "Why do you think there's something I'm not telling you? She's in there, and I need to get her out. It's very simple. Isn't that the sort of job you do?"

Her face might not show anything, but her aura swirled with tension. "No," he said. "Not anymore. I only take on projects I find interesting. Extracting some corporate pawn from a dangerous location isn't the sort of thing that interests me. And in any case, I'm not going in myself—just arranging the team. So I suggest you tell me what it is you're not sharing, or I'll be on my way."

When she didn't reply, he made as if to rise. "It's been good seeing you again, Olivia," he said. "I wish you the best of luck in—"

"She's my daughter," she said.

Winterhawk sat back down, slowly. "Your daughter."

"Her name is Victoria. She's nineteen, and she's a student at MIT&T. I lost contact with her when the—events—occurred in Boston, and the quarantine went up."

"I see." His gaze flicked down to the image again, then back up to Olivia's face. The resemblance wasn't strong, but now that he was looking for it, he could see it. "The quarantine has been in effect for some time. Surely with your connections, you could have found someone else by now."

"I've tried," she said. "I arranged a team a month ago, but they never even made it past the blockades."

"How did you find out I was planning an expedition?" Winterhawk asked. "Been keeping tabs on me, have you?"

"No. To be honest, I figured you'd probably been killed years ago."

That sounded more like the Olivia he'd known. "So, then—"

"I've...arranged with certain assets within my division to keep me apprised when they hear of groups planning to go inside. When I heard about this one—when I heard you were involved—I thought..."

"You thought what?" He sipped the wine again, wishing it were something stronger. "That I'd drop everything and take up your cause simply because we had a little fling twenty years ago? I'm sorry about your daughter, but what would possibly make you think I—"

He stopped.

He looked sharply at her.

Her face remained calm, but she didn't avoid his gaze.

With slow deliberation, he set his wineglass back on the table. He shook his head. "No. Don't even try it, Olivia."

"Do you think I *wanted* to?" she asked. "Do you think if I had any other alternative, I wouldn't have pursued it?"

"You're lying," he said dully. "You've got to be lying. Or else you'd have—"

"No," she said. "I wouldn't have. I didn't want her to know. After I left—after I found out—I knew it would be better for all of us."

He shook his head. "It's not possible," he said. "This is another of your games. Whoever this young woman is—whether she's your daughter or not—you're obviously keen on getting her out of the Zone. You've played these games before. They might have worked on me twenty years ago, but not now."

Her laugh was harsh. "Of course you don't believe it. You don't *want* to believe it. You're no different now than you were then. You never had room for anything that didn't have to do with magic or research. Even if I'd told you then, you'd have found a way to deny it."

"Assuming it were true," he said, and did nothing to attenuate the cold edge to his voice, "you didn't even give me the chance, did you? You constructed your own reality and assumed I'd conform to it."

He pulled the napkin from his lap, tossed it on the table, and stood. "It was a good try, Olivia, but you'll need to move on to another of your former admirers. I suggest you try one who's a bit more gullible next time."

"I can prove it," she said. She stood as well, and faced him across the table. "You can read my mind. I know you can. Do it. See if I'm lying."

He stared at her. The sort of magic that allowed the probing of another being's mind wasn't something anyone voluntarily consented to. That was especially true of mundanes: a lifetime of sensationalistic trid shows and other popular media had terrified most of them into believing they had no defense against mages who could sift indiscriminately through their deepest thoughts. The worst part was that in this case at least, their fears were both justified and valid. If Olivia allowed him into her mind, she almost certainly knew she had only the strength of his word that he wouldn't rip through, tearing open closed doors and examining anything he wished. That included any corporate secrets she might be privy to—secrets that, given her position within Ares, could be worth a fortune to the right people. Not to mention potentially devastating to her career—and even her life.

He almost gave her a pass. Almost. He glanced down at the holopic of the young elven woman, then back up at Olivia. "I don't need to read your mind," he said. "Not completely. I can use a spell to tell me if you're lying."

"Do that, then," she said. "Do whatever you need to do to convince yourself. If knowing the truth is what it takes to make you do this, then that's the way it's got to be."

He kept it quick and straightforward, but he didn't hold back. Even if she'd tried to resist, he was confident he could punch through her defenses like so much tissue paper. But she didn't. She sat back down, put her hands on the table, and waited as he cast the spell. Her aura still showed tension, but also determination.

He started with a couple of test questions, general things to calibrate her responses. She answered them without hesitation, and no duplicity showed in her aura.

Here we go. No turning back now. "Is Victoria, the young woman in this holopic, your daughter?"

"Yes," she said.

"Is she my daughter?"

She looked him straight in the eyes. "Yes."

The spell didn't waver.

He paused, gripping the edge of the table. His mouth went suddenly dry, and his heart beat faster. "Are you certain?" he asked with care.

Her eyes narrowed. "Of course I'm certain," she snapped.

Again, no wavering.

"Is she inside the Boston Quarantine Zone?"

"Yes."

"How do you know?"

"When the quarantine went into effect, I thought she might have somehow managed to get out. I hired a very talented mage to try to find her, and she was unable to do so."

"When did you last have contact with her?"

She hesitated a beat. "A little over two months ago."

He frowned. "The quarantine has only been up for six weeks."

Another beat. "We...didn't speak that often. She's...very independent, and resented what she called my 'helicoptering.'"

Briefly, he tried to reconcile the wild, free-spirited woman he'd known twenty years ago with the straitlaced, corp-hardened version sitting in front of him, and wasn't surprised at Victoria's relationship with her mother.

"Does anyone else know?"

"That she's yours? No. I had another relationship shortly after I left."

So far, the spell had not indicated any duplicity.

He could have left it at that. He believed her now: she was a mundane, and at his level of magical ability she couldn't hide anything so personal from him. Pursuing this further would border on pettiness—satisfying his own unnecessary curiosity at her expense.

Still, she'd volunteered. And he wasn't feeling terribly charitable toward her at the moment. "Did you know about her when you left me?"

Her jaw tightened. "Yes."

Something inside him froze, and he couldn't stop his next words: "Why, then?"

"Why what?"

"Why did you leave? Why didn't you tell me?"

Her expression shifted, hardened. "I could refuse to answer that. Your spell can't make me tell you anything—it just tells you if what I do say is the truth. Right?"

He nodded, once.

"And if I refuse to answer—will you force it out of me? Is that what it will take to make you get her out of there?"

He didn't answer for several seconds, but never broke her gaze. "No," he said at last. "I won't force you. But I do want to know."

He thought she'd look away then, but she didn't. Her face was still set, with only the barest quiver at the corner of her lips belying her calm. "I left because of you," she said.

"Because of me?"

"Because I didn't think it would be good for a child to grow up with you as a father."

"Why not?" He almost let the spell slip at her words.

Her eyes flashed, and her voice rose. "How many reasons do you need? Because you never wanted a child, and you know it. Because you were married to your work, and your magic. Because even back then you could never stay in one place, never settle down. If you weren't on the cutting edge of magic, chasing down ancient secrets, doing things that should have killed you by now, you weren't happy." She gripped the table more tightly and leaned forward. "Is that the truth you wanted to hear?"

He'd asked for it. And everything she'd said was true—it was just hard to hear it all in one place, stated so frankly. "Then why did you—" he began.

"Keep her?" Surprise traced her features and was gone. "Because I loved you at one point—or at least I thought I did at the time. I thought I could have a part of you—the brilliant, funny part that attracted me to you in the first place—without the... downsides."

Something in her expression caught his attention, and he barely noticed that he'd dropped the spell. "You didn't get what you wanted, did you?"

She sighed and only then did she lower her gaze. "No. I didn't. She's just like you, Alex. Maybe worse. Never satisfied. Never settled. Always pushing boundaries, just to prove she can. That's why I'm so worried about her in there. I'm afraid she'll get herself killed taking some crazy shot at getting out on her own, before I can help her."

He slumped in his chair, rubbing his jaw.

"I'll pay you well. I wasn't lying about the fifty thousand. I've got a fair bit of credit saved up. If that's what it takes—"

He shook his head. "I wouldn't do this for any amount of money, Olivia."

Her head snapped up, her eyes widening. She drew breath to protest.

"Tell me about her," he said, standing and holding up a hand to forestall her words. "Tell me everything you think is relevant. I'll want images, address, her course schedule if you know it, names of friends...and a ritual sample if you can manage it. As soon as possible. It will take me a few days to change the plans—as I told you, I wasn't intending to lead the expedition myself, so I'll need to smooth a few feathers."

She studied him for a long moment, then retrieved her commlink from the table. "I'm sending you a file with everything you need to know. If I've forgotten anything or you have any questions, my private contact number is in the file. And..." she opened her bag and pulled out a small box, which she offered him. "This is a ritual sample. As I said, my contacts didn't have any luck locating her from outside the barrier, but...perhaps once you get inside..."

He took it and stowed it in his jacket pocket. "I'll be in touch," he said. "Assuming I get out, of course. That's by no means a foregone conclusion."

"Surely you've got some sort of plan?"

He gave her a bitter smile. "As you well know, Olivia, even the best-laid plans have a way of going awry."

He'd made it all the way to the door before he stopped and turned back. "Olivia?"

"Yes?"

"Is she Awakened?"

She nodded, but it was more of a reluctant admission than an assent. "She's an adept."

He held her gaze a couple of seconds longer than he should have, then hurried out.

FOUR

"Smoothing a few feathers" back at the DIMR had been a bit of an understatement, just as Winterhawk had known it would be. He'd called Doris Wu into the cluttered temporary office he was using and broke the news as briskly and dispassionately as he could.

"What do you mean, you're coming along?" The dwarf was young for her position, a solid mage with impeccable credentials who'd risen through the DIMR's ranks by means of a combination of gutsy research, perseverance, and ambition bordering on the edge of unseemly. The trip into the QZ was to have been her first command of a field expedition, her first opportunity to prove herself in a practical setting, and the fact that she was originally from Boston and had studied at MIT&T made her an even better choice. Despite the well-documented danger inherent in trying to enter the QZ, she'd been quick to volunteer for the job.

She faced Winterhawk now across the desk, her expression full of astonishment and frustration and carefully veiled anger. "When was this decided?"

"It was rather sudden," he said. "I apologize—I'd have told you sooner if I'd known myself." When she drew breath to protest, he held up a hand. "Listen," he said, "it won't change much for you, honestly. You'll still have charge of the day-to-day operations and the research personnel. You've still got the local expertise. I'll be there more in an—advisory capacity."

"Why?" she asked. "We've been planning this expedition for months. We all know what's expected. We all know our roles once we're inside. What do you need to advise?"

"Ms. Wu, I'm sorry, but there's really no discussing it at this point. It's been decided."

She sighed, clearly attempting to hide her disappointment, and put on the corporate team-player mask. Then she met his gaze, her expression challenging. "Will you tell me something?"

"If I can."

"You chose me for this job. You put me in charge of this team when you assembled it. I know your reputation—I know why they decided to bring you in as an outside consultant instead of handling the whole thing in-house. And now you're demoting me." When he shook his head and started to speak, she continued quickly: "No, no. Don't try to sugarcoat it. You know as well as I do that if you come along, your presence will undermine my authority. Not officially, of course. I'm not saying you'll do it on purpose. But your reputation—"

"My reputation," he pointed out, "isn't just academic, Ms. Wu. The fact is, you might find my presence helpful. I know you've read all the reports—you've got all the most up-to-date information that can be provided. But that's just it—it's *data*. It's not real-world experience. You can read about it all you like, but if you've never actually been up against some of the threats we're likely to find inside, you've no idea how you'll react to them. I can help with that."

She sighed. "Yes, yes. I know all about your shadowrunning days. I've read *those* reports, too. But I guess it doesn't matter, does it? Like you said, nothing I say is going to change it. So..." she added with a shrug, "I guess what's done is done."

"Indeed it is," he agreed. "And at any rate, I was serious about your still taking charge of the bulk of the expedition. I've got to take care of a couple of separate matters while we're inside, so I won't even be onsite at the research station all the time."

Her expression sharpened. "Separate matters?"

"Nothing you need concern yourself with, Ms. Wu. Now, if you'll forgive me, I'm late for another engagement. I've got one more member I need to see about securing for our team."

"Another freelance mage?"

Winterhawk chuckled. "No. Not a mage. More—security."

He felt her gaze on him as he left the office, and hoped she wouldn't end up being trouble.

FIVE

Like many of the city's residents, the trendy little coffee shop in Dupont Circle, just outside downtown DeeCee, lived a double life. During the day, it played host to the hordes of workers who put in their time at the various offices in the area's high-rises. From early morning until after seven or so, a steady stream of mid-level sararimen and -women streamed in and out seeking a shot of something to keep them awake, and perhaps more importantly a chance to socialize for a few minutes with someone who wasn't their boss or the guy in the next cubicle. The place featured percussion-heavy music from indie bands, its AR imagery emphasizing its social consciousness and commitment to providing only the best sustainable, ethically harvested products. The cheerful baristas represented all the standard metatypes, and would make all sorts of off-the-menu concoctions for you if you tipped them well enough.

After dark, though, when most of the other trendy little coffee shops were already closed up tight in favor of the numerous nightclubs and bars, this place shifted everything, from its staff to its clientele. It wasn't obvious and it wasn't entirely planned, but when the owners caught wind that more than a few strange bedfellows were showing up to sit in the back and sip exotic brews to the accompaniment of the latest international tunes, they decided to make a few changes. Nothing that would upset the daily workers, who just thought they were modernizing—only a few alterations to the layout and security. It wasn't the kind of place where world-shaking deals were made, or high-nuyen shadowruns were arranged, but it cultivated a well-deserved reputation as a place where discreet biz could be conducted in relative privacy.

Even so, Doris Wu wasn't taking any chances. She'd switched from her usual high-fashion corp-mojo style into a neat leather jacket, tight jeans that made her short, stout legs look like a pair of blue sausages, and chic, high-heeled boots. A slouchy hat covered her short, dark hair, and mirrored shades obscured her eyes. She carried a leather shoulder bag of the type corporate deckers favored to cradle their cyberdecks. She looked like any of the hordes of quirky, successful codeslingers out for a few brews with friends.

She glanced around a moment as she entered the shop, then headed for the rear left corner and a small table wreathed in shadows. A woman sat there already—an ork from the look of her size and musculature, but her face was hidden.

Wu sat down across from her with a last glance around. She hated masking her aura and pretending to be a mundane; she was proud of her magical abilities, and not using them made her feel as she might if she didn't use her left arm. She paused to call up an AR window and order a mocha.

"I must say I was surprised to hear from you," the ork said. She leaned forward a bit, wrapping her perfectly manicured, red-tipped fingers around her own cup. Her features looked almost human, slim and sculpted, almost certainly the result of expensive plastic surgery. Aside from her impressive physique, the only features that revealed her true metatype were her pointed ears and two delicate tusks poking up from beneath lips that matched the red of her nails. "You were fairly adamant about your refusal to consider our offer last time we spoke."

"There've been...developments since then," Wu said.

"Indeed. May I ask the nature of these developments?"

"You may not. Not until we've come to an agreement, anyway. But I can assure you, I've reconsidered your offer, and in light of recent events, I'm ready to accept. I must insist on an additional condition, though."

The ork's elegantly sculpted eyebrow rose. "And what would that be?"

Wu smiled a tight smile. "I've evaluated my current career situation, and I believe that I'll be ready to make a move when I've returned."

The ork woman's face remained mostly impassive, but Wu didn't have to assense her to spot the slight tic indicating her surprise and approval. Still, she matched Wu's smile. "I think that can be arranged. Assuming you're successful." She pulled up an AR that Wu couldn't see and consulted it. Her cybereyes glinted briefly in the trendy overhead track lighting.

Wu remained silent, watching the ork. She wasn't entirely sure she was doing the right thing, even now. When an associate of the ork's had contacted her a month ago, she'd been indignant: she had been a loyal researcher for the DIMR since her MIT&T days. The Institute had funded not only a large chunk of her education, but several of her side research projects. She didn't know how they'd found out about the expedition into the QZ, but their offer had been highly tempting even when she hadn't been willing to consider it.

The caller hadn't given her details, except to say that all she'd have to do was make contact with someone behind the wall, take delivery of a datafile, and return said file—along with the results of any research into the ley line her team performed—to a location that would be specified once Wu returned. The data in the file, apparently, was vital to research being conducted by the people the caller represented. In return for providing the information, the caller had promised her an untraceable payment well in excess of a year's salary at the DIMR.

She'd turned them down, of course. It was a polite refusal—it always paid to keep one's options open—and she'd even filed away the caller's contact information on the remote chance she changed her mind. While Doris Wu was as motivated by cold, hard nuyen as the next person, mere monetary compensation wouldn't have been enough by itself to tempt her away from the prestigious position she enjoyed in one of the DIMR's high-profile research departments. Especially not after the trip to the QZ and the resulting research would poise her to take the next giant step along her ambitious career path.

Now, though, with Winterhawk's visit and the change of plans he'd sprung on them at the last minute, the situation had altered. He'd had his shot, made his reputation already—no way was she going to sit by and let him rob her of this plum opportunity.

"One other thing," she said, almost casually.

"Yes?"

"I'll need the assistance of your people to...make a couple of minor changes to the logistics of our insertion plan."

The ork's eyes glittered. "Let's finalize our agreement, and I'm sure we'll be able to work something out to our mutual satisfaction."

SIX

Bull did good work, Winterhawk had to give him that. Every detail of the English garden was perfect, from the individual blades of grass to the warmth of the filtered sunlight to the shifting silvery forms of fish moving through the stream that flowed lazily beneath the simple wooden bridge he stood on. Bull being Bull, the scene also included eerily accurate depictions of Winnie the Pooh and Piglet (the classic versions, of course) crouched over one edge, repeatedly dropping sticks into the stream and hurrying to the other side to see which one emerged first.

Ocelot showed up a few minutes later. His virtual self looked little different from the real thing—tall, blond, athletic, moving through the world like a jungle cat expecting trouble behind every tree. A bit younger, perhaps, but only a bit; Ocelot had never been one for artifice. He reached the bridge and indicated its other occupants. "They here for the meet too?"

Winterhawk chuckled. "No."

"You sure this is secure?"

It was a reasonable question, given Winterhawk's usual focus on magic over technology. "Oh, yes. I'll have to compliment Bull on the Poohsticks game next time I see him. Always nice to see someone who appreciates the classics." He stepped off the bridge and began a slow, meandering walk along the untidy garden's haphazard paths.

Ocelot fell into step next to him. "So what's this about?"

"I have a job that might interest you, and in any case, I'd appreciate your help."

Ocelot's ice-blue, cat-slitted cybereyes narrowed. "No poison this time?"

"No. Nothing like that. I'm preparing an expedition into the Boston Quarantine Zone, and I want you to come along."

He stopped. "'Hawk, are you fraggin' *nuts?*"

"I've been told so on more than one occasion, but no. Not in this case. I've been working with the DIMR for a while now, setting up a group to go inside and study the new ley line that's emerged." He set off walking again, confident that Ocelot would follow him. Bull had even gotten the light scent of primroses right.

"You—uh—*do* know nobody gets in there, right?" Ocelot caught up with him after stubbornly remaining where he was just long enough to make his point. "And even if they do find a way in, they don't get out?"

"Yes, but this isn't some poorly funded shadowrun. This expedition has some serious resources behind it. I'm confident we can manage it. Others have—you just haven't heard about them, because it's in everyone's best interests to keep it quiet." He shrugged. "We've been planning it for months. The only difference is, up until yesterday, I wasn't planning to accompany them."

Ocelot stopped again. "And now you are."

"I am. And, while I'm certain the security personnel we've got are well trained, highly competent, and expert in every way—well, I'd prefer someone with your...unique talents."

Before Ocelot could speak, the mage held up a hand. "It pays very well, I assure you. And this time I don't have to pay you out of my own pocket. I can get you on as a special security consultant—I've essentially got carte blanche to pick the team. You—what?" He paused when he got a good look at his friend. Ocelot was smiling—a tight, humorless little thing.

He resumed walking again. "Seriously, 'Hawk?"

"What?"

"Whatever you're not telling me."

"What makes you think I'm not telling you something?"

"Because I know you. I don't have to be able to read auras or any of that drek to tell something's up. This ain't just a case of you bein' your usual curious self, or you'd've been goin' all along. So, what is it?"

Winterhawk's smile matched Ocelot's—mirthless and amused. "Can't get anything by you, can I?" In truth, he expected it. He'd have been disappointed if Ocelot *hadn't* picked up on it. He made a gesture in the air and a holo appeared in front of them.

Ocelot studied it. "Who is she?"

"Her name is Victoria Crane. She's inside. And I'm going to get her out. That's not part of the approved expedition, hence my interest in...nonstandard assistance."

"You takin' side jobs? I didn't think you did that anymore."

"Not exactly. I have a more...personal interest in this one. A friend asked me to look into her disappearance while I was inside." He waved his hand again and the holo disappeared. He resumed walking. A fox darted across their path, disappearing into the tangled bushes. After several moments of silence, he said softly, "Apparently, she's my daughter."

Ocelot's double-take was almost comical. He stopped dead in his tracks and spun on Winterhawk. *"What?"*

"Long story. The short version is that I had a relationship around twenty years ago. It didn't work out. Her mother never told me after she left." Winterhawk sighed. This was unfamiliar territory for him. Normally, he made sure he was so busy that he didn't even have time to *think* about such things, let along talk about them with anyone else. He'd made a career of keeping his personal life—well—*personal,* and his close ties to other people as infrequent as he could manage. "Look—there's no point in going on about it. She's in there, her mother asked me to find her and get her out, and I plan to take my best shot at it. Will you help me?"

"You believe this woman? Seems pretty convenient, having some long-lost daughter show up right before you're plannin' to head into the QZ."

Winterhawk walked for a while, staring out over the garden, before he replied. "I believe her. I didn't at first. I thought the same thing you did. But...yes. I do."

Ocelot let his breath out in a long, slow exhale. "You realize this is a bad idea, right? You're probably gonna get yourself killed runnin' off lookin' for some random corp princess inside the Zone. You've heard the stories about what it's like in there, yeah?"

"Oh, I've probably heard more of them than you have." He turned and headed back toward the bridge without looking at his friend. Off in the distance, Pooh and Piglet darted across the bridge and flung themselves down on their bellies, gesturing with enthusiasm down toward the water. "So...are you in or not?"

"Yeah, I'm in," he said, jamming his hands in his pockets in resignation. "Somebody's gotta keep your ass outta trouble."

"Nice to see you've got such faith in me," Winterhawk said wryly.

SEVEN

Between the ten-meter-tall, highly fortified walls erected around the QZ, the military and corporate presence patrolling the shoreline, and the aircraft and drones constantly flying overlapping patterns along all sides of the border, one might think getting in or out of Boston would be impossible. Add the plethora of spirits and technological devices supplementing the Zone's lethal defenses to the mix, and anyone contemplating a trip might decide they'd be better off trying to break into somewhere safer—like, say, the Aztechnology Pyramid, or Ghostwalker's lair.

The thing about airtight defenses, though, is that they never are. No matter how carefully one might plan, no matter how much money and ingenuity one might devote to building the perfect containment system, there's almost always one avenue that can't be completely locked down: the metahumans who designed, built, and administer the system.

Everybody has a price, and as long as that remained true, the most perfect system in the world is only as safe as the weakest member of its critical staff.

In the case of the Boston Quarantine Zone, that weak link was Ares.

Ostensibly, the Zone's land defenses were coordinated by a non-corporate force: the UCAS National Guard, aided by their various corporate advisors. Most of the big corps, including NeoNET, Renraku, MCT, Saeder-Krupp, and Aztechnology, had boots on the ground, and even though they were all wearing the same uniform patch, everybody knew who was from where.

Due to some fallout from the Brookline incident, Ares, while reinstated as part of the security coalition, didn't get the preferred location assignments for securing the QZ perimeter. Which, in turn, meant that if you knew who to talk to, you might find their sections of the border a bit more porous than expected—for the right inducements, anyway.

Winterhawk pulled up the collar of his heavy armored coat. It was a couple hours before dawn, and the hangar wasn't heated. The late-fall wind blowing in through the wide, open doorway sliced through him like knives. At least they were getting in before the snows began. With luck they'd be in and out before they had to worry about that added inconvenience.

Not that luck ever had much to do with operations like this. It was all about planning, and how well the planners could anticipate potential pain points. In this case, that meant a lot of variables not accounted for.

Winterhawk stood off to one side with Ocelot, both watching closely as the workmen prepared the drops for loading into the battered cargo plane's hold.

"I don't like this," Ocelot said.

"I'm not fond of it myself." Winterhawk shifted his attention to Doris Wu, who was conferring with one of the workmen. A small group of others from the DIMR team huddled around a pile of gear, sipping soykaf. "But we investigated several possibilities, and this one's the safest. If we try to go in on the ground, we're likely to get shot down before we come anywhere near the wall. Same with a water approach—too many automated defenses."

"Yeah, but what's to stop the people inside from shooting us out of the air once they drop us? We'll be sitting ducks up there."

Winterhawk didn't respond; he'd known Ocelot long enough to know that grumbling was his old friend's way of letting off steam. Both of them had been fully briefed on the plan, including the security precautions: the crates in which they'd be riding were fully armored as well as warded to prevent detection by magicians or spirits inside or out. The pallets were equipped with sophisticated guidance systems designed to steer them toward the designated landing area, inside a small complex controlled by Ares. After that, they'd be on their own—their contact had made no promises or guarantees beyond dropping them inside.

The most problematic part of the whole thing, and the one causing all of them the most concern, was the fact that the drop target was nowhere near as close to Salem as they'd have preferred. Although the new ley line extended through most of Boston, Winterhawk's plan was to make arrangements with friends he had among the Salem witches, allowing them a better chance to establish a stable base of operations. With communications in and out of the Zone spotty at best and nonexistent at worst, he hadn't been able to make definitive contact, but as far as he was concerned it represented their best option once they got inside.

However, the Ares contact, a shadowy ork known only as "Sarge," had refused to discuss altering the route to drop them further north, claiming they'd come under increased scrutiny since the deal was negotiated, and it would look too suspicious for the cargo plane to deviate from its usual routes. "Take it or leave it," he'd said. "I'm pullin' enough strings to get you in there in the first place."

The crates were arranged on thermoplast pallets, tightly lashed down to ensure they'd remain stable. Sarge had given them a brief overview when they'd arrived an hour ago: each pallet was carefully balanced with a mix of large and small crates, and attached to a parachute that would deploy automatically when the pallet reached the preprogrammed altitude. "It's not an exact science," Sarge said, his cigarette bobbing up and down as he spoke. "We've had pretty good success dropping 'em down into the complex, but sometimes they go a little off course. You'll want to be prepared to defend yourself if that happens."

The team would enter the Zone inside five of the larger crates. Each one was designed to carry two people, depending on size. Doris Wu had seen to the logistics: each magical researcher would be paired up with a security specialist, and additionally the team's decker would ride with Wu in the largest of the crates.

The accommodations were far from posh. Winterhawk eyed the interior of the crate he was to share with Ocelot: it included a pair of narrow jump seats, both facing the crate's wall where sliding panels afforded a view of the outside (as well as a place to shoot or cast spells from if the need should arise). Their gear, secured with tie-downs, and a stack of boxes marked with Ares logo, took up the remainder of the space. Tight quarters.

He glanced at Ocelot. "It won't be for long."

"Yeah, that's what I keep tellin' myself. You bringin' Maya?"

Winterhawk indicated a small crate under one of the jump seats. "I didn't want her to come, but she insisted. There've been quite a number of reports of spirits being disrupted when they try to get in or out."

"So she's gonna ride in there?"

"It's heavily insulated, even more than our main crate. It should be nearly impossible to detect her. Once we're inside, she'll be fine as long as she doesn't try to leave."

"Okay, let's move 'em out," Sarge called. "Everything's loaded up and ready to go. Get yourselves settled and strapped in. Takeoff's in fifteen minutes."

Winterhawk opened the small crate. "*Are you sure you want to do this?*" he asked Maya. She'd been hanging out on the astral plane; he felt her presence nearby even though he couldn't see her. *"Last chance to back out."*

"Somebody needs to look out for you," she said, amused. Her shimmering form appeared inside the crate. She gazed up at him with luminous green eyes, then folded her paws primly beneath her and her plumy black tail around her haunches.

Winterhawk closed the crate and made sure it was sealed, amused by the absurdity of what looked very much like tucking one's cat into a carrier for a trip to the veterinarian. He slid the crate under his seat, cinched the tie-downs securely in place, then took his own seat and strapped in.

Ocelot did the same, checking to make sure his weapons—a Predator and a Defiance T-250 shotgun—were easily accessible. The space inside the crate was too cramped for him to use his AK-97, but he still kept it lashed to the wall next to him along with his katana.

Sarge's men closed the crate and several *snaps* sounded as they secured it. After a moment, dim lights switched on. Winterhawk felt Ocelot tense next to him—he'd never done well in confined spaces, and this place certainly qualified. "I could use a little trid spell to conjure you up an in-flight movie if you like."

Ocelot didn't answer, nor did his tension subside.

A few moments later, the crate shuddered and a muffled whining roar came though, and they began to move.

The comm crackled, and Doris Wu's voice came through: *"Comm check. Everyone getting this?"*

The other groups checked in. "Loud and clear," Winterhawk said. If necessary, he could cast a Clairvoyance spell so he could see what was going on outside, but he wanted to use as little magic as possible until they were safely inside, to further avoid the possibility of detection. He'd have to make do with the pair of small cameras mounted on the crate's exterior walls. They had a limited field of view, but at least they provided a picture of their surroundings.

"All right," Wu said. *"Everybody sit tight, and we should be inside in less than a half-hour. We'll regroup at the rendezvous point and make our plans for getting to Salem."*

The plane continued its rumbling approach, and a few minutes later they were in the air.

Winterhawk leaned back in his seat. It was impossible to get comfortable—there simply wasn't enough room inside the cramped crate to stretch out his long legs, and his back ached from pressing against the unyielding wall.

It already seemed like they'd been in the air for hours, but a glance at his chrono told him they should be crossing into the QZ in about fifteen minutes. Ocelot sat next to him, white-knuckled hands clenched around the shotgun in his lap, eyes closed, his entire posture radiating stress. Winterhawk decided not to try talking to him.

Instead, he pulled his commlink from the inner pocket of his coat and studied the holo Olivia had given him. The dark-haired young woman gazed back at him with that glitter of challenge in her eyes; he examined her face, looking for any resemblance.

Victoria. My daughter.

The words sounded strange to him—strange and implausible. Oh, it was certainly possible, biologically speaking. He'd had his share of relationships, especially back in those days: most of them brief, intense, and without strings attached from either his side or hers. But the thought that one of those relationships had produced a daughter—and one whose mother had kept secret from him for nearly twenty years—seemed like something out of a bad trid show. Had Olivia taken steps on purpose to increase the likelihood of a pregnancy? He couldn't believe she'd do that, but then, apparently he hadn't known her as well as he thought he did, even back then.

Despite his intentions to keep his thoughts focused on the mission, at least until the drop got them successfully into the QZ, his mind kept returning to Victoria. What was she like? Her mother had said she was "just like him," and hadn't sounded happy about it. What did she mean? Victoria was an adept, she said. The files she provided described the young woman as a gifted athlete, the recipient of a scholarship to MIT&T, highly intelligent, but an indifferent student.

Winterhawk paged through the file, noting the numerous citations she'd racked up during her early school career for pushing boundaries and defying authority. He smiled a little; the old Olivia, the carefree spirit he'd known, might have stood for that kind of thing—perhaps even celebrated it—but the modern-day Olivia, the ambitious corporate power player, would find it as problematic as—well, as the restless mage she'd spent a few months with all those years ago, the one she'd abruptly broken things off with just about the time he'd actually considered that they might be getting serious for the first time in his adult life.

Nineteen years old. Speaking of adult lives: at nineteen, Victoria was no longer a child. That changed things too. He'd never wanted to be a father. He'd never enjoyed being around small children, and the thought of having responsibility for raising one of them terrified him more than any of the horrific magical threats he'd faced. But hell, he'd done shadowruns—successful ones with team members Victoria's age. He hadn't decided yet whether he'd even tell her who he was, but if he did manage to track her down in that hellhole—if she were even still alive, which he had to admit, given the reports coming out of the QZ, was by no means certain—he'd have the chance to get to know her first. To gauge what kind of person she was, and whether he thought she'd benefit from further association with him.

Or him with her.

"So you're a dad."

Winterhawk looked up to catch Ocelot glancing at the holo. "Apparently so."

"Can't get over that. It just seems so...not you."

"Knowing your habits," he said, amused, "I wouldn't say much. Wouldn't be at all surprised to find a few copies of you running around Seattle."

Ocelot shook his head emphatically. "Not happening. That's why I rent my relationships." He nodded at the holo. "What's her mom like? She say why she didn't tell you?"

Winterhawk didn't want to discuss it, but given that the distraction meant Ocelot wasn't currently clenched around his shotgun, he conceded. "She was different back then. We weren't together long. I thought it was serious at the time, but in retrospect it was never meant to be. We had...mutually incompatible ambitions."

Ocelot considered that, staring straight ahead. He didn't look at Winterhawk when he said, "You know the kid could be dead, right? Or might get that way when we're tryin' to get back out."

"I know that."

"So...if we find her...are you gonna tell her?"

Winterhawk decided he shouldn't be surprised Ocelot had picked up on his thoughts. The two of them had been teammates long enough that they'd come to a strange kind of understanding, despite their wildly varying backgrounds. "I don't know yet," he said at last. "I think it will depend on her."

"On whether you think she can handle it, you mean."

He shrugged. "Who knows if we can even find her? One person in an area that's essentially a war zone, with spotty communications, growing anarchy, and CFD reaching epidemic proportions. Odds aren't good. I know people in Boston, but who knows whether they'll be able to help us with this?"

"Plus you have to do what you went in there for." Ocelot nodded. "That dwarf woman, the one in charge, doesn't like you, does she?"

"What makes you think so?" Winterhawk hadn't told Ocelot anything about Doris Wu, and this morning she'd mostly avoided the two of them as she directed the loading logistics.

"Pretty obvious. I caught her giving you the stinkeye a couple times earlier, while she was talking to that Sarge guy."

Winterhawk was about to answer when the comm crackled and the pilot's voice spoke: *"We're approaching the drop point. We'll circle the target area and drop the crates approximately thirty seconds apart, some on the initial approach, and the rest on the return loop. You'll feel a drop, and then a jerk a few seconds later as the chute deploys. The pallet's guidance system will get you as close to the target zone as possible, but it's not precise. When you land, your holding crates will open automatically to allow exit. If that doesn't happen for some reason, use the manual releases inside."*

"Copy that," Wu responded. *"Remember, everyone, stay in communication. If you end up outside the target zone, get yourselves to a safe area and report your position. We'll have to play things by ear, but the priorities are staying safe, keeping the team together, and securing the equipment, in that order. Understood?"*

The others responded affirmatively. Winterhawk wasn't entirely sure if the hesitation in some of their replies came from a bad comm connection or fear as it finally sunk in that they were about to ride a parachuting crate down into one of the most dangerous quarantine zones in the UCAS.

Either way, it was too late to back out now.

"Winterhawk, do you copy?" Wu asked.

"Ready to go."

EIGHT

"Something's wrong." Winterhawk pulled up an AR view and connected to the exterior cameras, trying to get a look outside, but all he could see was the dimly lit inner wall of the plane's cargo hold.

Ocelot's hands tightened on his assault rifle. He'd slung the shotgun over his shoulder and unlimbered the larger weapon as their drop time approached. "Why?"

"They should have dropped us by now."

"They said it would be thirty seconds or so between drops. Maybe we're last in line." Nonetheless, Ocelot slid his viewing port open. "Can you get a look around magically?"

Winterhawk cast a Clairvoyance spell and reached out beyond the plane. Below, all he could see was fog obscuring the city, tinged with the faint light of the approaching dawn. He activated his comm. "This is Winterhawk. Pilot, are you there?"

"Affirmative," the pilot said.

"What's going on? Why haven't we been dropped yet?"

"Stand by. We're experiencing a small technical difficulty. We'll be doing one more circling pass so we can correct it, then you're next in line."

Winterhawk tensed. "What about the others? Are we the last?"

"Yes, sir. Please stand by." The connection went dead.

"I'm telling you, something's wrong," Winterhawk said again. "Wu? Do you copy?"

No response.

"Damn."

Ocelot shifted in his seat. "I want outta here," he said through gritted teeth. "Now."

"That makes two of us." What was going on? "Wu! Please respond. What's happening down there?"

The plane bucked and shuddered, and the comm crackled again. *"This is the pilot. We're encountering some difficulty. Please be advised of a small change of plans."*

Winterhawk's tension grew. "What kind of change?"

"We're unable to drop you at the original target location. We've just been informed they're experiencing problems on the ground. We've identified an alternate location, south of the original."

"What the hell?" Ocelot demanded. He grabbed Winterhawk's wrist and yelled into the comm, "What kinda problems? Just put us down where you're fraggin' supposed to!"

"I'm afraid that's not possible at this time, sir. Please stand by and make sure you're strapped in. Drop in thirty seconds." The comm went dead again.

It had been a long time since thirty seconds had passed so slowly. Winterhawk sat, every muscle tense as the plane continued to shudder and bounce. Were they flying through turbulence? Were they under attack? He couldn't tell. Next to him, Ocelot's growing agitation was nearly palpable despite his stillness. He tried the comm again: "Wu? Do you copy?"

Still no answer.

There was a *thump* and the pilot's voice came through again. *"We're opening the bay doors now. Stand by. You'll feel a drop and then a jerk upward about ten seconds later as the chute deploys."*

"Where are we?" Winterhawk demanded. "Where are you dropping us?"

No answer. Instead, something jolted the crate and pushed it forward, and then they were falling.

"'Hawk...?" Ocelot's voice sounded tight. "What do we do if the chute doesn't open?"

That thought had already crossed his mind, but he hadn't mentioned it—Ocelot's claustrophobia was causing enough problems as it was. "I'll worry about that in ten seconds," he said, already readying a levitation spell. He didn't know how much the rest of the cargo on the pallet weighed, so he had no idea if the spell would be strong enough to keep them from crashing.

A sharp jerk pulled them upward, straining them against their harnesses. A few seconds later a low rumble began, sending a faint vibration through the bottom of the crate.

Winterhawk let his breath out, and only then realized he'd been holding it. "There," he said, relieved. "The chute's deployed, and the guidance system is online. Don't know where we're ending up, but at least it's likely to be in one piece."

"Unless somebody on the ground tries to shoot us out of the sky."

"Ever the optimist." Winterhawk tried to be amused by his friend's characteristic pessimism, but the fact was he'd had that thought too. None of this was going as planned—why had all the others been dropped at the designated location, but they had not? Why had the "technical difficulties" surfaced only after all the other crates were down?

He remembered the conversation he'd had with Wu back in DeeCee, how she'd responded when he'd told her he'd be accompanying the expedition. Had she—?

But no, that was absurd. Doris Wu was a professional, and a loyal longtime DIMR operative. He'd never worked with her prior to this mission, but he knew her reputation well. She wouldn't put the mission at risk because of a personal issue.

Still, though, why wasn't she responding to his comm calls? It could be nothing more than the notoriously uneven coverage inside the QZ—or it could be that something had gone wrong on their end. Not knowing was excruciating.

"How long until we touch down?" Ocelot asked. He had his AK-97 out and was peering through the sliding port.

"Couple of minutes, I think." Winterhawk leaned down beneath his seat and flipped the catch on Maya's concealment crate. At least she'd gotten past the spirit blockade without being noticed. "*Maya?*"

The crate was empty, but Maya's reassuring voice spoke in his mind. "*I'm here. You seem agitated. Is something wrong?*"

"*We're not sure yet.*"

"Can you send her out to do some scouting?" Ocelot asked, indicating the crate with a head movement, without looking away from the viewing port or moving his weapon.

"I don't want to do that until we land," Winterhawk said. "Too much chance someone will notice her."

"Great. So we—"

The crate jerked, and the low, steady rumble beneath them changed tone.

"What's that?" Ocelot demanded.

"I'm not sure." Winterhawk kept his voice calm, though he was anything but. The last thing he needed was Ocelot's paranoia and claustrophobia to combine into a full-blown attack. If that happened, his friend might well rip the crate open with his bare hands in his compulsion to get *out*.

The crate jerked again, first in one direction, and then in another, flinging them against their harnesses. Ocelot pressed himself against the viewing port, swinging his gun barrel back and forth. "I don't see anything out there," he said. "I don't think anybody's shooting at us."

The rumble changed tone again, taking on a high-pitched whine. The crate shuddered. "Damn," Winterhawk said under his breath.

"Damn what? What the hell's going on?"

"Someone on the ground is trying to take control of the guidance system."

"You mean they're hacking us? Steering us off course?"

"That's exactly what I mean."

"Can you do anything about it?"

"Not without a decker." And Wu had made sure the only decker on the team was in her crate.

"I want *out* of here!" Ocelot was already unhooking his safety harness. "No way in hell I'm gonna sit here while they drag us over half the damn town!"

Winterhawk pulled up an AR window and adjusted the view from the outside camera. The image was blurred and foggy, as yet showing nothing but sky and the far-off, shadowy forms of buildings.

"Strap in," he ordered. "We—"

Something hit the side of the crate, rocking them back and forth, and a loud *boom* sounded.

The camera feed went dead.

Beneath them, the low rhythmic rumble of the guidance system shuddered again.

"'Hawk, if you don't pop this thing open right now, I will," Ocelot said. Outside, more *booms* sounded as what sounded like rounds slammed into the sides of the crate. "Why the hell are they *shooting* at us?"

That was a damn good question. Winterhawk leaned against the wall and peered out through the viewing port, sending a Clairvoyance spell out to try to figure out how high up they were—if it could penetrate the fog.

A round hit the side only a few centimeters away from him. He jerked backward, slamming against the back of the crate, and struggled to keep the spell up.

Then something exploded above them, and they were falling.

"'Hawk?" Ocelot yelled, his voice bright with panic.

But Winterhawk wasn't listening. "*Maya, help me,*" he sent, gathering energy. He didn't have time to think or to plan—he'd have to count on his magic being strong enough that his levitation spell could get them down safely.

"*I'm here, boss.*"

He felt her strength add to his as the spell went off. The crate ceased its plummet toward the ground with an abrupt jerk and settled into floating. He focused his concentration on lowering it slowly and carefully down—he had no idea how far up they were, since it was impossible to see past the fog covering the ground. When he spoke, his voice was tight with strain. "Look outside. If you see the ground, tell me."

Ocelot gritted his teeth and nodded, moving to the viewing port. "Can't see a damn thing," he said after a moment. "Nothin' but fog or clouds or somethin'."

More rounds slammed into the crate's side, rocking it.

Winterhawk closed his eyes and blocked out everything but the crate. Already, holding the levitation spell was straining his magical strength. He didn't usually have trouble with levitation, but whatever was in the other crates on the pallet must be heavy—and the QZ's background count made it more difficult than usual to keep the spell going even at his power level. How did street-level magicians even get anything *done* in this spirits-forsaken place? He clenched his fists, squeezing his eyes shut. He couldn't break concentration now. The crate rocked back and forth as more rounds struck it.

"I think we're gettin' close," Ocelot called. "I can see the tops of some buildings now."

"How tall?" he rasped.

"Can't tell. Fraggin' fog is—look out!"

Winterhawk's concentration finally slipped at Ocelot's yell. The crate jerked, tilted crazily, and slammed hard into the ground.

NINE

Ocelot was already struggling with the catches on the inside of the crate. "Crash fragged 'em up," he muttered.

From outside, thumps and yelling voices. Winterhawk couldn't make out much of what they were saying, but he caught snatches of it: "*Get it open!*" and "*Hurry up!*" and "*Not much time–*" No way to tell where they'd come down—his Clairvoyance spell would be no help with that, and opening the viewing port would only give away their presence. But if these people were the ones who'd steered the drop off course, they could be anywhere. He unhooked his safety harness.

The thumping and pounding increased, and then the front side of the crate popped open to reveal a crowd of people clustered around it—mostly young, dressed in synthleather and ripped denim. Many were armed, with a motley collection of weapons ranging from crowbars and baseball bats all the way up to assault rifles and SMGs. Behind them, Winterhawk got a brief impression of blasted-out buildings with boarded windows, abandoned vehicles, and graffiti.

Wherever they were, they definitely weren't inside some Ares facility.

The crowd stared at Winterhawk and Ocelot. "What the fuck—?" one of them, a bulky bald ork in a CrimeTime T-shirt and a synthleather vest, demanded.

The others behind him began muttering, and some raised their weapons.

This was bad.

With a flick of his hand, Winterhawk raised a glowing barrier between him and Ocelot and the crowd, enclosing them inside the armored crate. They were outnumbered—if this turned into a firefight while they were still stuck inside, they were dead.

"Let's all be civilized about this," he called, projecting to be heard over the voices.

"Fuck, he's a spellslinger," one of the others said.

Behind them, on the other side of the pallet, Winterhawk heard more of the crowd ripping into the other crates. *"Maya, what are they doing? How many are there?"*

"They're carrying off the smaller crates," she said. *"And ripping open the big ones. About twenty of them all together. They're upset. This isn't what they expected."*

"Get outta there," the ork ordered. "Both of you."

"So you can shoot us?" Ocelot glared at him.

"We're takin' this stuff," said a human woman carrying an assault rifle. "Hand it over and we might let you go."

"What the fuck's goin' on?" yelled another man they couldn't see. "There ain't no food in here. No weapons."

"He's got weapons," said still another, pointing at Ocelot.

"Yeah," the ork agreed. "Hand over the guns, too, and maybe we won't kill ya."

"Like hell we will," Ocelot snapped.

"Others are coming," Maya said in Winterhawk's mind.

"How long? How many?" Over the comm to Ocelot, he added, *"We can't stay. I don't like leaving the gear, but we've no choice. We can't carry it with us."*

"I'm listenin' to any bright ideas." Ocelot indicated the area around them with a head motion. The open front of the crate was now ringed with ragged figures, about half of them armed. If they all started shooting at once, they'd blow Winterhawk's barrier down in seconds.

"Hold on," Winterhawk said. "I've got this." Aloud, projecting even more to be heard over the crowd's increased volume, he called: "Listen to me! You can have what's in the crates. But we're leaving here now, with our weapons and gear. You will stand aside and let us go." As he spoke, he reached out to the astral and gathered mana to him, weaving it into a subtle spell that settled itself around the crowd, slipping into their minds. "That's all we want," he said, his voice soothing, hypnotic, reasonable. "Just let us take our gear and go, and we'll be on our way."

It was harder to maintain the spell than it should have been, even against such a large crowd. The area's background count pushed against Winterhawk, forcing him to concentrate harder. Still, the crowd gradually stopped yelling as the spell's tendrils snaked out and took hold of them. They looked at each other as if trying to determine what they should do. They murmured and muttered among themselves. Several lowered their weapons.

"Uh...yeah, okay," the ork, who seemed to be in charge of the little band, said. "Yeah. You can go. We just want whatever's in the supply drop."

"Good, good," Winterhawk said soothingly. "That's right. We're no threat to you. None of you will be shooting at us, right?"

"Nah," the ork said. His eyes looked unfocused. "Nah, we ain't shootin' at ya. Go ahead."

"Be ready," Winterhawk said under his breath to Ocelot. "Don't threaten anyone overtly, but keep your gun ready. Grab whatever you can carry and let's be on our way. I can keep this spell going for a while, but not forever."

Ocelot didn't ask questions. He quickly gathered the rest of his gear and stowed it in the pockets of his coat, slinging his katana over his shoulder. "Let's go. These guys're makin' me nervous."

Winterhawk addressed the milling crowd again, many of whom now held some of the smaller crates. "I'm going to drop the shield now. We don't need it. You aren't going to hurt us."

"Not gonna hurt you," the ork agreed. Next to him, the woman nodded and shouldered her assault rifle. "You just get outta here and leave the stuff."

"You sure about this?" Ocelot whispered as the shimmering barrier that was the only thing between them the crowd's wrath winked out of existence.

"Shh. Come on." Now that the barrier was down, Winterhawk could devote more of his concentration to keeping the spell up on the mob. If he slipped now, if the group figured out what he'd done to them, they were dead for sure. "Just keep walking, and try not to distract me."

The ork and the woman stepped aside, and the others nearby did as well. After a moment, a few of the remaining group followed suit, leaving a narrow corridor through the crowd. Still others hurried forward to begin ransacking the inside of the big crate.

Winterhawk kept walking, slow but steady, following Ocelot as he kept his focus on maintaining the spell. If they could get away from the crowd, they could lose themselves in the dawn-lit streets while the ragtag group finished carrying off their treasures, figure out where they were, and then try to contact the other members of the expedition. All they had to do was—

"*Boss! Look out!*"

Maya's fearful voice came an instant too late as something flew into the middle of the group and detonated with a searing flash. A wave of force exploded outward, knocking them and the others off their feet.

A harsh male voice boomed over a loudspeaker: "*You're all under arrest! Everyone remain where you are. Resist and we will use force!*"

TEN

Winterhawk hit the ground and rolled. All around him, the crowd was yelling:

"*Fuck! It's the cops!*"

"*Run!*"

"*Grab shit and go!*"

"*I can't see!*"

He staggered back to his feet, looking around for Ocelot, taking a quick check of the crowd. Whatever had hit them—probably a flash-bang grenade, so he was thankful it had landed behind them or they'd both have been blinded—had blown his concentration, so the spell was down.

Fortunately the crowd seemed to have other things on its mind. The ones who hadn't been blinded were running, some of them still clutching smaller crates. Two of them carried a larger one, staggering off down the street toward an alley. They'd almost made it when a red line of rounds suddenly stitched across the rearmost of the pair. He jerked and shuddered, dropping his end of the crate with a scream as he fell. The other abandoned his burden and his friend and took off, disappearing into the shadows.

"Come on, 'Hawk!" Ocelot grabbed his arm with one hand, firing his shotgun with the other. "We gotta get outta here!"

"*Drop your weapons!*" the voice boomed over the PA again. "*Get down on the ground and place your hands on your heads! This is your last warning!*"

Whoever they were, they didn't seem inclined to wait for anyone to acknowledge their orders, though. Another small group from the crowd, running for cover behind an overturned dumpster, cried out as more rounds tore into them. Only one made it to the dumpster and immediately began firing back.

"*Maya—what do you see?*"

"*They're surrounding you. I don't recognize the uniforms.*"

"Not Knight Errant?"

"No. There's an opening to your right–see the alley there? You–"

Her voice cut off, and Winterhawk sensed fear in their link. *"What's going on? Maya?"*

"Spirits. Big ones!" Still fear. Maya was a powerful spirit, but she hadn't been designed for combat.

"Come on! This way!" Winterhawk urged Ocelot, pulling him toward the direction Maya had indicated. *"Maya, get out of here. Try to keep track of us, but if you can't, find our group. Tell them where we are. Go!"*

He felt Maya's presence leave his mind as he and Ocelot darted into the narrow alleyway between two decaying brick buildings. Littered with trash, discarded boxes, and overturned dumpsters, it made for slow going. Winterhawk was forced to slow down, following in Ocelot's wake as his more agile companion picked his way through the detritus. The stench of old garbage and rotted food hung nearly visible in the air.

They'd made it halfway to the other end of the alley when a pile of trash ahead began swirling up from the ground. Spinning madly, it formed into a vaguely humanoid shape nearly three meters tall, blocking the exit.

Ocelot pulled up short and whipped his katana off his back, arcing a powerful swing at the thing's midsection. It roared and leaped backward, then surged forward to take its own shot.

Winterhawk, a few steps behind, skidded to a stop and nearly lost his balance on a clump of slimy garbage. He didn't have time to think about where the spirit had come from, but he knew they had to get past it fast.

"Stop right there!" the booming voice called from behind him.

Winterhawk risked a fast look over his shoulder. *Damn!* Three figures stood backlit against the alley's entrance, their silhouettes bulky with armor. They carried what looked like riot shields. He threw himself sideways toward cover an instant before they opened fire.

"'Hawk!" Ocelot took another swipe at the spirit, sending part of its "arm" flying off to smash into the brick wall. "Change partners!" Without waiting for a reply, he leaped up, caught a corner of a rusting fire escape, and swung himself upward toward the building's roof, barely avoiding a blow from the trash-spirit. As he went, he sprayed covering fire toward the three cops, driving them off to both sides of the street.

Winterhawk didn't watch him go. Instead, he summoned a spirit of his own, forming it from the air around him, and directed it at the trash-spirit. It was harder to do that here, but he'd have an easier time banishing the enemy spirit if it wasn't trying to take him apart. Behind him, he heard more yelling and gunfire.

His spirit was even bigger than the trash-thing—despite the lingering effects of the flash-bang grenade, this was no time to go small. It surged forward and smashed into its opponent, driving it backward and out into whatever was at the other end of the alley. Winterhawk stayed low and followed, ducking around the corner of the building where at least he'd be out of the cops' line of fire. They'd send more, he was sure of it, but it would take time.

He allowed himself a couple seconds to take stock of his surroundings. The alley had ended at a narrow single-lane road spanning the buildings. Like the backstreet itself, it was full of trash, junked cars, and torn-up concrete, but seemed to be empty of other threats.

"Are you there?" he called to Ocelot over the comm.

"On the roof. Can you get up here?"

He glanced back toward the spirits. The trash-thing kept trying to duck past the air spirit, no doubt to reach its primary objectives: Winterhawk and Ocelot. The air spirit, however, was doing its job, moving with effortless grace to block its opponent's forward progress. The trash-thing was probably physically stronger, but with luck the air spirit would keep it busy long enough for them to escape.

"Coming," he said.

Damn, it was hard to cast spells here. He had no idea what was spiking the background count up so high; ideally he'd summon an illusion or an invisibility spell to conceal him as he went up, but the mana here felt *thick,* like he was trying to cast through sludge. His head pounding from the grenade and the wrongness of the magic, he didn't want to risk trying to maintain two spells at once. Instead, he ducked behind some cover and summoned a levitation spell. As he lifted from the ground, he stayed close to the building on his way up. He'd have to make this fast—if they spotted him before he reached the top, he'd be in trouble.

He'd made it halfway before he heard the *thunk* of something firing, and an instant later something slammed hard into his back, driving him into the side of the building. His head lit up with pain and the last thing he saw before everything went dark was the building's brick side careening past him as he fell.

ELEVEN

Winterhawk awoke into pain, disorientation, and cacophony.

It was hard to make sense of anything, or indeed even to think at all. His head throbbed, not just from the hits he'd taken, but from the fact that some kind of discordant screaming noise blared into his ears at a frequency that set his teeth on edge.

He was upright, seated in a hard chair. He raised his head, but when he tried to move further, his shoulders flared pain: his arms were wrenched backward, handcuffs digging into his wrists behind him. His ankles were likewise secured to the chair's legs.

Someone had gone out of their way to neutralize him—and done it the old-school way, too. He felt the heavy mask snugged over his head, complete with a tube shoved into his mouth that allowed him to breathe, but not to speak. *Magemask.* He'd heard of them, of course, and even seen them in use, but never experienced one himself. Nowadays, when someone needed to neutralize a mage without killing him, they generally employed a combination of drugs and VR to keep him so disoriented and distracted that he had no desire to fight it.

The magemask, on the other hand, was downright barbaric. When combined with the shrieking noise piped constantly into his ears, the thing did a damned good job of buggering up his concentration to make it difficult to even consider casting any spell.

Maybe impossible. He wasn't sure yet. That was for later, after he figured out where he was.

Where were the others? Was Ocelot here too, or had he been killed in the firefight? He struggled to remember when he'd last seen his friend, before everything had gone completely to hell, but between the noise and the disorientation, he couldn't. He wrenched his neck from one side to the other, trying to dislodge the mask's earbuds, growling in frustration around the thick plastic tube.

The blaring noise abruptly quieted to a manageable level, and a deep, harsh voice spoke. "We got four guns aimed right at your head, mage, and spirits on the astral keepin' an eye on you. You make one move that even *looks* sketchy, and we decorate the walls with your brains. Got it? Nod if you got it."

He nodded. They hadn't killed him outright—that meant they wanted something from him. Best to find out what it was before making any decisions.

"You're also under remote observation. They see anything they don't like, they flood this room with knockout gas and then they kill you. Nod if you understand."

Winterhawk nodded again. Whoever they were, they were scared of him. Very scared, in fact. He had no idea if they were telling the truth about the remote observation or the guns or the gas, but he didn't feel like testing any of it yet. Every bone in his body hurt.

"Okay. I'm gonna take the tube out so you can talk. Remember what I said. The guys with the guns have twitchy trigger fingers. Don't move."

Winterhawk didn't move. The room was oppressively warm and humid, and smelled of stale smoke, sweat, and old soykaf. The mask's clinging synthleather made the situation even more claustrophobic.

Someone—presumably the man who'd been talking to him—yanked the tube free without touching him. He coughed, his mouth suddenly dry. How long had he been here, trussed up to this chair? When he spoke, his voice cracked with disuse. "You don't have something to drink, do you?"

The man backhanded him, rocking his head back. "You answer questions, mage. That's all I want to hear out of you. Understand?"

Winterhawk tasted blood where the blow had cut into his cheek. "Who are you? What do you want with me?"

The man hit him again. "You ain't too bright, are you? I said *we* ask the questions. One more and I won't go so easy on you. Got it, scum?"

He nodded, spat blood, and shifted his jaw to make sure the guy hadn't broken it. "I've got it," he rasped.

"Good. Just so you know, you're under arrest."

"On what charge?"

Apparently, his captor didn't consider that a question worthy of further punishment. "Possession of contraband, and trespassing on corporate property. What's your name?"

"Michael Barnes." No point in lying to them—at least as far as they could know, based on the fake SIN the DIMR had set up for him. Damn, it was hard trying to talk to someone he couldn't see.

"Well, Mr. Barnes, you're in a lot of trouble." The man's voice held an edge of satisfaction. He cracked his knuckles.

"They'll be looking for me, you know."

"Not if they don't know where you are. The rest of the scum you were with are dead."

They don't know. They might be lying. He waited.

Heavy boots thumped, and the sound of the man's voice indicated he was circling the chair. "Where are the rest of your friends?"

"What friends? You just said they were dead."

A meaty hand grasped him by the hair and yanked his head back. "You know what we do to smartasses around here? Especially smartass mages?"

Around the room, metallic *clicks*.

So they were telling the truth about the guns, at least.

"I'm not being a smartass." He resisted the urge to jerk his head forward. "I've got no idea what you're talking about."

The man tightened his grip. "You know, we can do this the easy way or we can do it the hard way. I'm fine either way—my guys can always use the exercise. But why don't you just make it easy on yourself and give 'em up? It's not like they wouldn't do the same with you."

What was he talking about? "Sorry," Winterhawk said. "Even if I wanted to help you, I can't. Suppose you tell me what this is about." He braced himself for another blow.

This time, the guy hit him in the gut—a good, solid blow that knocked his breath from him and left him gasping. "Enough crap!" the man yelled, leaning in close to his face. "You tell us *now* where your chummers were divertin' those supply drops to, or you're gonna be in a world of hurt."

Winterhawk hid his immediate lack of answer behind an awkward coughing fit. So *that* was what this was about—they thought he was working with whoever had grabbed control of the crate and steered it off course. They had no idea that he and the others had entered the QZ inside the very crates they were supposed to be tampering with.

He shook his head. "You've got it all wrong. I didn't—" He paused. "Ah. I see it now. You don't want *them* diverting the drops because *you*—or more likely whoever you work for—were already diverting them for their own purposes." This got better by the moment—not only was he in the hands of some collection of grunts who fancied themselves law enforcement, but their little insertion had managed to run afoul of at least two warring factions bent on claiming the contents of the supply drops for themselves. "Have I got it right?"

"We're askin' the questions here!" the man yelled, and cuffed him again, twice this time. "One more chance—give up your friends, or we'll be forced to switch to a different approach. And trust me—you won't like it. You also won't like when we toss you in a cell somewhere and maybe just forget about you."

"Look," he said between sharp breaths. "You've got my identification. I'm a consultant for the DIMR. Why would I be hijacking bloody supply crates?"

The man snorted. "Yeah, right. And I'm Celedyr." He sighed loudly. "Okay, you wanna play it that way, fine. I'm done bein' nice."

This is nice? Winterhawk thought, testing his jaw again. Either the guy was good or he was lucky, because he still didn't think anything was broken.

"See what you can get out of him, Pinsky." His voice sounded farther back now, like he'd moved away. "Work 'im over good, but don't kill 'im. Not yet. When you're done, make sure he's all fixed up so he can't sling any mojo and toss 'im in 4D."

"Yes, sir," said another male voice: lower, gruffer. Maybe an ork. The voice held a certain pleasure that Winterhawk didn't like at all.

A heavy metal door opened and shut, and more footsteps sounded around him. He didn't need sight or astral perception to sense that more people had entered the room.

"Last chance," said the gruff voice. "I hope you don't take it, actually. Messin' up skinny norms always makes our time in this hellhole of a town a little nicer. Y'know?"

Without giving Winterhawk a chance to answer, he and the others set about following their boss's orders.

TWELVE

When Winterhawk awoke again, it took him several moments to work through the fog in his head enough to tell that he was lying on his side on a hard surface. The mask was still on, with the tube back in place, and his hands were still cuffed behind his back. They'd turned the soundtrack from hell back on as well. It wasn't as loud as before, but it didn't matter: the harsh, unpredictable chords clashed in a confusing mishmash of random sound, battering his brain, rendering any kind of thought beyond the basic level pointless and excruciating.

His body was a solid wall of pain. His captors had done what their commander had directed, falling to their task with the enthusiasm of mob enforcers or a pack of schoolyard bullies. Periodically they'd ask him again who his compatriots were, assuring him that all he had to do to make it stop was give them up, but they hadn't seemed terribly interested in whatever answers he gave. He suspected the questioning was only a formality, and what they really relished was their chance to practice their favorite mayhem-based skills.

Still, though—they'd been careful, at least as far as he could tell. He didn't think they'd broken anything, though the pain in his ribs told him they might have cracked a couple. His dry mouth tasted of blood, and it was nearly impossible to swallow around the tube.

Was he alone? How long had he been here, drifting in and out of consciousness? He had no idea. For all he knew he could be lying in the middle of a room full of people, all watching and waiting for him to awaken. He didn't think so, though—he remembered the commander's last words to his men: *"Toss 'im in 4D."* Was that a room? A cell? Had they done what the commander had threatened, and left him here to be forgotten until he died?

He struggled to concentrate. Nothing about the sounds they were pumping into his head remained the same for more than a couple of seconds—it was as if they had gathered a collection of the most distracting and irritating files they could find, tossed them into a routine that randomized not only the sounds but the volume level, and then mixed them all together. One second it was a bit of growling goblin rock, followed instantly by the high-pitched wail of a siren, followed in turn by a shrieking baby. Almost the worst part of it was the occasional second or two of something quieter, because his body remained on edge as it anticipated the inevitable return to chaos. He almost wished they'd submerged him in some drug-induced VR world.

Damn you, concentrate. *You're supposed to be good at this!* Winterhawk closed his eyes (even though the world was every bit as black when he kept them open) and began taking slow, rhythmic breaths. Entering a meditative state amid the constant the pain, hunger, exhaustion, and aural distractions wouldn't be easy, but it was his only chance. He could do this. Whoever his captors were knew he was a mage, but he had to bank on the fact that they didn't know exactly how *much* of a mage he was. He routinely masked his aura, and had been doing so when they caught him. Had they checked further once he was unconscious? Did they even have the means to do so? He had no idea, but it didn't matter.

Either he succeeded at this, or he didn't.

Deep breath.

Another.

Concentrate on slowing heartbeat, slowing respiration.

Try to block the pain. Ignore the sounds.

A high-pitched baby cry morphed into something that sounded like the squeal of pigs being slaughtered. He stiffened, jolted from his efforts, but let the sounds wash over him and renewed his attempt.

Carefully, carefully...

Focus...

Knowing if he had miscalculated they would certainly kill him, he shifted his body to the astral plane.

The sound and the pain and the exhaustion melted away with a sense of relief that was almost a physical sensation itself, but it was instantly replaced by its own set of horrors.

Grayness. Despair. Terror. Cruelty. He winced as the emotions hit him, almost retreating back to his body. Wherever he was, many people had suffered here.

He struggled against the extra load of astral suffering and looked quickly around, more than half expecting one or more angry spirits to converge on him and attack.

But they didn't.

He stood in a small box with solid walls, and he was alone.

He turned: his physical body lay on a shelf emerging from one of the walls, legs curled up, aura flickering weakly.

Tentatively, he tried to push his astral body through one of the walls. He'd have to be careful—if they had spirits on duty watching from the outside, he couldn't let them catch him.

It didn't matter, though—everywhere he tried to pass through the walls, he was stopped short. *Damn. They must have FAB or wards or something around here.* After a few more moments' examination, he decided it must be fluorescing astral bacteria, because there were places he could poke a hand through, or a leg—but nowhere he could get his entire body past. *Well, bugger. Even a badly-maintained prison is too much for me right now.* He moved back fully inside the cell, but didn't return to his body yet. It felt so good to be away from the pain...

"Maya? Are you there?"

No answer.

Where was she? Had some of the powerful spirits roaming the QZ captured her? Banished her? Disrupted her? No, he'd have felt it if she'd been destroyed.

"Maya?"

He looked around again—surely someone must come and check on him periodically, if for no other reason to make sure he was still there and still alive. When would they come back? Were they on some schedule of rounds?

"Please, Maya—if you're out there, please answer me."

"...Boss...?"

The mental voice was faint and astonished.

His astral form slumped in relief. *"Maya! Oh, thank the spirits... Where are you?"*

"...Hiding..."

"Can you help me?"

"...I can't get inside where you are," she said. *"...I can barely hear you now... You sound...wrong."*

"Do you know where I am?"

"...Yes. You're in a building. They've got spirits on patrol. I don't think I can take them all on..."

"Do you know who they are? A gang? Knight Errant?"

"...No. They have uniforms, but they act more like a gang... They like to hurt people. They've got several prisoners."

"Any other mages?"

"...No. I hid and listened to the spirits... The men are afraid of you..."

"Why didn't they just kill me, then?"

"...They think you know something... They want you to tell them..."

Winterhawk looked around again. *"Do you know if anyone else survived? Ocelot?"*

"I don't know... I've been trying to stay near where they took you. ...I couldn't sense you until you reached out to me. I think they've got you somewhere I can't reach..."

"I think I'm in a cell lined with FAB. But it's deteriorating. I can't get my astral form out, and my body's trussed up like a bloody Christmas turkey. Can you find someone to help? I'll have to go back to my body soon, before they catch me."

"I don't want to leave you..." Her voice was full of concern.

"I know...I don't want you to leave me either." Sending her—the first friendly contact he'd had in gods knew how long—away would be even harder than going back to his pain-wracked body. But he didn't have a choice if he didn't want to die here. *"But you've got to do it. Try to find someone who can get me out of here. Look for Ocelot, if he's alive. Go to the DIMR."*

"...I will," she said, resigned. Then her voice became more urgent: *"I have to go—I think one of the spirits saw me!"*

And then she was gone from his mind like she'd never been there, and all the fear and despair flowed back in and threatened to overwhelm him. For a few moments while she'd been with him, he'd managed to put it all aside, but that just made it worse than ever when it returned.

He was going to die here.

But before he did that, he would damned sure find a way to take some of them out with him.

THIRTEEN

Rough hands jerked Winterhawk up to a sitting position, and the shrieking in his ears quieted again. "Come on," a rough voice said, dragging to his feet where he stood, swaying.

He couldn't say anything with the tube in place, so he settled for making a questioning noise.

"Shut up and come with me." The man gripped his arm and tried to pull him along. "We got you covered, so don't try anything."

He staggered and pitched forward, his legs too unsteady to support him. He'd have fallen on his face if the man hadn't caught him. After a moment, another set of hands gripped his other shoulder, and together they dragged him along. With the noise volume lowered, he heard a heavy steel door open. They hustled him through it and slammed it shut behind him. He tried to keep his feet moving—walking hurt less than being dragged—but didn't completely succeed. His captors clearly had no patience for their prisoner's physical state.

After a few minutes, they threw him down into another hard chair. "Okay," the man said. "I'm gonna take off the hood. I'm also gonna warn you one more time: sit still and listen. My guys *will* shoot you if you try anything. Got it?"

Winterhawk nodded. At this point he wasn't sure what they expected him to try—though in truth he thought he could still cause them some trouble even in his current condition, if he so chose. It might still come to that, depending on why they'd brought him here.

They pulled the tube out, then hands fumbled at the back of his head and the snug-fitting magemask was pulled roughly free.

Winterhawk blinked as harsh light hit him, and coughing fit seized him.

"Here," the voice said. "Drink this."

A bottle was pressed to his lips, and he struggled to stop coughing long enough to swallow the tepid, metallic-tasting water. He opened his eyes, seeing his captors for the first time.

The man standing in front of him was human, but so big and bulked out he could have been an ork. His buzz-cut hair, rough, scarred features, and hard, narrowed eyes marked him as someone who solved most of his problems with fists rather than brains. He was dressed in an unkempt uniform with a logo reading *HARD CORPS*, and a name tag that read *Blakely*.

Behind Blakely was an even bigger and bulkier ork in the same kind of uniform. Spread out around the room, with guns trained on Winterhawk from at least three sides, more uniformed figures stood at anticipatory attention. It was clear from their expressions that they were hoping he'd make a move so they could shoot him.

"What's this about?" he rasped. It came out barely louder than a whisper. If they were intending to work him over again, why had they removed the mask? Was this something else?

"This is your lucky day, shithead," Blakely said. "I don't know how they found out you were in here, but you got somebody that wants you out."

Winterhawk stared at him. Had Maya managed to reach the DIMR? If Ocelot was still alive and she'd found him, rescue was more likely to come in the form of a heavily-armed mob storming the place.

"Where are they?" he asked. He wanted more water—or even better, something a lot stronger—but he wasn't going to ask this two-bit bully for anything. *Steady,* he told himself. Tempting as it was to do something like control the man's mind or try taking down the lot of them with a well-placed manaball, he could afford to wait.

"Just hang on. We're doin' this on our schedule, not yours."

Winterhawk shrugged, as best he could in his position. He assensed Blakely, reveling in the simple ability that he'd taken for granted for most of his life. The big man's aura radiated uncertainty and frustration—it looked like whatever orders had arrived to release him had come as an unwelcome surprise.

"So, then, what are we waiting for? I'm guessing whoever they are, if they can manage this they're not the kind who should be kept waiting." He kept his expression neutral.

Frustration flared around Blakely, and Winterhawk knew he'd hit a nerve. He almost backhanded the mage, but pulled the blow at the last second and didn't make contact. "Shut up," he said instead. "Spellslingers are a fraggin' pain in the ass anyway. Shoulda killed you before."

"Inconvenient," Winterhawk agreed. He looked down at the dirty, bloodstained, and torn remains of his shirt and trousers. "Plan to hand me over like this, do you? My benefactors might not take kindly to your...hospitality."

And then Blakely's gun was pointed at his head. "You know," he said, "I could just blow your smartass head off and claim it was an accident. Happens all the time in the Zone. Maybe I just tell 'em we found traces of CFD during a routine check, and couldn't take the chance. You want me to do that?"

Before Winterhawk could answer, there was a knock at the door. It opened to reveal another uniformed cop, this one a dwarf. "Sir," he said, "They're here for the mage. What should I tell 'em?"

Blakely snorted. "Fuck it. Let 'em have 'im." He grabbed a handful of Winterhawk's shirt front and leaned in close. "I know you got somethin' to do with those crates," he said. His breath smelled of beer and garlic. "Maybe we didn't get you for it, but you tell your friends if I catch any of 'em, they're dead. And it won't be quick, either. Got it?"

"If I see anyone, I'll be sure to pass that along." Winterhawk resisted the urge to draw back away from the cop's noxious breath.

"Get 'im outta my sight," Blakely ordered.

FOURTEEN

Winterhawk didn't recognize the woman waiting for him. She paced back and forth in the makeshift lobby, looking impatient and annoyed as she subvocalized into her commlink. She spun as the door opened. "If you don't—" she began, then stopped when she saw them. "About time," she snapped.

Winterhawk studied her as the cop behind him released the cuffs and feeling began to flood with pins and needles into his hands. Tall and slim, she had a tense, whipcord quality that made her seem like she was in motion even when standing still. Delicately pointed ears poked up through a mass of dark red hair. She wore black leathers that fit her like a second skin, a pair of twin Predator Vs hanging from her belt, and an Ingram Smartgun slung over her shoulder.

"What the hell did you *do* to him?" she demanded, glaring at the cops.

"He's a spellslinger," the big ork growled. He seemed to be the one in charge, now that Blakely had made himself scarce. "We ain't set up to deal with spellslingers. He's lucky we didn't blow 'im away when we caught 'im. He was tresspassin' on corp property. You want 'im or not?"

The woman didn't seem at all deterred by his hostility. She stalked forward and got right in his face. "You're *lucky* my employer found out he was here before you *did* kill him," she said, her voice low and even. Its utter lack of emotion made it sound even more threatening. "You don't want to know what might have happened to your pathetic little operation here if you had."

The ork paled a bit at the mention of her "employer." He released his viselike grip on Winterhawk's upper arm and shoved him toward the woman.

The human with him pulled out a commlink, tapped something into it, and offered it to the woman. "Sign here."

She did something with her own commlink, glared at the guy, then turned to address Winterhawk for the first time. "What did you have with you?" Unlike the way in which she spoke to the cops, her voice held polite respect when speaking to him.

Who *was* this woman? Did she work for the DIMR? It was the only reasonable explanation, though he wasn't sure why the mention of her employer would strike such apprehension into these thuggish cops. He decided to roll with it for now—whoever she was, she was getting him out of this nightmare, and that was good enough for the moment.

"Not too much," he said. "Armored coat, commlink. Oh, and a small box containing a ritual sample. Though I doubt I'll be getting that back, will I?" The cops—or whatever they were—had probably tossed it. No doubt the contents of the crate were long gone too, stolen and sold either by this bunch or one of the others involved in the firefight.

"You'd be surprised," the woman said. Then, back to the man: "You'll produce everything that you confiscated. And I mean *everything*. That includes any ritual samples you might have taken from him as well as the one he had on him."

Winterhawk raised an eyebrow. She was good. He must be slipping, if he hadn't thought of that. But then, he had no idea how long it had been since they'd taken him, and his brain was operating nowhere near peak capacity.

The man looked like he might protest, but the ork made a sharp gesture and he scurried off through the closed door. Less than a minute later, he returned carrying a box, which he dropped with rather more force than necessary on the desk.

"That's it," he said. "The ritual sample we got from the spellslinger's in there, but that's it. If he had another one on him, it might've gotten destroyed when we arrested him."

Winterhawk sighed. He'd expected as much, despite the woman's confidence to the contrary. Losing the sample was going to make locating Victoria a hell of a lot harder, but right now he had more immediate concerns.

"You sure about that?" the woman asked, watching the ork carefully. She turned back to Winterhawk, who'd lowered himself onto a bench, deciding he'd lose less dignity by sitting down than by falling down. "Are you satisfied he's telling the truth?"

He'd been assensing the ork ever since he'd sat down. His aura showed more than apprehension—it showed fear. A simple truth detection spell confirmed it. "That's all they took," he said. "I don't know what happened to the other sample, but they don't have it."

"Fuck, okay. Why don't we get out of here? This place stinks. And I'm sure you'll want to clean up and get something to eat in a more civilized atmosphere."

"Absolutely." He realized it was entirely possible that he'd just been sprung from one trap to walk, eyes open, into a more dangerous one. But right now, he didn't care.

He waited until they were outside before he said anything else. "I don't suppose you're planning to tell me who you are, or who your employer is." He struggled not to show how weak and ill he felt. This woman may have saved his life, but that didn't mean he trusted her yet. "Are you from the DIMR?"

"You can call me Anissa," she said. "Our ride should be here any minute. Think you can make it a couple blocks?"

He glanced at the stark gray building they'd just exited, not missing the fact that she hadn't answered his questions. "I want to get as far away from this place as I can. I'll manage." In truth, he had no idea how he intended to do that since his legs felt like limp spaghetti noodles, but the thought of getting away from Hard Corps spurred him to extra energy. Once they got wherever they were going, he could work on trying to find Ocelot, and figure out if Wu and the rest of the expedition had made it where they were trying to go. Assuming, of course, that Wu wasn't the reason he was here in the first place. He'd have to play that one carefully.

"Where are—" he began.

Anissa held up an urgent hand to stop him, clearly listening to something he couldn't hear. Her expression darkened. "Fuck!"

"What?"

"Our ride's under attack!"

FIFTEEN

Anissa tensed suddenly, primed for action. Her gaze shot between some point ahead of them and Winterhawk behind her. Moving fast, she plunged her hand into her jacket pocket and thrust something toward him.

"Sorry about this," she said, "but they need help, and I'm not leaving you here."

She offered a slap patch—stim, almost certainly. Something to get him moving. Not his normal choice, but this wasn't a normal situation. He'd deal with the aftereffects later.

He snatched it from her and slapped it into place on his arm. Instantly, the fog shrouding his brain cleared away like someone had hit it with a high-speed fan, and his heart began hammering in his chest as if he'd just run several times around the block. Some of the pain drained away, and the rest dulled. Useful things, stim patches—it was part of why he usually avoided them. He'd pay for it when the effect wore off, but if he couldn't get moving, he might not live long enough for it to wear off.

"Let's go," he rasped.

Immediately she took off, though he could tell she wasn't moving as fast as she might have if he wasn't with her. Winterhawk struggled to keep up with her. Even with the stim patch, he was still weak from his confinement and hunger.

"Be careful," she called without looking back, still obviously splitting her attention between him and her conversation with her unseen compatriots. "They ran into a mob of shamblers. If you can't fight, get out of the way till we give you the all-clear. A little mojo wouldn't hurt, though." She drew both Predators as she ran.

Shamblers! So he was about to get his first taste of the reason why Boston was locked down in the first place. The name had amused him when he'd first seen it in some of the reports coming out of the city: it made it sound like Boston was under attack by some kind of zombie apocalypse. But while the CFD-addled, mindless mobs had quite a lot in common with the classic walking dead (including their penchant for cannibalism to renew their bodies and energy), there was nothing entertaining about them. Especially not now, when he was running headlong into the middle of a group of them.

Ahead, Anissa leaped over something in the street. "Look out!" she called back.

He followed her lead and sidestepped the dark form huddled next to a clapped-out American missing two wheels. A brief look down as he went by revealed a human form—but clearly one beyond help. It was missing its head and one of its arms, and a pool of liquid, black in the single overhead sodium-vapor light, spread beneath it. At least some of the shamblers had clearly come from this direction. Winterhawk glanced around, half-expecting a crowd of them to come boiling out of the nearby darkened alleys.

Anissa slowed a little to let him catch up. "They're fraggin' hard to kill," she said. "We need to get to the vehicle and clear a path out. Be ready to move."

He heard them before he saw them. They rounded a corner and Anissa held up a hand in a sharp *stop* gesture. Winterhawk skidded to a halt behind her and stared.

"Bloody hell..." he muttered.

All the reports he'd read to help prepare the team for what to expect once they were inside the QZ did nothing to inoculate him against the real thing. A mob of perhaps twenty staggering, moaning scarecrow creatures in tattered clothes surrounded a small vehicle parked between two nonfunctional hulks. There were so many of them that they blocked out any light that might be coming from it: the only way Winterhawk could tell it was there at all was the blare of its alarm going off into the night, adding its shriek to the inarticulate cries of the shamblers.

"Come on!" Anissa ordered. "Remember what I said—stay out of the way if you can't fight." She started forward again, guns aimed at the crowd but not firing yet. They either hadn't noticed her and Winterhawk, or were simply more focused on getting into the vehicle.

Winterhawk hurried to catch up; he knew the stim patch wouldn't keep him moving for long.

Ahead, a victorious cry went up from the shamblers. With a loud metallic creak followed by a crash, the group on one side of the vehicle shoved it upward until it rested on its side. They continued pounding on it with their fists, yelling something Winterhawk couldn't make out.

"Fuck!" Anissa ducked behind a nearby derelict car, took aim, and squeezed off twin bursts from her pistols. She was good—two of the creatures' heads exploded in gory hazes, their bodies dropping, still twitching, to the ground.

But now she'd gotten the others' attention. "Can you use magic to get the car upright?" she demanded to Winterhawk, who'd joined her behind cover. More than half of the crowd of shamblers had redirected their attention to where they hid. Grunting with rage, the things abandoned the car and started toward them.

"Possibly. But what about—"

"Don't worry about me! We need to get that car moving!"

"Right, then." Nothing was ever easy, and this was no exception. "I hope you know what you're doing."

He muttered a small levitation spell under his breath—far less impressive than anything he'd normally do, but he couldn't risk drain—and lifted off the ground, aiming for the roof of a two-story building next to where the car was parked. Even despite his growing fatigue, it felt good to be using magic again.

"Hit 'em with electricity if you can!" Anissa yelled in between bursts.

Winterhawk didn't answer because two of the shamblers spotted him, bent to pick up debris from the street, and flung it at him. Their aim was every bit as bad as he'd expect from a bunch of bad zombie imitators, and good thing, too—what they lacked in dexterity, they made up for in strength. He dropped down on top of the building as something heavy and metal hurtled past him, slamming into the side of the building less than a meter from where he'd been. He ducked behind the brick lip surrounding the building's top and took quick stock of the situation.

Off in the distance, no more than a block away, another mob approached, even bigger than the first. For a second Winterhawk allowed himself to hope it might be help, but no, another couple seconds' scrutiny revealed the same staggering but surprisingly fast movements as the group below him. More shamblers, and he had no way to communicate with Anissa aside from yelling and hoping she'd hear him over the shrieking alarm and the grunts and moans of the attackers. He'd have to hope she noticed them.

But then again, if they weren't out of here before the second group reached them, it might not matter.

A cry rose above the shamblers' din. The creatures had gotten the van's passenger-side door open and yanked the man riding shotgun out, shrieking and flailing in panic. Gunfire split the air as Anissa tried to take them out, but she wasn't fast enough. Two more of them went down, but others grabbed the screaming man and, as Winterhawk watched in horror, ripped his arms free of his body and then fell upon his jerking corpse.

"Johnny!" Anissa yelled. She'd pulled out her SMG and was firing more bursts into the group approaching her.

Winterhawk blinked sweat from his eyes. No more time to wait. Anissa had said electricity affected the shamblers—now was the time to find out if she was right. This was going to hurt, but getting ripped to pieces would hurt a lot more.

He gathered mana to him and released it with a roar, carefully controlling its target area to avoid the car. They wouldn't get anywhere if he burned out its electronics or killed its driver. Even without his usual magical foci, and at a fraction of his normal power level, the effect was impressive. The air crackled as flashing bolts arced down, illuminating the area next to the car with a deadly, dancing lightshow.

The shamblers screamed and juddered as the lightning disrupted the nanites coursing through their bodies—if the situation had been less grave, it might have even been comical, the way they jerked like a crowd of bad backup dancers. One by one, the creatures clutched their heads and fell. The smell of ozone and burning flesh rose, competing with the ever-present stench of garbage.

"Go!" Winterhawk yelled. His head pounded, and he felt blood trickling from his nose. *I must be farther gone than I thought— that shouldn't have hit me so hard.*

But he wasn't done yet. As Anissa vaulted up, taking down shambler after shambler with precise, surgical headshots, Winterhawk used a quick telekinetic shove to topple the car back onto its wheels, crushing several of the creatures beneath it, then levitated himself down to the ground. He hoped the driver was still alive and the car still functional, or they were all about to be in a lot of trouble.

The second group of shamblers was getting closer. They were less than fifty meters away now, and appeared to sense their prey preparing to escape because they increased their speed. Anissa slapped a new magazine into her SMG and sprayed them with rounds; some dropped, but the rest kept coming. She ran to the van, jerked open the rear door, and clambered inside, climbing over the crushed and bleeding corpses of the shamblers Winterhawk had dropped the van on.

"Hurry!" she yelled, flinging open the door on the other side and plugging an approaching shambler in the head as it reached for her.

Winterhawk's head pounded harder. His body shook as he struggled to keep the spell going long enough to get to the ground. The stim patch was already fading, and when it went, it would go fast. With grim determination, he focused on the van's open door and put on a final jet of speed. He could hear the whine of the engine as the driver prepared to move out.

The shambler group was nearly upon them now.

"Hurry up!" Anissa yelled again, leaning out the doorway and reaching toward him with the hand not holding the SMG.

He lunged toward her, collapsing into the van's rear compartment, sprawled across the seat. "Go! Go! Go!" she screamed, shoving him aside, and then the deafening chatter of SMG fire again.

He barely heard Anissa slam the doors shut, nor the screech of the van's tires as it leapt forward into the night. And then the combination of the stim patch's chemical boost and his own raging adrenaline suddenly took a long step off a high cliff, and the world went away again.

SIXTEEN

Vyx felt their eyes on her as she and Virago pulled their bikes into the rear entrance to Kustom Rode Bykes. Falcon's modified Harley Nightmare was already there. It was late, but the naked overhead lights still blazed in the work area of the Ancients' home base, illuminating several other motorcycles in various stages of disassembly. Other bikes, both functional and not, lined the walls and the alley alongside the garage. The familiar odors of oil, rubber, and sweat overshadowed the ever-present stench of garbage wafting in from the street, but just barely.

A tall, tattooed elf with a shock of bone-white hair looked up from where he knelt next to a dismembered Yamaha Kubaraya up on a rack, wrench in one grease-covered hand. He nodded to Virago, and then his gaze settled on Vyx. His eyes were hooded, his expression guarded. "Liam wants ta talk to ya," he said around a cigarette poking from between his thin lips.

From the other side of the garage, a young male elf with long brown hair and a green jacket said something to his companion, a slightly older, rail-thin woman with an elaborate coiffure and a Concrete Dreams T-shirt. Both of them glanced at Vyx and Virago, and their expressions hardened.

"You chummers got a problem?" Virago asked loudly. "You wanna take it up with me?"

The elf working on the bike shrugged. "Nah, no problem." He bent back over his bike and resumed his wrenching.

"Tanner? Kendra?" Virago's expression practically invited them to come over and start something with her.

"No problem with *you*," Kendra said sullenly, picking at her fingernails and not meeting either Virago's or Vyx's eyes.

Virago pushed her way through the garage toward the door on the far side, and Vyx followed her. Tanner and Kendra had been two of Vyx's most vocal detractors among the Ancients, but Slyder had never said anything against her. She started to say something, but didn't; nothing she did could make this any better. None of her skills would be any good against this.

The showroom was closed this time of night, not that they did much business these days even during their inconsistent operating hours. Dim track lighting illuminated a trio of gleaming, tricked-out bikes in the center of the floor in front of an armored picture window sporting the shop's name. Shelves intermittently stocked with gear—synthleathers, boots, bags, and a few dusty helmets—lined the walls. Somebody had spray-painted an artistic version of Ancients' circled-A symbol in green on the back wall behind the counter. Without its neon-bright ARs flashing away, the place looked subdued and more than a little dingy.

Lucky Liam, the leader of the Boston branch of the Ancients, leaned against the counter, talking to another tall elf in the gang's colors. Others lounged around the showroom, including Falcon. None of them looked directly at Vyx, but the whole scene had the feel of a meeting—or a trial.

Liam finished his conversation and then looked up. "Have a seat," he said, indicating a couple more stools with the shop's logo. His expression betrayed nothing; his voice, with its normally pleasant Irish-accented lilt, was even.

"Look," Virago said, her gaze shooting around the room to skewer each of the lounging gangers in turn. "This is—"

"It's okay," Vyx said, touching her arm. She took the indicated seat. "Let's hear what he's got to say." Her heart pounded, but she held herself still. She'd screwed up—she knew it. This could go any number of ways, depending on how Liam decided to play it. The longer she could keep things calm, the more likely they wouldn't escalate into something they'd all regret. Still, her muscles were on edge, her awareness heightened as she kept subconscious track of the positions of everybody in the room. If the situation went south, she'd have to move fast. She'd seen firsthand in the past how quickly the volatile gangers' tempers could spark into violence. She wished she had a drink or a shot of Jazz to calm her jangling nerves.

"Heard from Mr. Johnson," Liam said, as if he were discussing the weather. "The train's cargo's been safely delivered. So good job there."

Falcon started to say something, but Liam pinned him with a glare, and he subsided. "Let's talk about the rest of the job," he continued.

"It wasn't her fault," Virago protested. "They threw three fraggin' *grenades* at her! How was she supposed to—"

"She's a fuckin' showoff!" Falcon said, pushing off the shelf he was leaning on, fists balled. "It damn sure *was* her fault! She got Grey killed!"

More voices rose into an unintelligible angry hubbub. Another made it above the din: "—told ya we never shoulda taken fraggin' breeders! You let Virago's little piece of tail in, and now one o' our best spellslingers is dead!—"

"—Whatcha gonna do about it, Liam?—"

"—kick 'er out on her round fookin' ears! More'n she deserves!—"

"Oughta kill 'er now!"—

Vyx didn't need magic to see which way the crowd's mood was headed. Their anger and grief had become almost a solid thing in the room, and every bit of it was aimed straight at her. She tensed, readying herself to move, plotting potential escape routes.

"Shut up, all of ye!" Liam's normally soft voice cut through with ease. He stood up straighter, emphasizing his height and the hard muscle under his green-and-black jacket. He turned to Virago. "Is Falcon right? Is it 'er fault Grey's dead?"

"No!" Virago said. She glared at Falcon. "You never liked Vyx. I get it. Neither did Grey. But she did her job. She did a damn *good* job! What was she supposed to do when that fragger threw those grenades at her? Let 'em hit her?"

"We're a *team*!" Falcon yelled back, taking another step forward, fists clenched. His jacket shifted to reveal an Ares Crusader II stuck in the waistband of his jeans. "That slitch has been nothin' but trouble since we took 'er in. She don't care about nobody but herself! She ain't got no loyalty to none of us except you, and that's only 'cuz you're bangin' 'er!"

Around him, the crowd rumbled agreement.

In an instant, Virago's Predator was in her hand and pointed at Falcon's face, and a split-second later his was aimed at her. "You wanna say that again, you son of a bitch?" Virago yelled, her face dark with rage.

"Okay, that's it!" Liam's voice boomed above them once again. "Everybody get the hell outta here except Virago, Vyx, and Falcon! *Now!* And put those fraggin' guns down before somebody else gets killed! We've lost enough people already! We don't need this kinda shite in our own ranks!" He pushed himself off the counter and stepped between Virago and Falcon. "Or are one o' ye gonna shoot me?"

For a moment, it looked like one—or both—of them might. Vyx held her breath, poised to act, to bolt, to dive in and take

Virago out of the line of fire before somebody put a spark to the precarious powder keg in the room and all hell broke loose. *I'm gonna get more people killed.*

But then Falcon let out a loud, frustrated sigh and lowered his gun, jamming it back in his waistband. "She's gotta go, Liam," he said. "That's it. I ain't gonna stay here and let some breeder bitch spit on Grey's memory. It's her or me." He raised his voice. "What about the rest of you?"

Several of the others made noises of agreement. Out of the dozen or so in the room, four more stepped forward. That included Tanner and Kendra, the two from the garage, who had drifted in earlier.

Falcon faced Liam. "Come on, *raé*," he said, sounding more reasonable. "You gonna take the side of a *goronagit* against your own people? Your own *family*?"

Liam stood up straighter. "Don't do this, Falcon." His voice was back down to its normal soft brogue, but there was a dangerous edge to it now. "Ye wanna stand up to me, do it right. Challenge me properly. Ye sure ye wanna take me on, *omae?*"

"You'd risk all that for—*this?*" Falcon spat, gesturing toward Vyx.

"Go," Liam said. "All of ye. Get out. You too, Falcon. I wanna talk to Virago and Vyx."

Falcon held his ground for another beat, then turned and stalked off. Everyone could hear his angry muttering. The four who'd stood with him followed him, back out toward the garage. The others drifted off in groups, casting furtive glances of suspicion and distrust back over their shoulders.

Liam looked suddenly tired, and Vyx knew why. The Ancients weren't numerous in Boston, and attrition after the walls had gone up had taken their numbers down low enough that they were forced to use smarter but riskier tactics to hold on to their turf. The constant pressure came not only from their traditional enemies, the Bane Sidhes and the anti-elven Knights of the Red Branch (for whom the name of Kustom Rode Bykes was a direct insult), but now also from the expanding crop of addled headcases roaming the streets.

"Look," Vyx said. "I screwed up. I didn't mean to, but that doesn't matter. Grey's dead, and it's my fault. You want me to go, I'll go."

They were bold words, but she had no idea where she *would* go if they kicked her out. Back to MIT&T? She hadn't been near there in a few weeks, but she'd heard the campus was still cordoned off. They might let her back in, but the idea of cowering behind yet another wall made her sick. She'd almost rather take her chances trying to sign on with some other group of survivors. There were plenty of them out there, and her skills would be useful. Maybe one of the urban tribes would take her, or the Wicked—those fraggers were batshit, sure, but they'd appreciate her abilities.

"No you won't," Virago stated. "You paid your dues. You got as much right to be here as any of the rest of 'em."

"But I don't, do I?" Vyx said bitterly. She ran a hand over the line of studs and hoops in her rounded left ear. "You know as well as I do, I don't have the right original equipment. The only reason anybody's letting me stick around is because you need the bodies. If the wall wasn't up, we'd still be sneaking around like we used to."

Liam sighed. "She's right," he said, and didn't look happy about it. Before Virago could get started again, he raised a hand. "Listen. I don't want 'er gone either. She's good. I get it. But—" He spread his hands. "I can't be 'avin' a mutiny in the ranks right now. We got too many things goin' south on us, and too many of our people are dead. If Falcon walks and takes that many with 'im—"

"He ain't gonna walk," Virago protested. "He's a chickenshit. Always was. Where's he gonna go? That crew wouldn't last a week out there on their own. It ain't like they can leave town."

Liam didn't answer. He paced the small office, moving with silent grace despite his heavy boots. After a few moments he stopped and perched tensely on the edge of the old desk. "I've got one idea, but I don't like it much."

"Let's hear it," Virago said.

"You know's well as I do that Falcon and his lot are a bunch o' hotheads," he said. "They'll cool off eventually, but it'll take time. And as long as they gotta keep looking at Vyx every day, the wound's never gonna heal. If we don't send 'er on 'er way, we gotta get 'er outta 'ere for a while. Give things a chance to cool down."

"So where would I go?" Vyx asked.

Liam pulled up an AR window and examined some figures. "You musta 'eard talk o' some o' our supply lines bein' compromised in the last few weeks."

"Yeah," Virago said. "The BADs aren't flowin' like they should. O'Rilley's pretty torqued about it, yeah?" Bioengineered Awakened Drugs, or "BADs" on the street, were what happened when mad science and magic got together and had babies. They were also highly lucrative for those who produced, supplied, and sold them.

"That's puttin' it mildly," Liam said. "Somethin' must be goin' on with the witches up in Salem. Either they switched sides and cut a deal with some other distributor, or they're not producin' the quantities they used to. There's also reports that people're gettin' hold of tainted batches—the kind o' stuff that's killin' people or drivin' 'em crazy. Whatever's goin' on, it's hurtin' biz. Bad enough O'Rilley's gotta take the leavins after Damon gets his fill, but now even that's dryin' up. He's gettin' impatient to find out what's going on, but he can't spare the manpower. I was gonna send Grey up there with a couple other guys in a few days to talk to 'em and find out what's happenin'."

"So you want *me* to go instead?" Vyx stared at him.

"Yeah. They don't know ye, plus ye got the advantage of bein' a woman. They wouldn't expect ye to be in with us since yer a norm, and they'd probably talk to ye easier than Grey since yer female. If ye can get on their good side, act like yer thinkin' about joinin' up with 'em, maybe ye can find out what they're up to. If they've switched sides and are dealin' with someone else, O'Rilley's gonna want to know that."

"And if they catch 'er," Virago said angrily, "They'll kill 'er. Or somethin' else out there will. It ain't safe for any of us to be on our own these days with the streets full of headcases." She glared at Liam. "You're sendin' her off to get cacked, is what you're doin'. This way you can solve your problem without gettin' blood on your hands."

"Ye got a better idea?" he asked. "I'm listenin'."

But she didn't have a better idea—or at least if she did, she didn't mention it. "If she goes," Virago said at last, her tone stubborn, "I'm goin' with her."

"Ye can't—" Liam began.

"Yeah, I can. And I will."

The Ancients' leader shook his head. "I can't lose ye, Virago. We need ye here. Nobody's got a problem with ye."

"Wait," Vyx said. "I can make this work!"

She jumped off the stool and rounded on Liam, surprised at the animation in her voice. Maybe there *was* a way to make things right. She couldn't bring Grey back, but maybe she could prove her worth to the Ancients so they'd cut her some slack. After all, it wasn't like she'd gotten Grey killed on purpose.

"What if I go to the witches and tell 'em I want to join up 'cause I got kicked outta the Ancients? I can even tell 'em the truth about why. They're gonna know something's up if I show up or if they do their research, but it makes sense I might try to join up with 'em if that happened. For protection, if nothing else.

Like Virago said, it's not safe for anybody alone out there. And I'm Awakened, so they'll probably let me in."

Liam pondered, rubbing his sharp chin. "Not a half-bad idea," he said at last. He examined a couple more ARs. "'Course, ye know to make this work we'll have to make it convincing. Ye won't be able to call on us for help if you get in trouble."

Vyx nodded soberly. "Yeah. I get it." It burned, the chance that she might lose the closest thing to a family she'd ever managed to find. It especially burned that she'd have to leave Virago. But choices were pretty thin on the ground right now, and if she did the job, she trusted Liam to take her back in and smooth over the problems with Falcon's people. If she played this right, she wouldn't have to lose her family.

She'd just have to make sure she played it right. "Let's make it happen," she said. With a bitter little chuckle, Vyx skinned out of her ripped, bloodstained green Ancients jacket and tossed it on Liam's desk. "Guess I won't be needing this for a while."

SEVENTEEN

Winterhawk jerked awake, still half in the grip of an uneasy nightmare where gibbering shamblers ripped his limbs free off his body and devoured them as he watched.

"Easy," said a voice from behind him. "You're safe—or at least that's what they tell me."

The voice was familiar. Winterhawk spun around. Ocelot sat on the other side of the cot he lay on, his chair tilted back on two legs. "You never do anything the easy way, do you?"

The mage didn't bother to try to hide his relief. "I thought you were dead." His voice still sounded tired. How long had he been sleeping? How long had he been here—wherever *here* was?

"I thought *you* were." Ocelot let the chair fall with a *clunk*. "You can thank Maya for that—she found me and brought me to where they took you. Took us a little longer, since you weren't there when we got back."

"*You're welcome,*" a prim, amused voice said in Winterhawk's mind.

He lay back, hand across his forehead. "Where are we? Who—"

"Sounds like you had all the excitement." Ocelot got up and began pacing the small room. "I met Anissa when I got here—she said you'd run into some of those zombie things. Shamblers, she called 'em. Said you did some pretty fancy mojo to get you guys outta there."

"But where is *here?*" Winterhawk sat up, even though it was probably a bad idea. He still felt lightheaded and dizzy, but most of the pain and numbing fatigue were gone. "How long have I been out?" His coat and other gear, he noticed, were piled on a table next to the cot.

"Few hours. We're in an abandoned church near Mission Hill." Ocelot nodded at an empty chair, where a clean shirt and trousers hung. "Your clothes were shot, so they brought you those. No shower facilities, though. I guess we're waitin' for somebody to show up, but she wouldn't tell me who."

"Her employer. I don't know who he—or she—is either." For the first time, Winterhawk noticed the room had no windows. "Are we prisoners here?"

"Nah, not as far as I know. We're in the basement. I haven't tried to leave yet. They got some damn good security here, but I think it's mostly for keepin' out the zombies. They almost blew me away when I showed up, until Maya popped in and explained who we were."

The cat-spirit shimmered into existence on the cot next to Winterhawk, rubbing against him and purring her ethereal purr. "How did you get away?" he asked as he idly stroked Maya's back.

"Thought they'd killed you," Ocelot said, and didn't look happy about it. "I figured even if they hadn't, goin' against that kind of artillery directly would get us both killed. I was tryin' to convince some of those gangers who took the crate to help me, but they took off too. When Maya found me, I was hiding out, tryin' to figure out a way into that place." He leaned down and rummaged in a bag on the floor. "You want somethin' to eat?"

He'd almost forgotten he hadn't had anything in—*bloody hell.* "How long has it been since the firefight?" He got up and began swapping his torn, bloody clothes for the fresh ones. A quick Fashion spell took care of fine-tuning the fit and adjusting the utilitarian shirt and trousers to something more to his usual style. People often mocked the Fashion spell, but it was bloody useful when your clothing options were limited and you didn't want to look like you'd picked your gear from an understocked thrift store.

Ocelot frowned. "You don't know?"

"No. Being trussed up like a damned Christmas goose and shoved inside a magemask plays hell with your time perception, trust me. I'm going to have nightmares for weeks."

"Damn. *That's* what they did to you? It was a little over two days. Maya told me she couldn't communicate with you for a while." He handed over a bottle of water and a couple of energy bars. "It ain't much, but it's a start."

Winterhawk had finished the water and was devouring the second bar with ravenous intensity when there was a knock at the door. "Yes?" he called, as Ocelot's hand went to his shotgun.

Anissa appeared in the doorway. She still wore her leathers, and her pistols were back on her belt, but she'd left the SMG elsewhere. "Finally awake," she said. "Good. You ready to meet the boss?"

"What I want," he said, "is to know what's going on, where I am, and when I can be on my way. Believe me, don't think I'm not grateful for the rescue, and I expect your employer will want something in return. I'm certainly willing to discuss that. But I've got reasons for being here, and friends I need to look for. Assuming they're still alive," he added bitterly.

"The boss might be able to help you with that," she said. "He wants to talk to you before you make any decisions or leave. Believe me, you don't want to be out on the street with nowhere to go, especially not this time of night."

She had a point. If those creatures who'd attacked the van were roaming the street, he didn't want to run into them—at least not until he had a lot more information, and more time to rest. He was already beginning to see that whatever data he and the DIMR had gathered about what it was like inside the QZ was incomplete and inadequate at best.

"Let's see what he has to say, then." Winterhawk got up, testing his balance, and discovered he felt much better than he had before. That was something, at least. He shrugged into his coat, stuffed his commlink into his pocket along with his ritual sample (*have to destroy that soon,* he thought), and headed out the door.

"I do owe you—and your employer, whoever he is—something for getting me out of there," he said. "I don't know what I've got myself into, but it's likely not worse than being at the mercy of that lot."

She nodded. "The boss was pretty surprised when he got word that you were in town."

"He's heard of me, then?" he asked, surprised. Speculation grew in his mind: the DIMR? Some other magical organization operating within the QZ?

"He keeps his ear to the ground," she said. "Not much in this town he doesn't find out about eventually."

Outside was a dingy brick hallway and a wooden staircase. She led them upstairs and down another hallway lined with broken pews. A tall, tattooed ork in an armored coat lounged at the end, smoking a cigarette. He nodded to Anissa and the others as they passed.

The church was neither large nor impressive by Boston standards—the sort of threadbare, well-used place designed more for saving souls on a small scale than enticing the flock into giving up their hard-earned nuyen to keep it looking sufficiently impressive. Most of the stained-glass windows lining both sides were broken, their openings covered with hefty plaswood barriers.

About half the pews were either gone or shoved up against the walls, and up at the front the only thing that remained was the altar, currently playing host to a slim figure who sat casually atop it, backlit by a series of candles.

"Well," said the figure. "I'd heard you had a knack for getting yourself into trouble, but I never expected to see you inside the QZ."

He swung around to reveal himself as a young human, early twenties at the oldest. His clothes were rough: a simple leather jacket and faded jeans, but his model-handsome face wore an amused grin. His glittering, ice-blue gaze was fixed on the mage.

Winterhawk froze.

Of course.

He would have kicked himself for not putting things together, but at least he had the excuse of not being at his best. "Hello, Damon."

"Damon?" Ocelot muttered beside him. "The dragon? Oh, fuck…"

Winterhawk had never met Damon in person, but he'd certainly heard plenty of stories. It was hard not to, given how often the young dragon was in the limelight. If he wasn't causing mob scenes by showing up at clubs unannounced or pitting himself against highly trained teams competing for the chance to hunt him down, his rumored romantic pairings singlehandedly provided livelihoods for half the gossip-rag publishers on both coasts.

After the blockades had risen and news from inside dried up, speculation ran rampant about whether Damon had succeeded in getting out, especially given that no one had heard anything from him. Odds were running about fifty-fifty each way, but nobody on the outside could prove anything.

Damon lounged back on the altar, sipping a drink he had next to him. "Would you care for one?" he asked. "You're welcome to it, of course, but I'm guessing you might want something a little more substantial after your stay with Hard Corps. Did Anissa take care of you?"

Winterhawk nodded. "Thank you." Whoever had worked on him while he'd been unconscious had been good, given his current lack of injury. Even considering the fact that the Hard Corps officers had been more concerned with beating a confession out of him than causing permanent harm, he'd still expected to be left with more lingering effects. He wondered if Damon had done the job himself.

In any case, it was a good thing: it wasn't a smart idea to meet with dragons, even young ones who preferred to stay in human guise, when one wasn't at one's top form. "How did you know?" he asked.

"Know what?" Damon took another sip.

"Everything. That I was here. That I was being held prisoner."

"I didn't know you were here until word got back to me that Hard Corps had picked you up." He arched an eyebrow. "Smuggling yourself in on a supply crate? Why would you do that? Most people try to get *out* of the QZ, not get in."

"Suppose we get right to it, shall we?" Winterhawk sat on a nearby pew, never taking his eyes off the dragon.

"Get right to what?" He smiled. "So suspicious. I've heard that about you. You don't trust many people, do you?"

"Not really, no. Likely why I'm still alive."

"And you don't like me very much." Damon didn't seem ruffled by this revelation.

Winterhawk shrugged. "I don't have an opinion of you personally. I'm not fond of some of your activities. But that's beside the point. I can't deny you've helped me out of a fairly dire situation, and I'm grateful for that. I've no idea *why* you did it, but—what do you want?"

"I won't insult you by saying I couldn't make use of your help, now that you're here. Though honestly, when your Maya came to me with the story, I felt helping you was the least I could do. I wouldn't wish Hard Corps's tender mercies on my worst enemies. Well," he amended, stretching his long legs out in front of him, "maybe my worst enemies. But certainly not someone of your... reputation."

Winterhawk blinked. Maya had come to *Damon* for help? He'd have to have a talk with her later about that. "What, then? Whatever it is, I'd like to take care of it and get on with why I'm here. Did Anissa mention I've got some friends I need to track down?"

"She did."

Winterhawk reminded himself again whom he was dealing with—it wouldn't pay to forget it, despite the fact that Damon had the whole human thing down much better than the other dragons he'd met in his career. Unlike the others, who always managed to give the impression, unspoken or not, that they might make a light snack of you if you didn't treat them with appropriate respect, it was easy enough to believe with Damon that you were merely chatting with a handsome young man who just happened to be curious about what you were up to. "I need to make some calls."

"You're welcome to do that." Damon sipped his drink again. "I warn you, the network inside the Zone is spotty at best, so you might have to try a few times before you're successful."

"Might want to check your 'link," Anissa said. "Some of those shamblers can fry electronics."

Winterhawk frowned, pulled out his commlink, and tried to power it up. Nothing happened. *Damn, damn, damn.* It was worse than simply losing his means of communication—all his files about Victoria, the local LTG codes of his acquaintances in Boston, and other important data were all stored on it. And he doubted he'd be able to access his backups from here. He shoved it back in his pocket with a growl of frustration.

"I'm sure we can find you a working commlink," Damon said. "But let's talk first, shall we? I won't take much of your time. I've got other obligations as well."

"'Hawk—" Ocelot began, his voice laced with an edge of caution.

Winterhawk held up a hand to stop him. "Yes, let's talk. You can tell me what the price of your help is, and we'll go from there, depending on what you want."

Damon's smile widened. He hopped gracefully down from the altar and began pacing the front of the church. "How much do you know about what's going on in here? I get reports occasionally from the outside, but they're hard to come by, and who knows if they're accurate?"

Winterhawk raised an eyebrow. "You want me to believe you're stuck in here, without any contact with the outside world? Or have you simply chosen to remain for some reason of your own?"

"Does it matter?" Damon asked with a shrug. "I'm here, at least for the moment. I'll admit to being curious about why *you're* here. I'd assume it would take a truly compelling reason to persuade someone like you to risk the blockades."

Winterhawk didn't see any point in withholding the truth— at least not all of it. "Research," he said. "The DIMR's sent an expedition in to study the new ley line."

"Ahh." Damon nodded in satisfaction. "Well, then. Our aims might coincide more than I'd thought. As it happens, the...favor...I intend to ask of you concerns a similar area of interest."

"I wouldn't think you'd need me for that," Winterhawk said. "From the reports I've heard, the line is already aspected toward dragon magic." He adjusted his tone to ask the question without asking it.

"True enough, it is."

"And given your reputed ties with the Salem witches—"

"Yes, well. That's true as well, as far as it goes. But sometimes there are advantages to a bit more...covert approach."

"Can you two stop talking past each other and get to the damn point?" Ocelot asked, frustrated.

From the back of the room, Anissa chuckled. "A man after my own heart, Boss."

Damon didn't appear annoyed by their words. He spread his hands in acquiescence and leaned against the altar. "You know about Eliohann?"

"Rumors," Winterhawk said, "Though fairly credible ones. From what I've heard, he broke free of some NeoNET facility where they were trying to use a specialized nanite treatment on him. Something went catastrophically wrong. He was the dragon who crashed into Fenway Park and started this whole mess."

"Correct. He infected thousands of people with a particularly virulent form of CFD, which is what set the whole quarantine into motion."

"Yes, we've run into a few more aggressive specimens of the afflicted," Winterhawk said. He glanced over his shoulder at Anissa. "My condolences on the loss of your friend, by the way."

"Thank you. It happens—too often these days. But it still sucks when it hits that close to home."

"Here's where it gets interesting," Damon said. "You're probably aware that my popularity among the Salem witches is a bit strained these days. At least with a subset of them."

"I've a few friends among them," Winterhawk said, "though I haven't been back to Boston in a couple of years." To Ocelot, he said, "There's a bit of a schism brewing. Some of them are in favor of Damon's continued interest in their area because he's good for business. Others think he's corrupting the purity of their magic by bringing in too many outsiders, and aspecting the area too much toward dragon magic."

"That's putting it mildly," Damon said. "And now, I've been getting reports that some of the witches on the pro-dragon side of the fence have been transferring their support to Eliohann. And further, that there might be some outside influences at work. Reports are quite sketchy, but lately I've also been hearing that the more zealous of the anti-dragon contingent might have come under potentially dangerous new leadership, though I haven't been able to turn up any specifics yet."

"Indeed?" Winterhawk raised an eyebrow. "That's unexpected. So what do you want me to do?"

"Investigate. Talk to your contacts and friends. Find out what's going on with the witches, what they're up to, and whether what I've heard about Eliohann and these new leaders is true."

"Why can't you just do this yourself?" Ocelot asked. "You're a fuckin' *dragon*. You're telling me you can't whip up a magical disguise that will fool these witches?"

Damon shrugged. "No doubt I could. But I've got a lot on my plate these days. And given that Winterhawk here has so conveniently crossed my path, and further given his history of friendship with representatives on both sides of the schism, it would likely be easier for him to discover what's going on than it would for me to go in there disguised as a stranger—or as myself. Especially considering that it's not widely known I'm still inside the QZ, and it's to my advantage right now to keep it that way."

"Settling down, are you?" Winterhawk asked wryly. "No more wild nightlife?" He narrowed his eyes. "And that doesn't even bring up the rather large elephant in the room."

"Which elephant is that?"

"Come on, Damon. You mentioned it yourself that I don't like you very much—and you bloody well know why."

Damon smiled and shrugged. "You're referring to some of my business interests, of course. I've...put those mostly on hold for the duration."

"Supply lines dried up, have they, now that you and the witches are on the outs?"

The dragon shrugged. "To some extent. But as long as the walls are up, I've got other concerns that take up most of my time. Let Morelli and O'Rilley fight over the scraps until things are back to normal. I doubt they'll make much headway, considering how many of their associates they've lost."

"So you're sure this little investigation into the witches' activities isn't more focused around getting your BAD pipeline up and running again than in finding out what Eliohann's up to?"

Damon smiled. "I wouldn't ask that of you. I don't need to. If I had such a desire, I've got plenty of other avenues to pursue. Why would I waste a talent like yours on such a commonplace activity?"

"But you can't deny that if I can get you solid intelligence on what's going on in Salem, it will certainly prove advantageous for your...ongoing plans."

The young dragon's smile widened. "Believe what you will. I'll tell you what: let me sweeten the pot for you a bit, if I can't soothe your conscience. Do this for me, and I'll do what I can to make sure that you and your friends can get safely out of the QZ when you're ready."

"We already have a way out," Winterhawk said. "That's all been arranged through the DIMR."

"No doubt." Damon pushed himself off the altar and finished his drink, and his expression sobered. "But one thing you can be certain of, if nothing else: nothing is a sure thing inside the Zone. You've been a shadowrunner—you know how quickly even careful plans can go wrong. Raise that by an order of magnitude here. You should never pass up an offered favor—in the end, you might find you'll need me after all."

EIGHTEEN

Vyx's plan was to make a quick stop at the place she shared with Virago to pick up her gear before she left. She didn't have much there—most of what she owned was back up at her dorm room at MIT&T, which meant that, with the cordons in effect, it might as well have been chilling in a crater on the Moon. Didn't matter, though—all the stuff she cared about was here.

The flat was on the second floor of an abandoned three-story building a half-block from Kustom Rode Bykes; several more of the Ancients currently in Liam's favor dossed here as well, and she hoped none of them would show up before she could get out. She wasn't afraid of any of them except maybe Liam (he was every bit as fast as she was, and had a drekload more combat experience) but a nice clean exit would be better for everybody.

Most of the items strewn around the one-bedroom flat were Virago's, so it took her a little longer to sift through them and gather hers into a small backpack and couple of saddlebags she could sling over the back of her bike. Vyx focused on packing, trying not to dwell too much on what had happened over the past several hours, and how much her life had changed because of a split-second mistake. Replaying it over and over in her mind now wouldn't change it. It was over, it was done, and she'd have to deal with the fallout.

A floorboard creaked behind her and she spun, reflexes primed to defend herself before she realized that her innate sense of impending danger hadn't fired off.

Virago stood in the doorway. She held up her hands. "Down, girl," she said. She stripped off her green-and-black Ancients jacket and tossed it over a nearby chair. "You okay?"

"Sure, I'm okay." Vyx stuffed a couple more pairs of jeans into her saddlebag. "Why wouldn't I be?"

"'Cause you're rollin' over like a whipped dog," she said. Her eyes flashed indignation. "This ain't like you, lettin' 'em run you off this easily. Who do they think they are? None of what happened was your fault. If it'd been Falcon or Blaine or any of those guys, they'd just write it off to biz. Only reason they give a fuck's 'cause you're not an elf."

Vyx shrugged. Virago's words were true, but they didn't change anything. "Doesn't matter. It happened. Besides, it's not like they're sendin' me off to try to get over the wall or anything. Just to do a little recon in Salem. I hear it's nice up there—might even be a little vacation." She didn't believe that, and she was sure Virago knew it. "I'll just do the job and come back, and if they give me any trouble after that, they can kiss my ass. Liam's got my back, and so do you. Who else do I need?"

Virago grinned. "That's more like it." She got up, kicked through a pile of dirty clothes on the floor, and came up with a duffel bag. She began tossing items into it with a haphazard lack of organization.

"What are you doing?"

"What's it look like I'm doin'?"

Vyx shook her head. "You're not coming with me."

"You gonna stop me? Like to see you try." Her words were light, but her expression was serious.

Vyx sighed and zipped up the pack. "Look. This is my problem, not yours. You're not on everybody's shit list. Liam told you not to go. You defy his orders, who knows what might happen? You might get kicked out too." She picked up her twin knives and stashed them in their sheaths, then strapped her katana to her back. Her girlfriend had used to tease her about her refusal to use guns, but after seeing her in action, she'd not only given up the teasing, but had given her the blade as a one-month anniversary present shortly before the lockdown. It wasn't pretty or ornamental, but had the sort of deadly, no-nonsense functionality Vyx loved.

"So? Fuck 'em, then. They flap their jaws about loyalty and all that shit, and then the first time somebody screws up they cut 'em loose?" She snorted in disgust. "That ain't the way it used to work."

"You didn't used to take norms," Vyx pointed out.

"Yeah, well. You're an honorary elf anyway. But it doesn't matter. They kick you out, they kick me out too." She flung open a dresser drawer and stuffed a pistol, a sheathed knife, and an HK-227 into her duffel bag, then dug under another pile of clothes for spare magazines. "So you gonna shut up and let's go, or do we wait for Falcon and the rest to get back?"

Vyx threw a wadded-up pair of jeans at her. "You know, you're not bad for a stuck-up keeb."

"Fuckin' right I'm not."

NINETEEN

"What weren't you sayin' back there, 'Hawk?" Ocelot asked.

A dreary, disconsolate rain fell. A few figures shuffled along the sidewalks, but no one approached as they drove by. Damon, true to his word, had instructed Anissa to find a commlink for Winterhawk. It was a bare-bones model, but included additional shielding that might make it less vulnerable to the shamblers' disruption. He'd also given them the use of the van Anissa had used to rescue him. Even its battered appearance wouldn't keep it from presenting a tempting target for thieves, but it would get them to Salem—at least if they went straight there without stopping.

Winterhawk had no intention of going to Salem without stopping.

"Hmm?" The mage was driving, since he was more familiar with Boston, at least under normal circumstances, than Ocelot was. They had to move slowly, picking their way around garbage, abandoned vehicles, and occasional roadblocks and detours; once, a small crowd of shamblers appeared ahead, and they took a quick left to avoid them.

"You didn't tell Damon about Victoria. You still plannin' to try findin' her?"

"Of course I am."

Ocelot paused. "Your 'link's bricked, so you don't have any of your info about her. And the Hard Corps guys took your ritual sample, so you can't find her that way. What's your plan? Don't we have to track down your expedition first? You know where they planned to set up, right?"

"I do. But I don't think that's going to help us."

"Why not? You can send Maya to find them, right?" He glanced into the back seat, where the cat-spirit sat with her paws primly crossed and her plumy tail tucked around her. She hovered a few centimeters above the seat, so the bumps and jars from the bad road surface didn't affect her.

"I don't think they're here any longer."

"What?" Ocelot twisted in his seat, interrupting his vigilant scrutiny of their surroundings to stare at Winterhawk. "What the hell you talkin' about? Why wouldn't they be?"

"We never intended to stay for long," the mage said. "That was why we'd have had to move fast to locate Victoria if things had gone as intended. The original idea was to spend two days studying the ley line, getting as much information as possible, then travel to a designated location near the Wilds where the DIMR had arranged for us to be retrieved. The plan was for them to have some operatives on the other side to help get us out under cover of darkness, but time was of the essence. It wouldn't have been safe for them to wait too long past the designated time."

"Wait, so you're sayin' we *can't* get out? But you told Damon—"

"I know what I told Damon. You don't think I trust that dragon with *all* our secrets, do you?" He shrugged. "I still want to check— there's a chance that Wu and the rest of them are still there. I need to have a conversation with her in any case, but that might have to wait. After that, we find Victoria, locate my friends among the witches, and get the information Damon is looking for. If he keeps his word, we'll get out using his method, whatever it is. And if we have time, I'll take a look at the ley line and take some notes. I should be able to get enough to make the Institute happy in a few hours."

Ocelot looked skeptical, but returned to his scrutiny. "So you know where to find Wu? Did you have a plan for where to set up? I thought you said you had to work something out with the witches once you landed."

"The DIMR maintains a safehouse in town not far from where the ley line is supposed to be. If they're still here, that's likely where they'll be, since as far as I know, Wu didn't have contacts with any of the witches. Without me, there'd be no need to go to Salem—it would just add unnecessary difficulty."

"So where is this ley line? Are we close?"

"About half a kilometer from here. They didn't want to have the living quarters too close, as the background count near it is significant. Since it's aspected toward dragon magic, it plays havoc with anyone not of that tradition." Winterhawk turned the car onto a narrow, winding street lined with small, neat houses separated by small, neat yards. In contrast to the areas closer to downtown, the street was heavily lined with trees, the yards weren't strewn with trash, and the whole neighborhood had a tranquil, suburban look.

Winterhawk parked the van in the driveway of a modest two-story home about halfway up the street, behind a large, beige Mercury Comet. Would Wu still be here? Had she been behind the diversion of their supply crate to a location so far from the designated landing site? If so, why? Had she been so angry and jealous of Winterhawk for taking the expedition away from her that she'd arranged to discreetly get him out of the way long enough for her to establish her command? That seemed a petty thing to do, but he'd seen enough ambitious corpers and academics that he didn't discount the possibility.

If she and her team hadn't left yet, they would have words—some of them related to the fact that she and the rest of the team were bloody well going to sit their arses down and wait long enough for 'Hawk to finish his recon before they left.

"That theirs?" Ocelot asked, nodding toward the Comet. "Maybe they *are* still here." He hefted his shotgun from the floor, covered it with his jacket, and got out. The neighborhood was quiet: no one walking along the sidewalks, no cars driving by, no sign of roving packs of shamblers.

"Not sure," Winterhawk said. He paused to summon an air spirit and instruct it to stay near the car and alert them if anyone came near it, then headed past the sedan toward the house.

No one answered their initial buzz. Winterhawk knocked loudly on the door. "Dr. Wu? Are you in there?"

No answer.

"*Something's wrong,*" Maya said suddenly in Winterhawk's mind.

He froze. "*What is it?*"

"*Inside. There are several people, and they're all dead. And I sense traces of magic.*"

The hairs stood up on the back of Winterhawk's neck, and a chill gripped him. This was not good. He grabbed Ocelot's arm. "Let's go around the back. Maya says there are dead bodies inside."

"And you want to go in and look at them." Ocelot sighed. "Of course you do."

"She also says she detects traces of magic."

The backyard had the look of a typical suburban family dwelling: plaswood deck, covered barbecue rig, and more trees. A sliding glass door leading out to the deck was covered by heavy blinds, so they couldn't see inside.

Winterhawk shifted to astral sight. "Hmm. The wards are down. That's not good. Maya, do you sense any spirits? Or anyone guarding the place?"

She was gone for a few seconds, then reappeared on the deck. *"No, no guardians, spirit or otherwise. But whatever happened in here was bad."*

"If Wu's people summoned any spirits and they're dead, the spirits wouldn't hang about," 'Hawk said aloud. He tried the door. Locked. *"Maya, can you open this?"*

A moment passed, and then they both heard the tiny *snick.*

Winterhawk slid the door open. He shifted back to astral sight before stepping inside, but saw no sign of anyone lying in wait for them. "Come on," he said. "But look sharp. And we'll need to make this quick. I've no idea if they've turned the mundane alarm on, or how long it will take for anyone to respond if they did."

Inside was a small sitting room with a pair of oversized sofas and a trid unit. Everything appeared undisturbed.

"What the hell?" Ocelot whispered. "Nothing looks messed up. The trid's still down there—thieves would've taken that."

"Where are they, Maya?" Winterhawk asked.

"Upstairs. In the bedrooms."

They hurried up, Ocelot with his shotgun at the ready. As they reached the second floor, the unmistakable odor of decay permeated the air. It got stronger as they approached the closed doors to the bedrooms.

Winterhawk tried the door to the master bedroom at the end of the hall. It was unlocked. He pushed it open and stared into the room. "Bloody hell."

With the door open, the stench that rolled out was almost visible to the naked eye.

"What—?" Ocelot asked from behind him. "What *happened* to her?"

It was a fair question, since whatever had befallen Doris Wu was clearly not a natural death, nor was it the typical bloody aftermath of a home invasion or the neat efficiency of an execution. The woman who lay on the bed was only recognizable as Wu by her dwarfish stature and familiar no-nonsense hairstyle. Her features were unrecognizable, twisted and obscured by what appeared to be an advanced case of decomposition. An oily dark puddle radiated out from beneath her, staining the neat geometric-patterned comforter and the pillow beneath her head. Next to her, as if she had been holding it in her hand when she died, was her commlink, also covered in rot.

"Holy fuck," Ocelot said, his voice distorted as he held his nose against the stink. "She looks like—I saw a body that looked like that once. They'd pulled it out of a sealed metal barrel after it'd been in the Sound for about a month."

Winterhawk nodded. "There's no way she could have decomposed that badly in this short a time if this were a natural death, or a simple murder." He ducked into the tiny bath attached to the bedroom, grabbed a handful of tissue, and picked up Wu's commlink, which he shoved into his coat pocket. "Anyone approaching, Maya?" he asked aloud.

"*Not yet,*" she said. "*You should hurry, though. The astral plane around here feels–wrong.*"

"Not surprised," he muttered. Then, to Ocelot: "Come on— let's check the other rooms. I want to see if the rest of the team are here too."

They were. Winterhawk and Ocelot moved through the remainder of the house's four small bedrooms and soon discovered that the rest of Doris Wu's research team had suffered the same fate. The two security men lay on their beds in one room, the remaining pair of researchers slumped over a desk and slouched in a chair in another. The decker they found in a puddle of goo in the last bedroom's bath, where he'd obviously pitched forward and crashed to the floor while seated on the toilet. His deck, its screen cracked, lay in a stinking puddle on the tile floor in front of him. With each door they opened the putrefying stench grew stronger, until they could barely stand to remain in the house.

"Is this all of 'em?" Ocelot asked, his fingers still clamped on his nose as he examined the corpse of the decker.

"Yes." Winterhawk grabbed another wad of tissue from the decker's bathroom and picked up the deck, swallowing hard against the reek.

"You got any idea what happened here? Whatever it is, it's not even close to normal."

"Not yet," Winterhawk said. "But you're right." He returned to Wu's bedroom. Her gear, in a pair of black shoulder bags, was stacked neatly next to the room's small desk. "Bring those along, will you? I want to see if the other researchers had anything as well."

"We should get the hell out of here," Ocelot said. He took the bags but kept moving with restless energy from window to window, as if certain that someone was waiting outside, prepared to jump them any moment.

"I want to find out what's happened," Winterhawk said. "Maya said something about the astral here being wrong. I want to know what she meant."

"How you gonna do that? Whatever you do, make it quick. The longer we stay here, the more likely somebody's gonna notice something. Like this smell."

"Just give me a few minutes. I think I can get some answers. Maya, go with Ocelot. Make sure no one comes near the place. His head will fly apart if he has to stand still much longer."

He heard Maya's chuckle in his mind, and the two of them headed out. "Make it quick," Ocelot said again.

Alone in the quiet room except for Doris Wu's unsettling presence, Winterhawk stood in the center and turned slowly around, assensing the area. It didn't take him long to pick up on what Maya had noticed—the astral plane in the room (and, he suspected, in the entire upper part of the house) felt...odd. Greasy. Rotten. It felt like a place he shouldn't be, like an old garbage dump or a long-forgotten charnel house. Just touching it with his astral senses nauseated him in a way the actual bodies had not.

None of the sensations were strong—whatever had happened here, he'd bet money it hadn't happened in the last day, so the worst of it had dissipated. Still, if this was what was left after the strongest of the impressions had faded, he could see how it had gotten the jump on three trained magical researchers, let alone two mundane security personnel and a decker whose consciousness probably hadn't been anywhere near the house when the attack had struck.

As he expected, there was no sense of fear or pain—whoever had killed the team had somehow managed to enter the house, get past whatever no-doubt formidable magical and physical protections Wu and her people had set up, and kill them without waking them. That implied some fairly serious power, not to mention planning. And that didn't make sense. Who would care about a small expedition entering the QZ to study the dragon ley line? Given the size of the ley line, it wasn't as if they couldn't get the same data themselves, if information was what they wanted.

He took a couple of cleansing breaths and sent out a call to the astral plane, reaching for contact with one of the spirits that hovered around homes and homelike areas. He still thought of them as "hearth spirits," even though most younger mages didn't call them that anymore. *Getting old,* he thought wryly.

When the spirit arrived, it seemed reluctant to appear. It was tiny, weak, and fearful—perhaps something the attackers had overlooked, or perhaps whatever had hit the house and the people inside had leached some of its power.

"*Come on,*" he urged it gently. "*No one's going to hurt you. I just want to know what's happened here.*"

He sensed its intent rather than felt it: it was willing to talk, but not for long. "*What happened?*" he asked, indicating the room. "*And when?*"

"*Day before yesterday,*" it said. "*In the night. A little bit before dawn.*"

"*How many of them? What did they do?*"

It paused a moment to think, then Winterhawk got a vague sense of confusion. That was the problem with small, weak spirits: they had a much harder time articulating their thoughts in a coherent manner than did more powerful ones like Maya.

"*Nobody came in,*" it said at last, still troubled. "*Something hit them. It came all at once, and they all died. They...*" He sensed a shudder. "*It was wrong.*"

"*What was wrong?*"

"*The astral plane. Something came through and found them.*"

"*Something? A spirit?*"

"*No.*"

And then, suddenly, he had it. It was the only thing that made sense. "*It was some sort of ritual, wasn't it? A sending. Someone hit them remotely.*"

He felt understanding, then agreement. "*I hid, but I saw it. I didn't want it to see me. I was scared.*"

That was certainly understandable. Any magic powerful enough to do this could have ripped the tiny spirit to shreds. "*What about their magical protections? Did they have guardian spirits? Wards?*" He hadn't sensed any wards around the house when they'd come in—was that because there hadn't been any, or because the sending was potent enough to destroy them?

"*I don't know.*" The little spirit's mind-voice sounded fretful, like a small child who'd been forced to stay up too late. "*The spirits left after the people died. They didn't like it here either.*"

Damn. The chill crawling up Winterhawk's spine increased. Somehow, Wu and her people had managed to piss off someone powerful enough to rain down this kind of destruction on them—and after only being here for a day or two. Who could it have been?

"'Hawk?" Ocelot's voice called from downstairs. "We gotta go! Maya says she saw a couple KE cars heading in our direction. The place might've had a silent alarm."

Frustration gripped him. He wanted to study the area further, but they couldn't risk staying long if the cops were on their way. "Coming!" he called. He closed his eyes and reached out with his astral senses, concentrating harder. He didn't want to—he already felt like he'd need to take at least four showers just from his previous contact with the place's tainted astral energy—but he had to know.

He didn't get it until he moved closer to Wu's body. As he did so, the feeling of unease increased until he felt his gorge rise. Whatever this had been, it was centered here. Some kind of twisted, unnatural energy swirled around Wu, almost like—

No.

It couldn't be.

It didn't make sense.

Still, once he'd identified it, he couldn't deny it was here. His breath quickened, and his heart rate increased until he could feel it thudding in his chest.

He had no idea how Doris Wu had managed to get on the wrong side of a powerful toxic magician, but somehow she must have done just that. The astral didn't lie. The impressions were fading, but the power was strong—they would linger for days before dissipating fully. He opened his eyes and stared hard at Wu's corpse again: the advanced, twisted decomposition was certainly in keeping with the vile kind of magic the toxics practiced.

But why?

"'Hawk! Get out here!"

"Coming!" On his way out, he ducked into the other researchers' bedroom and quickly grabbed as much as he could carry of their gear, then hurried outside.

TWENTY

Ocelot was driving now. Winterhawk sat in the shotgun seat, going through the bags he'd retrieved from the house. "This isn't making sense," he said under his breath.

"Still no idea why some toxic fragger would be after 'em?"

"I can't imagine why. They'd only been here a couple of days—hardly seems likely they'd have gone out of their way to anger a toxic shaman. A powerful one, too—I don't like to think about the level of power it would take to punch through the kind of wards that were likely on that house." He continued to sift through the bags.

"You think she was runnin' a little something on the side?" Ocelot steered the car around what looked like the aftermath of a three-vehicle pileup in an intersection. "Maybe that's why she had to get you out of the way—she had something planned, and was worried you'd figure out she was up to something and get in the way."

Winterhawk considered. "It's possible." He pulled Wu's commlink from the bag. "Actually, that's a damn good thought. I'll hold on to this—perhaps Damon's got someone who can crack it, or we can locate a decker. But for now, honestly, I don't care what she was up to. If her shady dealings got her killed, that's her problem, not mine. Shame about the others—unless they were in on it as well, of course. But right now, I'm more concerned about finding Victoria, doing Damon's little job, and getting the hell out of here."

"What about the ley line?"

"That's not a priority at the moment. If I get some time to grab a few readings, I'll do it. But we've already missed our ride, which means our focus needs to be on getting out now. I'm not putting my trust in Damon to make sure that happens."

"Good to hear you say that. So where we going?"

"Back into Boston for now. MIT&T is apparently on lockdown, which means if Victoria's inside, it will be tough to get her out."

"And if she's not?"

"Then we need to find people who know her."

"'Hawk, you realize she might be dead, right?" Ocelot spoke with care, but as usual he didn't dance around the hard truths.

Winterhawk nodded without looking at him. "If she is, that's one less thing we have to do before we can leave," he said, trying to sound brusque. He doubted Ocelot fell for it, though.

TWENTY-ONE

The reports Winterhawk had received from the outside hadn't been exaggerating: they weren't getting anywhere near the MIT&T campus without a lot more backup and recon. Whether the place was trying to keep something out or something in, the four layers of walls, cordons, and barriers were pretty clear indication that they wouldn't be getting onto campus without a lot more planning than they had time for.

"You think she's in there?" Ocelot asked, regarding one of the numerous roadblocks they'd encountered surrounding the area.

"From the way her mother described her, no." Winterhawk turned the car around and headed off down a side street, pointed north.

"So where are we going now?"

"Toward Cambridge. Fortunately for us in this case, she's probably got no reason to hide. Her mother said she lived on campus, but if what I suspect about her is true, she probably didn't spend much of her time at home, meaning she was likely caught on the wrong side of the cordon. If we can find someone who can track her, we might be able to find her—or at least where she frequented. I'll probably need to borrow some funds from you, since I can't access mine at the moment."

As Winterhawk had suspected, quite a number of students had been caught on the wrong side of the MIT&T cordon, and from the look of things many of them had long since found alternative housing arrangements and spent their evenings hanging out at the bars and eateries near campus.

"You know your way around here?" Ocelot asked after they'd parked the car in what looked like a relatively safe spot and the mage had summoned a spirit to keep an eye on it.

"Well enough. Keep a lookout—aside from students, rumor has it that this area's become a bit of a hub for local shadowrunners."

"Maybe we can find a decker to track her."

"Possible, though given the spotty nature of the Matrix inside the QZ, I'm not counting on that."

The first few places they checked netted them no success. No one recognized Winterhawk's description of Victoria, and Maya verified that none of them were lying or hiding anything.

"There's got to be a better way to do this," Ocelot said as they trudged toward the next place, a tavern-style bar with large MIT&T and Harvard AR banners flashing across the sidewalk near the entrance.

Inside, loud music played, several trid players showed sporting events, and the smell of beer, body spray, and hot wings filled the air. In other words, a typical university bar. Winterhawk swept the place with his gaze; most of the tables were occupied by either couples or groups of rowdy young men. He settled on one near the back. "Let's try them," he said, nodding toward it. They pushed their way through the crowd.

The table they headed for include an eclectic group of athletic-looking young people: a male elf, a female ork, and three humans—one female, two male. They looked up from their pizza, pitchers of beer, and animated conversation as Winterhawk and Ocelot drew closer. The ork, clad in a tight-fitting Harvard T-shirt that showed off her impressive arm muscles, eyed both of them with suspicion. "You guys want something?"

"We're looking for someone," Winterhawk said. "We were told you might be able to help us." He paused, and when none of them spoke, he said, "Her name is Victoria Crane. She's a student at MIT&T." He described her, wishing not for the first time that he hadn't lost his image when his commlink got fried. "She's an adept."

He assensed them as they exchanged glances. "Why you wanna find her?" the ork asked, eyes narrowing.

"I'm—a friend of her mother's," he said. "She's concerned about her, and asked me to look into her whereabouts."

The elf shrugged. "Never heard of her."

The others shook their heads.

"Sorry," the ork said, glancing around at her companions. "Guess we can't help you."

The twitch in her aura said otherwise, but Winterhawk's instincts told him not to push it. Instead, he gave them the number of the commlink Damon had given him. "I can make it worth your time if you happen to remember anyone who might know where she is," he said. "Give us a call if you do."

"Yeah," the elf said. "We'll do that." The rest were already turning away, returning to their conversation.

Ocelot waited until they were outside before speaking. "They know something," he said. "Why didn't you push 'em?"

"They do," Winterhawk agreed. "Or at least the ork woman does. But I sensed she didn't want to say anything in front of her friends. We'll see if I'm right. Come on—we've got a lot more people to talk to."

But none of the rest of their conversations with students and others in the clubs and restaurants around campus gleaned any useful information. No one they asked had ever heard of Victoria or recognized her description. The closest they came was one man who said he thought he'd seen her a few months back, before the quarantine had gone into effect, but he couldn't be sure.

"How long are we gonna do this?" Ocelot asked as they headed back toward the car. "Hell, even if she's still alive, she might have gotten out of town before the shit hit the fan. You don't know, and it's damn hard to find out—"

Winterhawk held up a finger as his commlink buzzed. "Yes?"

"I know somebody who's got some info you might want," said a voice Winterhawk recognized as that of the ork woman they'd first talked to. *"She won't stick around for long, though. You know where the the Purple Horse is?"*

He consulted his commlink. "Is that the gay dance club in the South End?"

"Yeah. I'll tell her to meet you there in an hour. She's an ork like me, only skinny and white. Crazy blue hair. Can't miss her. Name's Jazz."

"You can't just tell me?"

"Take it or leave it, chummer." The connection went dead.

They left Maya patrolling outside and another spirit to watch the car. The club was doing a brisk business: loud music pounded into the street every time the padded doors opened, and club patrons of all metatypes lounged along the walls chatting and smoking. Most of those outside were male, dressed to impress. They eyed Winterhawk and Ocelot as they passed, and a couple called out cheerful invitations.

Inside, the thumping synthpop music was so loud it was hard to hear oneself think. ARs were everywhere, advertising drinks, clothing, sex toys, and other wares; occasionally they'd glitch out and flicker off before reappearing. The clientele inside was still mostly men, but some women, in groups and pairs, sat at the tiny purple-topped tables and dotted the dance floor.

They spotted Jazz instantly—as the ork woman at the bar had said, it was hard to miss her wild shock of blue hair. She was seated at the bar, alone, her hand wrapped around a tall, nearly empty glass. Winterhawk indicated a vacant table off to the side of the dance floor, and he and Ocelot settled there. Winterhawk sent a text to the bartender, who a moment later placed another drink in front of Jazz and nodded at them.

She regarded them a moment as if evaluating them, then picked up her drink, moved through the crowd, and dropped down across from them. "I didn't think you'd show."

"Your friend said you had information about Victoria."

She took a long pull from her drink, watching the writhing bodies on the dance floor, and then her face twisted into an expression of distaste. "Yeah, I know her," she said. "*Knew* her."

"Knew her?"

She shrugged. "We were hooking up a few months back. Till she dumped me for that ganger slitch."

Winterhawk and Ocelot exchanged glanced. "Ganger?"

Jazz snorted. "Yeah. Vic's an adept like me, but she didn't fit in too well at school. Didn't even want to be there. You say her mom's looking for her?"

"She's asked us to find her, yes."

"Not surprised. From what she said, her mom's a bitch on wheels. Vic was only at school because Mom got her in on some kind of corp scholarship. She didn't give a fuck about goin' to class." She leaned forward, an anticipatory gleam in her eyes. "So whatcha gonna do when you find her? Drag her back home?" She looked as if the thought appealed to her.

"Not...sure yet," Winterhawk said. "Tell us more about this ganger."

"Can you believe it? We were out at this dive in the Rox—Vic always liked walkin' on the wild side, y'know? A buncha Ancients were there. I wanted to leave, but Vic spots this elf slitch in their colors and strikes up a convo with her. Next thing you know, they were at their own little table in the back, actin' like nobody else was even there."

"So she dumped you right there?" Ocelot asked.

"Nah. But she might as well've. After that she was always busy when I tried to meet up with her, and eventually I heard she and the slitch were a thing." She took another long drink and sighed. "So yeah, I'm not feelin' too much like I want to protect her, y'know? You want to track her down and drag her back to Mommy? You go right ahead. Let 'er try to explain why she blew off half her classes stayin' out late hangin' with a keeb go-gang."

"Wait," Ocelot said. "She's human, right? How's that work? The Ancients'll barely talk to anybody without pointy ears."

"Yeah, mostly," Jazz said. "That changed when the walls went up, though. Lots of things did. Word is they'll take anybody now, long's they got some mojo. I'm not sure whether Vic joined up or not, but I wouldn't be surprised. That's the kind of thing she's into—fast and furious, y'know? The faster the better." She rolled her eyes. "I don't care. She can do what she wants. Don't tell anybody I told you where to find her, though. I don't want to get on the bad side of any gangers. It's tough enough in here now, even if you keep your head down."

"Your name won't come up," Winterhawk assured her. "We—"

Off to their right, on the edge of the dance floor, something was happening. A crowd of people pressed in around something, but they couldn't see what it was. Ocelot tensed. "We should get out of here."

"It's chill," Jazz said, her eyes focused on something they couldn't see. "AR chatter says somebody probably got a bad batch of Chroma again." Her gaze shifted back to them. "Happening a lot lately. Last couple weeks. Stupid to even take the chance, you ask me. Stick to safe shit like novacoke." She finished her drink. "Anyway, gotta jet. You guys got what you need?"

"Thank you," Winterhawk said, getting up. Already, two burly club staffers were pushing the crowd aside while another carried a slender young man out. The young man's arms and legs flailed madly, and his screams were loud enough to be heard above the pounding beat of the music. Winterhawk assensed him as they went by. He only got a couple seconds' read before the group swept past and was once again swallowed by the throng. He got Ocelot's attention and pointed toward the exit.

When they got outside and could hear each other without yelling, Ocelot said, "So now we gotta find the Ancients? Great. They're gonna *love* us."

"Sounds like they're a bit more open-minded now."

"I'll believe that when I see it. They ain't gonna want to talk to us."

"We'll just have to be persuasive, then."

They got back to the van. Winterhawk dismissed the spirit, Maya settled into her spot in the back seat, and they picked their way around the abandoned vehicles clogging the street.

Ocelot had retrieved his shotgun and was scanning the area around them, as usual hypervigilant for potential threats. "So what was that back there? What's Chroma? Some kind of club drug, it sounds like. Must be new. I don't do clubs as much as I used to these days."

"It's only been around for a year or so," Winterhawk said. "Supposedly one of the more harmless of the BADs—mundanes use it so they can 'see the music.'" He frowned and shook his head. "One of these days, these fools will learn that there's no such thing as a safe BAD. They're playing with things they don't understand."

"Eh, you're just gettin' old," Ocelot said, grinning.

Winterhawk didn't answer. This was exactly the sort of thing Damon would be up to his scaly snout in—club drugs, designed to enhance the hedonistic experiences of the user, would be right up his alley. Especially magical ones. Had the bad batch the unfortunate young man had gotten hold of had come through the dragon's distribution pipeline? Even more than that, though, what he'd seen during his quick assensing of the victim troubled him. He couldn't be sure he'd gotten it right, because he hadn't been looking for it, and had only recognized the faint traces because it was so soon after he'd encountered them before. But if he'd seen what he thought he'd seen—

"Check something for me, will you?" he asked.

"What? And where are you going?"

"The Rox—the west edge of it, anyway. If memory serves, that's where their territory is. You can check that too, if you want. But before that, see if you can find anything else about anyone's experiences with bad batches of Chroma."

Ocelot stared at him. "'Hawk, you can't just go knock on the Ancients' door like you're lookin' for a lost puppy."

"I know. That's why you're here."

"What the hell's that supposed to mean?"

"You know gangs. You dealt with the Ancients back in Seattle, didn't you?"

"Yeah, but—"

"So you can do it again." He waved him off, impatient. "Look that up for me, all right? And Maya, keep an eye on us from the astral. I've got the van disguised, but let me know if you spot anything we should know about."

Ocelot looked like he was about to say something else, but instead let out a loud sigh and pulled out his commlink. "Network's shit," he muttered, but soon he was cocooned in a semicircle of AR windows as Winterhawk continued negotiating the smaller side streets heading south toward the Rox.

There weren't many vehicles on the road, and most of those were small, nimble motorcycles. 'Hawk kept most of his attention on the road, but focused a corner of his concentration to maintain the illusion he'd put on the van. He'd made it look like a clapped-out wreck covered in Bondo and dents, hoping it wouldn't appear tempting enough for anyone to mess with. He glanced over toward Ocelot periodically.

"The chica at the club was right," the samurai said after five minutes, shoving three AR windows aside to minimize them. "I only found a few things about bad Chroma—none of 'em anyplace like screamsheets. All just social-media stuff, people talkin' about their friends' bad trips. Maybe the bigwigs are suppressin' the story, or maybe it's not big enough to give a fuck about, with all the other shit goin' down around here. But anyway, just like Jazz said—nothin' older than about two weeks ago." He shifted in his seat, pausing to close the rest of the windows and scanning the front, sides, and rear of the car with careful concentration. "You expect to see that?"

"Any accounts of what happened?" Winterhawk asked. "Did any of the victims die?"

"A couple did, yeah. Most of 'em went crazy. One attacked a KE cop and got ventilated. Nobody's talkin' about anybody recoverin'." His eyes narrowed. "You sound like you're fishin' for somethin'. Out with it. Why do you suddenly give a fuck about bad drugs?"

"I don't, normally. People can do what they like, regardless of how stupid it is. But in this case, I noticed some odd traces around the victim back at the club when I assensed him."

"What kind of traces?"

"Twisted magic. Toxic, unless I miss my guess."

"What?" Ocelot's hands tightened on his shotgun. "You sure?"

"No. I only got a quick glimpse. No real detail."

"Isn't that what you said killed your researchers? Some kinda toxic ritual?"

"Yes. And now you're beginning to see what troubles me."

"You think the two are related? How can that be? Did Wu and her team stumble into something?"

"I still don't see how," Winterhawk said. He made a left turn. "It's probably nothing—Boston is a magic-rich area. I'm sure there are plenty of toxics lurking in the shadows. But something makes me wonder. With the walls up, I doubt anyone's smuggling many BADs in from outside the QZ, which means they're likely to be locally produced."

"So?"

"So—the most prolific producers of BADs in the Boston area are the Salem witches. They grow them out in the Wilds."

"You think the *witches* killed Wu's people?"

"No idea. They aren't a monolith—there are a lot of subgroups out there, from your garden-variety nature-loving Wiccans to… some that are considerably less wholesome. As far as I know, Wu didn't have any specific contacts among any of them—that was my job." He shook his head. "Anyway, we need to find Victoria. It's not to us to police the drug trade. Did you find anything about the Ancients?"

"Yeah. Found where their turf is. Still gonna say I don't think this is a good idea, though. You and gangs go together like fish and jet engines."

"Objection noted," Winterhawk said as an area of his AR map lit up. He turned again and headed toward it.

TWENTY-TWO

They entered the area Ocelot had indicated on the map in about twenty minutes, and it wasn't long before they began to spot the Ancients' telltale tags.

"This is a damn stupid idea," Ocelot said. His gaze was never still, though he walked with confidence and even a bit of swagger. "Walkin' into a gang's home turf is askin' for trouble."

"We don't have time to send them a calling card and wait for them to get back to us," Winterhawk said. "We'll be fine. We're not exactly defenseless."

He was right about that. After Ocelot's research had turned up the neighborhood that constituted the Ancients' central turf and identified their headquarters, a motorcycle shop called Kustom Rode Bykes, both of them had decided the direct approach was the best. They left the van parked in a dark alley two blocks away, guarded by only a single spirit this time since Winterhawk wanted Maya to accompany them along with another spirit.

The mage had used a Fashion spell to alter their clothes according to Ocelot's specifications. "We want to look confident, like we're not gonna take any crap, but not too cocky," Ocelot said. "The idea is to show them we can take care of ourselves, but we're not challenging them." To that end, Winterhawk now sported an elegant corporate-style suit, his heavy armored coat altered to a more subtle design. Ocelot wore the suit and more overt armor of a bodyguard, and had several of his weapons, including his monofilament whip, concealed within it.

As they walked, they couldn't help but notice that they were being watched. Some of it was obvious: pairs and trios of green-jacketed figures, overwhelmingly elves, lounging on street corners or watching from stoops. Some was less so: Maya reported more watchers inside buildings, and even patrolling spirits. "*They're interested,*" she said. "*Suspicious. But mostly waiting.*"

"They want to see why we're here," Winterhawk said. He'd taken Ocelot's advice: despite the fact that walking through gang-infested neighborhoods was not high on his list of favorite things to do, he carried himself with the authority and subtle arrogance of someone who expected respect. He allowed enough of his aura to show past the mask to let any Awakened observers know he was magically talented, but not enough to show the full extent of his power. No sense giving away all your secrets at once. He wasn't well versed on gangs and their spheres of influence, but the Ancients were well known to have a larger than usual percentage of magicians and adepts among their ranks.

As they walked, it became clearer that they were picking up increased attention. No one stepped out to accost them, and no one overtly followed them, but when you'd been in the shadowrunning business as long as Winterhawk and Ocelot had—not to mention when you had two spirits running overwatch for you—it wasn't hard to spot the heightened scrutiny. By the time they drew close to their destination, the spirits were reporting that at least twenty people were observing them from various concealed locations along the street.

Kustom Rode Bykes was in the middle of a long block of mostly defunct and shuttered businesses. Its front display window was gone, replaced by heavy plaswood reinforcement decorated with more Ancients symbols and other graffiti, and a roll-up door stood half open, revealing part of a lighted workspace behind it. Several motorcycles were lined up in front of the place, and a pair of male elves in green jackets leaned against the front wall, smoking, in attitudes of carefully feigned nonchalance. As Winterhawk and Ocelot approached, the pair stepped out and blocked their path.

For a moment, the four of them eyed each other in silence. "You want somethin'?" the elf on the left, a tall, gangly young man with a shock of white hair, asked around his cigarette.

"My boss wants to talk to your boss," Ocelot said, indicating Winterhawk.

They'd discussed their plans before they'd arrived: since many of the Ancients in this area were of Irish descent, 'Hawk had thought it best for Ocelot to do the talking as much as possible. He doubted his own British accent would make him popular.

The other elf, a little shorter and beefier with buzz-cut red hair, snickered. "That so, is it? Maybe ye can talk to us instead." He spoke in a thick Irish brogue.

Ocelot shrugged. "Whatever. We don't want any trouble. We got a job to do, that's all. We're lookin' for somebody, and word is you guys might know somethin'."

The roll-up door opened the rest of the way and two more elves, a male and a female, drifted out from the work area. Winterhawk got a brief impression of several more motorcycles back there, with more elves rising from their work to check out the situation.

The white-haired elf's gaze flicked toward the newcomers from the garage, then back to Winterhawk and Ocelot. "So whaddya want? You got balls, just walkin' right up to our front door, that's fer sure. Gimme a good reason why we shouldn't just take yer gear and sell the rest of you fer spare parts?"

"You got no problem with us," Ocelot pointed out. "And we got none with you. Just biz." His eyes narrowed. "And besides, you might have a little more trouble than you think doin' that, if you try. Sure, you might kill us. Probably will. But I guarantee you won't do it without losin' some of your guys. Way I hear it, you can't afford to lose people for no good reason these days."

Next to the white-haired elf, the redhead shifted, clenching his fists. Winterhawk sensed the two newcomers from the garage now behind them—they were surrounded. "*Keep an eye on those two,*" he instructed Maya. Meanwhile, the air spirit continued to report back the positions of the other nearby observers.

"Come on," Ocelot said. "We ain't got all night, and neither do you. Maybe we don't even need to talk to your boss. Maybe you got what we need. We're lookin' for a girl. Human. Word on the street says she might be runnin' with you guys."

The two exchanged glances again, and the woman muttered something to her friend that Winterhawk couldn't hear. "*She wonders if you're talking about someone named Vyx,*" Maya reported.

Winterhawk forced himself not to show any reaction, to maintain his imperious demeanor. Vyx? That was too close to Victoria to be a coincidence. If Jazz's intel had been correct and Victoria *had* fallen in with the Ancients, perhaps she was here now. He realized with a bit of shock that he'd been so focused on finding her that he had no idea what he would say to her if she actually turned up.

"Who the hell're ye, anyway?" the redheaded elf asked. "Why the fuck should we tell ye anythin'?" His hand fell to the butt of a pistol at his hip.

"It doesn't matter," drawled the woman from behind them. "What do we care if they know? She's gone. You lookin' for Vyx, yeah? Norm slitch? College girl?"

"That's right," Winterhawk said, forgetting he wasn't going to talk. "Is she here?"

"Lemme handle this, boss," Ocelot growled. He turned to face the woman. "She's gone, you said? Where?"

The woman grinned. "Got 'er ass kicked out, she did. Good riddance. Fraggin' round-ears don't belong here anyway."

"And neither do ye," said the redhead. He glared at the woman, then back at Winterhawk and Ocelot. "Now get the fuck outta here. We ain't got yer little norm slitch. By now, the headcases prob'ly got 'er. Not like anybody'd miss 'er. Nothin' but trouble, that one."

The white-haired elf nodded. "You got fifteen minutes to get off our turf. We still see you after that..." He pushed the front of his jacket aside to reveal a sawed-off shotgun.

Winterhawk was about to say something, but Ocelot shook his head. "C'mon, boss," he said. "Let's go. I got a couple more ideas for leads to follow up."

"Not a good idea to challenge them here," Maya agreed. *"I count at least ten guns aimed at you at the moment."*

So close! She'd been here, but now she'd slipped away. Winterhawk had assensed the Ancients as they spoke, and he had no doubt they were telling the truth about Victoria—Vyx, now, apparently—not being here. But did they know where she'd gone? Why had they sent her away? So many questions. He wanted nothing more than to force the elves to tell him what he wanted to know, but Ocelot was right—this wasn't the time. They'd have to regroup and approach the situation from another angle, and that would take more time.

He felt the elves' gazes on them as they retraced their steps back toward where they'd left the van. No doubt the other Ancients had gotten the update from the ones at Kustom Rode Bykes, because now the groups they'd passed on their way in weren't even trying to be subtle about watching them as they went by on their way out. Like Ocelot, he continued to walk with nonchalant disregard, as if the deadline they'd been given to vacate the area meant nothing to him. He'd run with Ocelot long enough to know you never showed weakness or fear to gangers—most of them were like packs of wolves, ready to fall upon prey at the first taste of blood. It was all a big dance—he could tell from his brief assensing that the Ancients didn't want trouble any more than they did, and as long as everybody played along with the game, nobody had to get hurt. Winterhawk thought it all rather pointless, but he had to acknowledge that it was nothing but a cruder version of the same psychological two-step practiced in nearly every confrontation with at least two sides, up to and including negotiations between nations, corporations, and dragons.

If playing the silly posturing games got them out of there faster and helped them find Victoria sooner, so be it.

They had almost reached the edge of the Ancients' territory (Ocelot had pointed out the border when they'd gone in—one side of the street awash with green paint and Ancients symbols, the other equally covered in Hellriders iconography) when the air spirit raised an alarm over the mental link it shared with Winterhawk.

"Someone's coming. Fast."

TWENTY-THREE

'Hawk didn't pause to ask for clarification. "Down!" he ordered over the comm, ducking behind a wheelless parked car. Then, to the group of three Ancients observing them from the edge of their turf: "You lot! Heads up! Someone's—"

That was all he got out before two vehicles came screaming in their direction, tires shrieking as they took the corner fast. The one in front was a boxy delivery van, the rear one an equally nondescript sedan with a blasted-out rear window. As soon as they rounded the corner, several gun barrels poked out from half-opened, blacked-out side windows and opened fire on the three Ancients. Whoops and war cries came from the unseen gunmen inside.

Their plan didn't go entirely as expected, though: rather than being the sitting ducks the gunmen had obviously been hoping for, the three Ancients had moved with liquid speed at Winterhawk's yell. One cried out as bullets stitched his side, but the other two made it to cover and were already returning fire.

Winterhawk made a fast decision. He didn't know if it was the right one, but at this point he couldn't take the time to consider. He fixed his gaze on a section of street about half a block ahead of the van's current position and formed the spell pattern in his mind, dropping a glowing barrier directly in front of it. The van's brakes screeched and its tires howled as the driver tried to haul it to a stop before impact, but the barrier was too close. The loud crash as the vehicle slammed into the glowing wall echoed along the entire darkened street. A second crash when the car hit the back end of the van wasn't as loud, but every bit as detrimental to the sedan's forward progress. Winterhawk braced himself against the astral feedback as the barrier flared and disappeared—he hadn't expected it to stand up to a hit like that, but it hadn't had to—it had done its job exactly as he'd planned.

The Ancients and Ocelot, meanwhile, hadn't been idle. As the van's and the sedan's doors opened and figures sought cover, the street erupted with the sound of gunfire. It wasn't just coming from the two unwounded gangers, either: as 'Hawk crouched behind the car and waited for his heart rate to return to normal, he picked out three different muzzle flashes from upstairs windows. One of the shadowy figures behind the sedan spun and fell, his assault rifle clattering to the street. More yells and calls from both the Ancients and the newcomers joined the gunfire to split the street's former silence.

The sedan's driver was still inside, obviously trying to get the car moving because the front wheels were spinning hard, throwing up bits of broken roadway. Another figure, moving so fast it was barely possible to follow it, swung down from somewhere above Winterhawk and dashed forward, wrenching the sedan's door open. From his vantage point, 'Hawk couldn't see what happened next, but a second later a triumphant *"One down!"* came over their link from Ocelot, and a second after that the dark figure had darted away to the other side of the street.

With the sedan's driver neutralized and neither vehicle moving, the remaining Ancients wasted no time in dispatching the rest of the assailants. The two from the street joined five more who'd dropped with nimble, deadly grace from upper windows, and soon the all but one of the vehicles' seven occupants lay dead on the wet street. The final occupant, a muscular human with a broken nose and a jacket sporting a green, orange, and white patch on the back, was disarmed and roughly hustled off, hands zip-tied behind his back, by three Ancients.

Two more approached Winterhawk, who was still observing from his vantage point behind the car. He held up his hands. "Don't shoot. Do I look like one of those idiots?" He sent mental messages to Maya and the air spirit to keep watch for any other approaching vehicles.

"Ye warned us," one of them said. "Why'd ye do that?"

"Are you complainin'?" Ocelot came up behind 'Hawk, moving so quietly the mage wasn't even aware he was there until he spoke. "I'd say we helped save your pointy-eared asses."

"We can't stay here," the Ancient said. His vision fuzzed out for a moment as he listened to an unseen voice, then he nodded as if in reply. "C'mon back with us. Lucky Liam wants to talk to ye."

'Hawk looked at Ocelot, who shrugged. With Maya and the spirit continuing to provide astral recon, they allowed the two Ancients to lead them back toward Kustom Rode Bykes. The others stayed behind, hovering around the two crashed vehicles.

"What about the other one?" Winterhawk asked. "Is he dead?"

"No, but he's gonna hurt like hell for a few days," the other one said. "Better a few busted ribs than a head shot, though."

"Who were those guys?" Ocelot asked. "I saw the colors, but we're not from around here."

"Bane Sidhe," the first one said. He didn't spit, but his tone suggested he'd like to. "Fookin' bastards. They're gettin' bolder, comin' into our turf like that."

Winterhawk didn't ask what would become of the prisoner they'd taken. In truth, he didn't care. "Who's Lucky Liam?"

The second of their Ancient escorts glanced back over his shoulder as if expecting to be followed. "Just come on. We gotta get back."

Activity around the bike shop had increased considerably since they'd left only a few minutes previously. The roll-up door was locked down now, and Maya reported several more concealed Ancient gangers hiding in strategic locations on both sides of the street.

"This way," the first Ancient said, indicating for them to enter the bike shop through a reinforced front door emblazoned with the shop's name. Beneath it, someone had spray-painted another of the ever-present green A-in-circle logos with more artistic talent than usual.

Inside, several more elves waited, their demeanors tense and watchful. Their gazes all instantly focused on Winterhawk and Ocelot as they entered, but only one of them stepped forward: a tall redhead with the muscular, lithe form of an athlete. His face was as youthful as all the others—elves were like that—but his shrewd, hooded green eyes spoke of both experience and intelligence.

"So," he said. "Yer the ones who tipped off my guys about the Bane Sidhe attack."

"Not exactly," Winterhawk said. "We had no idea who they were or what they wanted."

The elf's eyes narrowed and he frowned at Winterhawk's accent, but he didn't comment. "Name's Lucky Liam."

"So we've been told. As my friend mentioned, we're not from the area."

A few of the other elves muttered and shifted, but Liam raised his hand to wave them down. Instead of looking offended, he chuckled. "Fair enough, then. I lead the Boston Ancients. And it seems we owe both o' ye for saving some lives tonight. I also heard ye came by earlier, looking for some information about Vyx."

Winterhawk nodded. "I was told she's not here any longer. Is that so?"

Liam fixed a harder gaze on him. "Why d'ye want t'know? What d'ye want with her, anyway?"

"We've been hired to find her," Winterhawk said. "By someone who's very interested in seeing her safely home."

Another elf snorted. "Her mam want her back?"

"Shut yer gob, Blaine," Liam snapped. He considered a moment, then stood. "Come on. We'll talk."

"Boss—" the white-haired elf began.

"Shut up. Get on, all of ye—I doubt those assholes'll try again tonight, but I want patrols out along the perimeter, and tell Bree and Joker to get some more spirits out. You so much as see anything that looks wrong, make sure I know about it. Got it?"

"Yeah, I got it." He and the other elves stalked out, talking among themselves, leaving only Liam and two other elves alone with Winterhawk and Ocelot.

"Wait out here," Liam ordered the elves, and waved Winterhawk and Ocelot into a cluttered office. He closed the door behind them, though a window afforded the two guards a view inside. Winterhawk noticed they'd both drawn guns, though at the moment they held them loosely at their sides.

"Why d'ye want Vyx?" Liam asked again. He shoved aside an exhaust pipe and several empty soykaf cups and settled himself against the desk. His expression revealed nothing.

"I told you," Winterhawk said. "We've been hired to find her and bring her home."

"Home? Where's home? Who hired ye?"

Winterhawk paced the office. "We've not got time to dance around—we need to find her quickly. How much do you know about her?"

"If somebody hired ye to find 'er, why d'ye need us to tell ye where she is? Why not just give 'er a call? The network's spotty, but if ye keep tryin', ye can usually get through."

"We ran into a bit of trouble and lost most of our information. Images, address data—all of it."

Liam looked like he wasn't sure he believed that. "Well, she was at MIT&T. Didn't wanna be—didn't get along with 'er mam."

"They had certain...disagreements about her future," Winterhawk agreed. "But her mother cares about her very much. And she wants her home."

"And I ask again—where's 'home'?" Idly, Liam began gathering up the soykaf cups. When he had them all, he tossed them into an overflowing receptacle on the other side of the room. "If 'er mam's in the QZ, she's probably safer with us."

"She isn't."

Liam's eyes narrowed. "So, yer sayin' ye've not just been hired to take 'er home, but to get 'er out of the QZ? Ye got a way out?"

"We're...working on it. Things haven't gone quite as planned."

"Yeah, nothin' ever goes as planned in this hellhole." The elf's chuckle was utterly mirthless. He was silent for several seconds, obviously considering. Finally he sighed. "I can't tell ye where she is—not exactly. But I can tell ye where she went. I'm just not sure if I should."

"Why not?" Ocelot asked. "Is she here or not? That other guy said she left."

"She did. But not because she wanted to." He pushed himself off the desk and dropped into the chair behind it, leaning it back until it hit the wall. "Maybe you guessed she didn't fit in so well here."

"Because she's human."

"Yeah, that was a lot of it. Ever since the walls went up, we've had to...relax our standards some. Open membership to a few... shall we say...select individuals not of the elven race. But that didn't mean everybody was in favor of it. Vyx messed up and made some enemies. I had to make a choice—let 'em kill 'er, send 'er packin', or...the choice I ended up makin'. Which was to send 'er off, but with a job to do to get 'er away from here for a while till people cooled down. Figured if she managed to do it and make it back, she might make up for 'er screwup enough that the guys'd be willin' to let it go."

"Why would you do that?" Ocelot asked. "You're the leader. You're tellin' me you were okay with a norm in your elf gang?"

Liam shrugged. "Like I said, we didn't have a lot of choice. There's a lot of dyin' goin' on here these days. Vyx was good. Damn good. Plus, she'd taken up with my cousin, Virago."

"So," Winterhawk said, "As I told you—we're in a hurry. Can you tell us where you sent her?"

Again, Liam didn't answer for a long time. "I don't like it," he said at last. "But mebbe it's for the best. Even if she succeeds and comes back, she's still gonna cause trouble. That's just the way she is. Gettin' 'er outta here would be good for us, and good for her, too."

He stood. "She's gone to Salem. And Virago went with her." He pulled out his commlink and tapped something in. "Gimme your code—I'll send ye 'er LTG, and Virago's, too. Mebbe you can reach 'em if ye want—though if she finds out her mam's tryin' to track 'er down, she'll probably run."

Winterhawk stared. "Why?" Victoria was in Salem too? Coincidence, or was some larger plan he couldn't see yet in effect? "Why would you send her there?" He twiddled a setting on his commlink to receive the files Liam was sending.

"Wait a sec," Ocelot said. "I was doin' some research on you guys when we were tryin' to find your turf. You work for the O'Rilleys, runnin' drugs."

"I'm not sayin' anything 'bout that," Liam said, glancing toward the two guards outside.

"You don't have to," Winterhawk said, as things began to fall together. "This has to do with the BADs the witches produce, doesn't it?"

"That's a pretty big assumption," Liam said.

"It's the only thing that makes sense," Ocelot said. "Why would you send her on a mission up there if it didn't have something to do with biz? You didn't just send her off to stay with your sister or somethin', did you?"

Liam started to say something, then stopped and went still as he listened to some unheard communication. "We got more trouble," he said. "I need to go, so I'll make this quick. Yeah, yer right. I'm not mentionin' specifics, but I sent 'er to Salem to try and figure out why certain supply pipelines 'ave nearly stopped. O'Rilley's people are gettin' nervous and leanin' on us, so I figured I'd make the best of a shite situation all around."

"Salem's a big place," Winterhawk said. "Can you give us more detail?"

Liam was already heading for the door. "Not much. I told 'er to make contact with a chummer up there who goes by Beatrix." He sent Winterhawk an LTG. "That's a drop she uses for messages. Don't ask for any other info—I won't give it to ye. I didn't want anyone tracking 'er if they overheard anything, so I kept it vague on purpose. That's all I'm tellin' ye, so move along—I gotta go."

"One more thing." Winterhawk didn't step in front of him, but he did move in that direction. "We can find her, but it will be a lot easier if we had something to track her with. Have you got anything like that?"

"Vyx took all 'er stuff with 'er," Liam said, sounding impatient now. Then he frowned, seeming to remember something, and stalked back across the room to a battered metal file cabinet. He yanked open the lowest drawer and pulled out a green synthleather jacket, ripped and stained with patches of blood, which he tossed to Winterhawk.

"This is 'ers—she left it here a few days ago. Maybe ye can use that to find 'er." He swept out the door and gathered up the two guards with a gesture.

Winterhawk and Ocelot followed them out. A few other elves eyed them with suspicion, but most of the gangers had already left. The bass rumbles of several motorcycles firing up came through the wall from the garage next door.

"Salem," Ocelot said when they were back outside.

"Seems all roads lead there," Winterhawk agreed. "I'm not sure how I feel about that, but at least it narrows our choices."

TWENTY-FOUR

It took Vyx and Virago the better part of a day to make it out of Boston proper. Acutely aware of the interconnected mishmash of rival gang territories surrounding the Ancients' corner of the Rox, they elected to put aside the usual recklessness they reveled in when riding with the gang in favor of picking their way with confident care around the edges of the Hellriders' territory to the northwest. It was either that or try going straight through the middle of the Hub, and neither of them wanted to do that.

They barely avoided two potential confrontations on the way out of the area. The first was with the Hellriders, a go-gang that made the Ancients look like law-abiding commuters by comparison. Vyx didn't know what the gang was up to—they didn't usually ride in broad daylight—but neither she nor Virago wanted to find out. They had to make a fast detour, but better that than getting caught out. Even though they'd left their Ancients colors back at Virago's place, Virago's bright green hair was a dead giveaway for anyone looking their way.

The second was a crowd of shamblers that had gathered in the middle of the road just north of Cambridge. There had to be at least forty of them milling around, blocking a major intersection. Several Knight Errant vehicles were parked nearby, and the KE forces were trying to get them under control. Vyx and Virago didn't stick around to wait for the outcome, but altering their route to avoid this clusterfuck added still more time to their trip.

Normally, the pre-QZ trip from the Rox up to Salem would have taken less than an hour in decent traffic. To be fair, "decent traffic" wasn't a concept one often observed in the Boston 'plex, but even so, once they got out of the city proper they could make good time, especially at the speeds they normally rode. That all changed when the walls went up, though—between the ever-present metahuman threats, the patchy fog that had descended over much of the area, and the roads' general state of growing disrepair, it was wise to add significant padding to any itinerary of more than a couple kilometers. Most regular citizens didn't even bother traveling anymore unless they had to, opting to remain behind barriers in dozens of small enclaves, trusting the police, security forces, and an increasing number of armed private citizens to protect them and to help maintain the fragile illusion that they were safe.

That was pretty much Vyx's definition of hell on earth—far worse than anything the QZ could dish up on its own.

They picked up the Salem Turnpike just outside Boston and headed north. Neither spoke much, each one hyper-aware in case anyone tried to hassle them. These days, you could run into just about anything on the roads, especially after dark. The fog made vision treacherous, and the late-fall temperature combined with the damp air to make the ride uncomfortable.

Vyx had ridden with the Ancients enough to know that when they were doing a job or trying to put a little fear into the Bane Sidhe or other rival go-gangs, the adrenaline that coursed through her body made the cold a non-issue. Now, though, the chill crept through her gloves, down her back, and made her legs feel like two blocks of ice. She blipped the throttle a bit to catch up with Virago as they crossed through Revere. Beyond, the Turnpike cut a straight line for several kilometers through a swampy stretch called Rumney Marsh, which meant that even if they covered the distance at top speed, they'd still be away from civilization (such as it was these days) for a good twenty to thirty minutes.

Just stay sharp and you'll be fine.

Even so, she almost missed them when they attacked. Her danger sense twigged her an instant before two figures on bikes pulled out from a tiny hidden side road, catching up fast, engines whining hard. *Fuck!*

"We got company," Vyx said over the comm.

"Yeah. Let's see if we can outrun 'em." Virago didn't sound scared—in fact, she sounded pleased to have something to do besides dodge chunks of road and shamblers.

Vyx grinned. "Sucks for them if we can't." Already her body coursed with adrenaline, her muscles primed and ready for action. She jacked her bike's throttle and it leaped forward as Virago's did the same, opening more distance between them and the bikers behind them.

Vyx called up a view from her rear-facing camera and projected it into her glasses' HUD. It didn't look like there were more than two back there. They didn't have any lights on, but the heat of their bikes and their bodies blazed against the foggy darkness when she cycled the glasses from low-light to thermographic vision. "Can you tell who they are?"

"No colors I can see."

So at least it wasn't the Hellriders or Bane Sidhe out here on some kind of biz. If it was just a couple of freelancers thinking they'd found an easy score, they'd be in for a surprise. Vyx scanned the road ahead while keeping part of her concentration on the small vid window showing the approaching pair. The upcoming stretch of the Turnpike was deserted as far as she could tell, but there weren't many buildings or other roads out here. She didn't expect an ambush, but that didn't mean she wasn't scanning for one.

A sharp *crack* broke through the steady whine of the bikes' engines, and the two pursuers surged forward, closing the distance. One brandished a pistol, while the other had some kind of long curved blade. Both whooped into the night as they approached. They wore battered leathers crudely painted with symbols, dark goggles, and cloths wrapped around their lower faces. Their matted hair streamed out behind them.

Next to Vyx, Virago pulled out her own pistol and returned fire. The guy on her side dropped back and the shot missed. Up ahead, a bridge stretched over part of the marsh, though the fog made it look as if the road simply shot out into nothingness.

"Watch it," Vyx said. She hunkered down lower and presented an erratic pattern to make herself less of a target.

They darted across the bridge, the two other bikers only a few meters behind and still screaming something Vyx couldn't make out. A round spanged off the side of her bike, barely missing her leg. "Fuck!" she called over the link. In a smooth motion she'd practiced hundreds of times, she drew the katana from the sheath on her back and held it ready.

They were approaching another bridge, this one longer than the one they'd just crossed. *"Car up ahead,"* Virago reported.

Vyx saw it too, its lights dazzling, glowing bright against the fog. It was heading toward them, a short distance from the bridge on the other side. Its lights made it hard to see what it was, though: some random citizen braving the trip toward Boston? A cop? Would the bikers give up their pursuit? Her hand tightened on her katana, and her knees on the side of the bike.

As soon as she and Virago entered the bridge, they saw that the bikers had planned this ambush. The car, which had been coming toward them, slammed on its brakes and slewed sideways, coming to a stop across two of the bridge's four lanes, and two more bikers, their lights also off, erupted onto the far end from where they'd concealed themselves.

Even at their speed, Vyx and Virago barely had time to react. Vyx, in front, had only a split-second to make a decision, and it wasn't one she wanted to make: no matter how fast she moved, the bike was still governed by the laws of physics, and those laws said that a pair of dual-purpose tires and some heavy-duty brakes couldn't stop fast enough to avoid hitting the car.

Vyx braced her feet on the pegs and launched herself up off the bike in a controlled leap toward the car. Still clutching her katana, she flipped her body and rolled across the top of it, gritting her teeth as the bike crashed into the vehicle. She rolled a couple more times and leaped to her feet.

Virago, meanwhile, apparently taking a page from the Hellriders' playbook (one of their favorite stunts was playing chicken, but unlike most sane people they considered slamming into their opponents part of the fun), hit her throttle and headed straight at the two new bikers. They held their ground for an admirably long time, taking potshots at her that didn't hit, but at the last second they jerked their bikes to either side and Virago blew past, using her own pistol to let the one on her left have it in the face as she did so. She whooped in elation as she shot past the remaining biker.

Vyx whooped with her, but a second later dived to the side as the guy riding shotgun in the car opened fire on her with what sounded like an SMG. The rounds tore into the ferrocrete, sending up little puffs of smoke and shrapnel.

"Need a lift, babe?" Virago's voice came over the 'link. She'd spun her bike around and was coming back toward the fight, peppering the car with covering fire from her pistol. The vehicle's armored window held, but a network of spiderweb cracks appeared below the few open centimeters the occupant needed to shoot from.

Vyx grinned. As Virago passed by without slowing, she vaulted upward and landed neatly on the back of the elf's bike. The back wheel shimmied alarmingly as her weight landed over it, but after a second it settled down. Virago flung the bike back and forth to present a harder target, steering with one hand as she stowed one pistol and drew another. More *cracks* as the bikers kept firing, but now the guy with the SMG was at the wrong angle to hit them without getting out of the car.

"Get the hell outta here!" Vyx yelled.

Virago apparently had no argument with that. She gunned the bike again and zoomed off the bridge, keeping up her erratic pattern.

Vyx, whipping back and forth on the precarious pillion seat, glanced over her shoulder as the scene behind them faded into the background. A couple more rounds zinged by, and then the fog swallowed them. Vyx let her breath out, wondering what *else* was going to mess with them before they got to town.

They limped into a diner on the outskirts of Lynn a short distance later, Vyx perched uncomfortably on top of Virago's saddlebags and duffel. The bike bucked and wheezed, the harsh, metallic clanks emanating from somewhere in its innards not encouraging. Virago rolled into a parking space and Vyx tumbled off, stumping around to shake the kinks out of her legs. Her butt ached like she'd just ridden the last several kilometers straddling a steel rail.

Virago got off more slowly and crouched next to the side of the bike. Small puffs of blue smoke wafted up from the engine, mingling with the hot, acrid odor of smoldering oil. "Fuck," she said. "That was fun. Let's do it again next week, yeah?"

Virago didn't make a habit of showing fear, and most other people wouldn't have picked up the edge under her flippant tones. Vyx wasn't most other people.

"Think it's gonna make it to Salem?" She glanced back in the direction they'd come, surprised by her raw grief at the loss of her own bike. The Rapier had been a gift from the Ancients when she'd joined: the remains of a once-fast ride they'd appropriated from a Bane Sidhe who wouldn't be needing it anymore in whatever afterlife they'd sent him to. It didn't run when she'd gotten it, and with its blown engine, twisted front wheel, and mangled exhaust, it had barely maintained its structural integrity enough to remain upright.

She and Virago had worked on it over many weeks, using parts from the shop and others they'd lifted from the rides of rivals the gang had taken down. When they finished, they'd restored it to nearly as good as new—at least as far as functionality went. Aesthetically it wasn't pretty, and their attempts to paint over the Bane Sidhe colors and symbols showed that both were better at wrenching than artistic expression, but that was part of its charm. The other part was that it had been *hers,* and more valuable to her than the trim, proper little coupe her mother had given her before she'd left for MIT&T. That thing had probably been stolen or stripped for parts long ago by somebody behind the cordon, and she hadn't missed it for a moment.

Virago rooted around in her duffel bag and pulled out a toolkit. "Dunno," she said. "Go get us somethin' to eat, and I'll see what I can do with it.

When Vyx returned juggling a couple greasy wrapped soyburgers and paper cups of soykaf a few minutes later, Virago was just rising from the ground, wiping her hands on her grubby jeans.

"Best I can do," she said. "It's a damn good thing we got away when we did. Couple more shots like that and we'd've been road pizza. I think I got it patched up enough we should make it, but unless we find some parts up there, I ain't puttin' money on makin' it home."

They settled onto benches at one of the diner's two outdoor tables, where they could keep an eye on the bike. For several minutes neither spoke as they devoured their burgers and scanned the road in both directions for potential threats. The sun had gone down by now, the lights along the highway patchy and intermittent. Road maintenance, even along the main corridors, had become a much lower priority than it used to be, even when the crews could get hold of the parts. Vyx was glad for Virago's elven vision, which made spotting anybody approaching on foot or in vehicles without lights a lot easier. Between that and her own adept ability to sense approaching danger, she was fairly confident they'd be able to eat in peace. They couldn't stay long, though. The faster they got to Salem and found Liam's contact, the better. She hoped whoever it was, they could offer suggestions for a place to stay.

"Sucks about your bike," Virago said suddenly. "I'd like to rip those assholes a new one."

Vyx was about to reply when her commlink buzzed. Puzzled, she pulled it out. Who would be calling her? The LTG showed up as blocked. "Yeah, who's this?"

The voice was female, and sounded like it was coming from the inside of a crowded metal garbage can. *"Vyx, that you?"*

It took Vyx a moment to recognize who it was: Sky, one of the other female members of the Ancients. She was a quiet type, and Vyx hadn't had much chance to get to know her, but even though she was another elf, she hadn't shown nearly the same level of bigotry toward Vyx and the other non-elven recruits as most of the other elven rank-and-filers had. "Yeah. What's up? Why're you calling me?"

"I shouldn't," she said. *"I know you left. But I heard somethin', and thought you'd wanna know about it."*

Vyx held up a finger as Virago shot a questioning look her way. "Yeah?"

"These guys came by earlier tonight. They were lookin' for you. Two norms."

What the hell? "You sure? They were lookin' for me? You know why?"

"Yeah. I heard Tanner talkin' to Kendra about it. They came by and said your mom hired 'em to get you back."

Vyx froze in place, finger still in the air. *Holy frag.* Her *mother* was trying to get her back? After all this time? "What did they tell 'em?" *Calm down. Nobody knows where you went except Liam, and he wouldn't rat you out.*

"They just said you left, I guess. Liam talked to 'em for a little, I hear, since they helped us out in a firefight with the BS."

"What'd they look like?"

"I didn't see 'em much. Tall, one dark-haired and dressed like a stuck-up corper. Spellslinger. The other guy was blond and either chromed or else like you. Bodyguard, prob'ly. Hang on—I got a vid, but it's pretty bad."

A message popped up, indicating an incoming file. The transfer timed out twice over the spotty network before it finally got through. Vyx pulled up the short video and examined it: it had been taken from inside the garage, and showed the two figures from about ten meters away, from the back. The dark-haired man was thin and wore a dark gray longcoat, and the blond man stood like he was primed to move at a split-second's notice. Vyx recognized that stance; Sky was probably right that he was enhanced in some way, either magically or with 'ware.

Bad news, both of them.

Vyx paused to let the implications sink in. Gods, her mother not only sent people after her, but apparently some heavy hitters. And they might not be the only ones, either.

Even worse—what if it hadn't been her mother who'd sent them, but someone who'd hired them to act like they were working for Mom? Why, though? What would anyone want with her at this point? She'd been in the QZ for months, and aside from getting on the bad sides of a few of the Ancients' enemies (and a few of the Ancients themselves), as far as Vyx knew she hadn't pissed anybody else off enough to send that kind of talent after her. "Okay. Thanks for letting me know. I owe you one."

"Yeah. Gotta go now. Good luck. And don't tell anybody I called you."

Vyx blew out a long blast of air, slumping forward and letting her 'link clatter to the scarred table. "Well, fuck."

"What? Who was that?"

In a dead tone, staring down at her hands, Vyx repeated the conversation and replayed the video.

"Fuck..." Virago gripped her shoulder. "But hey, Liam won't tell 'em where you are."

"That guy's a spellslinger. They have all kinds of ways of finding people." She wished she hadn't slept through half of Thaumaturgy 101—she had a vague feeling magicians could use items belonging to a target to locate them. What if her mother had given him some kind of sample? Falcon and the other mages she knew in the Ancients were more about frying people with manabolts than heavy-duty ritual stuff, but that didn't mean this guy couldn't do it.

If he had a sample, though, why would he have to hunt up her chummers to ask where she was? Maybe he was trying to get hold of one somewhere else. Even as stressed as she was, Vyx couldn't help smiling at the thought of some high-class corp mage digging through her and Virago's mountain of dirty laundry in search of nail clippings or stray hairs.

"So, what're you gonna do?" Virago asked.

"Hell, I dunno. Right now I'm gonna finish my burger. If they show up, we'll deal with 'em. Maybe when we get to Salem, Liam's witch friend might be able to help us out."

Virago nodded contemplatively, sipping her kaf as she returned her attention to the road. "You never said much about your mom," she said at last.

Vyx shrugged. "What's to say? You know we don't get along. No big deal—she does her thing, I do mine."

"Sounds like maybe that's changed now."

"Doesn't matter. I'm not goin' back. Even if they figure out how to deal with the headcases and the wall comes down, I'm done with school."

Virago nodded, hands wrapped around her cup. "You ever know your dad?"

"Nah. He's dead, I guess. Good thing, too." She and Virago had never talked much about their parents—the subject just never came up, aside from Vyx's frustration with her mother's control-freak tendencies.

"Why's that?"

"He ran off on Mom when he found out she was pregnant."

Virago snorted. "Yeah, that ain't anything new. My dad was a beetlehead, and my mom was...let's just call her an exotic dancer.

One o' her 'customers' knifed her in a cheap hotel room when I was five." She spoke in the matter-of-fact tones of someone who'd long ago made peace with the memories. "Didn't think runnin' off was so easy in your crowd, though. She never tried to find him? Get some money out of him, at least?"

"Didn't want to, she said. He was some lowlife she had a fling with in college. Doubt he even *had* any money to get." She took another bite of her burger and didn't look at Virago. "She said he used to get rough with her. Said she was better off without him, and glad when she heard somebody cacked him."

"Bet you wish you coulda had a shot at him." Virago tossed her wadded-up burger wrapper gracefully into an overflowing trash receptacle in front of the diner's door.

"Like I said," Vyx said, rising, "It's a good thing he's dead. C'mon. We'd better get back on the road. Sooner we get there, sooner I can soak my sore ass in some nice hot water."

TWENTY-FIVE

Winterhawk and Ocelot were on the road again, headed north and back toward central Boston. Winterhawk was quiet as they drove.

"What next?" Ocelot had his shotgun in his lap and was, as usual, scanning the area around them. They had seen no further sign of the Ancients as they'd left the gang's turf—either they'd been off attending to the "trouble" Liam had mentioned, or they were making more of an effort to conceal themselves. "You have any luck getting through?"

Winterhawk shook his head. "No. Every time I try, it breaks up and I can't even get through to leave them a message. So we'll try plan B. More difficult, but harder to hide from." He patted the bag where he'd stowed the jacket Liam had given him. "We use this to track them down. If they're still together—and still alive—it should give us a better idea where to start."

"How you gonna do that, though? Don't you need some kinda ritual materials?"

"I do, yes. That's where we're going now. To visit an old friend."

Ocelot stared out the window. Even in the darkness it was obvious there weren't many vehicles on the road. So far, Winterhawk's magic had disguised the van sufficiently that nobody had bothered them, but the back roads they traveled, avoiding the larger arteries to stay away from go-gangs and other predators, were torn up, strewn with piles of garbage, and frequently blocked by the dead hulks of other vehicles, dumpsters, and metahuman-made barriers.

"What if she won't go with us?" he asked suddenly.

"What?"

"What if we find her, and she doesn't wanna come with us? Sounds like she and her mother don't get along so well. And if she's hooked up with this Virago *chica*, what if she doesn't want to leave her?"

"Who wouldn't want to get out of this hellhole?"

"You're not answerin' the question, 'Hawk."

"That's because I've got enough to think about right now," he said, trying to keep the edge out of his voice. Ocelot was right, of course. He'd been thinking about it from when Olivia had told him she hadn't spoken with Victoria since before the quarantine. If he and Ocelot simply showed up and told her they'd been hired to pack her up and take her home as if she were a runaway teenager, would she even agree to go with them?

"She's like you," Olivia had told him. Liam had also said she was trouble.

"You gonna tell her who you are?" As usual, Ocelot somehow managed, despite being as mundane as they came, to cut right to the center of Winterhawk's troubled thoughts.

"I don't know yet. Can you be quiet and let me drive?"

Ocelot subsided into silence, continuing to scan for threats. "I hope this friend of yours has somethin' to eat," he said a few minutes later, as they drew closer to the city's center. Ahead, Boston's iconic skyline rose into the heavens: Mitsuhama's twin corkscrewing spires, Aztechnology's massive pyramid, Ares's SkyTouch Tower, NeoNET's six soaring structures. In the Hub, Boston's downtown area and quite literally the hub of corporate activity, you could almost believe it was biz as usual if you squinted a little and suspended disbelief.

"I just hope he's still alive."

"Where is he?"

"Well, that's the interesting part," Winterhawk said.

"I hate it when you use the word 'interesting,'" Ocelot grumbled.

"Have you heard of the Catacombs?"

"No, but I have a feeling I'm about to."

"Cheer up. Only half of my friend's shop is underground."

"I need a drink," Ocelot said.

To Winterhawk's surprise, the shop called The Wandering Wizard not only still existed, but appeared to still be doing business. A brick-fronted, hole-in-the-wall place sandwiched between two other defunct businesses, it displayed its name across the front in eerie blue, both in AR and in meatspace.

"So what is this place exactly?" Ocelot asked, looking around. "Lore shop?"

"Yes and no. The proprietor's a chap who goes by Doc Belmont. He maintains a rather standard magical-supply shop on the upper level, but if he knows you—or if you bring in something that catches his eye—you might gain access to the lower half, where far more intriguing things go on."

They pushed open the door and entered the shop. A faint mix of aromas wafted out: incense, soil, several bits of things spicy and unidentifiable, decay, and even a brief whiff of what smelled like brewing tea.

The interior was lit by flickering candles in sconces along the dark, wood-paneled walls, and unseen speakers softly played an instrumental piece in a minor key that still managed somehow to sound sprightly. Colorful ARs thick with mystical symbols advertised various wares. The shop had no windows, but the feeling of being watched was so strong that Ocelot put his hand on his shotgun butt under his jacket. The place was packed full of carved display cases, bookshelves, and other furniture—if anyone had been lying in wait to ambush them, they'd have dozens of places to hide.

"Anyone here?" Winterhawk called. "Doc Belmont?"

"Doc's not here," came a reedy voice from behind one of the counters. There was a scrabbling sound, and then a young dwarf in an old-fashioned coat covered in colorful pins popped up. "Help you?"

Interesting. Winterhawk hadn't been to Boston for a couple years, but every time he visited The Wandering Wizard, Doc had been front and center. Especially this time of night, when most of his clientele did business. He'd started to wonder if the man ever slept.

"Where is he? I haven't seen him in a while. I'd like to say hello." Maya, who was riding on his shoulder, picked up on his unease. She nuzzled against his neck and then leaped down onto the counter, where she sat regarding the dwarf with her tail wrapped around her haunches.

The dwarf shifted from foot to foot. He glanced at Maya, back at Winterhawk, and then quickly over his shoulder toward a stout security door. "You sure I can't help you?" His entire demeanor radiated nervousness.

"Where's Doc?" Winterhawk asked again. He took a step forward and assensed the dwarf. As expected, he was Awakened—possibly a student working here as an internship or a part-time job to supplement his studies with some real-world experience. "We're in a bit of a hurry." Winterhawk let his aura masking drop for a moment, just long enough for the dwarf to get a look, then put it back in place. Next to him, from the corner of his eye, he saw Ocelot push aside his coat to reveal the shotgun.

"You just missed him," he said. "He went downstairs a half-hour or so ago to meet with some guy down in the Catacombs, but he hasn't come back yet. I'm startin' to worry that something's happened to him. He doesn't usually take that long."

Winterhawk froze. "Doesn't he usually transact that kind of business in the shop?"

"He does, yeah. I think it was a couple o' those urban tribe guys. He deals with 'em a lot these days. They get spooked easy, though. He said they wanted to see him about an item they found, but they'd only talk to him down there. If you really are an old friend, you know how he gets when he thinks somebody's got something interesting."

Winterhawk, unfortunately, knew exactly how he got. Pathological curiosity was an occupational hazard for certain types of mages (himself included). "And you couldn't reach him on the comm?"

The dwarf shook his head. "Tried a couple times, but the network's shittier down there than it is up here." He shrugged. "He's probably fine. He took a spirit down with him, and he's not exactly defenseless, y'know? I just don't like bein' up here by myself too long, is all. It's almost quittin' time."

Winterhawk's interest level in the dwarf's difficulties hovered only slightly above zero. "All right then," he said. "I need some ritual materials. Can you take care of that for us? As I said, we're in a hurry." He rattled off a list of what he needed from memory. He hoped the shop had them in stock; his glances around the shelves and displays revealed that apparently Doc had suffered as much from the quarantine as everyone else had—either that, or he kept more of his stock under cover than he used to in pre-lockdown days.

The dwarf began shaking his head ruefully halfway through Winterhawk's list, and by the time the mage had finished, he was looking scared. "Sorry," he said. "I can't help you. I've got some of that up here, but some of those reagents are downstairs. Doc keeps them in the vault, and I don't have the code. He's gotten a lot more careful since things went to hell. We had three attempted break-ins in the past month. I'm really sorry. You're welcome to hang around and browse, but until Doc gets back—"

Winterhawk held up a hand to stop the dwarf from babbling. Damn. This complicated matters. They could try to find another lore store—there were plenty in Boston—but most of the other good ones he knew were in Salem. He supposed at this point it would make more sense to just take their chances with finding a place up there. He was about to say something else when a voice spoke in his mind. *"Boss?"*

It was the air spirit he'd left guarding the van. This wasn't going to be good, he just knew it. *"What is it?"*

The spirit sounded almost as apologetic as the dwarf had. *"Somebody just crashed into the van."*

"What?" Something must have changed in his expression, because the dwarf was looking at him questioningly. He held up a finger to forestall him.

"Something big. I think something else was chasing it. It turned into the alley going fast, and crashed into it, then drove off."

"Is it still drivable?"

"Um...well, the driver's side is caved in, the back wheel is pointed sort of sideways, and a lot of smoke is coming out from the front..."

"Oh, bloody hell," he said aloud.

"What?" Ocelot demanded.

He sighed. "It seems we're going to be here a while. We might as well see if we can find Doc."

TWENTY-SIX

By the time Vyx and Virago limped into the outskirts of Salem on Virago's sputtering bike, it was full dark. Given the ominous noises the thing had made when they fired it up again after finishing their meal, they'd opted to leave the turnpike and head north on side roads. It added more time to the trip, but it was better than getting caught out by another go-gang when they couldn't manage anything more than about forty KPH without the front wheel shimmying like an epileptic devil rat.

Vyx perched on top of the saddlebags and duffel, kept watch for threats, and tried her best to get her mind off the ache in her ass by pondering what might go down in the next day or two. Ideally, if everything went according to plan, they'd meet with Liam's contact Beatrix, get the paydata on what was up with the BAD pipeline, then spent the next few days playing tourist in Salem, taking in the sights and generally staying away from the Rox long enough for Falcon and his chummers to calm down.

Of course, "ideally" and "everything going according to plan" were things that never happened, pretty much from the dawn of time. When you added the fact that a couple of corporate snoops were sniffing far too close to Vyx for her comfort, she'd accepted that a smooth ride wasn't the plan anymore. If they could convince Beatrix and her friends to hide them under a magical ward for a few days, maybe the snoops would go look elsewhere. That was a big 'if,' though.

Vyx forced herself to calm down, to let the tension drain from her body as much as she could while jouncing around on the back of a bucking Mirage. She hated running, being on the defensive, hiding. Her ideal solution to most problems was to face them head-on. She wanted to find these two corp flunkies and tell them to take a message back to Mom about where she could shove her nosiness. She was done with school, done with pretending to be a good little corporate cog on her way to some cushy entry-level drone job once she graduated. If Mom and her goons didn't like that, Vyx didn't give a frag.

"You wanna give her a call now?" Virago yelled over her shoulder as they pulled into the outskirts of Salem. "Or wait till tomorrow?"

"Now," Vyx yelled back. She wished Liam had given them more than an LTG number, but it made sense—if Beatrix was involved in something under the table, she probably didn't want her data getting out.

Virago pulled off the road, and Vyx gratefully tumbled off the bike. After staggering around for a couple minutes letting feeling come back into her legs and butt, she pulled out her 'link and made the call. She hoped the spotty reception would let her get through—maybe it was better out here with fewer people straining its capacity.

After two rings, she got voicemail. A female voice that didn't sound fake, even: *"Hey, you know who it is. Leave a message and I'll get back to you."*

"Uh...our mutual friend Liam sent us. We just got to Salem and we need to talk to you as soon as possible." Vyx decided minimalist communication was probably best, at least until they knew what they were dealing with. She continued to scan the roadway in both directions, periodically turning around to peer into the woods behind her. Virago was doing the same thing. Vyx's danger sense wasn't going off, but she'd heard plenty of stories about the woods around Salem. They'd always been full of things you didn't want to run into, but it had gotten worse since the wall went up.

She was about to slip her 'link back into her jacket pocket when it buzzed. Frowning at Virago, she pulled it back out. "Yeah?"

"Meet me at the Black Cat Tavern on Essex Street in a half-hour. Back room."

Vyx had barely connected the voice with the message she'd just heard when the connection broke.

"Who was that?" Virago was switching her focus between watching for threats and checking over the bike.

"Beatrix, I think." She relayed the message.

"I know where that is. We can get there early and scout the place out before she gets there."

"Let's go, then." Vyx was glad they were finally making progress, even if it did mean another ride on the back of Virago's clattering bike. The sooner they got this over with, the sooner they could find somebody to shelter them until the two corpers gave up and went looking elsewhere.

She didn't want to tell Virago (there were times that, despite their relationship and her acclimation to the Ancients' ways, she still felt like she hadn't completely left the life of the sheltered corp kid behind her), but the fact that her mother was sending people to track her down was making her nervous. She knew the kind of talent Mom could bring to bear if she got sufficiently motivated. Even though she doubted her mother would hire someone to physically grab her and bring her home, the idea wasn't completely out of the question. And with only Virago and a busted bike to help her stay out of their way, things could get ugly if they managed to find her in Salem.

The Black Cat Tavern was a quaint little place on meandering, tree-lined street lined with businesses catering to tourists. Most were closed at this hour, but the tavern itself featured a neon sign depicting a cat with an arched back, puffed tail, and almond-shaped green eyes. A jaunty witch's hat perched on its head. The building's weathered wooden front was dotted with ARs advertising local craft beers.

"Not many people," Vyx commented, noting the small number of cars and motorcycles in the lot.

Virago shrugged. "Slow night." She pulled into the parking lot and slid the bike into a space next to the back door, under a light.

Vyx slung her bag over her shoulder and followed Virago inside. Still no ping on her danger sense. She was probably being overly paranoid, but that didn't mean she planned to let her guard down. She'd do that when this was over.

Inside, the bar continued the "witch" theme, with a cheery fire burning in a large cauldron in the center of the room, more black cats, and rustic, battered booths and tables. A few patrons, mostly younger couples or groups of women, sat around some of the tables, but most were empty. Mostly they ignored Vyx and Virago as they entered, though a couple glanced up at them before returning to their drinks. A haunting, minor-key rock tune, loud enough to hear but not to disturb anyone's conversations, wafted from a hidden sound system.

When they asked for the back room, the slender, androgynous male bartender pointed them toward an arched doorway with "magical" runes painted around it. "Nobody back there, though."

"That's okay. We like our privacy." Vyx ordered beers for the two of them.

The back room was at the end of the hall past the restrooms; it was small, with only a few tables, a fireplace dominating one wall, and a pool table that had seen many better days crouching off to one side. A trid screen showed an Urban Brawl game with the sound off, and another speaker piped in the eerie tune from the front part of the tavern. The only windows were high up the two side walls, and the only other exit was a single door labeled *Emergency Exit – Alarm Will Sound.*

As the bartender had indicated, the room was otherwise empty. "We got ten more minutes," Virago said.

Vyx didn't sit still for any of those ten minutes. Instead, she paced the room, back and forth, back and forth, pausing to check the hallway and even to leap nimbly up on one of the chairs to look out through the high windows for periodic checks of the parking lot.

"You think those guys are gonna chase you all the way out here to Salem?" Virago asked, amused. She sat at one of the tables, feet up, sipping her beer.

"You don't know my mother when she gets her mind set on something."

"Hello?"

Vyx and Virago both spun to face the doorway, hands going to their weapons.

The petite young woman standing there raised her hands. "It's okay, it's okay," she said quickly. "I was supposed to meet you here."

Vyx eyed her with suspicion. She wore a brightly colored, flowing mid-calf skirt, a peasant blouse under a black leather vest, and her hair was tied back with a bright red scarf. She carried a shapeless synthleather bag over one shoulder. Her eyes, large and dark, followed the two of them with wary watchfulness, but no fear.

"Beatrix?" Vyx asked.

"That's me." She glanced around as if expecting that someone had followed her. "I can't stay long, so let's get right to it, okay?"

Virago swung her legs around and sat upright, indicating the seat across from her at the table. "You worried about something?"

"Not really, but it's never a bad idea to keep an eye out for trouble," Beatrix said. She took the offered seat and put her bag on the table in front of her. "What do you need?"

Vyx checked to make sure nobody else was coming down the hall, then leaned in close. "Lucky Liam sent us up here. He said you might be able to give us some info about the…supply line problems."

Beatrix frowned. "Yeah, I thought that might be it. Surprised he hasn't contacted me sooner about it, honestly. It's not as easy up here as it used to be, you know?"

"Well, yeah, with the walls and all," Virago agreed, nodding. "But that's been going on for months now. This is fairly new. Is something else going on? You heard anything?"

"Not really my area," she said. "I can do some checking around, though. How long are you in the area? You got a place to stay?"

"We just got here," Virago said. "Ran into a little trouble on the way up."

"Not surprised," Beatrix said. "Roads aren't safe these days." Her hands gripped the straps of her bag. "At least I might be able to help you out with a place to hang out while you're here. Couple of my coven-mates may have some space where you can crash."

"Yeah, thanks," Virago said. "We can even maybe do a little asking around on our own. We..."

Vyx stopped listening to what she was saying as her comm buzzed in her pocket. Seeing that the two of them were still in conversation, she triggered it without pulling it out.

The data flashed on her glasses. It wasn't a call—it was a voicemail message. The timestamp on it was fifteen minutes ago. That wasn't odd, though, even though she'd been right here in the back room at that time. The spotty nature of the Matrix in the QZ meant that sometimes calls didn't get through but went instead to voicemail, where they might take a few minutes, a few hours, or even a day or two to get through—if they got through at all.

What *was* odd, though, was that the sender was listed as *Beatrix.* There was no subject.

Vyx stiffened, but forced herself to maintain an expression of mild interest as she continued watching Virago and the woman talking. She opened the message.

It didn't have any text or voice component—just a file titled *Liam.*

The hairs beginning to stand up on the back of her neck, Vyx glanced across the table at Beatrix, studying her while appearing to be inspecting one of the beer-sign ARs on the other side of the room. She didn't take the time to look at the files, but downloaded them to her 'link for later perusal. Was something wrong, or was it just her paranoia again? After all, it made sense that Beatrix might have sent them the files to look over prior to the meet.

But why no message? Not even a *Hey, we'll talk about these at the meet.* And if something was up, why wasn't her danger sense pinging?

"—I can take you there," Beatrix was saying. "But we'll have to go tonight. Things are weird around here. Some of the covens are into some new biz—not sure what it is, but they kinda scare me, y'know? I don't want them finding out."

"Yeah, we can do that," Virago said. "Vyx, that cool?"

Vyx, who hadn't been listening to any of the previous conversation, nodded. "Yeah, sure. I gotta hit the head first, though. Come with me?" She punctuated her words with a hard squeeze of Virago's thigh under the table.

Virago was good—not only didn't she ask questions, but she didn't even change expression. "I gotta take a piss too. Too much beer," she said, grinning and indicating her empty glass. Back in a sec, Beatrix, okay?"

"Sure, no problem."

The two of them started to rise.

Beatrix changed.

TWENTY-SEVEN

The transformation only took a couple of seconds, but it seemed to happen in slow motion nonetheless—one moment Beatrix sat there at the table, a petite young witch with big eyes and a colorful outfit. The next, a...*thing*...erupted up from her chair, growing and spreading across the table as it lunged toward Vyx and Virago.

For just a second, Vyx could do nothing but stand rooted to the floor, staring in shocked horror, as the buzz of her danger sense suddenly went into overdrive. Beatrix's large, dark eyes had grown to grotesque size, going black and dead and somehow diseased. Her pale skin had gone fishbelly white, cracking and oozing with rot. Her slender body bubbled out of her stained, ripped clothing. More ooze, crawling with black, shiny forms, flowed from her handbag in front of her, and then the handbag itself writhed and propelled itself forward.

Worst of all, though, was Beatrix's mouth—grinning and impossibly wide, it bristled with pointy, yellow teeth. As she opened it even wider, something that looked like maggots poured from it, pattering to the red-and-white-checked tablecloth and rushing toward the two women across the table.

"Go!" Virago yelled, smacking Vyx hard on the back. "Back door!"

That broke Vyx's terror and she spun toward the rear of the room.

Light—greenish, sickly light—shone in around the door's cracks. The push-bar rattled, and then the door itself began to buck and shift as if something from the outside were trying to break through it.

The Beatrix-thing roared, a wet, warbling sound.

Vyx barely had time to fling herself sideways before a blast of something flew past her. It went through the AR of a dancing black cat and hit the wall, which immediately began to sizzle and ooze. The stench of decay, already strong from Beatrix herself, heightened.

What *was* this thing? No time to figure it out now—it was out of their league, whatever it was. And there might be another one outside. "Other door!" Vyx yelled, pointing toward the hallway where they'd come in. So far, nobody out front seemed to have noticed what was going on back here.

That wouldn't last long, though: Virago had her Predator out and opened fire on the Beatrix-thing. The rounds tore into it, ripping gobbets of rotten flesh loose and slamming into the wall.

The thing barely noticed. It made another of its horrific warbling roars—was it *laughing* at them?—and flung another stream of muck at Virago.

She got out of the way of most of it, but yelped as her jacket sleeve bubbled and sizzled. Jerking as if under attack by a squad of spiders, she shook her arm free of the sleeve and let the jacket dangle off her other side.

The Beatrix-thing had positioned itself in front of the hallway door now. To get out that way, they'd have to go through it. And it seemed to be growing even larger, ripping free of the young woman's clothes. It barely looked humanoid now. Everything it touched—the floor under its feet, the tables and walls it touched—blackened and turned to rot.

Vyx thought fast. This wasn't something she could fight hand to hand, which limited her options. She didn't even want to touch it, and the thought of sinking her fist or her foot into that soft brown ooze made her want to puke—which would probably make the damn thing happy.

Virago, meanwhile, had stowed her gun and drawn her katana, but hadn't moved in to attack. "What the hell *is* it?" she demanded.

The back door gave with a loud ripping *crack.*

Vyx spun sideways, her back against the side wall so she could keep an eye on both directions at once as her danger sense ramped up its intensity once more. "Another one!" she yelled.

"We are *so* fucked," Virago muttered, her hand tightening around her katana hilt.

"What's going on back there?" came a voice from the other side of the hallway, past the Beatrix-thing.

Vyx barely made out the form of the slim bartender, his eyes wide with confusion and terror, halfway down the hallway. "No! *Run!*" she yelled. "Get out! You—"

The Beatrix-thing sounded its wet roar again and flung a stream of muck at the man. He screamed and crumpled to the floor. Vyx got a quick impression of his flesh melting off his bones in blackened, rotten strips before she tore her gaze away.

But just for a second, its attention was off them.

And there was another way out of the room.

"Windows!" she yelled.

Without waiting to see if Virago understood, she snatched the nearest chair and flung it with unerring precision through one of the windows high up on the side wall. It was only about a meter tall, and if it was heavily armored they'd be in trouble—but no, apparently little taverns in picturesque tourist towns didn't face a lot of heavy artillery. The chair crashed through with little resistance. Cold air rushed in from outside, barely making a dent in the growing stench of decay.

"Go, go!" Vyx yelled.

Virago unleashed another barrage of gunfire at the Beatrix-thing and then vaulted backward. She leaped onto a table and launched herself through the opening. "Come on!"

Vyx wasn't far behind her. The Beatrix-thing shot another noxious stream at her, but she jigged sideways, slammed into the wall, then jumped on the table and followed Virago through the hole.

"Down!" Virago ordered. She was crouched behind a parked American, firing off rounds at two dark figures just coming around the corner of the building.

Vyx barely made it to cover before the *cracks* of more rounds split the air. She rolled to a crouch and then, before the two figures could react, leaped upward, caught the overhanging lip of the tavern's roof, and pulled herself up.

"We gotta get outta here!" Virago called. "Oh, holy shit—"

Vyx didn't have to ask what was going on—she could smell it. The Beatrix-thing was oozing out through the window hole. Still crouched low, she drew her knife and darted nimbly and nearly silently across the darkened roof. As Virago kept up covering fire, she reached the end and dropped down behind the two dark figures. One of them was still firing on Virago, while the other had his gun pointed upward, clearly trying to spot Vyx on the roof.

He spotted her, but too late. He'd only managed to turn halfway around when she drew up behind him and slipped her blade across his throat. He gurgled and dropped, and Vyx grabbed his SMG. She didn't like guns, but it wasn't as if she couldn't use them if she had to. They had to get out of here, and *now.*

The other dark figure had taken cover behind another parked car. Virago had used the chaos of Vyx's sudden appearance to duck down and change position, and their attacker was clearly caught off guard as he tried to keep track of both of them at once.

The Beatrix-thing oozed into the space between them, rose up and appeared to be sniffing the air, and then made a beeline for the car Vyx was hiding behind.

Vyx slipped back around the building—if the guy wanted to come after her, he'd have to follow her—and spotted the bike she and Virago had left there when they'd gone in. She keyed her comm. "Get ready," she said. "I'm coming around."

"Hurry the fuck up!"

Keeping an eye out for the remaining attacker—and checking to make sure no more were approaching—Vyx threw her leg over the bike and fired it up, hoping desperately that the time in the cold parking lot hadn't completed the job started earlier. But no, it flared to reassuring, albeit less than smooth, life instantly.

She gunned it and took off just as the second attacker poked his head and his gun around the corner. When he spotted the bike, he aimed his SMG and let off another barrage of rounds.

Vyx jerked the bike sideways. She still had the other guy's SMG in her hand, so she surged forward and fired at his lower face, the only part of him not protected by armor. Maybe she didn't like guns, but since right now she didn't have the luxury of preference, she was grateful Virago had made hear learn how to use one anyway. She didn't get a solid hit as she blew by, but his shriek of pain told her she'd at least made contact.

"Coming!" she called.

The Beatrix-thing, if anything, had gotten larger. It wasn't even remotely humanoid anymore—just a big blob of glittering, oozing muck spreading across the parking lot and over the car Virago hid behind. Everything it touched—tires, paint, windows—roiled and rotted, the tires' run-flat rubber melting into a stinking puddle, the paint cracking and peeling, the metal warping.

Vyx kept her eyes on it as she went by, holding her breath against the stench. Even out here in the open air, it was all she could do not to vomit. What *was* that thing? Was it Beatrix? Had it eaten her and taken her form? Was she alive somewhere?

She didn't have time to think about any of that now, though. She skidded the bike to a stop just past the car, counting on Virago to know what to do.

She did. Vyx had barely reached her when she leaped from behind the car and onto the back of the bike. "Go! Go!" she shrieked in Vyx's ear.

Vyx gunned it again. The back wheel slipped out from under her for a second, but Virago put her leg down and righted it long enough for Vyx to get her balance. And then they were off into the night, crouched low as another blast from the Beatrix-thing and another hail of rounds from the second attacker's SMG tried to take them out.

"Is it gonna follow us?" Virago demanded. Her voice held a touch of hysteria—as good as she was in a firefight or a running battle, her knowledge of magic and the things it spawned was pretty much limited to the stuff she'd seen the other Ancients doing. Everything else was from the trid.

"How the hell should I know?" It was a fair point, though—best to get as much distance between it and them as possible, and fast. Vyx flung the bike sideways down a narrow alley and kept going.

Inexplicably, she almost found herself wishing that the two heavy hitters her mother had sent after her had found her right about now. She suspected they'd make short work of that thing, and at least she knew how to get away from them.

TWENTY-EIGHT

"Have you been down here before?" Ocelot asked.

The dwarf, who'd introduced himself as Charlie Leary, had opened the security door for them and directed them down a steep staircase, accompanied by two of the shop's guardian spirits to ensure that they didn't touch anything on their way through.

"The door'll lock automatically behind you when you go out into the Catacombs," he told them. "It's warded and magically concealed on the other side. You won't be able to get back in without Doc, so if you don't find him, you'll have to find another way out. I suggest Monk's Tavern a couple klicks west of here— that's the closest and safest. Like I said, I can't stay here all night."

Winterhawk had made a mental note to say something to Belmont about the quality of his help—assuming they could *find* Belmont, that was.

"Sort of," he replied to Ocelot.

"Whaddaya mean, 'sort of'? Is it like the Ork Underground?"

"Yes and no." They were trudging down a brick-lined tunnel that passed a series of doorways, all closed and locked. "I doubt anyone truly knows the extent of where the tunnels down here go anymore. It started out as just the older sections of the underground transportation system, but since then the residents have expanded it to include a lot of additional tunnels, bits of basements, and quite a number of new areas dug out by the residents."

"And I'm guessing the residents aren't anybody we want to run into." Ocelot moved with his usual feral grace, one hand wrapped around the hilt of his ever-present monofilament whip, the other hovering in easy reach of his shotgun. His eyes were in constant motion, scanning the area in front of them and to both sides.

"Again, yes and no. The bits near the businesses are relatively safe—by 'relatively,' I mean you're not likely to be eaten by ghouls, at least not right away. And from what I've heard, since the quarantine went into effect, a lot of non-locals—commuters, tourists, that sort of thing—have found refuge in the more accessible parts."

"What about the other parts?"

"Well, if we have to go much further, we'll need a guide. That could be problematic, since the few I know of could be hard to find these days, if they're even still alive. Let's just hope we can locate Doc before that becomes an issue, shall we?"

The tunnels were far from quiet: the far-off rumble of subway trains, the incessant *drip-drip-drip* of water, and the dueling strains of at least three different types of music provided eerie accompaniment to their hollow footfalls as they continued down the wide main corridor. The area was lit by flickering fluorescents, but every few meters, another tunnel broke off from the main one, disappearing into darkness.

Occasional figures, huddled under blankets and heavy, threadbare coats, watched them go by with dead-eyed disinterest. The whole place smelled primarily musty and dank, mixed with the stench of garbage, unwashed bodies, and a faint, far-off hint of decay—whether the latter came from people, animals, or simply rotting food, it was impossible to determine. Whatever it was, it stunk.

"Keep an eye on them," Winterhawk murmured to Maya, who was currently sitting on his shoulder sustaining her own light spell.

"Already am," she replied. *"I don't like it here. It's cold and it makes my fur damp."*

"How much further are we gonna go?" Ocelot asked. "Where's this place the dwarf was talkin' about?"

"Not far, if memory serves. It's off one of these side tunnels up ahead—a place people apparently use for business down here."

Ocelot sighed. "I know he's your friend, but you know this is a bad idea, right?" He flicked his monowhip at a rat the size of a chihuahua that skittered along the tunnel's edge; the creature fell neatly into two halves, both sets of its now-disconnected legs pistoning wildly for several seconds before its body realized it was dead and it went still.

"I know it's a very bad idea," Winterhawk said. "But that's never stopped us before." He gestured at the pile of rat guts. "And we're hardly defenseless, either. Besides, I'm not doing it entirely because he's my friend," he added. "Doc can take care of himself, and he knows his way around down here. But if we can't get those ritual materials, we'll have a much harder time finding Victoria. Who knows what's going on with the shops in Salem these days?

That, and we're currently without transportation. He might be able to help us out in that regard as well."

He was about to say something else when a cry rang out ahead of them, followed by a flash of light and what sounded like a deep, throaty bark.

Next to him, Ocelot tensed, primed to move. "Is that the tunnel we were—"

Winterhawk touched his arm and nodded, holding up a finger. He gathered mana from the astral plane (*damn,* but this entire town had a nasty background count—casting spells here was like trying to throw a ball through a vat of pea soup) and sent it out.

Enhanced by the Clairvoyance spell, his vision reached out and flowed around the corner, following the narrower passageway until it opened out into a larger space. He took in the scene for a moment, stiffening as he dropped the spell and returned his attention to Ocelot. "Come on."

"Doc?"

"Yes. And it looks like he might need a bit of help."

They reached the end of the narrow passageway and Winterhawk took in the scene with a quick glance. The passage widened out into a larger room, maybe ten meters on a side. It looked like it might at some point have been a maintenance room, but whatever machinery that used to control it had long since been wrested free and carried off by scavengers. Currently it was full of trash, boxes, and piles of scraps.

On the far side, two figures had taken refuge behind one of the scrap piles. Winterhawk recognized one of them as Doc Belmont, but the other was crouched too low to spot. A glowing barrier spell in the shape of a dome covered the pile, but the mage could see at a glance that it was already flickering. It couldn't take too many more hits before it went down. He wondered how long the two had been hunkered down as Doc struggled to maintain the shield. Had the people he'd intended to meet with set him up for an ambush?

And if it went down, Doc and his companion would be in trouble, because several other humanoid figures—at least eight—surrounded it. Hunched and dressed in tattered clothes, the figures included the hulking form of what looked like an emaciated troll, who pounded on the barrier with massive fists. Next to him, an equally emaciated hellhound clawed at it as the others stood back, leaping and whooping. Occasionally one of them would fire a gun in a random direction. Next to them, several other prone figures lay splayed out on the filthy floor.

"He got a few of them at least," Winterhawk muttered to Ocelot over the link. "Get ready to move. Maya, tell Doc we're here."

He felt the cat's slight weight leave his shoulder as she shifted back to the astral plane, and then gathered mana for another spell. A second later, a small squadron of armored Hard Corps police shimmered into view on the other side of the room.

"*Drop your weapons!*" one of them yelled in a voice that sounded suspiciously like Ocelot's. "*Put your hands above your heads!*" Winterhawk was glad for the dim light—getting all the details right was hard enough when he was well acquainted with the subject of his illusion. Opting for Hard Corps instead of Knight Errant did allow him to add a few personalized touches, though.

The attacking figures whirled as one to face the new threat. "Fuck! Cops!" one yelled, and opened fire on the Hard Corps squad.

Ocelot vaulted into the room, a blur of motion now that the invisibility spell protecting him had dropped. He swung his whip and lopped off the head of the rearmost attacker. It hit the ground and rolled to a stop near the barrier.

The attackers were scattering now, trying to escape the cops. The hellhound, oblivious to the new threat, continued nipping and clawing away at the shield. From his vantage point at the entrance, Winterhawk saw Doc Belmont grin and drop the barrier, pitching the big black dog on its face in a flurry of flailing limbs. His companion, now revealed as an ork in some kind of gang jacket, let loose a point-blank burst from his machine pistol and the dog went still.

One of the smarter of the attackers had apparently either determined that the Hard Corps cops weren't real or that Ocelot was the bigger threat. He fired his pistol three times, but Ocelot was too fast for him: he leaped high, gripped a steel pipe still attached to the ceiling, and swung over the kid's head, landing neatly behind him. This time, the monowhip took off the guy's legs at just below the knee.

Bloody glad he's on my side, Winterhawk thought, dropping the illusion. Monofilament whips were nasty things—it was rare to find anyone with Ocelot's level of expertise and a full set of original-equipment limbs, because the learning process didn't allow for a lot of trial and error. Many would-be wielders, if they survived the early stages of training, either ended up with cyberlimbs to replace the ones they'd sliced off during practice, or resigned themselves to monikers like "Stumpy" and "Peg-leg."

He took quick inventory: five more attackers left. As he lined up on two of them trying to escape out the other side of the room and Ocelot spun gracefully around to take on the remaining three, Doc Belmont hadn't been idle. With a roar that was half-triumph, half-frustration, he hurled a fireball at the nearest one, a skinny elf, then cheered as the kid's greasy hair lit up into a bright blaze of flame. The kid ran screaming, clutching his head, until he slammed into a wall and fell, stunned.

One of the two heading toward Winterhawk, a short ork in a Red Sox T-shirt, yelled something that was probably obscene and flung a spell at the mage.

Well, isn't that cute. He wants to play. Given what had occurred over the past few days, culminating with losing their van, letting loose felt like just what the doctor ordered right about now. He let the kid's spell wash over him, his defenses easily deflecting it, then grinned at the ork. "My turn."

He pointed his hand, sending the ork flying headfirst and at high velocity into the nearest wall. His head made a dent in the bricks where he hit, and then he lay still.

"Doc," Winterhawk said, stepping into the room. "Good to see you. It's been a while." Doc, his ork friend, and Ocelot had already cleaned up two of the remaining attackers. He could just see the third disappearing down a passageway on the other side of the room.

Doc Belmont stepped out to meet him. "Winterhawk. Great timing." A tall, thin human with salt-and-pepper hair and a neat goatee, he wore a dark blue suit, now smudged with grime from their surroundings. Though his chest rose and fell with his recent exertion, his face was lit up with a broad grin. "We had that under control, but the help's appreciated."

"Yeah. Control." The ork clambered over the trash pile. He was wide, bald, and very ugly. What Winterhawk had mistaken for gang colors was revealed as a studded black leather jacket painted with bright images and symbols. One sleeve was torn, and blood ran down to stain his hand.

"Oh, be quiet. Some tough-guy enforcer *you* are." Doc's words were laced with amusement. "Let me take care of that for you, then we can chat with my friends here." He steered the ork to lean against the wall and began a healing spell.

"Uh...'Hawk?"

Winterhawk turned away from the scene to face Ocelot, who was examining the bodies spread out on the floor. They numbered eleven, including the ones they'd taken out and those that had already been dead when they got there. "What is it?"

"I don't think these guys were from the same group." Ocelot pointed to a couple of the attackers. "See? Dressed completely differently. These guys are wearin' some kind of gang colors." He indicated another body. "This one isn't. Neither are those over there."

Winterhawk studied them and was about to say something when Doc spoke again. "They're not. Come on—let's go back to the shop before anyone else shows up."

"We just leave these guys here?" Ocelot asked.

The ork, healed now, was on his comm. "I got some chummers comin'," he said, tucking it back in his pocket. "They'll take care of 'em."

Winterhawk didn't ask how they planned to do that—he didn't particularly want to know.

TWENTY-NINE

Vyx didn't stop the bike for twenty minutes. She lost count of the alleys, vacant lots, and patches of forest she'd driven through, and had even taken the bike across a narrow creek at one point on the off chance that the Beatrix-thing could track them by smell.

Finally, she pulled up in front of a brightly-lit Stuffer Shack and barely managed to get the bike on its stand before rolling off and sagging against a crumbling, graffiti-decorated brick wall. "Holy shit..." she breathed.

Virago didn't join her. She seemed wired up, unable to stop moving, so she began pacing ragged circles around the bike and the immediate area, with near-constant glances out into the darkness. "What the hell *was* that thing?"

"Some kind of spirit, I think." Vyx struggled to remember the Intro to Magic courses she'd dozed through most of last year, but the unit on spirits had mostly covered the basic concepts of conjuring and the usual spirit types—Fire, Air, Man, Beasts, that kind of thing. Whatever that thing back at the Black Cat Tavern was, it most certainly wasn't one of the standard spirit types. She pulled out her comm.

"What are you doing?"

"I'm gonna try calling Beatrix again."

Virago rounded on her. "Are you out of your mind, *chica*? She just tried to *kill* us back there."

"I don't think that was her." She told Virago about the file she'd received during the meet that had tipped her off to the fact that something was wrong.

"Wait a sec." Virago halted her restless wandering for a moment. "You're tellin' me that thing didn't set off your danger sense before you got that file?"

"No, and that's what's freaking me out. It takes pretty strong magic to get around it. I also want to know who those guys were that were with it. And why the hell are they after us?" She held up a hand and sent a call to the number she had for Beatrix. It went to voicemail. She didn't leave a message.

"Looks like we're on our own," she said. "We can keep trying, but I don't think we're gonna find her. She's probably dead."

"So what now?" Virago resumed her pacing. At this hour few vehicles went by, and only a couple figures shuffled around inside the Stuffer Shack, no doubt stoners or chipheads looking for late-night munchies.

"Go get us something to drink," Vyx said, nodding toward the store. "I'm gonna check out whatever Beatrix sent us. Maybe it'll help."

Nothing bothered Vyx as she stood leaning against the wall and accessed the files. Apparently either the horrific thing had been given specific instructions (attack them at the tavern) or its handlers had called it off for now. That didn't stop her from keeping a constant watch as she paged through them, though.

It didn't take her long—there were only a few, and most of them were text. The single exception was a brief video file, depicting a shadowy collection of figures circled around a fire in what looked like a twisted wood. Behind it, a blocky building covered in vegetation rose up, and past that a fence was barely visible. As she watched, something misshapen emerged from the wood and approached the circle, and the figures parted to let it in. The shot was taken from too far away to get any detail, though.

"Get anything?" Virago asked, appearing in front of her. She held out a tall can of soybeer. Vyx popped it and downed it gratefully.

"Not a lot. Beatrix has been tracking this stuff for a while now—she didn't know what's going on with the BADs, but she knew something was up. A lot of people acting weird. The only thing she's pretty sure about is that it's got to do with something out in the Wilds, and some of the covens are involved in it. There's a vid, and she kinda tried to explain where it was taken, but that part of the file is corrupted so it's not a big help."

"Isn't the Wilds where they grow the stuff in the first place?"

"Yeah. But she thinks somebody—or something—new has shown up in town and infiltrated the supply chain."

"Any idea who?"

"The Westhaven coven has recent new leadership. She thinks that's the best place to start looking. But she also says to be careful—she doesn't know who's involved, and whoever it is, they're dangerous. Several people have disappeared without a trace over the last month or so, and nobody seems to be doing anything about it."

"Fuckin' great." Virago finished her beer and tossed the can into the overflowing trash can. "So what do we do?"

"Tonight we find a place to hole up. Tomorrow, we contact Beatrix's coven—she gave us a couple names—and see if they know anything. Maybe she's not dead."

"You really think that?"

"No." She let her breath out. "You saw that thing. Do you think it would take her form if it hadn't killed her, or possessed her, or something?"

Virago examined the ruined sleeve of her jacket. Where the Beatrix-thing's stream of ooze had hit it, the leather had bubbled and cracked as if it had been marinating in a landfill for a couple of years. She ripped it free and tossed that in the trash can in disgust. "What about those guys your mom sent after you?"

"Right now, they're the least of my worries. At least we might be able to reason with them."

"You sure the guys with that thing weren't them?"

She hadn't thought about that. She recalled the details of the fight and shook her head. "Don't think so. If Mom sent 'em they wouldn't be trying to kill us—at least not me—and I doubt Mom would associate with anybody who could summon something like *that* thing. She'd pretty driven and used to getting her own way, but she's not crazy. Besides, if one of 'em was a spellslinger, why didn't he use any other magic?" Still, the tiniest of doubts nagged at her, and suddenly she felt very exposed. "C'mon. Let's see if we can find these people Beatrix mentioned. Maybe one of 'em will let us sleep in her garage or something."

THIRTY

Back at the shop (Charlie Leary had already left and locked up—Winterhawk suspected he'd high-tailed it out the instant he'd shut the door behind them), Doc put on a pot of soykaf and handed it around in mismatched cups. They'd left the ork behind to deal with whatever friends he'd called, so it was just the three of them.

He shook his head ruefully. "That's the first time that's happened," he said. "I may have to make some changes to the way I do business."

"Who were those guys?" Ocelot asked. "Why did they attack you?"

"It was an ambush," Doc said. "I was contacted by a representative of an urban tribe I do business with sometimes—the Parkmoors—with something they wanted to sell me. They often bring me interesting magical bits and baubles they find, since I give 'em a fair price or a good trade. Anyway, I showed up with Marco, but those others had already killed the Parkmoors. They attacked us, and managed to disrupt my spirit. I was about to try summoning another when you showed up. So thank you for that."

Winterhawk shrugged. "Glad to be of assistance."

Doc's eyes narrowed. "What are you doing here, anyway? I hadn't heard of you being in the QZ, and I'm sure word would have gotten back to me by now. I like to think I keep my finger on the pulse of magical happenings around here. Your presence would definitely qualify as a magical happening."

"It's—hard to explain," Winterhawk said. Before Doc could start firing off more questions, he added quickly, "And fairly recent. Listen—if you're sure you're all right, we're in a bit of a hurry. We came by to pick up some ritual materials. Your assistant said they were in the vault."

"Oh! Yes, of course." He took a long sip from his cup and closed his eyes for a moment, as if settling himself down. "Tell me what you need. I just got a shipment in a couple days ago. If it's not too unusual, I should be able to accommodate you."

Winterhawk gave him the list, once again from memory.

He nodded. "I believe I have all of that." Tilting his head, he eyed Winterhawk appraisingly. "It sounds like you're doing a tracking ritual. You looking for someone? Anyone I might know?"

Mages. Curiosity. They went together like bumps and trolls. "I doubt it. I hate to be rude, Doc, but—"

"Yes, yes, of course. I'll be right back." He got up and hurried toward the door that led downstairs.

They didn't talk while he was gone. Winterhawk leaned back in his chair and watched Maya wander back and forth along the counters, swishing her tail and occasionally stopping to sniff some item on display. With every step, their supposedly simple trip into Boston to gather data on a ley line had gotten more complicated. At least, as of a few days ago, Victoria was still alive, though, he reminded himself. That was more than he'd had before.

Doc Belmont returned in five minutes carrying a bag. "Here you are," he said. "No charge, of course." He dropped his voice to a murmur. "Even though we did have that under control, you know how these things can go sideways at a moment's notice. So I'm grateful for your help."

"That's appreciated," Winterhawk said.

"Where are you headed?" Doc asked, sitting back down after refreshing everyone's drink. "I can't imagine what would induce someone to enter the QZ voluntarily." He shuddered at the thought.

"Salem," Winterhawk said. "We've got some business up there, and from what we've been able to find out so far, the person we're looking for is there as well."

"We *were* headed to Salem," Ocelot reminded him. "No wheels, remember?" He glanced pointedly toward Doc, as if to refresh Winterhawk's memory.

He *had* almost forgotten about that. "You wouldn't happen to know where we could get our hands on a vehicle, would you?" he asked Doc. "We need to get to Salem, and apparently our van has been...incapacitated."

Doc shook his head. "Sorry, no. I rarely go anywhere beyond a kilometer or two from here these days, so I don't need one." He chuckled. "Amusing, really—the Wandering Wizard doesn't do much wandering anymore. I wish I could—" He paused, then held up a finger. "Wait a moment, wait a moment. I might know someone who can help you!"

"Who?" Ocelot asked.

"Marco."

"The ork? Your friend downstairs with the crime-scene cleaner chummers?"

"Right. Oh, of course. You don't know who he is." Doc looked pleased. "He's a member of Mama's Boyz."

"Who the hell are Mama's Boyz?" Ocelot started. "They—"

Winterhawk held up a hand to stop him. This wasn't good. This wasn't good at all. Especially given that Doc was probably right. "They're a gang," he said. "They control the Catacombs, and most of the other underground travel around Boston and its vicinity."

"Well, that's good then, right?"

"Er...no. From everything I've heard, they're a bit—well—unstable."

"Nonsense," Doc said. "I work with them quite a lot, actually—at least at the upper levels. I admit I've never been brave enough to venture down further, where some of their more...unusual members remain. But they've been invaluable at getting me around safely when I need to go somewhere. I admit they can be a bit unsettling, but as long as you pay them and treat them with proper respect, they're trustworthy."

"Unusual?" Ocelot asked.

"Ghouls...and others who don't show their faces above the surface," Doc said.

Winterhawk nodded. He had a pretty good idea who Marco had called to clean up the remainder of their battle scene.

"Listen," Doc urged. "You can say what you like about them, but they've never been anything but straight with me. It's how they make the honest part of their cred—running protection for people traveling in the Catacombs. And if properly induced, they'll even provide transportation. Shall I give Marco a call?"

Winterhawk and Ocelot exchanged glances. It was a risk, despite Doc's words: Winterhawk had heard stories about Mama's Boyz during his previous trips to Boston, and every one of them had been of the "stay as far away from them as possible" variety. The "Mama" who allegedly ran the gang had not been seen in years, and rumors swirled around not only her current location but her nature: claims ranged from a ghoul to an ancient vampire to some kind of powerful spirit, but nobody outside the gang had ever returned to tell the tale if they'd seen her. Supposedly she traveled the Catacombs in her own personal railcar, attended by a guard of ghouls and other types you didn't want to run into in a dark alley—or anywhere else.

Ocelot was consulting his commlink for information. "Great," he said. "Ghouls. So if we piss 'em off, we're snacks." He clapped

Winterhawk on the shoulder. "This has been a fun trip, man. We'll have to do it again sometime. You know, if we don't end up as our bus driver's main course."

"No sense of adventure," the mage said. "And you say *I'm getting old*." Truth was he didn't like it any better than Ocelot did, but Victoria was in Salem—or at least on the way there—and she was alive. They could try to find alternate transportation, but traveling underground with experienced guides (even if they might be ghouls) could well be safer than trying to navigate the surface roads, especially outside Boston.

"Let's do it," he said to Doc before he changed his mind. "Call Marco. And thank you."

THIRTY-ONE

When they exited the lower level of The Wandering Wizard a half-hour later, Marco was waiting, shifting from foot to foot in impatience. Behind him were three others: a chubby ork with red hair and florid skin so pockmarked it looked like a topo map of Mars, a dark-skinned, squinty troll who was barely taller than Marco, and a skinny, pale individual with milky eyes who hung back in the shadows and moved with restless twitchiness.

"You ready?" Marco asked. To Doc, he said, "Sorry it took so long. Lotta bodies to deal with."

"Quite all right," Doc said. "Will you let the Parkmoors know what happened? I mourn their loss, but I'd rather not be on their bad side if they think I was somehow involved."

"Yeah, already done," he said. "They're fragged off, but not at you. Any o' those fuckers left alive, they dyin' tonight."

"Enough talk," the troll said. He wore a ripped ork-smiley-face T-shirt that showcased his augmented musculature, a large smiley-face button, and his disproportionately large hands nearly engulfed a battered FN-HAR. "Let's go." He regarded Winterhawk and Ocelot as if trying to decide whether to mug them, ignore them, or eat them.

They'd started to follow when Winterhawk remembered something. He headed back over to where Doc stood waiting near the door. "I forgot to ask you," he said under his breath. "Have you heard anything about tainted BADs lately? Chroma, and possibly others?" He knew that for the right clientele, Doc did a small but brisk business in some of the more benign varieties of the Awakened drugs.

Doc looked troubled. "I have."

"Any idea where they might be coming from?"

"Come *on!*" the troll yelled. "We ain't waitin' all day!"

"Only rumors," Doc said quickly. "Be careful in Salem. As I hear it, there might be some nasty business going on up there. You'd better go, though."

Mama's Boyz clearly ran the show in the Catacombs, because no one accosted or even approached the group as they led Winterhawk and Ocelot on a circuitous, confusing route along abandoned railroad tracks, through narrow tunnels half-obscured by rockfalls and metahuman-made barriers, and across a couple of narrow waterways. Twice they descended sketchy-looking steel ladders set into walls, until by Winterhawk's reckoning they were at least twenty meters underground. The air was full of the smells of garbage, the deep green odor of mold, and general disuse. Down here, the overlay of decomposition was stronger, and the faint, echoing sounds off in the distance had an unsettling feel.

Even without magic, Winterhawk sensed they were being watched. He kept his senses open as they walked, both assensing the area and keeping an enemy-detection spell sustained. So far, the latter hadn't pinged, though the former picked out the glowing auras of forms observing from hidden nooks, alcoves, and passageways. Maya rode on his shoulder, watching from the astral plane and relaying information to him.

"You don't gotta do that," Marco said when he noticed Winterhawk's attention on the unseen. "Nobody fucks with us down here." He waved toward the skinny guy with the milky eyes. "Grief'd see 'em comin' a kilometer off anyways."

The little guy didn't answer that, but continued to creep along the group's periphery, his attention appearing to wander with aimless lack of direction as he drifted back and forth across the tunnel. As Winterhawk had suspected, he assensed as a ghoul.

"It's okay," Ocelot said. He too was watching, tense and primed for action. "We don't trust anybody to do our recon for us."

"Your call," Marco said, shrugging.

"Ya'd never get outta here alive if we left ya here," the troll said. He sounded like the idea appealed to him.

"You plannin' to do that?" Ocelot said. His grip tightened around the handle of his monowhip.

"Shut up," Marco ordered the troll, punching him in the arm with enough force to knock a human into the wall. The troll didn't appear to take offense; he just rumbled something under his breath and kept going.

Shortly after, they arrived at what appeared to be a dead end. The brick-lined hallway was narrow here, decorated on both sides with graffiti and crude artwork, and the ceiling was low enough that the troll had to crouch. It ended in a pile of rocks, trash, and other debris. "Okay," Marco said. "This is where we blindfold ya. And lose the spirits."

"What?" Ocelot demanded. "You outta your fraggin' mind?" He dropped into a defensive stance, his hand moving to his SMG.

Instantly, all three of Mama's Boyz did the same. Marco and the troll were in front of them, and Grief, the ghoul, was behind them.

"Wait," Winterhawk called, holding up his empty hands in a placating gesture. "Calm down, everyone. Ocelot, it's fine. We'll do it."

He'd been afraid this was coming, but hadn't mentioned it because he doubted he could have gotten Ocelot to come along if he had. They were far underground now, and despite the fact that he'd tried to keep all the twists and turns their route had taken straight in his mind, he was sure Marco and the others had doubled back and taken unnecessary detours several times to confuse them. He had no doubt that between himself and Ocelot they could take down their three guides with relative ease should it come to that, but it didn't matter—they'd never make it back to the surface alive without them. At best, they'd be hopelessly lost as they tried to retrace their steps; more likely, the denizens of the lower parts of the Catacombs—more of Mama's Boyz, as well as the other creatures of the night that made their homes down here—would kill them and strip them for their clothes, gear, and organs before an hour passed.

Probably well before an hour passed.

"I am *not* lettin' these guys blindfold me," Ocelot said.

"A moment, if you please," Winterhawk said to their guides. He waved his friend a few meters off and turned his back on Mama's Boyz.

"We haven't a choice," he told Ocelot. "It's their way of protecting their territory. I'll wager you've done it yourself, back in your gang days. I've known Doc Belmont for years. If he says we can trust them, I believe him. And remember, we *did* save one of their lives."

Ocelot glanced over his shoulder toward the three Mama's Boyz, all of whom were eyeing them with impatient annoyance, weapons held at the ready but not pointed at them. He clenched his fists and sighed. "Fine," he said. "But I keep my weapons."

"We don't want yer weapons," Marco said. "Somethin' gets brave enough to jump us down here, you're gonna help take it down."

"Or it can eat you first," Grief said in his whispery voice, tittering.

Marco produced a couple of grimy blindfolds and tied them tightly in place. They were crude and tattered, but they did the trick: darkness settled around Winterhawk, reducing his world to the smell old synthahol and rancid soyburgers, the unsettling sounds of dripping, murmuring, and shifting rock, and the almost palpable auras surrounding their guides.

"Stay close," he told Maya, then made a show of dismissing his air spirit as he felt the cat fade back to the astral. These guys might not want any spirits around to track their secret tunnels, which was fine with Winterhawk, but that didn't mean he'd let himself go completely unprotected. At this point, knowing where Mama's Boyz were taking them wouldn't help them get back topside, so he didn't give a damn about that, but having Maya running overwatch from the astral could prove valuable if anything went wrong. She was good at hiding herself, so unless the ghoul was better than he looked, he wouldn't spot her lurking.

"Come on," Marco said, and a hand—presumably his—locked around Winterhawk's upper arm. He turned the mage around and marched him back what felt like the way they'd come, then spun him several times before proceeding forward again. Up close, the ork's stench was nearly overpowering.

At least they hadn't tied their hands. As nerve-wracking as it was to walk along without seeing where he was going, relying on Marco's sure hand to keep him from tripping over something or walking off the edge of a drop-off, it could have been a lot worse. He consoled himself with the knowledge that he had at least a half-dozen ways to deal with the situation if things went sideways, and hoped Ocelot was doing the same. His friend's pathological issues with confinement could sometimes prove as detrimental to missions as 'Hawk's own bottomless curiosity.

He lost track of how long they walked, but it had to be at least a half-hour. Marco and the others didn't speak to each other at all, but led them stumbling and staggering through more doorways, over piles of what felt like scrap metal, and past one area reeking so profoundly of decomposition that Winterhawk had to hold his breath until Maya informed him they were past the area. *"You wouldn't have wanted to see that,"* she told him, her normally prim British tone sounding disturbed. "I *didn't want to see that."*

"Okay," Marco's voice said. "Step up. Time to roll."

Winterhawk allowed himself to be guided up a short set of metal steps, to a flat surface.

"You're on some kind of train car," Maya informed him.

In a moment that became obvious as someone snatched the blindfold from Winterhawk's eyes. He stood in the middle of a narrow room, its walls sprayed with tags and its floor covered in threadbare, grimy carpet. Several windows lined each side, but all of them were covered with armored barriers sporting more graffiti. After a moment, the room lurched and began moving forward to the rattling accompaniment of wheels on tracks.

Marco and Grief stood at each end of the car, Marco near the single closed door. The troll was nowhere to be seen.

Ocelot made a show of swiping his hand across his face. He glared at the two Mama's Boyz, but didn't speak. Neither did the gangers, though Grief eyed the two of them with undisguised hunger.

Wherever they were going, both the train and the tracks had obviously seen better days. The car rumbled and clattered, shaking as if it were trying hard to rip itself to pieces or leap free of the tracks and forge its own way to its destination. Several times it jerked hard to one side or the other, feeling to Winterhawk as if they'd just slammed into something on the tracks and knocked it aside. At one point something that sounded very much like high-velocity gunfire stitched the side, though the armor must have been better than it looked because nothing got through.

"Stay here," Marco ordered, leaping up and disappearing up through a hidden hatch in the roof. More gunfire sounded, and after a few moments he clambered back down without comment.

Winterhawk, who along with Ocelot had been keeping a particularly close eye on Grief while the three of them were alone inside the train car, asked, "How much longer?"

"We'll get there when we get there." Marco's patience with his courier job was clearly reaching its end.

Five minutes later, the train car rumbled to a stop. Marco threw open the door. "End of the line."

Ocelot beat Winterhawk to the door. "Where the hell are we?"

Winterhawk joined him. Outside the door, darkness stretched out in every direction, punctuated at intermittent and far-flung intervals by an occasional point of light.

"What, you think we're gonna just drop you in the middle of town like a fraggin' school bus?" Marco asked, contemptuous. He hooked a thumb north. "Salem's that way, couple klicks or so. Just follow the tracks and you'll be fine."

Winterhawk was glad to be done with the ork and his unsettling companions. He'd been watching their auras as they traveled, and it was becoming obvious that if they remained together for much longer, Doc Belmont notwithstanding, at least one of them had a good chance of starting something that could get ugly. He stepped out of the car and Ocelot followed, glaring behind him. For one of the few times in his life, he restrained himself from making a sarcastic comment regarding the quality of the ride.

They stood on a platform that looked all but abandoned as Winterhawk watched the receding lights of the train car. "Let's go," he said. "I want to get into town so I can do this ritual and find Victoria. And keep your eyes open. I wouldn't put it past someone—or something—to try to jump us on the way in."

"I hope they do." Ocelot's tone held a certain relish.

THIRTY-TWO

Using the information in the file, it didn't take long for Vyx and Virago to locate one of the members of Beatrix's coven. The woman agreed to meet with them, but only in a public place. Apparently, she was as nervous as they were, which struck Vyx as odd since she hadn't given her any information yet. Still, she didn't mind—meeting someplace well populated in broad daylight might not prevent more attackers showing up with more disgusting spirits, but she figured it was probably less likely.

They spotted her instantly as they limped up to the soykaf shop on Virago's increasingly failing bike: a plump, dark-skinned ork woman in a headscarf, black leather jacket, and ripped jeans. She glanced up as they approached, and her eyes narrowed. Her hand, the one not wrapped around a tall cup of 'kaf, twitched.

"Melinda?" Vyx called.

The woman relaxed—mostly. Her gaze flicked past them and out into the parking area; only when she seemed convinced nobody was following them did she wave them to chairs at her small table beneath a faded awning.

Vyx and Virago both positioned themselves so they too could watch the street, and Vyx introduced them.

"How'd you find out about me?" Melinda asked.

"From Beatrix. Have you seen her lately? Like, since last night?"

"No. I tried to call her this morning, but she hasn't called back. We were planning to meet today to discuss some coven business before our gathering tonight." The witch's eyes narrowed. "You know something about her?"

Vyx sighed. "Maybe. We were supposed to talk to her about some biz. But—I'm sorry to tell you this, but I think she might be dead."

"What?" Melinda's eyes flashed.

Vyx gave her the rundown of what had happened since they'd arrived in town. "She mentioned you in one of the files she sent me. I think she suspected something was up."

As she spoke, Vyx gripped the table, struggling to stay upright. She hadn't slept for over a day, her muscles ached from all the lurching around on Virago's bike and the fight last night, and she was getting sick and tired of constantly having to watch her back. Ambushes from other gangers, she could deal with. Freaky spirits and big-time corporate hunters on her tail were a whole new level of stressful. Hell, she half-expected Melinda to suddenly ooze out of her jacket and take a shot at them any second.

From the way Virago wasn't taking her eyes off the witch, Vyx suspected she wasn't alone in the feeling. She considered the Jazz ampoules in her bag, but didn't want to use one yet. She might need them later, and they always wiped her out after they wore off.

"What do you know about this?" she asked Melinda. "Anything? Beatrix said you were in her coven—"

Melinda sighed and took a long pull from her soykaf. Her shoulders slumped, and suddenly she looked tired too. "I don't know much," she said at last. "Beatrix was—is—right: something's going on. I think a lot of people suspect it, but everybody's afraid to talk about it."

"And whatever it is, it's affecting the...production?" Vyx glanced around to make sure nobody was listening to their conversation, but the outdoor seating area was deserted at this time of the morning.

Melinda nodded. "The coven's got a deal with the Ancients to supply them with product we cultivate out in the Wilds. Beatrix figured she'd hear from Liam soon, since she was the liaison. He liked dealin' with elves, y' know?"

"So what happened?" Virago demanded. "You guys decide you want more cred or something?"

"I wish that's all it was." The ork took another drink from her cup and checked the street again, then leaned in closer. "Like I told you, something's going on. One of the larger covens has a new leader, and she's making a lot of people nervous. Her and her right-hand spirit."

"How so?" Vyx asked.

"Hard to say. Nobody's sure what to think. This only happened a few weeks ago, and anybody who tries to poke their nose in too much either disappears or suddenly decides to leave town."

"So why don't you get a group of you together and confront them?" Vyx exchanged glances with Virago. That's what the

Ancients would do, if some faction started getting too big for their britches. "Take her out if she's makin' trouble."

"That's not the way we operate," Melinda said. "The covens are all...sort of self-governing. When people think of the 'Salem Witches,' they think of a big monolithic organization, but that's not the way it works. There are dozens of different covens, each one with its own priorities."

"So what are this other coven's priorities?" Vyx asked. "And have they changed since this new leader took over?"

"They're one of the anti-dragon factions." Melinda glanced at them. "You know about that?"

"Not much," Vyx said, and Virago shook her head. "Something about how some groups think it's cool that Damon's around because he's good for tourism, and other groups don't like him. That's about all I really know."

"So this new coven isn't dealing with Damon either?" Virago asked. "That's one of the things Liam was wondering about, thinkin' maybe they got a better offer from the wyrm."

Melinda shook her head. "They want him out. They'd work with us before they'd work with him, from everything I've heard. Speculation is they're tryin' to go into biz for themselves."

"So how does that stop your coven from doing what they do?" Vyx asked. "The Wilds are huge. Isn't there enough room for everybody?"

"The Wilds have gotten a lot more dangerous," Melinda said. "They've never been safe, but lately it's gotten worse. More corps are dumping their failed experiments out there, and—I'm not sure I believe it, but to hear some tell it, some of the critters have gotten hit with CFD."

Virago snorted. "Headcase critters? That's crazy."

"You'd think so, but you don't live out here. You haven't seen it, or heard the rumors from people who don't have any reason to lie."

"So what do we do?" Virago asked. "Liam—and the people he works for—are gonna be pretty fragged off if they find out their supply lines are peterin' out because somebody's messin' with your ability to produce. That could mean trouble for you."

Melinda snorted. "Liam's not gonna send a crew out here to deal with it. We pay attention, y'know—he's already stretched thin tryin' to keep hold of his turf in the Rox. He doesn't have the guys to spare."

"No, but O'Rilley does," Vyx pointed out. "Do you really want a bunch of mob guys up in your business?"

"Not my problem," Melinda said. "Sorry, guys. I can't help you."

Vyx sighed. She was afraid of that. Whatever was going down around here, it obviously had the witches spooked. "Can you at least tell us one more thing?"

"What's that?"

"When I told you what happened, you focused on Beatrix—that makes sense, since I know she's your friend. But what about the thing that attacked us? I've never seen anything like that before. Do you know what it might have been? Sorry I didn't get any vid—too busy trying to save our asses."

Melinda considered, looking troubled. "From the way you described it, it sounds like a toxic spirit."

A queasy shudder ran up Vyx's neck. "Holy shit."

"Who would send one of those after us?" Virago demanded. "That takes some pretty heavy-duty magic, right?"

"Not just that," Melinda said. "It takes a seriously fucked-up spellslinger to even conjure one." She shuddered. "I haven't heard anything about anyone messing with toxics around here. It's contrary to what we believe in. We work *with* nature, not against it. Even the hardcore anti-dragon people only want the wyrms out because they don't want the magic around here aspected in their favor."

She finished her soykaf and stood. "Listen—if I were you, I'd just get the hell out of Salem. Let Liam or O'Rilley's guys handle this one. I like you two, and I sense you didn't have anything to do with Beatrix's disappearance. I don't want to see you disappear, too."

"Can't do that," Vyx said. "We're kinda stuck dealin' with it. So if there's anything you can do to help us—"

"Leave me your contact info. If I think of anything, I'll call. But that's it. And if I were you, I'd stay the hell away from the Wilds. But I doubt you'll listen to me, so if you do go out there, be fraggin' careful."

Vyx sighed. She didn't miss the look of fear on the ork's face. It was the best they were going to get.

They left the shop and rumbled off on Virago's bike. "So," Virago said, "Wilds, huh?"

Vyx let her breath out through her teeth. "Sure looks like that's where the answers are."

"I was afraid you'd say that."

"I could just go out and take a look on my own," she said with a sly smile. "You know, if you don't want to go. Nothin's gonna sneak up on me. I wouldn't have to go far—just take a quick look around and come back. You could sit back and roast your toes in front of a nice fire. Maybe find a blanket and a cat..."

"Shut up, *chica.*" Virago snorted, grinning, and gunned the bike to join the light stream of early-morning traffic. "Let's make it quick, though. That nice fire doesn't sound half bad. And I want a hot bath, a stiff drink, and a long nap."

THIRTY-THREE

Winterhawk and Ocelot arrived in Salem just as the sun was coming up over the horizon. Ocelot found a cab, and on the driver's recommendation they selected a cozy, unassuming motel near the center of town.

"I'll call my friend when it gets to be a reasonable hour," Winterhawk said. "Until then, we should probably get a few hours' sleep. I don't want to bugger up this ritual, since we'll only get one chance at it."

When he headed to Ocelot's room two hours later, after a fitful sleep and a welcome shower, he found his friend fiddling with his commlink. "Couldn't sleep," Ocelot said. "So I've been checking out the news. You'll want to see this. Dunno if it's relevant, but it seems pretty coincidental if it isn't."

It was a news article describing an event that had occurred at a place called the Black Cat Tavern, the previous evening. Winterhawk scanned it, frowning. "A toxic spirit attack? This is getting more and more bizarre. First the hit on Wu and her people, and then the traces of toxic magic I noticed at the club, and now an outright attack in a public place? There's got to be a connection, but I sure as hell don't see it yet. We need to fix that."

"Yeah. But look at the rest. Two unknown women were seen in the area, but they took off on a motorcycle before anybody could figure out who they were. If Vyx and her girlfriend are here, they're probably on bikes."

"Good point. We should probably go out there today. Anything else?"

"Nothing useful. Seems pretty quiet around here, mostly. Lots of editorials about pro-dragon this and anti-dragon that. The Children of the Dragon are even here now—remember them?"

"Oh, yes. As I said, keep your eyes open. I'm going to give my friend a call—we need a space to do this ritual, and we can't do it here."

Winterhawk's friend, a serene elven witch named Althea Darrow, lived in a large cottage on the outskirts of town. When they arrived in another cab, they found her in her front yard dressed in a red hooded sweatshirt and jeans, levitating up a meter and hanging bird feeders.

"They have a hard time finding food this time of year," she said by way of greeting. She floated to the ground and enveloped Winterhawk in a hug, then pushed him out to arm's length and frowned, her smooth brow furrowing. "I'm so glad to see you. It's been too long. But what are you doing here? You didn't get caught in the Zone, did you?"

"No. We're here on a mission. A couple of them, actually." He introduced Ocelot as "my associate," then nodded at the house. "Is it all right if we go inside and talk? I've heard there's some strange business going on in town, and I'd rather not be out in the open until we get it sorted."

Althea's frown deepened. "Of course, of course. And you've not heard wrong."

She led them inside to a cozy parlor decorated in a combination of Early American style and magical symbols, and Winterhawk was pleased to sense the buzz of powerful wards as they passed through the doorway. No one would magically overhear them as they talked. A fat orange tabby lay curled up on an overstuffed ottoman; Maya manifested and settled with satisfaction down next to him, and purrs soon rose from the pair of them.

Althea returned with glasses of iced tea. "You don't look well, old friend," she said. "Tell me what's troubling you."

It felt good to unburden himself to someone who understood. For the first time in days, Winterhawk allowed himself to relax as he told Althea the story of the original mission to study the ley line, their experiences following their arrival in the QZ, and their growing concern about toxic magic. The only thing he didn't tell her was the identity of Victoria—he merely described her as someone he'd been hired to locate once he got inside the Zone, and told her he'd need to borrow or rent a ritual space soon.

Ocelot, meanwhile, paced the room and remained watchful, occasionally stopping by the window to peer out into the garden. Winterhawk didn't try to make him stop—it wouldn't have done any good.

If Althea sensed any duplicity in Winterhawk's story, she didn't comment on it. Her expression grew more serious as he spoke, however, and she nodded when he had finished. "Of course you can use my ritual space," she told him. "But what you say about the toxics troubles me. I hadn't heard about the attack on the Black Cat. Poor Sylvan, such a shame." She sighed. "Your words reinforce something I've been suspecting for a while now."

"What's that?" Ocelot asked, turning back to the conversation.

Althea glanced at him, but addressed Winterhawk. "The schism's getting worse."

"Between the pro- and anti-dragon forces?"

"Yes. Before, it was all fairly civil—as you know, the covens squabble quite a bit, and we all have our own opinions about things, but up until recently we've kept our disagreements mostly to the level of discourse, with the occasional minor spat now and then."

"And that's changed now? Why?"

Althea spread her hands. "I think it's a mix of things. The other dragon—you heard about him, right?—has caused more of a rift between the factions. Even the pro-dragon groups are split over it. Some of them want Damon to stay, but they're fearful of the new dragon. Others have embraced the new dragon and believe the Children have cleansed him of his virus, using the power of the ley line that's becoming more and more aspected toward their magic. There's a truce between the pro-dragon forces that have aligned themselves with the Children—they've claimed some land north of town, and haven't caused much trouble since—but under the surface nothing has really changed. I keep expecting things to erupt any day now, but I keep my head down and hope they don't."

"This new dragon—where is he now? Is he still here?"

Althea shook her head. "He's disappeared. Nobody knows where he went—or if they do, they're not telling. Even some of the Children I'm friendly with claim they have no idea where he's gone, and that troubles them. Some of them have left and gone back to Boston, though most are still here, up north."

Winterhawk nodded. He'd heard some of these stories as part of the intel that had trickled out of the Zone over the last couple of months, but it was good to have confirmation. He'd definitely have to find time to do some serious examination of that ley line before he left.

If he could leave, he reminded himself.

But that still wasn't the main problem. "What about the toxics?" he asked. "What do you know about them? Is someone trying to attack the witches by tainting the BADs you're cultivating out in the Wilds?"

"It's all rumors," she said. "There's *something* going on out there. I'm not convinced it's connected to the production, though—not directly, anyway."

"What do you mean?" Ocelot asked, pausing in his pacing.

"I mean I don't think anyone's trying to interfere with production any more than they ever did," she said. "There are always the rivalries, and sometimes someone will send somebody—gangers or shadowrunners, usually—up here to try to disrupt things, but we deal with them fairly effectively."

"What, then?" Winterhawk asked.

Maya, sensing his tension, lifted her head, opened one eye, and regarded him with concern.

Althea shook her head. "It's all just rumor. No one's been able to prove anything. But ever since the new leadership took over the Westhaven coven, it's gotten more dangerous than ever out in the Wilds."

"Who's this new leader?" Winterhawk asked.

"Her name is Sabeetha. She's a troll who follows Wolf. She's powerful enough on her own, but she's never seen without a massive Wolf spirit—and I mean massive. That's when she's seen at all, though—in the last few weeks, no one sees her but her own coven members."

Winterhawk frowned. "Interesting. No one's been able to assense her?"

"Nobody's gotten past her defenses. She's good at keeping herself hidden, both magically and physically. But she's not bothering anyone—despite the fact that many of us think she's got something brewing out in the Wilds somewhere, nobody wants to mess with her. They claim it's because it's not their business, but I think they're afraid."

That was the last thing Winterhawk needed right now: another puzzle to solve. Was this Sabeetha related to the interruption of the BAD pipeline? What about the toxic magic—where did that fit in? And there was also the matter of what had happened to Wu and her team.

He stood. "Right now, my number-one priority is finding the woman I'm looking for. After I do that, on to the next problem."

"Are you sure you wouldn't like to sleep for a while?" Althea asked, looking concerned. "You both look exhausted, and I've got a spare room and couch space..."

"Later. After. Could you show me your ritual space?"

She didn't look convinced, but she and Winterhawk had known each other long enough for her to know it was a losing battle trying to pry him from his purpose. "I'll show you where it is, and then see about fixing something to eat."

"If you could just give us a moment..." Winterhawk indicated Ocelot.

"Of course. I'll be in the kitchen." She hurried off, and after a moment her ginger tom uncoiled himself lazily and trotted after her, no doubt thinking he was about to be fed.

"You got a plan?" Ocelot asked.

"It's going to take me a while to set up this ritual—as I said, I want to make sure I get it right the first time. I'm planning to ask Maya to do a little astral recon—talk to the other spirits around the town and see if she can get them to tell her anything. Meanwhile, since I'm sure you'll be bored stiff watching me set up a ritual circle, perhaps you could do a bit of investigation of your own. Starting at the Black Cat Tavern."

"On it," he said. "Anything else?"

Winterhawk shrugged. "Stay reachable—once I find her, I want to get there fast. If you can find us some transportation, that would be helpful as well. Don't steal it, though," he added. "Believe me, they don't call this 'The Most Magical Town in North America' for nothing. Even the bloody doghouses have wards."

"Fuckin' great."

Althea volunteered to help with the ritual to find Victoria, and Winterhawk took her up on it after giving Maya instructions about the investigations he wanted her to do.

They moved around the circle in companionable silence, setting up the components and preparing the reagents. As they neared completion, Althea stopped and regarded Winterhawk with a gentle, appraising expression. "So—are you going to tell me the truth about this woman you're looking for?"

He stopped, startled. "What?"

"It's none of my business, of course, but I can help you more if I know what's really going on."

"I told you," he said, paying too much attention to the reagents he was inspecting. "I've been hired to locate her and get her out of the QZ." After a pause, he added, "What makes you think there's more to it than that?"

"Because you've been doing a terrible job of hiding your aura while you were working on the circle," she said, chuckling. "I've seen you work before—I know how careful you are. But with this, you look like a surgeon getting ready to operate on his own child."

He didn't answer, and hoped she didn't see him stiffen.

No such luck, apparently. "Wait a minute..." She put a hand on his shoulder, gently pulling him around so she could meet his eyes. The question in hers was clear. "I've hit a nerve, haven't I?"

He sighed, bowing his head. "All right. Yes. She's more than just a job. But that's all I'm going to say, Althea, so don't ask me for more. I've got more than a professional interest in finding her—and soon, since it sounds as if she's already got herself embroiled in whatever mess is going on up here." He indicated the circle. "Let's get on with it, shall we?" He knew he sounded more abrupt than he should.

Althea didn't appear to take offense. She squeezed his shoulder. "All right, I won't pry. Let's do this."

Winterhawk pulled out the Ancients jacket Liam had given him and regarded it for a long moment. He only had the single item—if this didn't work, he'd have to hope Ocelot's inquiries at the Black Cat Tavern had provided some useful information, and that Victoria hadn't left Salem—or hadn't been killed before they could track her down the old-fashioned way.

Pushing those thoughts aside, he stepped into the center of the circle, nodded to Althea, and began the ritual.

He shifted easily to the astral plane and paused a moment to orient himself. Here in Salem it was positively alight with color and vitality—the high concentration of magically active individuals and the astral energy they generated made for the kind of mystical light show that drew the curious—magical and mundane alike—from all over the world, or at least it used to before the containment went into effect.

Fortunately, Althea's cottage was far enough from the draconically-aspected ley line that its interference barely affected the ritual. It felt good not to be casting spells through a thick haze. The homey, well-lived-in aura of the house, as well as Althea's comforting and confident presence, supported Winterhawk's efforts as he reached out, took hold of the jacket's essence, and wove the magic to follow it to its source. The spell was a simple one—assuming that the target wasn't behind wards or otherwise magically protected—but he nonetheless wove the strands with great care. Althea's words hadn't been entirely wrong: he felt exactly as he imagined a surgeon might feel when beginning an operation he'd performed hundreds of times before—but never on someone from his own family.

Instantly, the jacket's astral presence began to glow, the familiar thread shimmering into being and snaking out of the circle. Even more encouraging, the glow was strong and steady:

wherever Victoria was, she wasn't far from his current location. She was almost certainly still in Salem, or at least nearby.

"Hold it steady..." he murmured to Althea. "I've got it..."

He moved with care even though he didn't need to: the strength of the connection was like an astral superhighway, pointing him to the south. Was she holed up somewhere, hiding from someone chasing her? Or perhaps moving around the town with Virago, looking for the information Lucky Liam had tasked her to track down? But no, it quickly became clear that the thread he followed was indeed nearby, but it wasn't in Salem. As he continued to follow it, it headed outside the town and toward the Wilds.

"No, no..." he murmured. "Why did you go out there?"

Nearby, he sensed Althea's tension.

He moved a little faster. If she was in the Wilds, he'd have to get out there and find her fast. No doubt as an adept she could take care of herself under normal circumstances, but it sounded as if the woods surrounding Salem weren't safe for anybody, especially nowadays.

His breath picked up as he zeroed in on the signal, and a few moments the astral thread terminated at the familiar glowing aura of his target. *Yes!* She was there, and she was alive! Next to her he spotted another aura, strong but more diminished—probably Virago, Vyx's cybered ganger girlfriend. Good—if they were still together, that meant—

Althea's fearful voice interrupted his thoughts: "Look!"

He was reluctant to take his attention off Vyx, afraid if he did, she'd slip away from him again, but he pulled back a little to take in the scene.

He immediately spotted what his friend had seen:

Vyx and Virago weren't alone.

THIRTY-FOUR

"I don't really see what you're expecting to find out here," Virago said. "This place is huge, and we barely have a fraggin' clue where to look."

Vyx shrugged. "I dunno. I just feel like we oughta be doing *something,* y'know? I don't want to go far—if anything spots us, I'll notice before it gets close, so I'm pretty sure we can take it down or outrun it. Don't you think so?"

"Yeah, probably." Virago adjusted the strap of her SMG on her shoulder and trudged along next to Vyx. "But I'm not crazy about the idea of wanderin' around out here until something tries to jump us. Do you even know what the plants they harvest to make BADs look like in the wild?"

"Hell no." Vyx grinned. "The only plants I recognize are the ones that died in my dorm room, and the Deepweed some of the girls used to bring up." She shrugged. "Just humor me, okay? We'll look around a little bit, then go back to the bike and head back into town. Maybe we can persuade Melinda to give us some more intel, or at least point us at somebody else who can."

It was late morning by the time they'd found a place to hole up and set off on their recon mission. They left Virago's bike concealed in some underbrush just off a narrow dirt road snaking into the forest from the main road, and marked on their AR maps so they could find it again if they had to get out in a hurry. Now, ten minutes later, they slogged through damp green ground cover as thin sunlight poked its way through the pale gray, overcast sky.

"What if those guys come after us? I'm not so sure we could take them down, from the sound of it." Virago glanced around as if expecting someone to be following them already.

"What guys? The ones my mom hired?"

"Yeah."

"I don't think they're trying to kill us, remember? And if we find 'em out here, maybe we'll teach 'em that we're not the easy prey they probably think we are." As they walked, Vyx had been keeping track of the trees they passed; most of them had branches big enough to support her weight—if anybody attacked them, she could be ten meters up before they even figured out where she'd gone. Virago wasn't quite as fast as she was, but she made up for it with firepower. Let 'em try, if they wanted to.

Virago, wisely, didn't pursue it. "So we're looking for—what?"

"Anything weird, I guess."

"This whole *place* is weird." She looked around, her slim nose wrinkling in distaste. "Give me the city any day—buildings, roads, devil rats, pizza delivery...frag, even the smell of garbage. This is...creepy."

Vyx had to allow that it was, in fact, creepy: in her childhood and early teens, she'd been on vacations with her mother or to summer camps where she'd spent time outside the city, but none of the forests she'd ever seen were anything like this. The bit of research she'd done before they'd left had pointed out that the Salem Wilds didn't necessarily follow a natural growth progression—all the magic in the area had resulted in a much thicker concentration of trees, some of them huge and twisted and downright spooky. Even though she'd never admit it, she was glad they hadn't come out here at night. Between the creepy trees, the constant low-level noises from far-off wildlife, and the ever-present ground fog that made seeing where they were stepping difficult—let's just say it didn't sound like her idea of fun.

To take her mind off the area's eeriness as she scanned the fauna for anything unusual, she asked in an offhand tone, "Do you really think they'll take me back?"

"Huh?"

"The Ancients."

"Why wouldn't they?"

Vyx rolled her eyes and made a point of stroking the top of one rounded ear. "Oh, I dunno, let's think: I'm not an elf. I fucked up and got somebody killed. Half the gang doesn't want me around. Not lookin' good, you have to admit."

"Eh, they'll get over it." Vyx shrugged. "They're hotheads, just like you are. Stuff blows over. Yeah, some of 'em are snobs, but they've also seen what you can do. Besides, you're with me. And just let 'em try to kick *me* out." Her voice took on a challenging edge.

Vyx wouldn't be mollified, though. She stared at the ground as she walked. "Would you go, if they did?"

"What do you mean?"

"If they kicked you out—or if they won't take me back. Would you go? I mean, come on: the Ancients are like your family. How long have you been with 'em?"

"Doesn't matter."

"How long?" she pressed.

"Started runnin' errands for 'em when I was seven," she said, with some reluctance. "Mostly because of Liam. He wasn't in charge then, but he was on his way up."

Vyx nodded. "That's what I mean. You wouldn't leave all that for me. I wouldn't want you to. I'd never ask."

Virago gripped her arm and brought her to a halt. "Listen, *chica*," she said, and her normally soft voice had a hard edge to it. "I make up my own mind about what's important to me, *so ka?* They ain't gonna kick you out. I'll make sure of that. But if they do—I'm comin' with you." She grinned. "Hey, maybe the Hellriders are recruitin'."

"You know, that's not a bad idea," Vyx said, tilting her head. "They've got some sweet bikes..."

Virago punched her gently and shoved her away. "Come on, drekhead. Let's finish up this bug hunt of yours and get the hell back to town. My feet are gettin' cold, and—"

Vyx's danger sense buzzed. *Fuck!* She held up a finger.

"What?"

"Something's out there," she whispered. "Run!" She grabbed Virago's arm and pulled her down into a crouching dash.

An instant later, a series of dark, shadowy forms burst through the trees behind them, at least fifty meters back—but between them and where they'd left the bike. The clearing rang with the sound of automatic fire, followed by an unearthly, warbling howl.

THIRTY-FIVE

Five minutes later when Winterhawk reached the meeting point, the side of a winding, narrow road near the north side of the Wilds, Ocelot was already waiting. The mage pulled Althea's little car onto the shoulder behind a battered, olive-drab, four-wheel-drive Jeep Trailblazer. Up ahead, an overgrown, even narrower dirt road, little more than a single-lane track and barely wide enough for a car, snaked off into the forest.

Winterhawk wasted no time swapping vehicles. "Where did you get that?" the mage asked, climbing into the Jeep's shotgun seat. "You didn't steal it, did you? We've got enough problems already."

"Rented it. Found a local—procurement guy." He nodded at the back seat, where a large duffel bag took up most of the space. "Picked up a few things, too. Few guns and some ammo. Where we goin'?"

Winterhawk pointed out the direction. "I don't think it's far. It was hard to tell from the astral, but it looked like they were near some kind of little farmhouse. Abandoned, most likely." He drummed his fingers on the armrest and tried to slow his racing heartbeat as the Jeep seemed to crawl with agonizing slowness toward its destination. *They can take care of themselves,* he reminded himself. "Did you talk to anyone at the Black Cat?"

"Yeah." Ocelot steered around the moss-covered husk of a fallen tree; clearly this road hadn't been used recently. "Place was closed—looked like something had torn out half their back room—but I tracked down one of the waitresses. She said two women, one human, one elf in a green jacket, showed up last night and met up with another woman she's seen before—one of the local witches. *Chica* named Beatrix. She doesn't know what happened next, since she wasn't in the back room, but she said some kind of enormous freaky thing busted out of there, and then a firefight started in the parking lot. By the time the cops showed up, though, everybody'd taken off."

"Were you able to locate this Beatrix?" Winterhawk kept his gaze fixed ahead of them, periodically levitating small objects out of the way so their forward progress would be slowed as little as possible.

"Nobody saw her at all. They didn't find a body, and nobody saw her leave."

"That's not good." He reached out to Maya; he'd recalled her after completing the ritual and sent her off to scout ahead. *"Do you see anything?"*

"They're here," she said. *"They're in trouble. Hurry."*

"Are they in the house?"

"No, they're trying to run. A huge wolf-thing is chasing them, along with a couple of hellhounds and men with guns. I think they might be out of ammo, because they aren't shooting."

Damn. If they ran too far away, he and Ocelot might have trouble finding them—or they might run into even more trouble out in the Wilds. He made a fast decision. *"Maya—I want you to show yourself to them. Tell them help is on the way, and steer them toward the farmhouse. We'll be there fast."*

"I'll try," she said. *"I don't think they're too inclined to trust anyone at present."*

"Hurry!" Winterhawk urged Ocelot. By his reckoning they were less than half a kilometer away. He summoned an air spirit and gave it a mental picture of the farmhouse and of Vyx's aura, then ordered it to go to them and assist them against whatever was attacking. He felt its acquiescence as it streaked off. He hoped it would be enough until they got there.

THIRTY-SIX

Vyx skidded to a stop, ducking behind a thick tree and waiting for Virago to catch up. Her danger sense wasn't pinging strongly at the moment and no one was shooting at them, but they could hear their pursuers crashing through the trees off in the distance. They couldn't stop for long.

"What the hell's going *on*?" Virago demanded, bending over to grasp her knees while still maintaining her scan of the forest behind them. "Why is everybody suddenly fuckin' *after* us?"

"Good question." Her gaze darted around, then she pointed upward. "We need to get back to town. I'm gonna climb up and see if I can spot a road."

"Yeah. Do that. I'll—" She stopped. "Oh, fuck!"

The glowing figure of a large, long-haired black cat with a plumy tail shimmered into being on a branch in front of them.

Vyx whipped out her knife, and Virago swung her katana around, slashing at the cat. The blade passed harmlessly through and sank into the tree's trunk.

"Stop, please." The cat spoke in Vyx's mind. Its mental voice was prim and feminine, with—a British accent? Seriously? *"I'm a friend."*

"What the—" She swept her gaze around again, but her danger sense still wasn't going off. She didn't attack the cat, though she did keep her knife raised.

"I'm a friend," the cat repeated. *"Help is coming. You need to follow me."*

"Like hell!" Vyx glared at it. "What do you mean, 'help'? What help? Who sent you?"

"Are you *talkin'* to that thing?" Virago demanded, looking as if she were trying to decide if her girlfriend had gone crazy or if she should take another shot at this weird cat.

"We don't have time for this," the cat said. There was no desperation in her voice, but urgency tinged it. She indicated a

direction with a head gesture. *"There's an old farmhouse nearby. My master and his friend will meet you there. Please—your pursuers are getting close."*

Vyx froze. "Your master and his friend?" *Oh, fuck...Oh, holy fuck...* "They're the guys who've been looking for us, aren't they?" Why did every damn thing in the world have to go wrong at once?

The crashing in the distance was growing louder. She could hear voices now, calling back and forth to each other. Worse, she thought she could make out the massive, loping form of the wolf. Her danger sense buzzed a little harder.

"They're not your enemies," the cat said. *"They mean you no harm. Please—if you don't hurry, they won't be able to help you."*

Two of their pursuers broke through the trees less than fifty meters away. "This way!" one shouted, pointing toward Vyx and Virago's direction.

Vyx exchanged glances with Virago. "Gotta make a choice," she said, talking fast. "The cat says it's with those guys who are looking for us, but they're not enemies."

"You believe it?" Virago glanced around the tree again, then jerked her head back. Her grip tightened on her katana.

Vyx hoped she wasn't making the biggest mistake of her life. "No choice," she said. "We'll deal with 'em if we have to." To the cat, she said, "Okay, let's go."

The cat seemed to nod. *"Follow me,"* she said. *"I'll try to conceal you, but stay low and move fast."*

"That's what I do best." Vyx bared her teeth in a fierce grin. She was trying not to think about the old phrase 'out of the frying pan and into the fire.'

THIRTY-SEVEN

"Here!" Winterhawk called, pointing.

Ocelot almost missed the overgrown turnoff, but whipped the Jeep off the narrow dirt road and up the rutted track. A rotting and broken wooden fence traced the path along their right side, probably all that was left of a long-abandoned horse corral. None of the buildings were visible yet. "You sure this is it?"

Winterhawk didn't answer. Instead, he reached out to Maya again. *"Did you find them?"*

"Yes, we're coming. Almost to you."

"How many pursuers?" He extended his senses further to the air spirit, trying to follow its progress.

"At least three metahumans. And the big wolf spirit. I didn't want to get too close to it, but I think something's–off about it."

"Off?" He glanced up as the two-story bulk of the abandoned farmhouse came into view around a bend.

"Hold on–I can see the house now. We're coming around the back."

"Get them here safely, Maya. We're there now."

He broke contact and leaped out of the Jeep as soon as Ocelot screeched to a stop around the back. "Let's get inside under cover. Maya says they're coming."

Ocelot snatched his duffel bag out of the back seat, slung it and his AK-97 over his shoulder, and took off for the door.

Winterhawk barely got a good look at farmhouse's interior as they pounded up the rickety stairs: graffiti, trash, and the remains of old sleeping nests told him drifters or chipheads had frequently used it as a crash pad, but none of it looked recent. The place smelled of dust, disuse, and the distant hint of squatter funk.

"Up here!" Ocelot yelled, ducking into one of the bedrooms facing the back part of the house.

By the time Winterhawk joined him, Ocelot had already dropped down below the room's single window. The glass was long gone; he'd braced his rifle with the barrel propped against the sill, scanning the thick forest beyond the backyard. "I don't—wait! Something's coming. Two o'clock!"

Winterhawk crouched on the other side of the window and peered out, assensing the area for any sign of living beings. For a moment he didn't see anything, and then a small, dark form streaked out of the trees followed by two young women in ripped jeans and leather jackets. Both ran faster than mundane humans, zigzagging and crouching low. Behind them, gunshots rang out.

He lost sight of them all as they darted inside the house. *"Bring them up here to us,"* Winterhawk told Maya. *"Quickly."*

A couple seconds later, more figures broke free of the treeline. Winterhawk counted three dark-clad humans, all armed with rifles, all running uneven patterns similar to their quarry.

"They went into the house!" one yelled. "Surround 'em! We—"

That was all he got to say before Ocelot squeezed off a burst of rounds. The man spun and dropped.

One of the remaining men quickly turned tail and plunged back toward the cover of the trees. The other paused, whipped something from his armored vest, and fired at the house. A quick *whuff* sounded, and then a louder *BOOM!*

The old house shook on its foundation.

Winterhawk roared and flung a manabolt at the man, who clutched his head and pitched forward to his knees, scrabbling at the ground as he tried to continue his forward progress. Another burst from Ocelot's rifle felled him.

Maya zoomed into the room, not even bothering to pretend she was running. *"The house is on fire!"* she said, her normally cultured British tones full of fear. *"They've hit it with some kind of grenade."*

A second later, the two women skidded to stops just inside the door, panting and dirt-streaked. They both stared at Winterhawk.

Winterhawk stared back at them—or rather, at Vyx.

Ocelot fired yet another burst into the trees.

"The house is on *fire!*" Vyx yelled. "What the hell are you doing? We gotta get outta here!"

"Grenade," Winterhawk said. "We've got time. We have to deal with your pursuers first. How many were after you?"

"Three guys," the other woman, an elf—Virago, most likely—said, still panting. "And one big fuckin'—"

"Holy shit!" Ocelot cut her off. "Look at the *size* of that thing, 'Hawk!"

Winterhawk spun back around. "Bloody hell..." he whispered.

The thing that broke free of the trees was a wolf. Or, it would have been a wolf if it had been anything approximating wolf-sized. This creature was the size of a small bus—three meters at the shoulder at least. Its shaggy black fur looked matted and sickly, its eyes burned an unholy red, and thick ropes of saliva dripped from its yellow-fanged jaws. It snapped at Winterhawk's air spirit, which cruised along beside it attempting to slow its forward progress. As 'Hawk and Ocelot watched, it lashed a massive paw out at the spirit, which already looked diminished from previous attacks. The spirit made a reedy little astral shriek and winked out.

Without looking back, Ocelot snapped, "You ladies know how to shoot?"

"Yeah," Virago growled. "Outta ammo, though."

"In the bag."

Winterhawk flung another spell at the approaching spirit as he heard Vyx and Virago going through Ocelot's duffel bag in search of weapons. The spell hit it and it yelped, but the sound was more one of anger than of pain. The remaining metahuman attacker, a beefy ork, used it as cover to fire toward the window. Rounds *spanged* off the rotted wood.

From below, the faint smell of smoke began to grow more pungent. They couldn't remain here for long.

Virago joined them at the window. She'd selected an SMG, but hesitated as she got a good look at the wolf-thing. It lasted only a second, though, and then she opened up with a flurry of rounds that stitched along the thing's side with deadly accuracy.

It barely slowed the beast's movement.

"Holy fuck..." she breathed.

It was almost at the house now. Winterhawk, switching gears, sent another manabolt at the ork behind it. Unlike the wolf, the ork didn't seem to have any unusual protections against magic. He clutched his head and fell, dropping his gun.

"'Hawk, how do we fight that thing?" Ocelot demanded. "What the hell is it? It—"

He stopped, and stared.

The massive wolf-thing had stopped. It looked up at the house, sniffing the air and cocking its ear as if listening to something. Then, with one last baleful glare up at the second-floor occupants, it turned and trotted at high speed back into the forest.

Ocelot didn't relax, nor did he move the gun barrel. "Okay..." he said. "Is anybody else as fuckin' confused as I am?"

Winterhawk didn't answer him. At that moment, a more pressing concern had presented itself in the form of a katana blade against his throat.

"Okay," Vyx said coldly. "Now we're gonna talk."

THIRTY-EIGHT

Ocelot moved even faster than Vyx had, whipping his rifle around and leveling it at Virago's forehead. "Drop it," he ordered.

"Hold on." Winterhawk remained still. He kept his voice calm and even, acutely aware of how fast this situation could go to hell if anybody made a wrong move. "Ocelot, please, don't do that. She's right—we absolutely need to talk. But we need to get out of here before the whole place goes up around our ears."

Vyx's cold tone didn't change, nor did she lower the blade. "I know my mother sent you guys after me, and I'm not goin' anywhere with you. Thanks for the assist, but we're outta here and you aren't comin' after us. If that means we have to take you out, we'll do it."

"'Hawk..." Ocelot began. Tendrils of smoke were beginning to drift up through the moldering floor.

"That might be more difficult than you think," Winterhawk said. "Either way, we do need to go somewhere else, and quickly. Even if the house weren't on fire, there's no guarantee that wolf-thing won't come back. And I'm not entirely certain we can cope with it just now."

"You two stay," Vyx said. "Give us a couple minutes' head start, then go."

"Is that really what you want?" Winterhawk asked. "You both look exhausted. You were out of ammunition when you got here. Unless I miss my guess, you no longer have a vehicle. I give you my word—if you come with us so we can discuss this, neither of us will make any effort to compel you to do anything."

He glanced around, and sniffed the air. "Please, though— decide soon. We've been through a lot these last few days, and I've no desire to end my existence in this dump of a house. Joining forces—at least temporarily—seems the wisest course of action at present."

Vyx's expression wavered.

Winterhawk assensed her, and wasn't surprised to see that her aura was as troubled as her face. "Please," he said again. "You have my word. Ocelot? Please lower your gun."

With obvious reluctance, Ocelot did as requested. "Yeah, my word too. This is 'Hawk's show anyway—I got no dog in the race. I'm just along for the ride."

Vyx exchanged glances with Virago. Unspoken communication seemed to pass between them, and then finally Vyx's shoulders slumped and she, too, lowered her blade. "Yeah, okay. Let's go. You got a vehicle? Our bike's a long way off, if it's even still there."

Ocelot was already gathering up his gear and was slinging it back over his shoulder. "Out back. We should go out the window. 'Hawk, anything nasty out there?"

"Maya says no. Let's go before that changes." He pulled out his commlink. "And Vyx, let me give you my LTG in case we get separated or you need to contact us."

They all clambered out the open window. Winterhawk, levitating down, watched Vyx as she climbed. Even as obviously tired as she was, she moved with effortless grace and speed, showing neither fear nor hesitation.

The four of them piled into the Jeep and hurried off. In the distance they could hear the growl of sirens—the fire department was on the way, and possibly more people they didn't want to encounter. With a combination of Ocelot's reckless driving and Winterhawk's illusion magic, they managed to get clear of the area before they were spotted.

"Where to?" Ocelot asked when they were back on the main road. He glanced around, first at Winterhawk in the shotgun seat, then at the two women in the back.

"I don't want to go back to Althea's," Winterhawk said. "None of us are terribly safe right now, and I don't want to put her in danger. I'll call her and see if she has any ideas."

As it happened, she did. After first protesting that of course they were all welcome back at her place, she grudgingly conceded that might not be the best idea. Instead, she gave Winterhawk the code to another place her coven owned. "I'll tell the spirit guards to let you in," she said. "But we need to talk later. I want to help you."

The house wasn't much more than a small cabin, but it looked solid and defensible. True to her word, Althea had instructed the two spirits—one earth, one air—that guarded it to let them pass, and soon all four of them were pacing restlessly around the cabin's spare interior.

"Okay," Vyx said, glaring at Winterhawk. "So my mother sent you after me. Why, after all this time? What does she want?"

Winterhawk studied her a moment, then glanced at Virago, who'd stationed herself next to one of the windows. He noticed she hadn't returned Ocelot's SMG. "There's no mystery to it. She's worried about you. She hired us to get you out of the QZ."

"And do what?" Vyx let out a loud sigh. "What are you supposed to do with me once you get me out? Deliver me to her?"

"She wants to know you're safe. There wasn't actually any discussion regarding any next steps once we got you out." Tiring of pacing, he sat down, confident that Maya or the cabin's spirits would warn him of any approaching threat.

"What if I don't *want* to get out?" Her expression hardened. "Does she even give a fuck about what I want? Because that'd be a first."

"Why *wouldn't* you want to get out?" Winterhawk waved a hand, indicating not just the cabin but the area in general. "You don't enjoy living in this hellhole, do you?"

"It might be a hellhole, but it's home," she said. "It's home a hell of a lot more than all those fancy schools my mother used to send me to."

"What about MIT&T? You just walked out on that—for what? To join a gang that wouldn't even take you if it weren't for—circumstances?"

Virago whirled. "Shut your mouth, shithead. Ain't none of your business what Vyx does."

Winterhawk continued, unfazed. "I'm right, though, aren't I? We spoke with your people back in the Rox—that's why you're here in Salem, isn't it? Trying to get away from those who don't approve of your being there?"

"Look," Vyx said, clenching her fists. "I'm not talking about this anymore. It's none of your business what I do or who I do it with. I'm not goin' back with you, and if you try to force me, I'll find a way to take you out. That's the truth. I'm not some soft little corp baby, okay?"

Winterhawk raised his hands in a conciliatory gesture. "Fair enough. As I said, we've no intention of forcing you to do anything you don't want to do. I might ask you to record a statement for your mother, since we've been hired to get you out, and if that doesn't happen I'll have to explain why, but aside from that—

frankly right now I'm far more concerned with what's going on around here."

Vyx looked like she might protest further, but then nodded, looking troubled. "Yeah. I guess if you talked to Liam, you know *why* he sent us up here, right?"

"To check up on what's going on with the BAD production," Ocelot said. "Yeah. You find out anything yet? What were you doin' at the Black Cat last night?"

Her eyes narrowed. "Guess I shouldn't be surprised you know about that too."

"You met with a witch named Beatrix," Winterhawk said. "From what we heard, you were ambushed by a team that included a toxic spirit. Who was this Beatrix, and what happened to her? Was she part of the ambush?"

Virago shuddered. "She *was* the spirit. Or at least it looked like her."

"What do you mean?" He stopped pacing again.

"She was sitting there talking to us, and suddenly she... *changed.*"

Vyx nodded. "And she didn't even ping my danger sense up until the end. That's hard to do."

Winterhawk resumed pacing, trying to put all the pieces of this puzzle together. Clearly, one or more toxic magicians were at the core of the problem, but that still didn't tell him how they were connected both with the BAD production in the Wilds and Doris Wu and her team. If their aim was to produce toxic-tainted BADs like the Chroma they'd encountered back in Boston, then what was the reason for it? Were they trying to destroy the market for the drugs by making people distrust them? Were they trying to bring down the wrath of the gangs and crime organizations that distributed the BADs on the witches? As far as Winterhawk knew, Doris Wu didn't even *know* any of the Salem witches, let alone have any connection with the Boston drug trade. In fact, it had been pretty clear when they'd set their chosen base of operations in Boston rather than in Salem that once they'd diverted Winterhawk off course, they hadn't intended to contact the witches at all regarding their ley line research.

"Were the group chasing you today the same ones you encountered at the Black Cat? Did you see the wolf before?"

"I don't know if they were the same group," Vyx said. "Definitely never saw that wolf before."

"So you don't know anything about a coven led by a troll woman, possibly with a wolf ally spirit?"

"Nah. We haven't been here long enough to find out much."

"We should call Melinda back," Virago said.

"Who's Melinda?" Ocelot asked.

"She's from Beatrix's coven. She was helpin' us out a little."

"Perhaps we should," Winterhawk agreed. "We'll contact my friend as well, and perhaps between us we can start making sense of all of this." Suddenly, a memory returned, and he mentally kicked himself for forgetting about it before.

"Let's go," he said. "We need to find a decker. Perhaps your friend or mine knows of one."

"Why do you need a decker?" Vyx asked.

He pulled Doris Wu's commlink from where he'd stashed it in an inner pocket. "I'm trying to trace another thread of our little puzzle," he said, holding it up. "And this might be the key."

THIRTY-NINE

Althea didn't know any deckers, but Melinda did. Vyx spoke with her from Althea's place while Winterhawk paced around in a fair imitation of Ocelot's impatience.

He'd sent Ocelot and Virago out to pick up some more gear from Ocelot's "procurement guy." The two returned an hour later bearing more guns, ammo, grenades, and upgraded armored jackets for Vyx and Virago.

"Any trouble?" Winterhawk asked.

"Nope. No sign of 'em."

Given Ocelot's usual level of paranoia and awareness of his surroundings, Winterhawk found that at least somewhat comforting.

"Where's the decker?" Virago asked as she and Vyx shrugged off their mangled jackets and donned the new ones, stowing their gear in the many pockets. Winterhawk noted Vyx's pleased expression when she saw Virago had made sure to get her a light jacket she could move in.

"We're meeting him and Melinda at her coven hall," Vyx said. "She's still spooked about what happened to Beatrix, so she wants to make sure we're behind some good wards."

"Prudent," Winterhawk said. He had no idea if Wu's commlink contained anything useful, or if her death was connected with what was going on in Salem, but hoped it would provide at least some usable data. In any case, since they'd lost the rest of the equipment they'd picked up from Wu's team's safe house when their van had been destroyed back at Doc's, it was the only chance they had.

Melinda's coven was based out of a combination meeting hall and arts center on a tree-lined street not far from downtown. She and the decker, a skinny, nervous elf barely out of his teens with pale, pimply skin and flaming red hair, met them inside.

"This is Flea," she said as she led them past weathered brick walls decorated with paintings, old-style photographs, and framed holoprints depicting Salem history. "He's the brother of one of our circle. He helps us out occasionally with Matrix business."

Flea grinned, showing silver-capped teeth. "Pleased ta meetcha," he said with a jaunty salute. Unlike Melinda, who favored a hippie aesthetic, he wore ripped jeans and a weathered Concrete Dreams T-shirt that looked old enough that it might have been purchased at one of their concerts back in the Fifties. Either he was older than he looked, or he spent a lot of time digging around in obscure thrift shops. He carried a bag covered with patches slung over one shoulder. "Whatcha need, and how much it pay?"

"Just a moment," Winterhawk said. Shifting to astral sight, he scanned the decker carefully, looking for any sign of toxic taint or duplicity. He saw nothing but a strong aura, muddied slightly by his cyberware. Satisfied that Flea wouldn't repeat Beatrix's performance at the Black Cat Tavern, he pulled out Wu's commlink.

"This belonged to a...friend," he said. "I need to know what's on it—specifically, what she was up to just before and the few days after she entered the Zone. Whatever you can find: records of comm calls, journal entries, anything like that."

Flea snorted. "I thought you'd have something worth my time. But hey, whatever. You're the boss. I can do that for a couple hundred, assuming there's no serious ice or heavy-duty encryptions."

"If there are, we'll renegotiate," Winterhawk said. "But she was a magical researcher. I doubt you'll find anything to tax your abilities."

The elf unzipped his bag and pulled out a battered deck covered in more stickers. "Gimme a few minutes," he said. "Talk among yerselves or somethin'."

Winterhawk settled back in a nearby chair where he could keep Flea in view in case anything went wrong. He watched as Ocelot and Virago resumed their pacing, chatting in low voices. It didn't surprise him that the two would find common ground, given their gang backgrounds. Though he doubted the Ancients and Ocelot's old gang had been friendly, strange situations made for strange bedfellows, and at least they had something they could talk about while both of them scanned the area compulsively for threats. It was definitely better than having them at each other's throats, which was the other possibility.

He turned his attention to Vyx. She stood slumped against a wall, her hands jammed into her pockets, appearing to examine a sculpture of a sinuous cat perched on a plinth, even though it was obvious her thoughts were far away. She didn't appear to notice him watching, so he took the opportunity to study her.

It was easy to see her elven mother reflected in her tall, lithe body, delicate but angular features, and pointed chin. She looked as if she were in motion even when standing still, and despite her exhaustion and several layers of grime and bruises from her travels, she had a confidence about her that reminded him of why Olivia had originally attracted him.

There was more, though. Part of him, even up until now after he'd seen her image on the holopic and then met her in person, hadn't wanted to believe what Olivia had told him. Some corner of his mind refused to accept that for all these years this woman who was every bit as much a part of him as she was of Olivia had been in the world, and he'd known nothing about her. He'd half-convinced himself that Olivia was deluded, or had found a way to fool his truth-detection magic, that the child wasn't his but had been the product of her time with one of her other lovers after they'd parted ways.

But now that he looked at her, really *saw* her, he could no longer deny it. He could see it in Victoria's—*Vyx's*, he reminded himself—eyes, in her strong jawline and straight nose, in the way she carried herself. The physical resemblance wasn't a strong one—certainly not strong enough that someone would notice it at a casual glance—but he couldn't deceive himself any longer. He took a long deep breath and let it out slowly as the enormity of the situation finally sank in.

"What're you lookin' at?"

Lost in his own thoughts, he hadn't noticed her turn toward him. Now, she watched him with narrowed eyes, her posture stiff and wary. "Nothing," he said. "Sorry. Just...thinking."

"About what?" She didn't approach him, but she did push herself off the wall in a fluid motion. "Looked to me like you were staring at me. You some kind of perv, too?"

He gave a grim chuckle. "Hardly."

"Coulda fooled me." She pulled a knife from her jacket and perched it on the tip of a finger, holding it with effortless balance as she continued to watch him. "So how much is Mom payin' you to drag me back home?"

"I told you—dragging you home was never the intention."

"Yeah, right." With a flick of her wrist, the knife flew into the air and came to rest on her opposite finger. "You're lying."

"I'm not," he said. "I don't know how I can prove that to you, but all we're to do is get you out of the QZ, and provide proof that we did so. After that, it's up to you what you decide."

She snorted. "Maybe so, but I know Mom. Once you tell her I'm out, she can set her usual corp dogs on me. So why the hell would I wanna go?"

Winterhawk glanced over to the other side of the room, where Ocelot and Virago had moved to give them some privacy. The two of them stood with their backs to the room, looking out the window toward the center's inner courtyard. "We can get her out too, you know," he said softly. "If that's what you want."

Her expression hardened for a second, then went back to narrow-eyed suspicion. She flicked the knife across again. "She wouldn't go," she said, her voice less confident than before.

"Why not?"

"Her family's here," she said with a shrug. "The Ancients. She'd never leave 'em."

"Not even to go with you?"

She glared. "I'm not goin' with you, so it doesn't matter, okay?"

"Are the Ancients your family too, Vyx?"

"That's none of your business!" She whirled, gripping the knife as if preparing to fling it at the wall, but then stopped herself and pocketed it instead. "You ask a lot of questions," she said, resuming her slumped posture against the wall. "Maybe it's time you answer some instead."

"If I can."

She studied him. "You never even told me your name. Your friend calls you 'Hawk.' That some kinda shadowrunner name?"

He chuckled. "It's short for Winterhawk. Ocelot favors economy of syllables. I suppose if I had it to do over again I'd have chosen something shorter, but it's too late to make a change now."

"You're a little old for a shadowrunner."

"That's not a question."

She threw herself down in a nearby chair. "Never seen a shadowrunner old enough to be my dad before, is all. I thought most of 'em got killed or retired before they got that old."

A tingle ran down Winterhawk's spine at her words. "I'm not exactly a shadowrunner—not anymore."

"Yeah? What are you, then? Mom got something on you? It'd either take that or a drekload of money to get *me* to break into the QZ if I wasn't already stuck in here."

"Looking for you is sort of a—side job. The original intent was to come in here to study the dragon ley line. When your mother found out about the planned expedition, she contacted me and asked me to look for you."

"How'd she know?" She frowned and pulled out the knife again, this time using the tip of the blade to clean beneath her short fingernails. She looked up at him, her features wreathed in suspicion. "She didn't just call you randomly, did she? She *knows* you."

Winterhawk couldn't decide whether to be dismayed or proud that she was that quick even after everything that had happened to her. He figured that, at least, was worth a bit of truth. "Yes. We've known each other for a while. I've...done some work for her in the past."

"Really?" Maya's amused voice spoke in his mind as she shimmered into visibility in his lap. *"That's what you're going with?"*

"Hush, you."

"So you used to be a shadowrunner," Vyx said, eyeing the cat.

"I still dabble occasionally. These days I'm mostly a researcher."

Almost as if realizing she was relaxing her guard around him, she glared again. "Well, whatever you are, you're not takin' me out of here against my will. If you try, you'll regret it."

She glanced toward Ocelot and Virago, then past them to the window. "You got any idea why those other things were chasin' us? Why Beatrix turned into that...thing?" She shuddered. "I've never seen anything like that before, and I don't wanna ever again."

He shrugged. "It sounds like you might have stumbled into something they didn't want you involved with. If the toxics are doing something out here related to the BAD trade, having someone show up asking questions about it wouldn't sit well. I'm sure they didn't expect you to get away from them."

"So you think they'll still come after us," she said. For the first time, she looked uncertain.

"I think we'd better do what we can to deal with them," Winterhawk said. He followed her gaze over toward the window. "I won't lie to you—your help, and your friend's, will be appreciated. We might be able to deal with whatever it is on our own, or with the help of some of the witches if they're willing—but I can't be sure of that until I know what we're facing."

Vyx got up and jammed her hands back in her jacket pockets. "So what happens if we don't help? If I just said thanks for the save and the gear, but we're outta here? Would you try to stop us?"

Winterhawk stood as well, and Maya drifted to his shoulder. Vyx was so much like him—stubborn, restless, never still. He understood now why she dismayed her mother so much, why the two of them could never see eye to eye on anything.

"No," he said at last. "I wouldn't. You're free to do as you like. But I'm asking you to help us, and save your decision until after we've found out whether we need to deal with this situation. It might be that we don't. Technically, nothing that's happened so far has been our concern. I can do my study of the ley line, you can go back and report to Lucky Liam about what you've found, and we can go our separate ways."

"You'd let me do that."

"Of course I would. As I mentioned, I'll ask you to record something I can take back to your mother. I think you owe us that, for saving your arses out in the Wilds."

"Yeah..." she muttered in obvious reluctance. She let out another loud sigh. "Yeah, I guess we do. Okay, then—temporary truce. But I'm tellin' you—if you try to make me do anything, or try pervin' on me—"

"Trust me," he said, chuckling. "You're not my type. You needn't worry about that. And you have my word, I told you. No coercion. I—"

"Hey, guys?"

Flea was looking up from his deck, frowning. His bright red hair looked even redder against his pale face.

All four of them hurried over next to where he and Melinda had been seated at a small table. "Did you find something?" Winterhawk demanded.

"Yeah. You guys are gonna owe me more than two hundred for this."

FORTY

"Let's hear it," Winterhawk said. "We'll discuss terms after we know what you found."

Flea looked at Melinda, who shrugged. His fingers danced over the keys on his deck, and an AR window flashed up. "Some of this was hard to make sense of," he said. "She had more encryption on it than you said there'd be, but I'm not sure it was hers. I think it might have been put on there by somebody else."

"Like somebody gave her the comm?" Ocelot asked.

"Yeah. Anyway—she kept a journal, just boring stuff like her work plans for the day and that kind of thing. But she also had another, hidden journal. That was where the encryption was. It sounds like she was keepin' progress reports for somebody."

"The DIMR?" Winterhawk leaned in for a closer look. "That's who she worked for."

Flea shook his head. "She referred to them a lot in the regular journal. She didn't mention anybody else in the secret one, but it was pretty clear from the entries that they weren't the same corp. Also that she wasn't workin' for the other one for long, far's I can tell."

"Interesting," Winterhawk said. "Makes sense, though—she wasn't happy about my coming along on the trip, and she didn't make any secret of that."

"You think somebody made her a better offer?" Vyx asked.

"Quite likely." He studied the AR window, which was flashing text by faster than the naked eye could follow it. "Flea, can you tell what she was doing? The original mission was to study the ley line—do you see any data on that?"

A different file popped up, showing columns of numbers and rotating charts. "She came to Salem," he said. "Looks like she's got a lot of data here, but she found something that she didn't expect. Here's where it gets interesting, and why you're gonna owe me more money." He waved his hand, and a second AR window joined the first. Like its counterpart, it included figures and charts, but the new ones didn't look the same. A video appeared below it, showing Doris Wu in a room they didn't recognize. "This is a partial file. Looks like some of it was corrupted."

The recording quality was choppy and the audio was bad, but Flea made a couple adjustments and it improved somewhat.

Wu began speaking in mid-sentence. *"–initial scans tend to support your hypothesis. Readings aren't strong at this distance, and likely wouldn't be noticed by anyone not looking for them specifically. I have made contact with a local female mage who was quite concerned at the information I shared with her. She has set up a meeting for this evening with several of her fellow coven members to discuss the situation further."*

Flea hit a key. "Here's the next one, from later that day."

Wu appeared again, against a different background. *"Meeting tonight went well. The coven members are concerned about the level of toxic magic detectable in the ley line's aspect, even to such a minor degree. I must go back to Boston tonight–a few hours are all I can spare without arousing the others' suspicions. I should be able to get away for a while tomorrow to come back and get some actual readings. I plan to reach out to my contact here again and see if I can convince her and perhaps others to accompany me into the Wilds long enough to get better data."*

"What's the date on that file?" Winterhawk asked. When Flea flashed it up, he nodded. "That's consistent with the attack. It's not possible to confirm the exact date of the attack since the bodies were compromised—but it sounds as if she returned to Boston so the others on the team wouldn't be suspicious of her actions."

"So how did they hit her with that sending?" Ocelot asked. Then his eyes narrowed. "One of the witches she met with was a plant."

"It appears that way," Winterhawk said. "At least one. In order to pull this off, the toxics would need to have agents in other covens, to keep them up to date on any possible opposition. They probably worked out a way to get a ritual sample from her while she was here." He met Ocelot's gaze. "But that's not the frightening part of all this."

"What is?" Virago asked.

"What they're trying to do. The ley line is currently aspected toward dragon magic, due to Damon's influence, and the witches are divided between those who support that and those who don't. But now we've got a third group in play, who are apparently trying to—"

"Change it to toxic magic?" Ocelot stared. "Holy drek, 'Hawk, that's insane. I don't know that much about magic, but wouldn't it take a massive amount of energy to change a whole ley line's aspect?"

"It would indeed," Winterhawk said. He paused a moment, trying to get his mind around the enormity of the situation. "They can't be that far along yet, or someone would have noticed. And likely they're not trying to change the entire ley line—that would be nearly impossible—but just a subset of it. Even so, the energy required would be immense. They've got to be planning something big."

"Like what?" Vyx asked, looking interested in spite of her obvious plan to maintain her studied indifference around the two shadowrunners. "What could they do to get that kind of energy?"

Winterhawk pondered, considering the possibilities before answering. He knew of several methods that might work, but most of them wouldn't be practical for the situation at hand—they would require the kind of preparation that would be difficult to miss, materials that would be impractical to obtain within the QZ, or a truly staggering number of participants to pull off.

He was convinced that, despite their infiltration of at least some of the other covens, they were still a relatively small group— the various Salem covens weren't known for their cooperation, but most of them were wise enough to put aside their differences against a truly dangerous threat. The fact that they hadn't meant either that something had changed regarding their level of potential cooperation, or they were simply unaware of the threat.

So if none of those methods were plausible, that left only one other that fit the parameters as he knew them. A chill ran up his spine and settled at the base of his skull. "I think they're using the spirit."

"What spirit?" Vyx asked.

"The big wolf thing?" Ocelot stared.

Winterhawk nodded, still trying to work out the possible details. Every time he added something new, the situation got worse. "I didn't get a good look at it before it ran off, but I'll lay odds that if it's that big and conceals its nature that well, it's a powerful great-form toxic spirit. Probably free. I've heard rumors of its existence before, but nothing substantiated. In fact, I wouldn't be the least bit surprised if it's actually the spirit, not the head of that coven, who's running the show. If that's what Wu was investigating and she found out the truth, it's no wonder they killed her."

"Wait a sec," Virago said, frowning. "Sorry—not really a magic girl. Our guys pretty much shoot fireballs and stuff, and the spirits they summon help us out in fights. I don't get how a spirit's gonna help them...do whatever it is you're talkin' about with this ley line thing."

"Some spirits—and at that level, this one is almost certainly one of them—have a gateway ability. They can open portals to other metaplanes, and allow others to use them to pass between our plane and that one."

"So—" Virago pressed.

"Oh, blessed spirits," Melinda said, gripping the edge of the table where Flea was still tapping away at his deck. "You think the plan is to open a gateway to whatever toxic plane that thing comes from."

"And use the energy, probably along with some kind of ritual, to shift the aspect of that part of the ley line," Winterhawk confirmed, nodding.

"And maybe bus in a few more of those things in the process?" Ocelot asked.

"Almost certainly," Winterhawk said. "Except that it's probably a lot more, not a few. And I doubt they'll stop with their little bit of the ley line, wherever it might be. Eventually, they'll have their sights on Salem as well, and possibly more."

FORTY-ONE

"So what do we do?" Ocelot asked. "Is there even a chance we can stop this?"

"Depends on a lot of factors we have no way of knowing." Winterhawk was back to pacing. "How powerful that spirit is, how far along they are in their plans, and how many others they've managed to recruit. From our side, we've got to take into account how much help we can get, and there's also the matter of actually *finding* where they're setting up. I'm betting it's out in the Wilds, and they'll have it well guarded."

"We know the general direction," Vyx said. "Beatrix—the real one—sent us a file. That's why we were out there in the first place. But bits of it were corrupted, so we don't have the exact spot."

"It's a start," Ocelot said.

"We should be able to get a lot of help, right?" Vyx asked. "This is a pretty big threat, if you're right. And it's right in their fraggin' backyard. If that's not enough to get them off their asses—"

"Yes," Melinda said, looking troubled, "but remember—there are a lot of witches around the area, but relatively few of them are trained or even prepared for something like this. Just because they can do magic doesn't mean they have any idea what to do in a fight. I'm not sure how many of them you could count on."

"Or even if we'd wanna bring them along, if they can't fight," Ocelot said. "Not only would they be useless, they'd get in the way."

Winterhawk had to reluctantly agree. He'd been a shadowrunner for so long that even now, when he was mostly out of the business, most of the magicians he interacted with when traveling the world hunting down magical phenomena were at least somewhat combat-ready. He knew a few among the Salem witches who could handle themselves well in a fight, but most of them, as Melinda had said, were merely everyday citizens who happened to have magical ability. If he tried to take them into a fight like this, even if they were willing, he'd be leading them into a massacre. And there was also the matter that apparently the toxics had infiltrated agents into at least some of the other covens, which meant trusting anyone without careful vetting could be dangerous.

He sighed. "Give me a few minutes," he said. "I need to think about this. Please keep an eye out for anyone who might be approaching."

As he expected, Ocelot followed him. Winterhawk didn't acknowledge his presence until he'd drifted off down the hall and into a side room containing a small conference table and several chairs. He leaned his forehead against a window that looked out into a wooded glen and sighed.

"There's something you're not saying," Ocelot said. He joined Winterhawk at the window.

"There are a lot of things I'm not saying."

"Wanna share any of 'em with the class?"

He didn't, not really. But he knew from experience that Ocelot wouldn't let it go, so he pushed himself off the window. "One of them is that we're laboring under a core assumption that might not even be accurate."

"What's that?"

"That we even *should* be doing anything about this."

Ocelot's eyes narrowed, but then he nodded slowly. "Yeah," he said after a pause, glancing at the door and then back at the window.

Winterhawk threw himself into one of the chairs. "This isn't our problem. No one's paying us to hunt down and root out a nest of toxic spirits in Salem. Our job—*my* job—was to study the ley line and report back on it."

"And get Vyx out," Ocelot added.

"That's a side consideration, and not related directly to what we're doing here. But I've got enough readings and notes on the ley line already that if I report my findings back to the DIMR, I'll have more than earned what they're paying me. At that point, it's up to them whether they want to mount another expedition to do something about it."

"What about Damon?" Ocelot didn't turn back toward Winterhawk. "You don't want to piss off a dragon. You gonna tell him anything?"

"Of course. We can report back to him as well. Perhaps he might have a vested interest in dealing with someone trying to re-aspect the ley line to toxic magic. And he's certainly better equipped to do it than we are."

"You think he'll keep his word and find us a way out?"

Winterhawk shrugged. "He's a dragon. Who knows what he'll do? But despite my disapproval of some of his business choices, everything I've ever heard about him indicates he honors his word."

"So, what, we just say, 'Sorry, witches, you've got some kind of toxic apocalypse brewing up in your backyard, but we're outta here. Good luck!'?" Ocelot's tone indicated that, despite his flippant words, he wouldn't necessarily have a problem if Winterhawk decided to take it that way.

"I don't know yet." Winterhawk stared down at the table under his hands. It was made of real wood and probably at least two hundred years old, scarred and worn but lovingly polished and maintained. "On one hand, we could be marching to our deaths with our eyes wide open if we go after them. On the other—if they don't know we're coming, we might be able to catch them by surprise, which might be our best chance of dealing with them. And there's also the matter that I have friends in Salem—and no illusions that if the toxics are successful in re-aspecting the ley line, they're not going to settle for corrupting BADs. That's not the way toxics work. They'll want to spread their influence."

Ocelot studied him for several seconds. "Okay, that's one thing. What's the rest?"

Sometimes, Winterhawk wished his friend didn't know him so well. There were few people in the world who knew him well enough to see through him when he was trying to hide something; unfortunately he'd been through too many nasty situations with Ocelot to even make a token effort. Ocelot might be about as magically active as your average heavy pistol, but he was one of the most perceptive mundanes Winterhawk had ever encountered. You didn't get much past him.

"Vyx," he said heavily.

"What about her?" Ocelot glanced toward the door.

"This is even less her fight than it is ours."

"Lucky Liam *did* send her up here to check out what was up with the BADs."

"Not really, and you know it. He wanted to get her the hell out of there before someone killed her or forced his hand and made him turf her out of the Ancients. The BADs were just an excuse to give her a place to go while the hotheads cooled down."

Ocelot leaned against the table and shoved his hands into his jacket pockets. "So you don't want to take her along if we do this."

"I don't know." Winterhawk shrugged a shoulder. "She's capable, that's certain. So is Virago. They'd be good to have around in a fight. They've got the right to make their own decision, once they know what they're likely to be up against."

"I think you're gonna have a hard time keeping her away. She's prickly enough about us as it is—if she thinks we're tryin' to hide something from her..."

"I know." Winterhawk sighed, bowing his head. Suddenly, all his exhaustion from the past few days was catching up with him, and the compulsion to crawl under the table and sleep for two or three days was overpowering. "I know. But..."

"But she's your daughter, and you want to keep her safe," Ocelot said quietly.

He nodded without looking up. He had no idea where this feeling was coming from, and it was more than a little bit disturbing. All his life, he'd had no parental instinct whatsoever. He'd been far too much of a free spirit, too addicted to new experiences, world travel, and variety to ever consider tying himself down even with a serious relationship. The thought of ever having a child— and further, actually *caring* about that child to the point that he'd risk his own life for her—was so foreign to him that it seemed as if another consciousness had invaded his brain. Hell, he barely knew Vyx. He'd only known she even *existed* for a few days, and had only met her face to face less than a day ago. How could these feelings be so strong already?

It didn't matter how, though. "Yes," he said, his voice full of resignation and weariness. "I don't—"

"Uh—'Hawk?"

Winterhawk glanced up at Ocelot's odd tone. His friend wasn't looking at him.

He was looking at the open doorway.

Vyx stood there, staring at him, eyes wide, fists clenched. Her face was a mask of rage.

"You fuckin' *bastard!*"

FORTY-TWO

Before either Winterhawk or Ocelot could react, Vyx was a blur of motion. In an instant she was in front of Winterhawk, and in the next instant she'd picked him up by the front of his coat and flung him across the room. He crashed into the wall with a *thud* and slid down, stunned.

"Vyx, I—" he began raggedly.

"No!" she screamed. "*Shut up!* I don't want to hear a damn thing from you, you lying shitwipe! Why didn't you *tell* me you were my father? And to think I was gonna *trust* you! I should kill you right now!"

Ocelot was another blur as he vaulted toward her, but Vyx was ready for him. She ducked under his grab and dashed out the door. "Don't fuckin' *follow* me!" she yelled, and slammed the door so hard the walls shook. The sound of her fast-moving footsteps faded quickly.

Winterhawk struggled back to his feet, shaking his head to try to clear it. She hadn't hurt him badly—his armor, both physical and magical, had taken the brunt of the impact—but his head reeled. He didn't think it was entirely from hitting it on the wall, either.

Ocelot hurried over and dragged him the rest of the way up, dropping him into a chair. "Well, fuck," he said, glancing toward the door. "Want me to go after her?"

Winterhawk shook his head and quickly got up. "Bloody hell," he murmured. "I was a fool. I should have thought she might be listening—set Maya to watch the hallway—" He was already moving toward the door. "Come on—we have to hurry."

He half expected Vyx to still be out front, venting her rage to Virago, but she wasn't. The ganger was already moving fast, gathering her gear—including a couple of the guns Ocelot had provided.

"What the hell did you *do* to her?" she snarled at Winterhawk and Ocelot.

"It doesn't matter," Winterhawk said. "We have to find her."

"Like hell *we* do." Virago zipped up her bag and slung it over her shoulder. She pulled a heavy pistol from her pocket and pointed it at the two runners. "Sounds like you assholes have done enough. I'm goin' after her. You stay here."

"Virago—" Winterhawk began.

She looked at the gun, looked at the two of them, and obviously thought better of her idea. "You stay here," she repeated more quietly, stowing the gun back in her pocket. "Vyx can be a hothead sometimes, but if she senses you two on her tail, she'll just run. Lemme find her and talk her down."

Winterhawk wanted to protest. He wanted to run out there, find Vyx, and explain things to her. Damn the mission. And twice-damn Olivia, who'd obviously been feeding her daughter all sorts of lies about him. Probably for most of the girl's life. If they got out of here, he would have words with her, and they wouldn't be pleasant ones.

But Virago was right, and he knew it. "Go," he said wearily. "Find her. Bring her back. Tell her it's not the way she thinks it is."

"And be careful," Ocelot added. "Those things are still out there."

Virago nodded and was gone.

Winterhawk turned back to Melinda and Flea, who'd been watching the scene with wide-eyed confusion. "Come on," he said. "We need to go back to Althea's place."

"What are you planning to do?" Melinda asked. She glanced toward the door. "And what about those two?"

Once again, 'Hawk shoved down the feeling that he should forget about the toxic threat until Vyx was back safe. "They'll be all right," he said, and hoped he was right. "I'll leave a spirit here in case they come back. If they're not back by the time we get over there, I'll send Maya after them."

He wanted to do it now, but reluctantly sent his ally spirit the instruction to wait. Vyx already didn't trust him—sending spirits to stalk her would be almost as bad as going himself. For now, he'd just have to make himself useful and count on Virago, who knew Vyx far better than he did, to handle the situation. "We have to let the others know what's going on—if we can figure out who we can trust."

FORTY-THREE

Vyx ran.

She didn't pay any attention to *where* she ran. She didn't care.

That wasn't entirely true: she *did* care. Anywhere was fine, as long as it was as far away from *him* as possible.

Her feet moved by rote, eating up the distance with swift efficiency as her brain screamed with a rage that threatened to overwhelm her. She couldn't form a coherent thought through the red haze of anger. Her fists clenched as she ran, and her mind flashed visions of *his* face as she closed them around his neck, squeezing the life from him.

How had she been so *stupid*? She'd been wrong to trust him even before she knew the truth. Her mother had sent him and his friend after her—why had she expected that they'd keep their word and not try to drag her back home? Shadowrunners did what they were paid to do, and they didn't have any problem lying about it if it made their targets easier to deal with.

She'd almost fallen for it. Thank the spirits she'd begun to have second thoughts after they'd gone off to talk privately—why would they have anything to hide from the rest of the group if they didn't plan to double-cross them? She'd drifted down the hall, silent as a light breeze, counting on the fact that they trusted her more than she trusted them.

And when she'd heard what the other one had said... *"She's your daughter, and you want to keep her safe."*

That British bastard was her *father*! The one who'd left her and her mother when he found out she was pregnant. The one who used to beat Mom up—or maybe even worse.

The one who was supposed to be dead.

And now here he was, working for her mother to get her out of the QZ.

She slowed, just a bit, as another realization hit her:

Was he?

Some of the rage ebbed away—she never could maintain that kind of anger for long—to let in a thrill of dread. What if her father *wasn't* working for her mother at all? What if he'd somehow found out she existed and was coming after her for his own reasons? What if Mom didn't know anything about this?

She skidded to a stop, only now taking notice of her surroundings. She stood in the middle of a derelict residential neighborhood full of small apartment buildings and tiny, ramshackle homes. A light rain fell, and a couple of kids stood on the other side of the street, staring at her. She had no idea how far she was from where she'd started, but knowing how fast she could run, she'd put a good bit of distance between them.

Growling in frustration, she spun away from the kids and pounded her fists on a gnarled oak tree. What the hell was she going to do now?

She was glancing around to see if anyone other than the kids was paying attention to her when her comm buzzed.

Was *he* trying to call her? Did he honestly think there was anything he could say that would lure her back now? She snatched the device from her pocket and glared at the incoming number.

It wasn't him. Virago's familiar code flashed on the screen.

"What?" she demanded, and instantly regretted her confrontational tone. As much as everything had gone to hell, none of it was her girlfriend's fault. "Sorry," she mumbled. "Little stressed out right now."

"Ya think?" Virago drawled. *"Where are you?"*

"I dunno."

"So you just took off like an idiot in some random direction and got lost? Vyx, you know those toxic guys are after us. What the hell is going on, anyway?"

"Hang on a second." Vyx pulled up an AR map window and studied it for a moment, noting the positions of her own dot and Virago's. "Okay, we're not far apart. I'll come to you." She started walking as she talked. "But I'm not goin' back there to *them*."

"Dammit, Vyx, tell me what's going on! Why did you run off like that? Did they try to attack you or somethin'?"

"What'd he tell you?"

"Who?"

"*Him!* Winterhawk! Who the hell *else*?" Subconsciously, her pace quickened as her heart began pounding faster again. "What'd he tell you?"

"Nothing! Vyx, get a grip, damn it! I told 'em to stay there and wait. Now are you gonna tell me what–"

"He's my father."

"What?"

"You heard me." Vyx watched the dot move closer to Virago on the AR screen. They were less than two blocks away from each other now. She hoped Winterhawk hadn't sent that damned cat-thing of his after her. "I heard him talkin' with that other guy, Ocelot. He's my *dad*."

"I thought your dad was dead!"

"Yeah, well, so did I. Listen, Virago—we gotta go. We gotta get out of here. We know what's going on with the ley line and the BADs now. We can go back and tell Liam—"

"How're we gonna do that? We don't even have—"

Static popped and crackled on the line.

"Virago?"

"Hey! What the hell—" Virago's voice punched through the static, bright with fear.

The sound of screeching tires.

Gunfire.

"Virago!" Vyx took off in the direction of Virago's dot. Adrenaline and magical power surged through her body, submerging aches, pains, and exhaustion. Her feet barely touched the pavement as she dashed headlong toward her girlfriend. "I'm coming!" she yelled. "Get away from there!"

Only a few seconds later she heard the gunfire in real time, just ahead of her. Skidding around a corner, she spotted a black van, its back door open and two figures in black armor leaning out, on top of where Virago's dot still showed up on her AR window. As she watched in horror, one of the men hit Virago with something that made her slump to the ground. The other one grabbed her and hustled her into the van, which was already moving off and gaining speed. The red dot disappeared.

"Virago!" Vyx screamed. She poured on more power, more speed, running so fast she wasn't sure she could stop without tumbling head over heels or smashing into a tree or a parked car. Her vision was fixed on the van's receding form, ignoring everything else around her.

Gunfire sounded again, this time from the back of the van. Something flashed, and something tore into Vyx's shoulder, slipping in past the open front of her armored jacket. Pain lit up her right side as she stumbled, lost her balance and went down, rolling over and over until she slammed into something hard.

The last thing she saw before she blacked out was the van fading into the distance and disappearing over a rise.

FORTY-FOUR

Althea's place was only ten minutes from the community center, but to Winterhawk it felt like they were taking all day to get there. He sat slumped in the Jeep's shotgun seat, fighting the increasingly more difficult urge to send Maya or some other spirit out to find Vyx and bring her back.

"That isn't helping, you know," Maya said gently in his mind. *"She can take care of herself. She's a tough young lady."*

"I know that," he said wryly, rubbing the back of his head where his daughter had tossed him into the wall. *"But this isn't a normal situation. She's a university student. Even if she's been running with the Ancients for a few months, that doesn't prepare her to deal with something like these toxics."*

"She's only been gone a few minutes. You know I'll find her for you if she doesn't—"

His comm buzzed in his pocket.

For a second, insanely, he thought it might be the spirit calling from the community center with news that Vyx had returned. He snatched it up. "Yes?"

"Help..."

The voice was weak, fading, but terrifyingly familiar. *"Vyx?"*

"They got Virago...Please..."

"Vyx, where are you? What's happened?"

A long pause, and then: *"Dad...please. You gotta help me..."*

"Vyx!" Everybody in the Jeep was staring at him now. He ignored them. *"Maya. Find her!"*

"On it, Boss."

"And be careful! It might be a trap."

Maya found her almost immediately, huddled in some bushes a few blocks away. Ocelot broke several speed laws getting there, but slowed down as they got closer. "You sure this isn't a setup?" he asked, trying to look everywhere at once.

Inexplicably, the police hadn't arrived yet. Perhaps they were understaffed, dealing with crimes in other parts of town, or—as in many larger cities—it took more than scattered gunfire to draw them out.

Even with his mind screaming for him to get to Vyx as fast as possible, Winterhawk hadn't forgotten the situation they were dealing with. He was already assensing the area, and in the back seat Melinda was doing the same thing.

"I don't see anything," he said. "Cover me." Without waiting for a reply, he leaped out of the Jeep and ran toward the wild clump of bushes in a vacant lot between two apartment buildings.

She was right where Maya said she was, her back pressed against the side of a building where she'd clearly dragged herself. He wondered how far she'd had to go—the light rain had already washed away any blood trail she might have left. Her legs were drawn up tightly to her chest, and the right side of her jacket was dark with blood. She'd torn off the bottom part of her T-shirt and fashioned a makeshift compress she held in place with a shaking left hand, and her right hand clutched her commlink.

He burst through and dropped down next to her, heedless of the muddy ground. "Vyx!"

Her expression was a mix of apprehension and relief. "You came."

"Of course I came. The others are here too. Come on—let's get you somewhere safe so we can take care of that shoulder."

"They've got Virago!" She tried to struggle up, but paled and sank back. Sweat stood out on her forehead and her voice shook with fatigue. "We have to find her!"

"We will," he said. "But it's not safe here." He stood and used a gentle levitation spell to lift her free of the bushes. "I promise— we'll find her."

"I didn't know if you'd come," she mumbled as he directed her floating form toward the Jeep and the waiting hands of Melinda and Flea.

"Why wouldn't I come? You know the truth now—I'm your father."

"Mom told me...you..." Her voice was fading now. She winced as Melinda carefully helped lower her into the back and covered her with a blanket from the cargo area.

Winterhawk waved Flea into the front and took the back seat next to her. "Yes, well, we'll be needing to have a conversation about your mother and what she's told you. But not now. Let's get you sorted out and get Virago back first, shall we?"

"Yeah..." She drifted, her head in Melinda's lap. The witch's eyes were closed, her lips moving. She was already beginning a healing spell. "Yeah...Thanks."

Winterhawk sent a spirit ahead to let Althea know what was happening, so by the time they reached her house and helped Vyx inside, she'd prepared a spot on her sofa.

"I'm okay," Vyx said, waving them off. She still looked pale and tired, but Melinda's healing spell had taken care of the worst of the gunshot wound. "We're wasting time. We need to find Virago before they kill her! I tried to call her...I think they messed up her comm...no signal. They probably already *have* killed her!"

"I don't think so," Winterhawk said. "Sit down and tell us what happened. Quickly, but don't leave anything out."

As Althea fussed around her, setting her up with a cup of hot tea and a bowl of soup, she told them what had happened after she ran away from the community center. "They were in a black van," she told Winterhawk and Ocelot, who were both listening intently to her story. "They hit her with something and dragged her into the van. I couldn't catch them. I wasn't fast enough..." she stared disconsolately into her soup, poking at it with her spoon.

"None of us are at our best right now," Winterhawk said. "And they'd probably have killed you if you got closer. The good news is, I don't think she's dead. Not yet."

"Why not?" Her gaze came up. "They've already tried to kill us twice before. Why wouldn't they now?"

"If they wanted her dead, they'd just have killed her," Ocelot said. "Dumped her in the street to find, and probably wouldn't have left until they were sure you were dead, too."

Winterhawk nodded. "They want her for something. Possibly to lure us to come after her. Possibly something else. I don't know. But it means we've got some time." He looked around the room at Althea first and then at Melinda and Flea, who sat off to the side, clearly unsure of what to do. "Melinda. Althea. We can't do this alone. This affects everyone around here. Trust me—if the toxics are able to finish their plans, it won't end well for anyone who isn't on their side. You've got contacts among the other covens—do you think you can call them? Convince them to meet with us?"

Melinda looked skeptical. "I know some people, sure—I mean, most of the witches know each other at least in passing. But getting them to work together? That'll be harder."

"I'm afraid she's right," Althea said, nodding ruefully. "Most of them have never been involved in anything like this in their lives. I doubt you'll be able to convince them to—"

Winterhawk stood and began pacing the room. He knew both of them were right; this wasn't going to be easy. "Can you try? This affects them—they have a right to know, at least, even if all they want to do is leave town. Just contact them, the leaders of the largest pro-dragon covens. Don't tell them why, though—don't mention the toxics. And don't go in person."

"Why pro-dragon only?" Melinda asked.

"Just a hunch—I think the pro-dragon covens would be less inclined to want to re-aspect the ley line away from dragon magic."

Althea nodded. "That makes sense. Though they could have spies among them as well. Remember Beatrix."

"I don't think that thing was really Beatrix. And I know, we've already established that there are spies everywhere. But we've got to do something, and soon."

"You're gonna have to tell them where the meeting is," Ocelot pointed out. "If some of them *are* spies—"

"We'll meet somewhere first," he said. "Once we move, we'll have to do it fast—not just to find Virago, but to move on them before they know we're coming and have time to prepare."

"Move *where,* though?" Ocelot asked. "You don't know where they are. You can't do a ritual to find Virago—you don't even know she's wherever they are."

"Somebody will know," Winterhawk said. "Hell, if we *do* discover a spy in the group, that might work in our favor."

"How so?" Althea asked.

"Because they'll know where the base is," he said grimly. "And at this point, there's no way they'll be able to keep that knowledge from me."

FORTY-FIVE

Melinda, Althea, and Flea got the word out to trusted leaders of the largest pro-dragon covens, and were able to set up a meeting at the community center an hour later. By they time they headed over in Ocelot's Jeep, the sun was going down and the day's drizzly rain had turned into a brisk downpour.

Vyx sat in the back seat next to Winterhawk, who'd given up his usual shotgun spot to ride with her. "I don't like any of this," she muttered.

Winterhawk nodded. "It's a lot to take in. You've had your worldview well and truly buggered up over the last few days."

Her eyes came up to meet his, and her face was troubled. "I don't even know what to think anymore. About you, about me—about anything."

"We'll talk later—I promise. I want to know what your mother's told you about me. But I can tell you almost certainly that most of it isn't true."

She glared at him. "Why should I believe that? Mom and I might not get along—well, at all, really—but she always treated me well enough. She tried to do what she thought was best for me, even though she never even tried to understand what I was about. But you—where were you?"

"We don't have time to go into that properly now," he said, glancing out the window. He had Maya and another spirit on patrol around the Jeep to make sure nothing approached them without warning, and had sent another ahead to talk to the guard spirits at the community center. As much as he wanted to put everything else on hold and take the time to give the conversation with Vyx the attention it deserved, that wasn't a luxury they could afford right now. His theory about Virago—that the toxics had taken her for some reason—was only that: a theory. For all he knew, they could have killed her already and dumped her body somewhere it would never be found. But if he was right, the longer they waited to act, the higher the chance that something would go wrong.

He put his hand on Vyx's shoulder and turned toward her. "I promise you, Vyx: we *will* talk. And I will tell you my side of the story. Every bit of it. After that, you can make your own decision about what you want to do going forward. All right?"

She nodded miserably. "I just keep feeling like if I hadn't been such an idiot and stormed off like that, none of this would have happened. That's why I'm up here in Salem in the first place—because I do stuff without thinking and get other people killed. If Virago's dead because of me—"

"Enough of that," he said. "Learning the truth the way you did was a shock—that wasn't the way I planned to tell you. I don't blame you for being angry."

"*Were* you planning to tell me?" Again, she glared at him. "Would you have, or just got me out of there and let me go on thinking you were just some guy my mom hired? Or did she even hire you at all?"

"She did," he said. "Though 'hire' isn't the proper word, since I refused to take her money once she told me who you were." He rubbed the back of his head and smiled ruefully. "If I had any doubt before that she was telling me the truth, I don't now. It appears you've inherited *something* from me, at least."

"Uh...sorry about that," she mumbled. "When I get mad, I kinda—go off."

"Oh? I hadn't noticed."

She didn't exactly grin—it was more a faint exasperated smile—but that was all right for now.

Winterhawk refused to reveal the reason for calling the coven leaders together until all of them had arrived. They sat now—seven of them, five women and two men—looking uniformly suspicious and confused.

"All right, we're here," an imperious-looking elf man in a black collarless jacket said from the front row. "What's the meaning of all this? "

"I apologize for the short notice and the lack of information." Winterhawk paced back and forth across the front of the room while Maya, sitting on the lectern, followed him with her glowing green gaze. "I'm sure you'll forgive me when you hear what I've got to say."

"When did you even get into town?" another, a dwarf woman with flowing blond hair, asked. "I hadn't heard anything about you being in the QZ."

"And why have you got all these new spirits here?" asked a young, slender human woman in a T-shirt featuring a cartoon cat on a broom. She glanced around, clearly assensing the room.

"Time is short," Winterhawk said, "so I'll get right to it." He resumed his pacing, exchanging glances with Althea and Melinda, who sat in the back row, and Ocelot, who slouched near the door keeping watch out one of the side windows. Flea sat all the way in the back, tapping away at his deck, cycling through nearby street cameras to ensure that nobody could sneak up on them. Vyx stalked back and forth along the back wall like a caged animal; her impatience and concern couldn't have been more obvious if she'd been waving signs. "You're all in danger, and I don't think any of you know how much."

The elf man snorted. "Danger? Of course we're in danger. We have been since the walls went up. What's new now?"

A few of the others murmured in agreement.

"I assume you've heard about what happened at the Black Cat Tavern recently?"

That sobered them up. "Rumors," said the dwarf woman. "Something about toxic spirits. But I don't know if I believe it."

"Believe it," Ocelot said from the back of the room.

"And you are?" the elf man asked, wrinkling his elegant nose in contempt. "Winterhawk, this is all very—"

"And you know about the Westhaven coven's new leader, and her wolf companion, yes?" the mage interrupted, pitching his voice louder to get over the elf's.

Again they nodded, muttering to each other. "We don't know much about her," said a chubby ork, the only other male in the group. "There's a lot of suspicion that she's bad news, and it's just about been confirmed that the wolf is actually a spirit, but they keep to themselves."

"The wolf is more than a spirit," Winterhawk said. "We believe it's actually a great form toxic spirit—possibly free—and Sabeetha is a toxic shaman. It's possible that the wolf is actually running the show."

They stared at him. "You can't be serious," said the dwarf woman. "Surely we'd have known—"

"Would you?" Melinda asked from the back row. "It's good at hiding itself, and you said yourself that you never bothered to check. I didn't either. None of us did, because even though we can be a bunch of busybody gossips about everyday things, we stay out of each other's way for the serious stuff. Even the big stuff, most of the time, like the...dragon issues."

"So what's this all mean?" the ork asked. "Yes, okay, toxics are a danger. Sounds like we need to find out more about this coven, and take care of 'em if they cause trouble. But why is this a big deal all of a sudden? They've been here for a while now—at least a few weeks—and nothing's happened. Why now?"

Winterhawk took a deep breath. This was going to be a lot for them to swallow, and he had no idea how they would take it. He also couldn't be completely certain none of them were spies, though after being scanned by himself, Maya, two more of his spirits, Althea, Melinda, and their own summoned spirits, he figured they'd have to be doing some world-class deception to hide any toxic traces. "Because we've found out some other information about their plans. An associate of mine was killed by a toxic ritual sending after she tried to investigate, but we were able to obtain her commlink, containing her suspicions and findings." He paused his pacing and faced them. "This is bad, people. They're trying to re-aspect the ley line toward toxic magic."

For a moment, all they could do was stare at him. He'd instructed his spirits and Maya to keep a close eye on them when he revealed the truth, to look for anyone who didn't appear surprised, or who responded with anything other than shock and amazement.

None of them did.

The elegant elf was the first speak, after silence hung in the air for several long seconds. "You...can't be serious."

"I can show you the video file if it would help."

"That's impossible," the dwarf woman said. "How could they hide something like that from us? They couldn't! Someone would notice."

"We think whatever they're doing, they're doing it out in the Wilds somewhere," Winterhawk said. "There's no way they could do it with a single ritual, or even a few—even if we're right and that *is* a great form toxic spirit directing the activity. I've been told nobody goes out into the Wilds anymore, at least not very far. That it's gotten too dangerous. Is that right?"

Another witch, an ork woman with multicolored hair and tattoos running up and down both arms, nodded. "The magic's gone wilder than usual out there since the wall's gone up—not to mention the corps are using it as a dumping ground for their failed experiments. Most of the covens I've talked to have taken to doing their rituals closer to town, to be safe."

"So you think they're out there someplace doing—what? Multiple rituals designed to change the ley line? How could they even *do* that so quickly?" The dwarf woman slapped her hands on the table. "That's *crazy.*"

But a simply-dressed, older troll woman who'd so far been silent was looking contemplative. "Maybe not," she said. "I can think of one way they could do it. And even how they could hide it."

"A gateway," Winterhawk said.

She nodded. "Yes. If they've got a spirit that big, it could just open up a gateway to whatever toxic metaplane it came from. As long as they have enough power to make sure nothing they don't want comes through, they could bleed off the power from the metaplane into the ley line, and keep the whole thing warded until they were ready to release it. Theoretically, they could do it faster than they should be able to, if they had enough extra power."

"They'd need someplace enclosed, then," the ork woman said. "That's not something they could just do out in a clearing in the forest. Even that far out, *somebody* would notice."

"I agree," Winterhawk said. "Do any of you know anyplace like that? Probably well into the Wilds, to discourage anyone from blundering into it. And obviously it would have to be near the ley line—probably on it, to get the best effect." He waved toward Flea in the back. "Flea, can you give us a map, please, including the information Beatrix sent Vyx and Virago?"

The decker typed something, and a few seconds later a large AR map flashed up, showing the town, the Wilds, and the path the ley line cut through both. One section of it lit up with an overlay.

As they all focused their attention on it, Vyx stalked to the front of the room. "This is taking too *long!*" she whispered harshly. "Even if Virago isn't dead, they've still got her! We need to go *after* her!"

"I know," he whispered back. "Just trust me. This isn't something we can just go running into with no planning. If she's alive, we'll get her back. But it won't do her any good if we get ourselves killed trying."

She let out a loud sigh. The witches were now talking among themselves, pointing at various parts of the map's highlighted section, asking Flea to zoom in first on one area, then on another. "I want to *move.* I want to *do* something! All this sitting around is—"

"I think I know where they might be," the elf man said suddenly.

Everyone focused on him. "Where?" Winterhawk demanded. "And how do you know?"

"Not the exact location," the elf amended. "But—" He pointed to a spot on the map, and immediately it lit up with a red dot. It was nearly a kilometer out into the Wilds, situated dead center within the meandering path of the dragon ley line. "A few weeks ago, a woman I know, not a member of my coven but a friend, mentioned that she thought something was going on in that area. She said something about an abandoned corporate facility. We didn't think anything of it—and then she disappeared."

"Did you try to find her?" Ocelot asked.

The elf glared at him. "Of course we did. But perhaps you don't know what things are like around here these days. Even if her comments about the Wilds were related to her disappearance, you don't simply go *out* there anymore. The Wilds are full of rogue spirits, dangerous creatures—even more dangerous now that the corps are dumping their failed experiments out there to kill each other where no one will know—and warped magic. It would be suicide unless you had a large, well-armed and -equipped group."

"Well, we've got that!" Vyx said loudly, waving to indicate the room's occupants. "If that's where this is going down, let's *go*."

The witches exchanged glances, and the troll woman's expression, when she turned back to face Vyx, was kind but troubled. "I don't think you understand, my dear," she said. "While this is certainly terrible news Winterhawk has revealed to us, it's out of the question for us to go out into the Wilds. At least not without significant preparation."

"What?" Vyx nearly vibrated with stress and anger now. "What do you mean? Did you *hear* him? Even if they didn't have my girlfriend out there, doing spirits know what to her, this is your *home!* Do you want those toxic fraggers fucking with your ley line? I know some of the people around here don't like the dragon messing with it, but this is *different!*" She whirled on Winterhawk. "You gotta make 'em *see!*"

Winterhawk took a deep breath. In truth, this was what he'd feared would happen. He'd known many of the Salem witches for years—attended their festivals, shared drinks with them when he was in town, and had long, esoteric conversations with them about magic that lasted deep into the night. They were, for the most part, good people, and he was sure they had no desire to see their town corrupted by toxic magic.

However, they were also civilians. Their power levels varied, everything from simple hedge witches up to initiates of the higher mysteries who had visited numerous metaplanes on astral quests and who could match him spell for spell. But almost none of them followed the path he did—they'd never been shadowrunners, they'd never travelled this world and others into dangerous locations, fighting magical threats and seeking long-lost treasures.

In short, they were afraid. And he didn't blame them. In their place, he'd be a fool not to be as well. "Vyx—"

She stared at him, her face full of horror and accusation. "You're not gonna do it!" Her fists clenched. "I should have known—all that talk about promises was just *bullshit*, wasn't it?" She spun, back toward the elf. "Well, if you're not gonna do it, I am. Tell me where this place is. I'll go myself!"

"*Vyx!*" Winterhawk pitched his voice to a commanding level that stopped her in her tracks. "*Listen* to me, damn you, before you do exactly what you said you didn't want to do and get both of you killed!"

"*What?*" she yelled, spinning back. "What are you—"

"I didn't say I wasn't going," he said. "I never said that. I gave you my word, and I'll keep it. But there's more at stake here than Virago. Somebody's got to deal with this."

"I'm sorry," the troll woman said. "I wish we could help you, but that still doesn't mean—"

"You don't *have* to go out into the Wilds," Winterhawk said. His voice still held the commanding tone, but its animation grew as a plan began forming in his mind. He didn't know if it was a *good* plan, but he had to do something. He was on the verge of losing some strong allies due to fear—but he realized they could still be helpful even if they didn't go along. "Listen to me, all of you! You want to help, right? You want to deal with these toxic bastards before they succeed?"

"Of course we do," the human woman said, and the others nodded in agreement. "We'd be fools not to. But—"

"But you don't have to go into the Wilds at all to help us," Winterhawk said.

"How the hell are they gonna—" Ocelot began.

'Hawk began pacing again. He always maintained that his mind worked better when he was moving, and this was no exception. The words tumbled from him as he walked, and he attacked the small crowd with the fervor a carnival barker trying to coerce them inside his tent to see the freakshow. "This place—this corporate facility—it will be well guarded. Magically, for certain. Spirits, wards—they'd have to have done, to keep anyone from catching on to what they're up to. No doubt they'll have made some progress with the ley line, and that will work in their favor as well. There'll be physical security too, but we can deal with that. What we need is a way to take out some of their magical protections—level the playing field a bit."

"A ritual," the troll woman said. Her wide troubled face crinkled into a knowing smile as she nodded.

"Exactly!" Winterhawk stalked the aisles, fixing each person in turn with his intense focus. "I know you lot don't like to work together, but I also know you're bloody good at it when you do. I've seen some of the ritual work you've done together during some of the festivals. If you can convince enough of your coven-mates to work together, do you think you could put together a ritual that would attack their defenses, even temporarily? You might not be able to take them out—not without a lot more preparation, but anything you can do will help."

The others nodded slowly as the light dawned, and Winterhawk allowed himself a triumphant mental fist pump. They were afraid, but they weren't fools, and they weren't cowards.

"We could do that," the elf man said. "It would take a bit of time to prepare—a few hours to get everyone together and set it up—"

"That's fine," Winterhawk said. "We're going to need some time as well."

Ocelot pushed himself off the back door. "'Hawk," he said, and now *he* looked troubled. "Listen—this sounds like a good idea, and you know I'm in, but—do you really think this is gonna work? We got you, me, Vyx—maybe Melinda and Flea if they'll go—that ain't exactly the kind of force I'd want to take in to a place like that, especially since we don't have much gear."

Winterhawk nodded. "Quite true. Which is part of why we need time—I need to implement the other part of our plan."

"Which is—?"

He was sure his grin was a bit manic, but he didn't care. "We were sent up here to figure out what was going on with a dragon-aspected ley line," he said. "I think it's about time for the dragon in question to take an interest in it himself, don't you?"

FORTY-SIX

"Do you think she's still alive?"

Winterhawk turned away from the transport vehicle's window, where he'd been staring out into the rainy darkness. It was hard to see much: a thick, persistent fog hung over most of the Wilds, reducing trees and other geographic features to indistinct haziness. It was an eerie, unsettling feeling, even for him.

Vyx sat across from him, watching him. She wore a mid-length armored jacket over jeans and a hooded sweatshirt. He couldn't see her eyes behind her tinted glasses, but he could tell even without assensing her that she was troubled.

"I hope so," he said. No point in arguing with her—she'd already proven to be skilled at seeing through duplicity. *"We'll know soon enough."*

"Maybe," she said, dropping her gaze to her hands in her lap. *"I just can't help thinking that if she'd dead, it's my fault. She'd never have run out of there by herself if she hadn't been chasing my stupid ass."*

"It's done now," he said gently. *"We'll do what we can."*

She glanced around the compartment, and he followed her gaze. It was meant to be a cargo hauler, so the accommodations were sparse even by transport standards, but beggars couldn't be choosers when time was of the essence. The others—Ocelot, Flea, Melinda, and the rest, sat pressed together shoulder to shoulder, watching as best they could through either the vehicle's armored windows or their AR hookups to the driver's view out the front window. They rarely spoke aloud, as it was hard to hear each other over the engine's rumble and the pounding of the rain; any conversations, like Winterhawk's and Vyx's, took place over private comm channels.

It was now three hours after the meeting at the community center, and approaching midnight. Winterhawk studied the silent group and began to think they might have a chance to pull this off.

Not a good one, mind, but a better one than they'd had when they were nothing but a ragtag, badly geared group in need of several hours' sleep and a good meal.

He hadn't expected to get through to Damon—with the communications grid as spotty as it was inside the Zone, it would have been a miracle simply to get through at all, but apparently the shielded, no-frills commlink Anissa had given him had more punch than he'd expected. It still took a little help from Flea, but after only three attempts he'd managed to reach Anissa. He'd given her the bare-bones version of what was going on in Salem, leaving out the part about Vyx and Virago, and asked her to put Damon in touch with him as soon as possible.

The dragon had called back in ten minutes. He listened in silence as Winterhawk provided him with a more detailed account of the last couple day's events, and when Winterhawk finished, he remained silent for several more seconds.

"I...see," he said at last, just as Winterhawk began to wonder if they'd lost their connection.

"Can you help us? This is bigger than you led us to believe—if we try to deal with it on our own, we're likely buggered. If you can come—"

There was a pause. *"I can't. Not personally."*

"Why the hell *not*?" Winterhawk couldn't help the edge that seeped into his tone.

"I'm—currently in the middle of something I can't postpone. If you could wait—"

"We can't wait. We have to do this now, before they realize we're on to them."

Another pause. *"All right, then. I can't come myself, but I'll send you some help. I've got a few people on retainer. I'll call them and send them up there right away, along with whatever gear they can gather on short notice. I'll come when I can."*

Winterhawk didn't like it, but it was the best they were going to get. You didn't simply call up a dragon and force him to do your bidding—even if this whole thing kind of *was* his fault.

"Fine," he said. "We'll take it. And one other thing."

"Yes?"

"You said you could get us out of here. I'd like to request you get on that. As soon as we've sorted out this situation, I want out of here. Be prepared for myself, Ocelot, and two others."

"Two?"

"Two," Winterhawk said firmly. "Details later. Send me the data on who we're expecting and when."

He'd never hung up on a dragon before. It was strangely satisfying.

Damon had been as good as his word: the team he'd sent had arrived less than two hours after the call, and now sat with Winterhawk, Ocelot, Vyx, Flea, and the others in the back of the rigger's modified GMC Bulldog. He studied them from behind his darkened glasses; it still looked like a woefully small group to go up against what he expected to see, but he'd faced some pretty tough odds with smaller groups than this.

There were five of them in all, bringing the group's number to ten. The rigger, a dark-skinned dwarf named Gus with close-cropped hair and a cynical grin, was driving at the moment, but Anissa had assured Winterhawk that his real talent was with drones. Anissa, decked out in her all-black combat armor and holding an assault rifle across her lap, sat next to a massive blond troll named Henrik, similarly dressed with a large duffel bag full of weapons between his feet. The team's decker, a willowy elven woman named Tweak, was across from Flea, and the two of them had tuned out the rest of the group as they coordinated their resources. Tweak had already managed to locate a floor plan of the facility in the Wilds, though she warned them that it was quite old and, since it came directly from its original owner Shiawase, might include deliberate errors.

"We'll take it," Winterhawk had said. "It's better than going in blind."

The last member of Damon's team was Bronwyn, a stocky ork shaman with wild dreadlocks and various a riot of colorful feathers and fetishes attached to her armor. She, Melinda, and Winterhawk had summoned several spirits before they left, keeping some in reserve while directing others to conceal and defend the Bulldog as they rumbled through the heavy forest on the way to the toxics' facility.

Maya, with her superior abilities to remain hidden, was playing scout. Winterhawk had sent her out ahead of them to watch for threats and report back, but thus far all she'd reported was that she'd located the facility.

"Not going near it," she told Winterhawk. *"It looks deserted, but they've got heavy magical defenses. And be careful—there are some nasty-looking things patrolling around the outside."*

When Winterhawk relayed that to the rest of the group, Ocelot asked, "What kind of nasty?"

"She says she doesn't want to look too closely at them. Abominations, she calls them."

"Fuckin' wonderful."

Winterhawk had left most of the spirit coordination to the Melinda and Bronwyn, focusing on maintaining communication with Althea and her team back in Salem. He had to give them credit—once they had a viable plan that didn't require them to leave town and face whatever was out in the Wilds, they'd done an admirable job of mobilizing their forces. By the time the team left, they were well into the construction of a massive ritual circle in the gym of one of the local high schools. It wasn't the optimum location, but in order to be effective against such a large threat, the required circle was too big for any of their covens' ritual spaces. Althea had assured him they'd be ready to go when he gave the word.

He glanced at Vyx again. She looked older now, barely recognizable in her multi-pocketed armored jacket and dark glasses, her jaw set and her fists clenched in her lap. Her aura vibrated with tension—he suspected if she thought she could get away with it, she'd bust out of the back of the Bulldog and run off in search of Virago herself.

She caught him looking at her and frowned. *"What?"*

"Nothing," he replied, and returned his attention to the others.

If Vyx had to sit still for much longer, she was certain she'd explode.

Sitting on the narrow bench, pressed between Winterhawk on one side and the enormous troll on the other, she felt as if the world were closing in on her. All around her the low murmurs of voices, the smell of sweat and armor and gun oil, the sudden jounces as the Bulldog bumped over the uneven terrain all served to remind her that every minute longer it took to reach the toxics was another minute when they could be torturing or killing Virago. *What if she's already dead? What if she isn't even there?*

She studied Winterhawk out of the corner of her eye, wondering if he had some kind of magic way to tell she was looking at him. He appeared to be deep in thought, leaned back against the wall. *Probably communicating with something in the astral plane,* she thought. She'd watched him as he coordinated the mission, taking in reports from Ocelot, from Anissa, from the other team's shaman, adjusting the plan based on the changing intelligence they'd received from the spirits, the deckers, and the witches.

Whatever she might think of him—and she wasn't anywhere near drawing any definitive conclusions yet—he was clearly good at what he did. People respected him. They listened to him.

She'd never worked with shadowrunners before. She'd met a couple as a young teen—a hard-eyed pair who'd chatted briefly with her mother while the two of them had been out to lunch one day—but aside from that, all of her (woefully limited, she was beginning to realize) real-world experience had been with the Ancients. She'd admired Lucky Liam, the way he led the gang with a combination of even-tempered strategy and occasional bouts of passion when they were warranted, but this group of shadowrunners made them look like a disorganized mob by comparison. There was no anger, no emotion, simply a laser focus on the business at hand. She was pretty sure they wouldn't all get out of this alive—and she was pretty sure they all knew it, too—but they didn't act like that was even a factor.

Would they be able to do this? She'd been on hand when they'd formulated their plan, though she didn't have much to offer. It was deceptively simple: the witches back in Salem would use their ritual to weaken the wards around the toxics' base and try to counter some of the ley line's background count, and the team on the ground would gain entry—either by infiltrating or storming the place, depending on whether the toxics anticipated their arrival—and stop whatever the toxics were doing to the ley line.

And get Virago out, she'd reminded them.

A small part of her wondered if they were only humoring her with their assurances that Virago's rescue would be an important part of the plan. Funny how they never spoke about her girlfriend when discussing their strategies.

It didn't matter, though—they didn't have to care. She cared. And she was damn well gonna get Virago out, or die trying.

"Are you all right?"

She started, discovering her father turned toward her again. She thought she could feel the heat of his arm against hers, but it was probably her imagination, given the armor they both wore. *"Why wouldn't I be?"*

He shrugged. *"This is all new to you."* Smiling ruefully, he added, *"Your mother would kill me if she knew I was bringing you into something like this."*

"Fuck Mom." She clenched her fists in her lap. *"I'm sick of her trying to keep me safe from everything. That's why I left in the first place."*

"That's why she did too, you know," he said. He wasn't looking at her now; his gaze was pointed at one of the armored windows, watching the dark, twisted hulks of trees rolling by.

"What the hell does that mean?"

"That's why she left me, and never told me about you. She was afraid you might turn out like me. That I might be a...bad influence."

She snorted. *"Worse than running with the Ancients? Wait till she hears* that *story. You can't–"*

She stopped when Winterhawk raised a sudden, urgent hand. *"What?"*

"Something's coming," he said, all business now. All around him, the others tensed. *"It's–"*

The Bulldog rocked and bucked as something large erupted from beneath it.

"Hang on!" the rigger yelled over the link.

An instant later, the Bulldog canted sharply to the right, tilting on its wide off-road tires as it tipped over. Yells and shouts filled the air as Vyx, Winterhawk, and the others were flung sideways, slamming into the walls as it crashed into the trees and came to a stop at a crazy angle, its wheels spinning uselessly.

"Out! Out!" the troll's voice boomed, and something hit them again.

FORTY-SEVEN

Voices erupted over Winterhawk's comm as everyone scrambled to extricate themselves from the disabled transport.

"What the hell was that?" he asked Maya. Already Henrik and Anissa had thrown open the rear doors and the runner team was pouring out.

"Holy shit!" Ocelot yelled. Of course he'd been one of the first out of the vehicle. "What *is* that thing?"

Winterhawk grabbed Vyx's arm and dragged her after him, clambering over the boxes, duffel bags and other disarrayed gear. Gunfire chattered around them, the runners using the overturned Bulldog for cover against a bulky, misshapen form looming in the moonlight.

It didn't take Winterhawk more than a second to identify it: a toxic earth spirit, and a big one. Clearly, the opposition either knew they were coming, or they'd set traps for anyone unwise enough to approach their base. He could try to banish it, but banishing spirits was tough, draining work. They'd barely arrived— he couldn't afford to risk the drain this early.

Fortunately, it didn't look like he needed to. The runner team, banged up but mostly unhurt from the spirit's assault, had fanned out and were opening fire on the thing with weapons, drones, and magic.

The spirit roared—a wet, burbling sound that Winterhawk felt as much as he heard—and rose up a good three meters while stretching its long, grasping arms toward Henrik. It was hard to see clearly in the faint moonlight, but it appeared to be formed of shifting, stinking mud enrobed in writhing plant tendrils.

It lunged at the troll, who stood his ground, bracing himself as he fired a long burst from his machine gun. The spirit roared again and staggered back a few steps, chunks of it flying in all directions. One hit Winterhawk's armored coat and sizzled.

The runners in Damon's team moved like they'd worked together for years, focusing their assault on the core of the spirit. They pounded it with guns and magic, but it barely seemed to notice their efforts.

"We can't stay here," Ocelot told Winterhawk over the comm. "They're tryin' to delay us."

"I know, I know." 'Hawk couldn't see his friend in the meat, but Ocelot's reassuring red dot appeared behind the toxic earth spirit on the AR display. He glanced to the side. "Vyx, we—"

She wasn't there.

Damn it, if she's run off again—

"Up here," came her voice on the comm.

He glanced upward and spotted her crouched on a branch high overhead. She pulled something from her pocket and flung it with unerring accuracy toward the spirit. It exploded with a flash that lit up the dim clearing, tearing more chunks from the thing.

It screamed again, directing a stream of what looked like sludge from its hands at Vyx. She vaulted off the limb, grabbed another two meters higher, and disappeared into the branches. Whatever the spirit had sprayed at her hit the branch she'd been on, and it broke free with a loud sizzle, crashing to the ground not far from Winterhawk.

We can't waste time with this. He reached out to Althea, back in Salem. *"Are you ready yet? They're on to us—we need to get inside!"*

"Not quite. This is a tricky ritual—something's fighting us. Give us a little more time."

"We may not have much more time." He couldn't tell them to hurry up—rushed rituals were failed rituals, and he knew they were working as fast as they could.

"We need to get in there!" Vyx urged from her perch high in the tree. *"If they know we're—Wait! Incoming!"*

"Got 'em!" Henrik called, and dots lit up Winterhawk's AR view. An instant later, a huddle of dark bodies appeared among the trees, their low growls seeming to come from everywhere at once.

At first, he couldn't tell what they were through the fog and sleety rain. More spirits? If the toxics had summoned that many and sent them after the team, they were in trouble. But as they drew closer, and he got a better look at them, he stared in shock.

"Bloody hell—are those *bears?*"

Already the air was full of the staccato patter of weapons fire and the flash-*boom*s of grenades. Two of the things jerked and staggered as rounds hit them, and a grenade blew another to pieces, but the rest didn't stop. As they burst through the tree line, it quickly became clear they weren't just bears.

Vast and black and shaggy, they were half again as large as normal bears. Angry red patches showed through their clumped, matted hair, and their stretched-open mouths drooled greenish slobber and sported yellowed, broken teeth. Winterhawk flung a spell at one of them and it screamed, rising up on its back legs and tearing at its head with its front paws.

More gunfire erupted, and another of the bear-things went down. Another leaped forward, paws outstretched, and slammed into Henrik before he could dive out of the way. The two rolled, wrestling on the leafy wet ground, until he could bring his machine gun around and ventilate its guts with a burst of automatic fire. Winterhawk waited only long enough to watch him stagger back to his feet before redirecting his attention.

What the hell were they *doing* in there? These things, whatever they were, were more than simple bears. As he watched another one taken to pieces by one of Gus's deadly roto-drones, he realized what he'd noticed subconsciously before, and it chilled him.

"They're working as a group!" he sent over the link. "How are they doing that?"

"Damned if I know," Ocelot sent back.

"I've seen that before," Anissa said. She was across the clearing, providing covering fire as Bronwyn directed her spirits against yet another of the creatures. *"The corps dump their CFD failures out here. Sometimes the headcases coordinate—even the animals!"*

This was getting worse by the minute. So the toxics had figured out how to make use of the failed headcase experiments out here? Toxic spirits were bad enough. If they had to face waves of nanite-addled creatures before they even reached the front doors, they'd never make it. They didn't have enough firepower for a sustained assault.

"Head for the entrance," he ordered. "They're trying to keep us out."

"What about the ritual?" Bronwyn asked. *"Are they ready in town?"*

"Go," he said. "They'll be ready. We need to get inside."

Next to him, Vyx swung down from her tree perch, swinging her staff to crash into the head of an approaching bear as she did. The bear screeched in pain and swiped at her, but she was too fast. She caught hold of a branch, arced her body in a graceful spin, and landed lightly on a thick branch of another tree, several meters up. "I'll meet you there," she called, and then she was gone, swinging through the trees like a monkey.

"We'll play rear guard," Gus said. "Go!"

Winterhawk didn't wait for a second invitation. With Ocelot and Mellnda behind him, he flung Manaballs to slow the bears and then took off toward the facility, using the trees for cover. *"Anything else?"* he asked Maya.

"Not between you and the fence," she said. *"But...boss?"*

"Yes?"

"I don't feel well."

A chill ran up Winterhawk's spine. *"It's the toxics. They're affecting you."* He should have thought of it before: normal, healthy spirits didn't like being around their toxic brethren—if they remained in close proximity too long, the corrupted astral energy could cause irreparable harm. And they hadn't even gotten inside yet. If the toxics truly were trying to re-aspect the ley line, he couldn't feel it out here, not yet. The background count from the dragon magic was bad enough, but at least it wasn't harmful to Maya and the other spirits.

"'Hawk?"

Winterhawk realized he'd slowed down while he was talking to Maya—Ocelot was ahead of him now, looking back. *Damn.* He hated losing the overwatch provided by his ally spirit, but he wouldn't take chances with her well-being.

"Maya—go back to Salem. Find Althea, and help relay information between us."

"I'm sorry, Boss. I'll stay if you'd like—"

"No. Go." He accessed the comm. "Flea, are you there?"

"Right here," the kid replied. *"Still back with the other team—they're rippin' hell outta these bears, and—"*

"I'll need you to hack into the facility's grid once we get inside," he said. "We can't take the spirits in, and we need recon." Assuming, of course, that toxic magicians even bothered maintaining a Matrix connection.

"On it," he said. *"Me an' Tweak'll be right there. And she says Gus can send in a couple of his mini roto-drones too."*

"Good. Anissa, bring the others along after we've mopped up."

The facility's perimeter fence wasn't far ahead, though it was difficult to spot through the underbrush, trees, fog, and rain. Winterhawk didn't know how long it had been since Shiawase had occupied it, but the toxics had clearly let its exterior go wild in an attempt to conceal it from prying eyes.

Stopping behind a thick tree about ten meters from the fence, he waved the others to a halt as well. He flashed up the facility's plans on the AR screen. They'd already discussed their approach on the way over—if the floorplan was accurate, only one area inside was large enough for the toxics' spirit to erect a gateway and for them to perform the ritual needed to re-aspect the ley line. He wondered how long they'd been at it—normally, changing the aspect of a mana line took months, during which the ritual needed to be periodically reinforced to maintain its potency and gradually increase its power and influence. Had the toxics figured out a way, perhaps with the help of the free spirit, to increase the speed of the ritual? Or had they been at this for months, quietly working under the witches' radar, and had only been discovered due to the combination of Doris Wu's and Winterhawk's investigations?

"Goin' in quiet or loud?" Ocelot asked.

"No point in being quiet now. They know we're here. But we need to wait for the group in Salem."

"We can't wait forever," Vyx said. *"We need to get in there."*

"I know. But we can't—" He stopped as his comm buzzed. Althea's LTG popped up on his AR display. "Althea. Are you ready?"

"No. We've got trouble." Her voice was steady but stressed. *"They've found us. They're attacking. I don't know how long we can hold them off!"*

FORTY-EIGHT

Damn, damn, damn.

They might be able to go in without support from the witches' ritual—Damon's team was good, and the toxics were probably better set up to deal with magic than with some of the toys they had brought along, but without knowing what else was waiting for them in there, it was a dangerous risk.

"Hold on, Althea," Winterhawk said, then switched comm channels. "Bronwyn. Are you there?"

"Right here. On our way, almost to your location."

"I don't want to send the spirits in—too much chance they'll be corrupted if there's as much toxic energy as I expect in there. Althea's in trouble, though. I want to send them to help."

It was another thing he didn't like—he'd been counting on the spirits to at least protect their exit—but if the witches' ritual was disrupted, they'd be in worse shape.

"Yeah," Bronwyn said promptly, and Melinda nodded too.

The others had reached them by now, concealing themselves behind trees outside the fence, reloading their weapons, preparing to go in. Winterhawk glanced up again, but only by assensing could he spot Vyx's form high above.

"Right, then. Instruct your spirits to follow Maya's lead. They'll go back to Salem and help take out the attackers, then come back here if they can."

An image flashed up on his AR screen, showing the outside of the high school where the witches were set up. There was no sound, but the occasional flash of light in the foggy dimness revealed the location of the toxics' team. "Althea. Any magic?"

"Not that I can tell." Her voice still sounded shaky. *"But we're not well protected here—I've sent a couple of spirits out, but everyone else is focusing on the ritual. We didn't think they'd find out about us this fast."*

"Help is on its way," he said. "Maya should be there already, and more spirits are coming. Hold on. And let me know as soon as the ritual's finished."

He broke the connection and motioned Ocelot, Henrik, and Anissa over. "This is your part of the show," he said. "How do you suggest we get inside?"

"We're into their system," Flea said triumphantly. "Their electronic security is drek. Basic level stuff. Easy-peasy. Bad news is, their Matrix connection is drek too, and a lot of the system's disabled—they're probably not maintaining it."

"Can you pop the door?" Ocelot asked.

"On your signal," Tweak said.

"No cameras I can access, unfortunately," Flea said. "But we should be able to get past any locked doors."

"I'll send the roto-drone in first once the front door's open," Gus said. "And the Fly-Spy on ahead. It can give us some intel."

Winterhawk took one last look around at the group. This was it. No more time to waste—every minute they spent out here gave the toxics more time to regroup their defenses.

"Let's do it," he said. "Get ready to move."

Another AR window popped up, this one showing a view from Gus's roto-drone, which had moved into position beyond the fence. It showed a small, blocky concrete building overgrown with greenery—the forest was obviously well into the process of reclaiming it after Shiawase had abandoned it. At a closer look, though, the greenery didn't appear healthy; its ropy, bloated tendrils and sickly gray-green hue spoke to the influence of the toxics. A wide metal door stood shut, its once-smooth surface marred by rust and scarring.

He switched the comm channel again so he could speak to Vyx privately. "Listen. Do *not* just run in. I know you want to find Virago, but let's not get you both killed. Understood?"

"Yeah." Her tone was the tiniest bit sullen. *"I'll play by your rules—long as I know you're lookin' for her."*

"Somethin's comin'," Ocelot broke in, and marked a new dot on their AR, off to the right of their location, inside the perimeter of the fence.

"Go," Vyx urged.

Winterhawk broke the connection with Vyx, hoping his words had gotten through to her, and fearing they hadn't. "Pop the door."

FORTY-NINE

Despite its ravaged appearance, the thick metal door smoothly slid open in response to the deckers' commands, revealing a wide, darkened hallway behind it. At the same time, Henrik launched a grenade at the fence. It hit squarely and detonated, taking out a three-meter-wide chunk.

Gus's drone went first, rumbling through the breach on its tracked wheels, its twin guns already firing at the dark shapes heading toward it. Two more drones, a medium-sized MCT-Nissan Roto-drone and a tiny Fly-Spy that Winterhawk could only pick out because its progress was painted on one window of his AR display, surged forward and hovered just outside the door.

"Hellhounds," Bronwyn said.

"Whole fraggin' pack of 'em," Ocelot added. He had his T-250 in one hand, his monowhip in the other, and a fierce grin visible beneath his shades.

"They look...weird," Vyx said.

Winterhawk adjusted the magnification on his glasses for a closer look, and frowned. She was right.

Normal hellhounds were massive black dogs, sleek and broad-shouldered, with glowing red eyes. This bunch was oddly misshapen, their usual smooth, loping gaits replaced by periodic awkward staggers. They still moved fast, but every few seconds their heads made little sideways jerks. That would have been creepy enough, but it appeared they were doing it in unison. A definite aura of "just not right" hovered around them. A quick shift to assense them told Winterhawk why: "Toxic magic. Might be more headcases. Careful."

Vyx swung down from her perch on the branch and landed lightly next to him, her katana held at the ready. In her other hand she gripped a handful of minigrenades.

"Take 'em down," Henrik ordered. He, Anissa, and Ocelot hurried through the fence breach, spreading out to face the approaching hellhounds. As the dogs drew closer, eyes blazing red and teeth bared, the group opened fire.

Meanwhile, Winterhawk, Melinda, and Bronwyn, levitating a few meters up and out of the hounds' reach, rained magic down upon them. Once again Winterhawk cursed the background count, which was making their spells significantly less effective. If the three of them hadn't been as powerful as they were, he doubted their magic would be much help at all.

"Maya, report," he sent as he watched his teammates take the dogs apart before they got close. With the additions of Vyx's unerringly accurate throws and another of Gus's armed drones, the hellhounds didn't have a chance. It struck him as particularly odd that they didn't turn tail and run, but they surged forward into the barrage as if directed by some unseen force. First the bears, now the hellhounds—how were a bunch of mad toxic magicians harnessing the local headcase paracritters to play guard-dog for them?

"Opposition down," Maya sent back promptly. *"The spirits helped, and the witches summoned some more of their own. They're back to the ritual now. Shouldn't be long."*

"Keep me posted. We've got to go inside, but I don't want to go against the toxics directly until they've taken down some of their power."

"Got it, Boss. Be careful." As always when he put himself in danger, he heard the faint tinge of worry in the cat's prim British tones.

"I'm always careful," he reminded her.

"I still don't believe that."

"Right, then," Winterhawk said to the others. "The situation back in Salem is in hand, so the ritual should go off soon. Let's get inside. We'll take out any ancillary opposition we find, and when we get the word, we'll go after the big bads."

"Sounds like a plan to me," Gus said. "Let's go."

The hellhounds lay strewn across the ground a few meters away, dead or dying. Up closer, their strange, misshapen bodies showed significant signs of illness and decay: missing patches of hair, clusters of white, swollen pustules and running sores, and angry red skin.

All three drones changed direction and headed through the open door. A few seconds later views from their cameras popped up on everyone's displays, showing a wide, empty hallway lined in what looked like cracked, corroded plascrete. The lights inside were a dim, sickly green, so it was difficult to make out detail, but nothing appeared to be moving.

The runners followed the drones inside, and the heavy metal door slammed shut and locked behind them.

"Nobody else is getting in," Flea said. "Not fast, anyway. And we set it up so we'll know if they do."

The corridor was nearly four meters wide, enough that they could spread out to avoid being sitting ducks for any hidden gun emplacements or area-effect magical ambushes. Anissa and Ocelot went first, sweeping their gun barrels right and left behind Gus's rumbling drone. Winterhawk and Vyx followed, then Melinda, Bronwyn, Tweak, and Flea. Henrik brought up the rear, since he was tall enough he could see (and shoot) over the others if necessary.

Winterhawk consulted the floorplan the deckers had provided as they all crept down the darkened hallway. Everywhere around them the place showed signs of rot and decay—more of the toxics' work, no doubt. A strong stench—equal parts rotting vegetation, putrefaction, and stagnant water—permeated the air.

"Everything we need is underground," he said. "There should be an elevator around here somewhere."

"Here," Gus said, flashing up a view of a pair of pitted elevator doors. "About ten meters up, turn right." Two corresponding dots appeared on the map.

"I don't like it," Ocelot said. "If they know we're comin', they could have booby-trapped the elevators."

Normally Winterhawk would have chalked it up to Ocelot's well-known dislike of enclosed spaces, but this time he had to agree his friend had a point. "Stairs, then."

Another dot lit up the map. "Door's here," Tweak said. "Looks like the place only has one underground level. Big, but not huge as corp places like this go."

"Probably some secret R&D lab," Anissa said. "Doesn't need to be big."

The door to the stairs was next to the elevators. They reached it without further opposition.

"Too damn quiet up here," Ocelot said.

"They're probably all downstairs," Winterhawk said. "They can't have a massive group—someone would have noticed before this."

The door was locked, but Tweak and Flea made short work of it. It opened onto an unadorned, corp-standard stairway leading downward, also with no light except for the weird green glow. The walls here showed signs of decay as well. Gus sent his Fly-Spy down first to scout and found no sign of anything alive other than encroaching mold.

The team made the trip to the lower floor in tense silence, once again spreading out in case they'd missed any traps.

"I don't like this," Ocelot said. "Makes me nervous when they go too long without shooting at us."

"My danger sense isn't pinging," Vyx said. "Maybe D— Winterhawk's right, and they're just focused on the ritual."

This door wasn't locked. They pushed it open a few inches, and Gus sent his Fly-Spy out into the hallway.

"They know we're here," Winterhawk said, watching the tiny drone's progress down another empty hall. "No doubt about it." Down here, the background count grew not only stronger, but more unsettling. The dragon-magic aspect he was used to made it difficult to cast spells, but didn't make him feel physically uncomfortable. But as he drew closer to the toxics' influence, the sensation of things crawling on his skin, nausea, and the overwhelming compulsion that he needed a long shower increased. He glanced at Melinda and Bronwyn and suspected from their expressions that they felt the same way. Further, though it was hard to pick it out through the miasma of toxic astral energy, he was certain the group had erected a powerful ward or circle of protection around their ritual area.

He reached out to Maya again. *"How's the ritual going? I can't reach Althea from down here via the comm, so we'll have to rely on you to relay messages."*

After a few seconds, the cat responded: *"She says they're almost done. Just a few more minutes."*

"What's the plan?" Anissa asked.

"The Salem team is almost ready," Winterhawk said. "I don't know how much they'll be able to help, but we'll need to be prepared to move when they weaken the background count."

"We need to find Virago," Vyx urged.

"Wouldn't hurt to sweep the place for hostiles," Henrik said. "Especially if we gotta wait. Maybe we can find her before the party starts."

They edged out into the hallway. It was narrower down here, only a little over two meters wide. The stench was stronger, wet and earthy and oddly cloying, as if a sewer had backed up through a garden full of rotting flowers.

Off in the distance, several *slams* sounded, one after the other, followed by low-pitched growling and shrieks that almost sounded human. A faint rumbling ran through the floor, like a distant earthquake.

"What was that?" Ocelot demanded.

"Trouble," Vyx said quickly. She gripped Winterhawk's arm. "Something's coming."

"Frag, they've opened a bunch of doors!" Flea said.

"Can you close them?" Anissa swung her gun barrel around, focusing toward the sounds.

"Yeah, but I think whatever was inside got out already. Damn!"

Winterhawk quickly shifted his attention to the feed from Gus's Fly-Spy drone, which he'd sent down the hallway to the left. He barely got a chance to spot a series of humanoid forms charging down the hallway when they erupted from the left-side corridor.

"Look out!" the troll yelled.

"There's more!" Vyx called, pointing. "Other end!"

She was right. More figures poured from a hallway further down. These weren't animals, though, and they weren't spirits. Their twisted, misshapen forms ran on two legs—everything from the slender figures of elves to the massive ones of trolls. These were metahumans—what was left of them.

They were fast, too. The first group was upon them almost before they could act, shrieking, flailing their arms, swinging makeshift clubs and swiping with long, hooked nails. Winterhawk got a good look at one of them as it lunged toward him, its eyes alight with madness: it was an ork, his bulky frame riddled with oozing sores and bulbous tumors that shone with a sickly sheen in the low, weird light. He opened his mouth to scream again and ooze poured out.

"Don't let them touch you!" Winterhawk yelled, sending out a wave of magical force to drive the ork and the others near him back down the hallway. Even that small expenditure made his head pound as the horrific background count sapped his power.

Gus, Vyx, and Melinda backed off, but Tweak wasn't so lucky. She stumbled, her foot slipping on a patch of ooze on the floor. Before she could right herself, three of them were on her. She screamed as their claws and teeth ripped at her exposed flesh, scrabbling to get through her armor.

"*NO!*" Anissa screamed. She took careful aim with her Ares HVAR and hit the nearest of the creatures ravaging the decker with a burst, pulping its head and spraying blood and brain matter around the small hallway.

Gus yelped as some of it hit him, his hand flying to his face. "It burns! Get back!"

Fighting in the narrow hallway was tough—the creatures seemed to have no self-preservation instinct, and flung themselves with equal fervor into melee and into bursts of automatic-weapon fire. It was hard enough not to hit friends among the flailing limbs and flying bullets, but trying to avoid being hit by the things' burning blood and having next to nowhere to maneuver made the situation nothing but worse.

Winterhawk backpedaled, flinging another spell that, in combination with Melinda's, acted as a wave to push them farther back down the hall, where more were coming. He focused on one of them, trying to get a better look. *Were* they metahumans? Their faces were so contorted in agony, their bodies so ravaged with growths and seeping wounds, that it was difficult to tell for sure—but then one staggered backward, rearing up for a second as a neat trio of rounds from Anissa's rifle stitched its chest, and Winterhawk got a clear view: the figure was human, or had once been—a solidly built woman wearing what looked like the remains of a CrimeTime T-shirt and jeans.

What was going *on* in here? "Is there anyone else down that corridor?" he asked over the link. Maybe if they could duck left into the hallway this group had come from, they could get more maneuvering room. But the last thing he wanted was for them be caught between two approaching groups of mutant toxic freaks.

The Fly-Spy was still cruising in that direction, but the light was so erratic it was hard to see anything definitive. Though it appeared that several doors along the corridor had been opened, it was impossible to see inside any of the rooms.

"Not sure," Gus said. *"I—wait!"*

"What?"

"Hang on, lemme boost the audio."

A second later, everyone heard a terrified sound over their comms:

"Help! For God's sake, if you're out there, help *me!"*

It was a female voice.

FIFTY

Vyx spun. "*Virago!*"

Winterhawk's gaze flashed between the creatures, Vyx, and Flea. "Where?" he demanded to the decker.

A dot blossomed in front of one of the doorways along the side hall.

"Go," Henrik said. "We'll hold 'em here." Suiting action to words, he fired another burst from his machine gun, cutting down two of the creatures.

"Hurry!" Anissa urged.

Vyx was already moving, tearing headlong around the corner. "Virago!" she yelled again. "We're coming! Hang on!"

Winterhawk took off after her. "Vyx, wait!"

"Like hell!" She was already halfway down the hallway, skidding to a stop in front of the room with the dot. She stopped and stared.

Winterhawk ran up behind her. "What did you—" Then he too stopped as he got a good look at the woman in the room.

It wasn't Virago. She was a middle-aged ork—or at least that was the metahuman race she most closely resembled. She lay writhing on the floor, reaching out toward the doorway as if imploring someone to approach her.

"Holy *shit,*" Ocelot said as he came to a stop behind Winterhawk.

The woman might have been an ork at one point, but now she was an abomination, same as the creatures attacking the team in the main hallway. Her skin, a pallid, unhealthy shade of gray peppered with angry red welts, was pockmarked with growths ranging from a few centimeters to one massive bulbous outcropping, bigger than her head, sprouting from her shoulder. Some of these had burst and oozed blood-streaked green-white fluid, while others strained at the skin covering them as if they might erupt at any moment. In spots, her skin had rotted through to the point where blood-slicked white bone was visible. One of her eyes, still with the light of sanity, focused on the newcomers, while the other one, a filmy white, wandered in its socket like an unseeing beacon.

Vyx started to enter the room, but Winterhawk grabbed her arm and yanked her backward. "No," he snapped. "Don't get close to her."

For once she obeyed him, but her expression was troubled. "What did they *do* to her?"

Winterhawk glanced at Ocelot, met his friend's gaze, then cut to Vyx, in a clear message: *keep her out here.* Aloud, he said, "Watch the hallway. Both directions." Then he stepped into the room. "Can you hear us?" he called to the woman.

For a moment, he thought she wouldn't answer, but after a few seconds her moans of agony faded until they were barely audible. Her single good eye, bloodshot and infinitely weary, settled on him. "Help...me..." she whispered. Blood and worse dribbled down from the corner of her mouth, staining her yellowed tusks and pooling up on the filthy floor beneath her.

"What's happened to you?" He moved a little closer, but kept enough distance that if she lunged at him, he could back off. Her aura roiled with disturbance.

"Don't!" she said, her good eye sharpening. "Stay back!" Her voice, mushy and indistinct, bubbled out along with another runnel of milky drool.

"What did they do to you?" he asked again. He glanced over his shoulder at Ocelot and Vyx; both of them stood in tense readiness, each one switching attention between Winterhawk and one end of the corridor. The muffled sound of gunfire, along with more shouts and screams, filtered in from the main hall. Another rumble, stronger this time, shook the floor. They wouldn't have much time here.

"Ask her about Virago!" Vyx urged.

Winterhawk ignored her, focusing on the woman. "Tell us. Let us help you."

A brief, strange expression flashed across the ork's face, almost as if something rippled beneath her skin. "You can't..." she whispered. "Too far gone. Dead...already... Don't...touch me."

She was right, of course. There was no way they could get her out of here, even if they had the time to try. "Why did the toxics do this to you? Did they kidnap you?" He remembered the story the witches had told about one of their number who had disappeared from the streets of Salem.

"No..." She reached out to clutch his arm, but then yanked her hand back. "You don't understand...they're...they're *infecting* people. I...got it by accident, but it didn't matter."

"'Hawk! We gotta go!" Ocelot called from the hallway.

"Just a minute!" he snapped back. Then, to the woman: "Got what?"

"CFD..." she whispered. "They're trying to...cure it with magic. Burn it out. Toxic..."

Winterhawk stared at her, uncomprehending. What the hell did she mean? "The toxics are trying to *cure CFD?*" That was so absurd he almost wouldn't allow himself to speak the words aloud.

"It all went wrong...Everything went wrong..." The ork was sobbing now. "Check the files. Notes. Lab...end of hall...You have to...destroy this place..." Her good eye fixed on him again. "Please...kill me. Please...I don't want to become like...them..." Her hand fluttered feebly in the direction of the fight in the main hall.

"Ask her about *Virago*!" Vyx yelled again. "Is she here? Where is she?"

Winterhawk doubted this poor wretched woman had any idea who or where Virago was, but he asked quickly, "Have there been any new captives? Just today?"

"I don't know...I don't know..." she moaned. She writhed on the floor, arms clutched tightly around her middle. One of the growths on her arm burst, slicking the floor with bloody discharge. "Please...dear God...make it stop...make it stop..."

Winterhawk backed off and nodded to Ocelot. They couldn't do anything for her—they couldn't even make her comfortable. And if the creatures in the main hall were any indication, she didn't have a bright future if they left her alive.

He moved out into the hall as Ocelot pulled out his Predator, took careful aim, and put a bullet in the ork woman's forehead. She stiffened and then went limp, her face going slack.

As Vyx turned away from the scene and pointedly fixed her attention on the hallway, Winterhawk got back on the comm. "Flea, are you there?" The sound of gunfire and yelling had faded in the last few seconds.

"Right here." The young decker's voice sounded shaky. *"Tweak's dead. Gus's hurt. Melinda's...trying to help him."*

"Do you need us back there?"

"No, they've got it under control now. Those things are dead or dying...unless there's more somewhere."

"Come here, then."

"What's going on? I thought we were gonna—"

"This is fast. Come to me. Tell the others to keep watch and kill anything that moves and isn't Virago. And tell them to stay well away from them—even the dead ones. They may be infected with CFD."

Another powerful rumble shook the corridor. A long crack appeared high up on the wall opposite the doorways, with more of the sickly greenish energy spilling out of it. Far off, something crashed down.

Ocelot glanced back and forth. "'Hawk, it sounds like this place is comin' down. We don't have time for—"

"We do. But we have to go quickly. This is important."

Flea came pelting around the corner and ran up to them. "What?" He glanced in the open doorway, his face twisting in disgust at what he saw. "The frag—?"

"There's a lab here," 'Hawk said, ignoring his words. "End of the hall, she said. We've got to find it and get the files inside. Quickly."

Like just about every other decker when presented with a problem, Flea got down to business immediately. "On it." His fingers flew over his keyboard.

"*Maya, how are things going?*"

There was a pause, and then the cat replied: *"Althea says soon. She can't promise they can completely counteract the ley line's aspect, but she says they can temporarily deal with the worst of the background count. They can't hold it long, though. You won't have more than a few minutes."*

"If everything goes as planned, we shouldn't need long. Keep me and Melinda posted." Then he shifted over to the comm. "Melinda and Bronwyn—get to the entrance to the ritual area and see if you can weaken those wards so we can get a look at what we're up against. We'll be along in a couple of minutes."

"Hurry," Melinda said.

"Got it!" Flea said. He pointed at a featureless door at the far end of the hallway. This one was still closed. "It's there. I can't reach anything inside, though."

"Probably off the Matrix," Ocelot said. "Let's get in there fast." He glanced nervously at the ceiling, but for now the rumbles seemed to have ceased.

Moving quickly but cautiously, they approached the door. The other open doorways revealed small, empty rooms similar to the ork woman's cell. All were featureless, with stained floors and corroded walls. Winterhawk noticed Vyx peering carefully into each of them as she went by.

When they reached the end of the hall Ocelot, Winterhawk, and Vyx all spread out, weapons ready as Flea popped the door's lock. "This one's tougher," he said. "They don't want anybody in here." He grinned. "Like that matters."

The door slid open, and they all tensed.

Nothing came hurtling out at them. The door opened on a dark space that Ocelot's light revealed to be a small lab, just as the ork had described. Several workstations lined the walls, with a pair of benches in the center and desk on the wall opposite the door. As with the rest of the facility, rot and decay had taken over, staining and cracking the furniture and lab equipment.

Ocelot stepped inside and swept the area with his light and his gun. "Looks clear."

"What am I looking for?" Flea asked.

"Offline files," Winterhawk said. He spotted a terminal on the desk. "Probably in there. Anything pertaining to CFD and toxic magic. Grab anything that looks remotely interesting, and hurry. We'll sort it later."

"And anything about Virago, or prisoners," Vyx added.

Winterhawk was beginning to suspect Virago wasn't here at all, but he didn't think it was wise to tell Vyx that. He waited tensely with the others until Flea pushed himself back from the desk, an odd expression on his thin face.

"Did you get it?"

"Yeah...I think I got it all. Some of it might be corrupted, though—this rot isn't good for electronics." He continued to look troubled.

"Problem?"

"No. It's just..." He let his breath out and swiped his hand over his face. "This is heavy stuff, chummer. Do you know what they were tryin' to do?"

"Yeah," Ocelot said. "Just like the ork said. Tryin' to cure the headcases. Come *on*. We gotta go."

Flea stowed his deck in its bag and followed them out. "There was some serious protection on that stuff. But I can see why they kept it off the Matrix."

"I didn't think these toxic fuckers were Matrix-savvy," Ocelot said. He'd taken point along with Vyx, and together the two were scanning the halls and doorways as they headed back toward the rest of the group.

"It's not the toxics," Flea said. His tone was as odd as his expression. "Not *just* them, anyway."

"What do you mean?" Winterhawk looked sharply at him. "Who else is it?"

"I'm not sure," he said. "But whoever they are, they're working with a corp. It'll take more digging to figure out which one."

"Wait a sec," Ocelot protested. "You mean a *corp* is working *with toxics?*"

"If they thought they had something to use against CFD?" Winterhawk frowned. It was plausible—especially if it was some renegade executive or small research team, desperate or ambitious enough to take a big gamble for a lot of potential glory.

"Looks like they didn't succeed," Vyx said.

"Maybe that's what the ork meant about everything going wrong," Ocelot said.

Winterhawk was about to answer when Maya's voice spoke in their link. "*They're ready,*" she said. "*They're not confident, but they're ready.*"

"Right, then," he said aloud. "Let's get back to the others and do this. Flea, take good care of that data. If nothing else, we should be able to leverage it for a good payoff."

They met the rest of the group at the main hallway. They were around another corner now, gathered outside a set of double doors. They'd brought Tweak's body with them; her bloody form lay against the opposite wall, her jacket covering her face. Gus hung back, leaning against the wall, his dark skin ashen.

"This is where they are," Melinda said. "There's a circle of protection around the room—a big one. Going to be hard to punch through it with this background count, so I hope Althea and the others come through."

"Better hurry," Henrik said. He indicated the wall a few meters down, where another crack had opened up. This one, like its counterpart in the other hall, oozed green energy, and a dark stain crept out from its edges so quickly the group could see it move.

The floor shifted again, and a chunk of ceiling came down, barely missing Melinda.

"*Go,*" Winterhawk sent to Maya. "*Tell them to do it. Now!*" He waved the others back. "Get ready to open up on that door when I give the word."

"Can you shield us?" Henrik asked. "If so, I can take it down with grenades." Gus nodded, moving his drone into position.

"That wise?" Ocelot asked, glancing up at the ceiling as another rumble passed through the hallway. "You don't want to bring the place down on our heads."

"We'll contain it," Bronwyn said. "Put them in place. We'll put up barriers around them so most of the energy will reflect back on the door."

"Not bad," Henrik said. He pulled a couple grenades from his pocket, set them just outside the wide, pockmarked door, and stepped back.

Bronwyn, Winterhawk, and Melinda began casting. Glowing barriers sprang, up, forming an enclosure around the area.

"Stand back," Gus said.

And then, as suddenly as if a curtain had been lifted, the overpowering feeling of pressing interference faded from Winterhawk's brain. "They've done it!" he called in triumph, though he could see he didn't have to tell Melinda and Bronwyn. They, like him, appeared abruptly energized by the sudden damping of the majority of the astral interference from the warring dragon and toxic energies.

He didn't think it would last long, though—from this point forward, every second was a gift. "Go! Now!"

Henrik's and Gus's nest of grenades detonated with loud *boom*s, though not as loud as they would be if not for the magical barriers surrounding them. The explosion blew a two-meter hole in the door, its energy reflecting back just as Bronwyn had predicted. Metal and debris blew outward, where they too smashed against the fading barriers, but at least for the moment the walls and ceiling of the hallway remained stable.

"We need to punch through their circle!" Winterhawk called, spotting another glowing, semi-translucent wall a meter inside the door.

The others fell to the task, glad to have something to attack. With all of them shooting, casting spells, or otherwise pummeling it in a small, concentrated area—not to mention the temporarily reduced background count adding power to their efforts—it lasted only a few seconds before flaring up and winking out.

"Go!" Henrik yelled, as more small chunks of plascrete rained down from the ceiling. "Spread out!"

The group poured through the opening, moving fast in an effort to get inside and separate so they weren't sitting ducks for any spell that might be headed their way. For one brief second, Winterhawk allowed himself to hope whoever was on the other side was either surprised or focused on the ritual, giving them enough time to get into position.

He got most of his wish.

As he tumbled through and dived to the left side, he got a brief impression of the room: huge space, high ceiling, more eerie green light, walls cracked and coated with slime and crawling tendrils of diseased plant life, overwhelming stench of decay.

And in the center, surrounded by shadowy figures, loomed the vast, misshapen form of the toxic wolf spirit. Behind it, a glowing gateway hung suspended, casting its own sickly light into the cavernous room. Winterhawk only got a fast glance at it, but it was enough to fill him with nausea and profound unease. He wanted nothing to do with whatever was on the other side of that gateway.

That was all he could take in, though, before Vyx yelled, "Look out!" and shoved him sideways before vaulting half the distance to the left-side wall.

The wolf-thing roared, a loud, wailing howl that spiked into Winterhawk's bones, and flung a wide swath of liquid toward the group like some kind of vile tidal wave of rot.

Winterhawk hit the ground and rolled, jumping back to his feet as a shriek sounded from his right. "*Melinda!*"

Most of the team had avoided—or mostly avoided—the wave. Ocelot had leaped free to the right, along with Anissa and Flea. Bronwyn was safe next to Winterhawk, but slower to rise, gripping her wrist and wincing. Henrik didn't move as fast, but his heavy armor and the group's magical protection had shrugged off most of the damage.

Melinda screamed again. For a moment Winterhawk could only stare in horror.

She must have slipped when trying to avoid the wave—they'd never know the truth at this point. It had directly hit her, washing over her, punching through her magical armor. Her scream grew to an agonized crescendo as the substance simply consumed her, eating through her flesh, dissolving muscle. Her body juddered for a second, and then what was left fell in a wet, steaming heap to the cracked floor.

He couldn't think about it now. He couldn't think about the fact that he'd brought a noncombatant into the kind of fight that would challenge seasoned shadowrunners. If he stopped to think about it—about the fact that Vyx was a noncom too, by his standards—he'd freeze and get more people killed. Instead, he made sure the magical defenses he was providing to the group were shored up to the maximum and dived behind a pile of rotted desks that had been shoved to the side of the room.

Meanwhile, the toxics hadn't been idle. Using the wave of decay as a diversion, they'd abandoned their ritual and taken cover on the other side of the room behind more derelict furniture and fixtures.

The massive Wolf spirit remained defiantly in the center of the room, the troll shaman standing behind it, making mad gestures.

She was tall even for a troll, dressed in ragged, stained robes. Her hair, matted and crusted with dirt—or worse—stuck out in all directions, and her eyes burned with an insane light.

Behind them, but in front of the shamans, two amorphous, barely humanoid forms shimmered into being from clumps of reeking vegetation on the floor.

Winterhawk took it all in with growing dismay. Unless he'd missed his count, they had six shamans counting the troll, two "normal" toxic spirits, and that Wolf abomination they'd been unable to make a dent in so far. Two of their own number were already dead, and even though it was reduced, he and Bronwyn were still fighting the hostile background count.

Things weren't looking good for the home team.

And then Gus had to go and make it worse. *"We gotta do this fast,"* he said over the comm, his voice full of an urgency that hadn't been there before.

"Why?"

"Take a look at the walls. I'm not feelin' good about how long this place is gonna stay up, 'specially with all this rumblin' and crackin'."

"And the doorway!" Anissa added.

Winterhawk didn't have much time to look at anything for long, but he took a quick glance up and behind him. They were right. The toxics had no doubt been here for a long time—probably months—if they'd gotten this far with the ley line. This place had certainly been a state-of-the-art corporate facility a few years back, which meant even when abandoned, its construction should have been robust enough to outlive all of them. But that was what toxics *did*–they brought ruin and decay wherever they went. And it was increasingly clear that their activities here, along with the presence of the gateway to whatever vile metaplane that spirit originated from, had accelerated the process.

And now they'd thrown around grenades, not to mention adding *different* types of magic to the mix and probably destabilizing whatever uneasy equilibrium that had existed before they'd arrived.

Bringing the place down might be the best way to take out the opposition, but it wouldn't do them any good if they went with them. Yeah, they had to get out of here. "Take down the shamans," 'Hawk called over the comm. From the astral plane, he could see which two were responsible for the two spirits, and he marked them on the team's AR. "That'll get rid of the spirits."

"Roger that," Anissa said, already moving. Henrik and Gus's roto-drone likewise began firing toward where the shamans had taken cover.

The Wolf spirit roared and flung another toxic wave toward the group, but all of them were moving fast, spreading out far enough around the vast room that hitting more than one of them at a time would be impractical.

The troll shaman glared at Winterhawk and pointed her hands at him, screaming something in a language that made his mind recoil. He dived sideways as a stream of acid hit the desk he'd been hiding behind, cutting it into two sizzling pieces.

"Want to play, do you?" he called. She might be good, but so was he. Hitting her directly wouldn't be the best use of his power—her protections in here had to be impressive. Instead, he picked up a heavy workbench from the other side of the room and flung it with all his considerable telekinetic strength at her.

She did flinch—that was something. But the Wolf spirit easily knocked it away...and then focused its baleful glare on Winterhawk.

FIFTY-ONE

Vyx concentrated on moving fast, letting her body's natural instincts override conscious thought, leaping and dancing over bits of fallen rubble and broken fixtures like a child skipping through a playground obstacle course. If she didn't do that, she was sure her fear would paralyze her—both of the situation in general and of the fact that if Virago was here, she was probably either dead or turned into one of those hideous things they'd been fighting in the hallway.

This was nothing like what she'd been doing with the Ancients. They were a go-gang—they rode their bikes fast, fought fast and hard, and took down anything in their way. But the things in their way were usually other go-gangs, maybe low-level mobsters or KRB operatives—the magic they faced was usually garden-variety combat spells, normal types of spirits, and stuff that boosted combat abilities. She'd never even *seen* anything like this. Sure, she'd heard of toxic magicians—everybody had—but to her, they were the stuff of horror trids, not something she ever expected to fight.

She watched the others taking this in stride, as if it were something they did every day. Were they bluffing? Were they as scared as she was, but just better at hiding it? She glanced across the room in time to see her father fling an enormous workbench toward the Wolf spirit, making it look effortless despite his obvious exhaustion. His friend Ocelot, as fast as she was and a lot more experienced, leaped and twisted like a mad gymnast, sweeping the room with his shotgun, flicking his hand as he went by—

A toxic shaman, not one of those Winterhawk had marked as the spirits' summoners, crumpled to the ground, his severed head dropping a second after the rest of him, and then Ocelot was gone again. *"One down,"* he announced over the comm.

Holy shit, was that a monowhip? Even with her legendary speed and confidence, she'd never been brave enough to try learning to use one. The only other Ancient she'd ever seen with one had been Lucky Liam, and even he rarely used it. But this guy swung it like an extension of his arm.

She gritted her teeth and gripped her katana. She was *not* going to be the weak link in this group. She wouldn't let them down—not her father, not the rest of the team...and not Virago. Whether her girlfriend was here or not, whether she was dead or alive, Vyx owed it to her to take down as many of these fraggers as she could get her hands on.

She ducked behind cover, focusing her mind, feeling the magic and the adrenaline singing through her body. Her danger sense wasn't much use to her here, since danger was everywhere, but she concentrated on picking up subtle nuances that might warn her of imminent threats. Maybe if she could get to the other side of the room, she could take out one of the summoners who'd be too focused on the bigger guns to see her coming. She fixed her attention on one and made her move.

Winterhawk threw himself behind another workbench, bolstering his defenses a second ahead of another toxic wave from the enraged Wolf spirit. They had to take that thing out! It was more powerful than the rest of them combined, and as long as it was here, it and the others could just wear them down until they were all dead.

He checked the AR map, picking out the dots indicating his team. The flickering green light and the sickly glow from the wavering gateway made it hard to see, but they were all over the room now. Ocelot had just taken out one of the shamans, but not a summoner. The spirits had taken off in two different directions, heading toward Henrik and Bronwyn. "Cover Bronwyn," he told Gus. "Maybe she can banish it if she gets enough time."

Immediately, the dot representing the roto-drone moved into position, its twin guns blazing as it fired burst after burst into the blobbish, reeking thing.

"We gotta move,*"* the rigger said again. *"Gettin' hard to breathe in here."*

He was right. At first, Winterhawk had thought it was nothing more than the overpowering stench from rotting vegetation and the rest of the decay in here, but it was becoming increasingly difficult to draw a deep breath. His heart pounded, and sweat ran down his back. They had to make this quick—but how? They were already outmatched.

"Boss?" Maya's voice spoke in his mind. *"Althea says something's strange. They can't hold the ritual much longer."*

"Yes, we know," he said, trying not to sound impatient. *"Working on it. Tell them to hold it as long as they can."*

"Something's resisting them. She said it felt like the magic is... twisting."

"As long as they can!" he sent.

He rolled again as the wolf, which still hadn't moved away from the gateway, threw more toxic muck at him. It hit the wall and sizzled. Another rumble ran through the room, and more chunks of 'crete rained down. If they didn't bring this place down soon, the decision would be taken out of their control.

Winterhawk saw an opening. He picked up another chunk that had landed near one of the shamans and, once again using a powerful telekinetic punch, aimed it and hit the shaman square in the gut, driving him backward and through the gateway. He screamed as he went through, and didn't reappear. One of the spirits immediately dashed after him and disappeared into the gateway, returning to its home plane as soon as its connection to its summoner severed.

"Shaman and spirit down," he called as their corresponding dots faded from the map. The one thing—the one tiny thing—that they might have going for them was that these shamans—probably even the troll—weren't combat-trained. They were like most of the other witches back in Salem: powerful, but unused to dealing with the kind of split-second thinking necessary to survive in a firefight. After months of frightening off, kidnapping, or killing anyone brave enough to come near their hidey-hole, they probably hadn't expected a team of shadowrunners to drop into their backyard.

"Press them," he said. "Don't let up. We can do this."

He wasn't sure he believed his own words—which was probably why he wasn't usually the one giving the pep talks.

Vyx leaped nimbly from one pile of broken fixtures to the next, running along the wall, looking for a shot. The Wolf spirit was fixated on her father, while the other four shamans, including the troll woman, and their remaining spirit battled the rest of the team.

Anissa, Henrik, and Gus had two of them pinned down behind cover with heavy fire. They'd been throwing around a lot of ammo—she knew they'd have to finish this soon, or they'd run out and then they'd all be screwed. Flea crouched in the far corner—she knew that only because his dot was on the AR display. There probably wasn't much he could do in here—as a decker, the place's lack of Matrix connectivity and the opposition's lack of technological gear made it hard for him to affect the fight. Maybe he was just trying to stay out of the way, which was probably smart. That left Ocelot, also out of sight except for his dot, and Bronwyn near the door. She wasn't throwing spells—maybe she'd tired herself out, or was focused on protecting the group. Vyx wasn't sure which.

She was about to move again, intending to slip up behind one of the other shamans and jump her, when the troll woman in the ratty robes turned toward Winterhawk. She snapped something to the Wolf spirit, who suddenly rose on its hind legs and began to howl, its gaze still fixed on her father.

But the troll had her back to Vyx now.

She wouldn't get a better chance. Everyone was ignoring her because she hadn't done anything yet—now was the time she could prove she could handle this. "I've got an opening," she said over the comm. "Going in!"

"Vyx!" Winterhawk's voice rose above hers. *"No. Don't–"*

She leaped.

It was one of the things she loved most about being an adept— the way she could jump great distances and land, feather-light, exactly where she wanted to. It was almost like flying. She used it a lot with the Ancients, sailing across the gaps between buildings, or from bike to bike, and never once had she lost her balance or fallen. She supposed she *could* fall—of course she could—but she refused to believe it. This was what she was meant to do.

She fixed her eyes on the troll. It wasn't hard—the shaman had to be three meters tall, taller than even the male trolls Vyx had met, with a wide, broad back and long, greasy hair. As Vyx got closer, she raised her katana.

One of the shamans spotted her and yelled something, but he was too late. Vyx was moving too fast—she knew she was only a blur to anyone moving at normal speed, and these slowpokes didn't have a prayer of stopping her now. She landed neatly on the troll's back, caught her shoulder with one hand, and, in a smooth and fast movement, sliced her katana across the troll's throat.

For an agonizing second, she thought it might not work, and once again her recklessness would get people killed—and probably herself as well. The katana's sharp blade encountered resistance: magical armor, the troll's natural physical defenses, or both.

The troll screamed a series of guttural syllables, raising her huge, clawed hands, trying to grab Vyx and throw her off. A stream of steaming, reeking liquid shot from her fingers, but once again Vyx was too fast for her: instead of hitting its mark, the stream shot upward toward the room's high ceiling.

Vyx redoubled her strength, as some of the liquid pattered back down onto her armored coat, sizzling and burning holes into it. She pressed the slash hard, pulling back with everything she had. Prodigious strength was not one of her adept abilities, and she certainly couldn't match physical power against a troll, but she didn't need to. Her dislike of guns had forced her to learn the right places to slash if she wanted to injure, to maim—or to kill.

Her blade, honed to an impossibly sharp edge, slipped beneath the troll's chin and sliced her throat open, sinking in deeper and deeper until the troll's head nearly separated from her body. Blood, looking black in the unhealthy green light, sprayed out in a fan in front of her.

"*YES!*" Vyx yelled, raising the bloody blade and riding the troll's body down as it toppled. She prepared to leap free and return to cover, suddenly aware of how exposed she was out here. An instant before she did that, though, she happened to glance directly upward, where the shaman's toxic magic stream had gone wild.

The ceiling was cracking apart.

As she stared in horror, a massive fissure formed and widened, shooting out smaller tributaries. Bits of acid-etched plascrete rained down on her, and an instant later, another loud rumble passed through the room.

Oh, holy shit...we're all gonna die in here!

A growl sounded, closer to her, and a fetid, hot stench filled her nostrils. She jerked her head around to face the source.

The Wolf spirit had turned away from Winterhawk, and its glowing, malevolent stare was now fixed on her.

Winterhawk had braced himself, reinforcing his magical defenses and preparing to once more leap out of the way of the Wolf spirit's attack—it was getting harder now, as the air got worse— and hurry to Vyx's aid before she got herself killed, when suddenly someone screamed behind it.

"Vyx!" *Oh, spirits, the shaman had killed her–*

But she was there, crouched on top of the troll's body. The troll's twitching, *dead* body. "She's done it!" he announced over the comm. "The shaman's dead!"

But then Winterhawk's world compacted to only two things as the Wolf spirit whirled away from him and fixed its attention on Vyx. If he'd had any hope that the spirit would dissipate at the troll's death, it was gone now. Whatever else was going on around them—the gunfire, the yells, the stench, the rumbling—he didn't care. That thing wasn't going to hurt his daughter, not as long as he was alive.

Roaring in rage, he gathered magical energy and flung a fireball at the Wolf spirit. It might not kill it—it might not even hurt it—but it would get its attention. If he could keep it focused on him long enough for the others to finish mopping up the other shamans, then—

The fireball fizzled and died, as the curtain that had lifted away dropped again, filling his head with magical static.

"*Boss!*" Maya's voice was urgent. "*They can't hold it anymore! The ritual's collapsed!*"

He hadn't needed Maya to tell him that.

The Wolf spirit was still facing Vyx.

Right, then—this is going to hurt.

He gathered more energy—more than was safe. He didn't care. He had to get its attention. He had to get it away from Vyx.

And then her voice was on the comm: "*Run! Guys, we have to go! This place is coming down any second!*"

He looked up, and froze. She was right. The ceiling fissure was widening as he watched, and more plascrete pelted down. The shamans continued fighting, apparently oblivious to the danger. The gateway shimmered and shifted.

All at once, he he saw his opening. It might not work, but nothing else was working and they didn't have time for subtlety. "Get out, everyone! Head for the door! Go! Go! Henrik—get ready to hit that ceiling with everything you have on the way out!" He marked the fissure, even though he didn't think it was possible to miss it.

"*You got it!*" Henrik's voice was triumphant as he caught on to Winterhawk's plan.

The Wolf spirit leaped toward Vyx, but she was already moving. It was fast, but she was faster. By the time it landed hard where she'd been standing, its massive diseased paws crushing the body of the troll shaman, she was already nearly to the door.

"Come on!" she yelled.

Ocelot joined her an instant later, shoving Flea and Bronwyn toward the door. Gus's roto-drone continued to lay down covering fire as he too backed toward the door. By this point, the whole wall was starting to come down, and the intermittent rumbling echoed like a heavy cargo train rolling through a tunnel.

Winterhawk ran. Flea, Anissa, and Bronwyn were already through and out in the hallway. Ocelot and Vyx slipped through next. Gus followed, but not fast enough: one of the shamans' toxic streams hit him a few feet from the door. He fell, screaming.

"Now!" Winterhawk yelled to Henrik as he too darted through the doorway. More hunks of 'crete crashed down onto him, hitting his shoulders and back. He whirled just in time to watch what happened next.

Henrik pointed his grenade launcher at the fissure and let fly. The little orb flew unerringly upward and disappeared into the crack; an instant later an earth-shattering *boom* shook the area. For a second, it seemed as if the explosion wouldn't have the power to take the ceiling down fast enough, but then the rumble grew louder and louder until it was almost deafening, and the whole thing cascaded down. The Wolf spirit made one last desperate leap for the door, but it was too big to get through. The last thing Winterhawk saw before he turned to leave was the thing going down under a pile of plascrete chunks, each one as big as a small car.

"*Run!*" Ocelot yelled. "*Go! Go!*"

"*Wait!*" Vyx screamed, skidding to a stop as all around her the other runners pelted down the hall in the direction of the stairway. The floor under her feet shook; bits of the ceiling out here began to fall as well. "*What about Virago?*"

"*She's not here!*" someone yelled back.

She almost didn't recognize the voice—it sounded very young and very scared. *Flea?* "You're lying! You don't know!" Tears streamed down her face, as much from the bad air and dust as from her despair.

Winterhawk grabbed her arm and was trying to drag her down the hall. "Come *on*," he urged. "We have to get out of here before this bloody place comes down around our ears!"

She yanked her arm back. "I'm not leaving without her!"

Flea looked as if he were about to go to pieces. "She's not here, Vyx! I promise!" He held up his deck. "I was searching the files I found! She's not here!"

A head-sized chunk fell toward Vyx, and Winterhawk swept it away with a spell. He reached for his daughter again, but she danced away.

"How do you know? Where is she?" she demanded, whirling on the young decker.

"I don't know where! Somewhere in Boston! Come on!"

This time she did allow her father to drag her along after the others. She felt suddenly numb. "Boston? Why—" Why would they take her there?

"They're gonna infect her," Flea said, hurrying along next to her. Behind them, a massive, muffled crash signaled the rest of the ceiling falling in on the huge room, and the hallway behind them was starting to go as well. Choking dust filled the air, mingling with the stench from the toxics. Everyone coughed now, doubling over, staggering along as fast as they could manage.

They reached the stairs and hurried up. "Infect her?" She stared at him—at least as much of him as she could see—in terror and disbelief. "With what? Is she gonna be like—" She thought of the malignant, disgusting abominations downstairs.

Flea didn't answer, dissolving again into a coughing fit. He stumbled up the stairs, clutching the railing with one hand and his deck with the other, his eyes streaming. Vyx grabbed his arm and helped him.

Virago wasn't here. She could wait for the rest.

FIFTY-TWO

They burst out into the clearing a few seconds later. It was still dark—Winterhawk felt as if they had been underground all night, but it had only been less than an hour since they'd gone in. Rain poured steadily down, but it felt good, washing away the muck and the stench and the dust. He dropped to his knees and took deep, gulping breaths of the fresh air.

He took quick inventory of the group as they did the same. Ocelot, of course, didn't let himself rest, leaning against a tree in watchful wariness as if expecting someone else to jump them. Henrik, Anissa, and Bronwyn had dropped into heaps next to each other.

Melinda and Gus and Tweak, of course, would never come out. He'd mourn them later.

Where was Vyx? For a moment he didn't see her, but then he spotted her across the clearing, focused on a slumped Flea. What were they talking about? He'd heard her yelling something at him on the way up, but couldn't make it out over the rumbles and cracks of the dying building. He dragged himself to his feet and moved toward them.

His comm buzzed.

"CFD," Flea told Vyx. He looked miserable, his pale face streaked with muck, his bright-red hair hanging limply over his forehead in the rain.

She stared at him. "No! No way! They—"

"They planned to use her as a test subject." He broke into a fit of coughing, then indicated his deck. "It's all in here. They infect 'em someplace in Boston. It just refers to their 'Boston lab.' I think that's the corp end of things, not the toxic end. Then they send 'em down here so the toxics can try to cure 'em."

Vyx's whole body went numb. CFD? Those toxic fraggers were going to turn her girlfriend into a *headcase*? "Oh, god..." she moaned, and gripped his arm.

Flea shook his head. "I'm sorry..." he said. "But maybe they haven't done it yet. Or...you know she might be able to fight it off. It can be done—you know that. Everybody knows that. If they get her and she can make it through seventy-two hours—she's strong, right?"

Hope—a faint little thing, fragile and tentative—welled up within Vyx. "She's the strongest!" she said fiercely. "And the most fuckin' stubborn bitch there is! If anybody can fight it, she can! We'll—"

She stopped as something caught her eye. Her father was approaching her, but he suddenly stopped, his expression going unfocused as if he were paying attention to something else. Who was he talking to?

The buzz wasn't a call—it was an indicator of urgent voicemail. Three of them, in fact, all from the same LTG. He listened to the last one first, and went still at the sound of the voice on the other end.

"You're a hard man to get hold of," Damon's voice said. *"You must contact me as soon as you get this if you want a way out of the Zone. I've secured transportation for four as you requested, but it's very time-sensitive. If you can't get back to Boston in four hours, I'm afraid it will be forced to leave without you. I might not be able to get something else put together for weeks–it's not easy to get people out without a great deal of preparation, even for me. Call me as soon as you can."*

Winterhawk glanced at the chrono in the corner of his glasses' display: They had less than two hours to make the rendezvous. That would be cutting it damned short.

Quickly, he returned Damon's call. The dragon himself didn't answer, but he told the person who did that he and the others would be on their way. The woman, who seemed to know exactly what was going on, sent him the coordinates to a rendezvous point in Boston, near the harbor. *"Don't be late,"* she cautioned. *"They won't wait for you."*

"Got a way out," he told Ocelot over a private comm channel. "But we have to move fast. See if you and the others can get that Bulldog functional again. I need to talk to Vyx."

His daughter was still sitting with Flea when he approached them. She looked shell-shocked, but he couldn't tell if that was because of something the decker had told her, or merely because the enormity of what had just occurred was finally catching up with her and she was in shock. "Vyx..."

Her gaze came up to meet his, but she didn't speak. She looked pale beneath the rain-streaked grime on her face.

Flea got up and gathered his deck. "I'll give you two some space," he said, and hurried after the others.

"Are you all right?" Winterhawk asked her. He crouched down next to her, mindful of time ticking away.

She shrugged. "I dunno."

"Listen," he said. "I just got a call—we've got a way out, but we need to act quickly. The transport leaves in two hours."

She stared at him. "You're leaving?"

"*We're* leaving," he said gently. "All of us. We're getting out of the QZ. Back to civilization."

"In two hours?"

"Yes. In Boston. We have to get moving."

She shook her head. "No. I'm not leaving."

Now it was his turn to stare at her. "What do you mean, you're not leaving?"

"I can't go!" she said, glaring. "Virago—"

"Virago's gone," he said, keeping his voice gentle. He put a hand on her shoulder. "I'm sorry, Vyx. Truly I am. I wish it weren't so. But staying here won't help—"

"She's *not* gone!" she protested, flinching away from him. "She's alive! She's somewhere in Boston, in some lab, and I'm gonna find her! Flea found the records in that stuff he grabbed. They're gonna infect her with CFD. They're gonna make her into one of those—*things*." She gestured toward the ruin of the lab. "But maybe they haven't done it yet! Maybe if I can get to her before they do—I can't just leave her here!"

Winterhawk rubbed his forehead. "Vyx, listen. You can't stay in here. Once you're out, you can do whatever you like. You don't have to go back to your mother. I can talk to Damon—his people can find Virago. Maybe they can even get her out, if she wants to go. But—"

She leaped to her feet, her smooth brow furrowing in anger. "You don't *get* it, do you? You don't just abandon the people you love because it's easier for you! Even if she doesn't turn into a headcase, she'll never leave here. The Ancients are her family. I told you that! And I belong with her!"

Winterhawk studied her face. Her eyes, the stubborn set of her jaw—so much like his own. For a long time, he didn't say anything; then he let his breath out. "All right," he said softly. "If that's the way you want to do it—I'll stay too. I'll tell Damon to get Ocelot out, and fill the other spots with anyone else who wants to go. I'll stay here and help you find her."

Her eyes widened. "You're not serious. You can't do that."

"You just told me you don't abandon the people you love because it's easier..." he pointed out.

"Yeah, but—" She gripped his arm. "No. You can't do it. You have to go. I *want* you to go. But I can't go with you. Not now. Not yet."

"You want me to go?" he asked, puzzled. "Why?"

She thought about it for a long moment, then shook her head. "You don't belong in here. Maybe later, when the wall comes down and Virago and I can both get out—I'll look you up again. I want that. I want to get to know you better, find out what lies Mom told me about you. But not now."

"Vyx—"

"No arguments, Dad," she said with a faint smile. "Remember before, you said you'd never make me do anything I didn't want to do? I'm an adult now. Mom doesn't want to accept it, but I gotta make my own way." Her smile widened, just a little, though her eyes glittered. "I'll be fine. I've gotten by this long okay. And we'll see each other again. You're not gettin' rid of me now that I know you're out there."

Winterhawk had no idea what to say. Part of him—rather more than a small part, if he were honest with himself—wanted to hit her with a stunning spell to knock her out, then pack her off to the transport. Sure, she'd be angry with him when she awakened. Maybe she'd never speak to him again. But she'd be *safe.*

She wouldn't, though. Vyx was like him: she'd never be safe, no matter where she ended up. *Safe* was just another word for *boring.* Her mother would never understand that, but it was in his daughter's blood, same as it was in his.

Still...

"No," he said firmly. "If you're staying, I'm staying too. We'll sort this out somehow, and—"

His comm buzzed. When he saw the name on the display, he tensed. Had the whole matter just been taken out of his hands?

"Damon. Why are you calling? Is the transport—"

He listened a moment, then smiled, relief flooding him. "Good. Brilliant. Thank you, Damon. I think we all owe you and your people one. Probably more than one." He ended the call and focused on Vyx. "Well. Some good news, for a change."

"What is it?" She leaned forward in breathless, terrified anticipation.

"That was Damon. They've got Virago. They picked up the transport in Boston. She's fine—which apparently is more than I can say for the people who had her."

She stared at him in disbelief. "What? How—"

"I'm not going to ask. Best not to dig too deeply into how dragons get things done."

Her eyes narrowed, and something dark flashed across her face. "Wait. You wouldn't lie to me, right? Just to get me to come with you? Because—"

"Vyx..."

"You *wouldn't,* right? Because—"

He bowed his head, then raised it and looked into her eyes. "Vyx...I would never lie to you about something like that. Look at me and tell me you don't believe me."

Her gaze bored into his. She held it for several seconds, and then her shoulders slumped and she let her breath out. "Thank the spirits...oh, gods...when can I see her?"

"Soon. I promise." He gripped her shoulders. "But Vyx—don't you see what that means? We don't have to stay here. You can come with us. Both of you can."

To his surprise, she shook her head. "No. We can't."

"What are you talking about?"

When she looked up again, she wore a faint, brittle smile. "I'm so glad they found her—that she's safe—but Virago would never leave Boston, Dad. And I'm not leaving her. Like I said before—this is her home. And it's mine, too." She pulled him into a hard hug. "You go. Tell Mom I'm okay, and I'm happy. You don't have to stay and help me now. We got this."

"But—"

"Go," she said. "I promise—this is what I want. And I know this is what Virago wants. We both owe you a lot for getting us out of this. Maybe we'll even find Damon and see if there's anything we can do to pay him back. But this isn't where *you* belong. You know it, and so do I." She grinned, and it lit up her grimy face. "Come on, Dad—we'll see each other again. You can count on it. When the walls come down, you won't be able to hide from me. But until then..." She spread her hands. "This is my home, but it's not yours."

He didn't want to admit it, to acknowledge it. He still wanted to pack her off home like she was a small child with no choice. He *could* do that, if he chose to force it.

But he also knew if he did that, he'd lose her every bit as much as if he'd let her die in the toxics' lair.

When he spoke again, his voice was ragged, resigned. "You're sure this is what you want? Absolutely sure? Once I get outside, I probably can't do much to help you."

"Yeah." She got up and pulled him into a hug. "Yeah. That's what I want."

His arms went around her, holding tight as the rain pelted down on both of them. "Right, then," he murmured, and managed to keep his voice from shaking. "We'd best get going. We've both got things to do. And people to see."

FIFTY-THREE

Four Days Later

Winterhawk sat in the same DeeCee bar where he'd first spoken with Olivia, toying with his drink and trying to decide if he hoped she'd show up on time, or be late so he'd have more time to prepare himself for seeing her again.

It had been four days since the frantic ride out of the Containment Zone. Damon's remaining team had dropped him and Ocelot off at the rendezvous point, under cover of darkness and heavy magical concealment, with only ten minutes to spare on the two-hour deadline.

It had been hard to let Vyx go, but also easier, because he knew it was what she wanted. She'd already spoken to Virago, and the two of them had made plans to return to Boston and see how Lucky Liam would respond to their news. She hoped he'd take her back in, but if he didn't, they always had Damon to contact. And someday... The walls, inevitably, would come down, though nobody knew when that would be. It could be weeks, months, or even years before he saw her again.

He hadn't gotten a chance to speak with Damon directly, as the dragon had other urgent business he was attending to, but he left the data they'd gathered about the ley line, the toxics, and what was going on in Salem with Anissa, who promised to deliver it personally. Flea had decided to remain, partly because he wanted the payoff from the data, and partly because Anissa and the others had asked him to stay on for a while as their decker since the loss of Tweak.

Before they parted ways, Winterhawk had taken Anissa aside briefly. "Look after her, will you?" he asked, nodding toward Vyx, who sat on one of the benches in the back of the transport. "Don't let her know, of course, but just—"

The samurai nodded. "Don't worry. We've already been talking to Virago. I think I can convince him to throw some work their way, and keep an eye on them from afar." She shrugged. "Kid's good. Lot of talent. Both of them, in fact. Need training and experience, but that's the easy part. If she doesn't make it with the Ancients, maybe both of 'em might want to join Damon's organization. You know, at least till they can find a gig of their own."

Winterhawk hadn't thought of that, but it wasn't a half-bad compromise, especially since he knew Vyx's chances of going back to MIT&T like a good little corporate student were somewhere between slim and none at this point.

"Thank you," he said. "I appreciate it. I just—"

"You feel guilty for leaving her here," she said gently. She put her hand on his shoulder. "Don't. We all gotta make our own choices, and she's made hers. She'll be fine. She's got exactly what she wants. And you've got things you still need to do out there."

That didn't help much, but he didn't say it. And then there was no more time, and he couldn't say it even if he wanted to.

He spotted Olivia before she saw him, walking through the early evening crowd, dressed in her chic, designer corp-wear. He watched her as she approached, noting the anticipatory expression on her face. His heart beat a little faster, his body tensing. She wasn't going to like what he had to tell her—he had given her no information when he called, beyond that he wanted to meet, because he wanted to tell her in person. He owed her that, at least.

As she reached his table her gaze swept back and forth, obviously trying to spot anyone who might be with him. When she saw he was alone, she frowned, then her expression crumpled. "She's dead, isn't she?" she asked bleakly.

He waved her to a seat; an unobtrusive server instantly set a glass of wine in front of her and slipped off.

"Tell me," she said, eyes glittering. "Is she dead?"

"No. She's not dead." There was no easy way to deliver this news; he focused on keeping his expression neutral.

"Then—where is she?" She looked around again, as if expecting her wayward daughter to pop out from behind another table, or suddenly leap out onto the small stage where a jazz combo played soft background music.

In answer, he removed a data chip from his jacket pocket and slid it across the table to her.

She looked at it, then back up at him. At his nod, she picked it up with lacquered fingernails and popped it into her commlink.

Winterhawk watched her as she watched it. He could neither see nor hear the message, but he didn't need to: he'd been there when Vyx had recorded it, still in her thrashed-up armored jacket, grimy-faced and full of resolve.

"*I can't come home, Mom,*" she'd said. "*I know about Dad, and it's not his fault. He wanted to get me out, but I told him no. I know you want the best for me, but let's face it—we've never really agreed on what that is. I love you, and I'll see you someday. I'm serious—don't blame Dad. He tried.*"

He knew Olivia had reached the end when her brow furrowed, and her eyes shone with glimmering tears. When she spoke again, her voice shook, though he couldn't tell if it was with anger or despair—perhaps a bit of both.

"You found her," she said in a monotone, "and you just—*left* her in there?"

He closed his eyes briefly. There would be no reasoning with her, but he tried nonetheless. "What was I to do? She didn't want to go. Should I have drugged her? Forced her? Is that what you'd have wanted?"

"I want my *daughter* back," she snapped. One spasmodic hand crumpled a red cloth napkin. "You were supposed to bring her back to me. You said you'd get her out of there." Her gaze came up to meet his. "She's your daughter too, Alex. How could you just...walk away from her? What kind of father does that make you?"

"I don't know, Olivia," he said. It was getting harder to keep his tone even. "You tell me what kind of father I am, since I never got the chance to find out."

She stared at him, clearly shocked by his words. "I told you why I didn't tell you. And I was right, wasn't I? She *is* just like you. And when she gets herself killed in there, it will be your fault. I hope you can live with yourself for that, Alex." She stood, tossing the napkin back on the table. "I should never have contacted you. I'm no better off than I was before, and now thanks to you I know Victoria's in even more danger than I feared."

"Vyx," he said quietly.

"What?" Her eyes narrowed, and her tone sharpened.

"Her name is Vyx," he said.

She held his gaze for another beat, and then whirled and stalked off in the direction she'd come.

Winterhawk watched her go, but didn't call after her.

Sometimes, it just wasn't worth trying to make someone understand.

LOOKING FOR MORE SHADOWRUN FICTION, CHUMMER?

WE'LL HOOK YOU UP!

Catalyst Game Labs brings you the very best in *Shadowrun* fiction, available at most ebook retailers, including Amazon, Apple Books, Kobo, Barnes & Noble, and more!

NOVELS

1. *Never Deal with a Dragon* (Secrets of Power #1)
      by Robert N. Charrette
2. *Choose Your Enemies Carefully* (Secrets of Power #2)
      by Robert N. Charrette
3. *Find Your Own Truth* (Secrets of Power #3)
      by Robert N. Charrette
4. *2XS* by Nigel Findley
5. *Changeling* by Chris Kubasik
6. *Never Trust an Elf* by Robert N. Charrette
7. *Shadowplay* by Nigel Findley
8. *Night's Pawn* by Tom Dowd
9. *Striper Assassin* by Nyx Smith
10. *Lone Wolf* by Nigel Findley
11. *Fade to Black* by Nyx Smith
12. *Burning Bright* by Tom Dowd
13. *Who Hunts the Hunter* by Nyx Smith
14. *House of the Sun* by Nigel Findley
15. *Worlds Without End* by Caroline Spector
16. *Just Compensation* by Robert N. Charrette
17. *Preying for Keeps* by Mel Odom
18. *Dead Air* by Jak Koke
19. *The Lucifer Deck* by Lisa Smedman
20. *Steel Rain* by Nyx Smith
21. *Shadowboxer* by Nicholas Pollotta
22. *Stranger Souls* (Dragon Heart Saga #1) by Jak Koke
23. *Headhunters* by Mel Odom
24. *Clockwork Asylum* (Dragon Heart Saga #2) by Jak Koke
25. *Blood Sport* by Lisa Smedman
26. *Beyond the Pale* (Dragon Heart Saga #3) by Jak Koke

27. *Technobabel* by Stephen Kenson
28. *The Terminus Experiment* by Jonathan E. Bond and Jak Koke
29. *Psychotrope* by Lisa Smedman
30. *Run Hard, Die Fast* by Mel Odom
31. *Crossroads* by Stephen Kenson
32. *The Forever Drug* by Lisa Smedman
33. *Ragnarock* by Stephen Kenson
34. *Tails You Lose* by Lisa Smedman
35. *The Burning Time* by Stephen Kenson
36. *Wolf and Raven* by Michael A. Stackpole
37. *Born to Run* (Kellen Colt Trilogy #1) by Stephen Kenson
38. *Poison Agendas* (Kellen Colt Trilogy #2) by Stephen Kenson
39. *Fallen Angels* (Kellen Colt Trilogy #3) by Stephen Kenson
40. *Drops of Corruption* by Jason M. Hardy
41. *Aftershocks* by Jean Rabe & John Helfers
42. *A Fistful of Data* by Stephen Dedman
43. *Fire and Frost* by Kai O'Connal
44. *Hell on Water* by Jason M. Hardy
45. *Dark Resonance* by Phaedra Weldon
46. *Crimson* by Kevin Czarnecki
47. *Shaken: No Job Too Small* by Russell Zimmerman
48. *Borrowed Time* by R.L. King
49. *Deniable Assets* by Mel Odom
50. *Undershadows* by Jason M. Hardy
51. *Shadows Down Under* by Jean Rabe
52. *Makeda Red* by Jennifer Brozek
53. *The Johnson Run* by Kai O'connal
54. *Shadow Dance* by Aaron Rosenberg
55. *Identity: Crisis* by Phaedra Weldon
56. *Veiled Extraction* by R.L. King
57. *Stirred* by Russell Zimmerman

ANTHOLOGIES

1. *Spells & Chrome*, edited by John Helfers
2. *World of Shadows*, edited by John Helfers
3. *Drawing Destiny: A Sixth World Tarot Anthology*, edited by John Helfers
4. *Sprawl Stories, Vol. 1*, edited by John Helfers
5. *The Complete Frame Job*, edited by John Helfers

NOVELLAS

1. *Neat* by Russell Zimmerman
2. *The Vladivostok Gauntlet* by Olivier Gagnon
3. *Nothing Personal* by Olivier Gagnon
4. *Another Rainy Night* by Patrick Goodman
5. *Sail Away, Sweet Sister* by Patrick Goodman
6. *The Seattle Gambit* by Olivier Gagnon
7. *DocWagon 19* by Jennifer Brozek
8. *Wolf & Buffalo* by R.L. King
9. *Big Dreams* by R.L. King
10. *Blind Magic* by Dylan Birtolo
11. *The Frame Job, Part 1: Yu* by Dylan Birtolo
12. *The Frame Job, Part 2: Emu* by Brooke Chang
13. *The Frame Job, Part 3: Rude* by Bryan CP Steele
14. *The Frame Job, Part 4: Frostburn* by CZ Wright
15. *The Frame Job, Part 5: Zipfile* by Jason Schmetzer
16. *The Frame Job, Part 6: Retribution* by Jason M. Hardy
17. *Tower of the Scorpion* by Mel Odom
18. *Chaser* by Russell Zimmerman
19. *A Kiss to Die For* by Jennifer Brozek
20. *Crocodile Tears* by Chris A. Jackson

Made in the USA
Middletown, DE
08 October 2020